Singing in Silence

Gather the Women

A Novel
By
Karen Clark

ISBN-978-1-945526-33-6
Library of Congress No. 2017948971

Written by: Karen Clark
Cover design by C. L. Cannon, Fiction-Atlas Author Services
Edited by Melanie McDonald, Rhonda Abbott, Sarah Burton, Carol Tietsworth

www.SinginginSilence.com

Dedicated to my mother
Joan "Jody" Alexander Roediger
She loved Mary and was 'there' for me
on this journey

PREFACE

I didn't grow up wanting to be a writer, though perhaps I've always been a storyteller. However, my journey changed on the Spring Equinox of 2005.

Driving on I-80 in Northern California, I was gazing at freshly planted fields and listening to NPR. It was the second anniversary of the Iraqi war. Being perimenopausal, it didn't take much to upset me. "Over 600,000 Iraqis dead, many of them children," they reported. A grandmother, I sobbed in my car for the now-childless mothers. I daydreamed about what the world would be like if the mothers and grandmothers ran the world. I envisioned women gathering— at the Click Café. I had no idea the Click Café would become *Singing in Silence*.

I thought *What can I do?* "Be careful when you ask questions," they say, "Just might lead you to your destiny." I had no idea my journey for the next twelve years was to write this book.

"Have you heard about the Third Secret?" my fellow Artist Way student asked at our meeting. "You know, Fatima, where the Virgin Mary appeared to three children? The Church was supposed to reveal the Third Secret, but they didn't."

That was enough to hook me. An avid researcher, I read about Marian Apparitions (visions of the Virgin Mary), the history of the Catholic Church, quantum physics, history of wars, Dior—and water, and entered all into a spreadsheet. And then I let the story come to me.

As the book evolved, I realized we needed a *Harry Potter* book for midlife women. Suspense sprinkled with magic. A novel not only for change but one you could get lost in.

This journey has not been easy. I wrote before work, after work, on the weekends. I wrote when my brain was injured due to workplace bullying, by a woman. I kept writing in libraries when I lost my home at age 60. I kept writing through each life challenge because I wanted a peaceful world for my grandkids.

Now, after twelve years this story is ready to be shared with the world. I hope you enjoy the journey and give it some "thought."

Trust the Journey

Karen Clark

June 29, 2017

Episode One

~

The Calling

Another world is not only possible, she is on her way. On a quiet day, I can hear her breathing.
~ Arundhati Roy

February 13, 2005—She stepped lightly across the icy well-worn stone patio, cradling her steaming Haviland Limoges cup in her age-weathered hands, bundled up in her favorite scarf and cape. The morning air was now settled after last week's violent mistral. She enjoyed her morning ritual—herbal tea with her morning newspaper, overlooking her beloved Provence village of Callian. *Today it begins,* she mulled, as she spread the newspaper across the mosaic table top with a knowing smile. In a small two-paragraph story at the bottom of page three, byline Coimbra, Portugal, she read of her dear friend's passing.

She wasn't at all surprised or saddened by the news. The dead woman had spoken to her one last time before drawing her last breath. They had never met in person, but had been "communicating" since 1960. It started the day the pope had refused to reveal the Third Secret to the world as instructed. The Frenchwoman had known that the secret would not be revealed at that time or now—but soon. She had been well schooled by her ancestor on the outcome. Feed the Field. That's how the nun found her.

She closed her eyes as she reflected on the last message. "Time to gather the women," the blind and deaf ninety-seven-year-old nun relayed from her simple cell. The nun was finally at peace with her part in the magnificent plan that started the morning of May 13, 1917, in Fatima, Portugal. Neither the threat of being boiled in hot oil nor being sequestered all her life by the Church could stop it. It had been destined for 500 years. The Frenchwoman had practiced well for her part.

* * *

February 14, 2005—"Seal it!" Cardinal Muench ordered. He knew it was imperative that everything contained in the cell be passed through the sieve of loyal trusted theologians and monsignors. "We think she experienced other apparitions in here. Called them 'mystical intuitions,' according to her diary," the deceased nun's bishop warned, as he oversaw the packing up of all her papers and belongings. The Church could not take the chance of anyone reading something that wasn't for their eyes—not this late in the game.

But it was more than tangible items Cardinal Muench was worried about. He had learned his lesson with the bungled clean-up after Pope John Paul I's sudden death.

"All plumbing is to be turned off. Every drop of water in the convent must be confiscated!"

Chapter One

______∞______

"I tap—I'm from Marin!" Stella sputtered, launching silver-streaked blond wisps of hair skyward. She glared at her daughter's reflection in the bathroom mirror; the familiar rolling of her eyes, the mocking "here she goes again" look—made Stella's arched eyebrow twitch. Why do daughters feel the need to mock their mothers? Should have named her Rainbow! Then she could roll her eyes like a shorted-out penny slot machine stuck on a jackpot.

She kicked the bathroom door closed with such force, it jiggled the vaporous face that skimmed the murky sink water.

Tap, tap, tap on her eyebrows . . . "even though I'm a menopausal divorced woman, I choose to totally and completely love and accept myself."

Tap, tap, tap, on the side of her eyes . . . "even though I feel fat and ridiculous going on a blind date" . . . tap, tap, tap under her eyes, her breath still shallow and rapid, sweat droplets trickling into the soft fluffy collar of her cashmere robe.

"Even though I'm fifty-seven" . . . tap, tap, tap under her nose . . . "husband left me" . . . tap, tap, tap on her chin . . . "haven't had sex in two years" . . . tap, tap, tap on her breastbone.

She tapped another round of her EFT, or Emotional Freedom Technique as her therapist had taught her, the calmness starting to edge out her panic. Deep breath in, then out. *Maybe I'll get through this ordeal without a pill. Maybe not.*

"I really need you to be a little more supportive right now, okay?" Stella yelled through the door. What was wrong with her only child? Nicki had been raised in a liberal household. Hell, she even lived in Napa Valley and was a dedicated meditator. *Why the cynicism?*

Maybe her daughter's passive-aggressive behavior was evidence of residual pain from her parents' divorce. Thanksgiving was just a few weeks away. The first big family holiday since the divorce became final. The first holiday since Stella's mother killed herself.

Nicki and her husband Carlos would be spending this year's holiday with Stella's ex and his lover, leaving Stella completely family-less. *Maybe I deserve her anger*, Stella thought. She could hear her therapist's voice telling her she did guilt well.

"Fine!" Nicki yelled from the bedroom. "If that's what it takes to get you on this date, I promise not another critical word. I *am* your biggest cheerleader right now, Mom."

Stella knew Nicki just wanted her old mom back, the fun-loving one. Both Nicki and Dibrovna, her long-time assistant, had been more-than-patient as they helped her recover. Sometimes, though, they were "too helpful," like now. She narrowed her eyes and watched Dibrovna carefully as her assistant fought for space among the Kilimanjaro of pillows piled four deep on Stella's bed as she laid out more clothing choices for Stella's date. A few months previously, Dibrovna tried to remove some of the pillows while Stella was taking a shower. When Stella returned and saw the vast emptiness of her king-sized bed, she ran and tightly swaddled herself in her down comforter as she furiously rebuilt her down cocoon fort, her eyes crazed like a feral cat.

"Even though," tapping on the crown of her head, "my husband left me for another man, I completely and profoundly love and accept myself—mind, body and soul." She finished with a slow deep release of breath. She estimated her anxiety level as a "four," down from a "ten." No pill needed—at least not right now.

She wished Maggie was here; her best friend since they worked as teenagers at I. Magnin's, the premier San Francisco department store. She smiled as she drained the basin, remembering what Maggie's mother used to say: "You two girls are as close as a coat of paint." Indeed. She could use a coat of paint tonight. *And maybe some new air freshener*, she thought, scrunching her nose. Oddly, the cloying scent of old fashioned roses filled her bathroom.

"Do you smell roses?" she asked, walking into her bedroom, unaware the scent was growing more intense in the gathering night fog. The two women continued to arrange outfits on the bed as if Stella were invisible.

Fine. Ignore me, she thought, taking short constricted steps into the bedroom. "Okay, I've got on two pairs of Spanx, so let's see what I can wiggle my old fat ass into this lovely evening," Stella said, the elastic cutting into her fleshy belly. If doubling up on medication helped her brain, she figured it ought to work on her middle-aged girth as well.

"What is wrong with you American women?" Dibrovna asked as she watched an obviously irritated Stella rummaging through the clothing selection. The Croatian war refugee was Stella's assistant at her Mill Valley clothing boutique, Third Act. She and Nicki had urged Stella to get back out into the dating scene. Return to normalcy, they said.

"You are a beautiful woman. There is nothing wrong with your looks. We European women don't want to turn back the clock, to be foolish young girls anymore. Our men find experienced women very sexy and desirable, you know. A little jiggle is sexy. You must stop looking to others for acceptance, Stella. Waste of time!" she ended, shooting Stella a silencing glare as she pushed her black-rimmed glasses up on her nose, then placed her strong hands firmly on her wide hips.

"Yeah," Stella sighed in what once was a sultry voice now aged to a husky, whiskey-smoked tone. "Well, I wish we could have more of your European men's influence here in the Bay Area. We mature women would adore being treasured. Instead, it feels like we're invisible, disposable—past our expiration date. You know, in my very brief experience since recklessly exposing myself to the online dating jungle, it's not long before they cut to the chase of what they are looking for: tits on a stick!" She cringed and slapped her hand over her mouth, unable to halt her last careless utterance. "I'm so sorry."

She knew Dibrovna was deeply religious and sensitive to vulgar remarks. *What the hell is wrong with me?* These days it seemed she was a little too slow pushing her self-edit button when voicing her opinions. She had always prided herself on her ability to be both charming and refined. Now she was just blunt and clumsy.

She wished she could be like Maggie, a scrappy wise ass whose sharp words slid easily over her lips, delivered with such Southern smoothness the recipient would just grin, eager for more. *Maybe it's my frontal lobe,* she thought. She read that when women go through the Change, their frontal lobe changes. They lose their filter. *Well, maybe not such a bad thing,* she thought. She might not be in her present state if she hadn't been so damn polite when she saw Todd's subtle signs through the years.

Maybe her crude ranting about men helped, as her anxiety noticeably receded. Or maybe it's the tapping. Either way, it was welcome relief. Being back in the single dating scene after a hiatus of almost thirty years had left her awkward and meek around men—definitely not her style.

"I'm so glad you two are here tonight." They both had been paramount in her healing, and she was grateful. Stella prayed, in her own way, that they wouldn't leave her.

She wasn't a religious woman—not now. Church had ended for her long ago. Memorial Day 1968, when they came and knocked on her family's door; only bad news delivered on a holiday. Her Catholic-raised mother was informed that Stella's father was missing in action in Vietnam. Not one person from their church had come to console them, bring them a casserole, thank them for their family's sacrifice for their country. Not one.

Her neck tightened as her pulse thumped hard in her ears. *No, not now!* She focused on the clothing to stop the flood of memories from triggering an attack. It helped, but not in a good way. She wasn't all that crazy about their style suggestions. At least there were a couple of black selections. She wasn't ready for color yet. Living in a black and white world was easier, felt safer. Helped her stay in the background. Still too shaky to shine as she once had.

Reflecting on her indifferent mostly sex-less marriage with Todd, she wondered how it could have lasted as long as it did. She had been happy; well, *happy enough* anyway. They enjoyed an almost-robust sex life in the beginning, until they had Nicki. Then it dwindled to occasional holidays. She hadn't minded much since he had been attentive in other ways. But when she hit her forties, her needs changed. Hormones surging, she desperately needed to feel sexy, lustful—desired. She wanted to be ravaged like in a romance novel, though she never told him. Couldn't he sense she needed affection? But Todd just kept pulling away, even slapping her hand when she reached for him in the early morning hours.

Unable to see that it had nothing to do with her, she believed society's message that it was her fault for being thicker, older, less than. For years, they avoided any meaningful discussion of their feelings, existing in a deepening vacuum-sealed silence. Maybe if he had done more, been more, "manned-up," she'd still be desirable. It felt good to lay all the blame on him. Her therapist might even call it progress. Now she just had to figure out a new routine, a new way of being.

"Mom, I think you'll look stunning in whatever you decide to wear," Nicki said sincerely.

"Stella, look at these. We just received these lovely dresses in jewel tones. Why not try this one?" Dibrovna tried to hand her the purple Oscar de la Renta, with just a slight hint of ruching at the waist.

There they go again. Color pushers! One thing she could no longer tolerate was someone telling her how to dress. Todd had done that, and what once was constructive criticism had turned cuttingly vicious. Her heartbeat pounded against her ribs, sweat beading through her brow, before slithering down and finding a home in the crevices of her crow's feet, stinging her eyes. She saw Nicki push her favorite black Armani under the pillows. Unable to stop, her defense mechanism kicked in.

"Hey! Remember me? The one with the Fine Arts degree? I worked at I. Magnin's, for crying out loud! And, may I add, I own a very successful high-end boutique!" They both turned towards her—their faces saying it all. They were not impressed or willing to entertain a narcissistic temper tantrum.

Inwardly ashamed of reverting to her old patterns when she felt unvalued, she couldn't help wanting to get her own way, like in the old days. "Well, at least I didn't add co-ownership of the art gallery to my list of credits. See? Progress—moving on," she said, stomping over to the bed as she rescued the kitten-soft cashmere Armani from under the now-flattened body pillow.

It ticked her off when people ignored her experience, treated her as infantile and fragile now because she had "cracked open," as she termed the day her life changed, and she had crawled into bed for a year. It hadn't been easy to recover. She had developed as many protective layers as the ancient redwoods in Muir Woods not far from her house just to survive. To cut through that steely bark revealing each tender layer would take the indulgence of time.

Opening her store had helped. Stella had always loved fashion, growing up and watching her mother drape patterns of the latest French couture fashion at I. Magnin. She had even met Christian Dior's original assistant, who would bring Dior patterns from Paris to replicate for the store's customers. It was the store's owner, Grover Magnin, who had introduced Dior to the world, giving him both financial and personal backing to start his own design house. Her mother had adored Dior because he brought femininity and beauty back after the ugliness of World War II. Those days held very special memories for her.

Memories were all she had now of her mother. She had died exactly three months to the day of the finalization of the divorce. It was the realization of being both an orphan and a divorcee that had caused her to finally "crack." She hadn't been able to leave her bedroom for months. She only left to rummage for food and occasionally shower. Even tonight with the heavy rose scent, she could still smell her crazy stench enmeshed in the bedroom's walls.

Her thoughts were drifting again—that seemed to be her perpetual state of mind now—fogginess, probably hormone-related; certainly not because of the Xanax. *Focus, Stella,* she silently admonished herself as she unsteadily stepped into the Armani.

"So, he's a nice guy, right, Mom?" Nicki asked as she zipped her mother into the elegant black silk wool dress. The dress was cut exquisitely, engineered to skim the curves of her body delicately but strategically.

Stella turned to look at herself in the full-length mirror. She didn't see what the other two saw. She had been avoiding mirrors for quite some time, easily shocked by her reflection. The mirror's image was of a puffy-faced, stocky woman with coarse blond and silver locks that Maggie once referred to as "kick-ass chinchilla" and a saggy neck she simply could not be friends with. That wasn't her. *Where did that alluring vixen go?* She twisted and tugged at the dress in an effort to stretch it, apprehensive of its snugness.

Nicki, frustrated by her mother's inattention to her question, raised her voice. "Mom?"

"What? Oh, Chet? He seems nice enough in his emails and from when we talked," Stella absently replied. She turned her back to the mirror, while she fussed with her hair. *Have I lost my looks,* she wondered? *Would I be able to be enticing yet once again? There had to be some kind of magical spark left, right?* She didn't realize how fatigued she had become from her constant measurement of her own self-worth by the number on the scale or from constantly comparing herself to other women. Exhausted, she really just wanted to crawl back into bed, smoke some pot and binge watch *Law & Order.*

"Well, he sure seems to light up your boat when you see email from him," Dibrovna added in her thick Croatian accent.

"Dibrovna, it's either light up my life or float my boat. You know I love you, but you might want to work on your metaphors, okay?" Stella kidded. It amused her when Dibrovna bungled the English language. Only speaking English for a decade, Dibrovna always accepted Stella's corrective ribbing in her good-natured way. If it hadn't been for Stella, her family might not be with her now.

Dibrovna had been Stella's rock since they met fourteen years ago, after fleeing Croatia during the fall of Yugoslavia. She first met Stella in San Francisco when Stella was running the art gallery with Todd over on Geary Street. When the split came, Dibrovna proved her loyalty to Stella. Dibrovna kept the Third Act running smoothly, while Stella did what she could from her office bed.

"Mom, you look stunning."

"Yeah, right," Stella lamented, still tugging her wavy locks in an effort at some kind of style.

"Can't you ever say anything nice about yourself?" Nicki asked wearily. She sometimes didn't know if the lack of self-esteem was real or a way to manipulate a compliment. She knew her mom was a clock stopper in her day, from what Maggie had told her after her grandmother's funeral:

> "Your mom always had those sparkly gas blue eyes, so devilishly teasing. Perfectly arched eyebrows, especially the one that popped high on her face when she was displeased. Yep, you know: *that* one. And the silkiest blond hair, like spun gold. And if that wasn't enough—and it was, believe me—she had such a luscious curvy body on top of pins that would throw a guy into next week. But you know what bewitched the men? Her flirty indifference. Drew them like bees to honeysuckle," Maggie had finished. "She was *always* noticed."

Nicki hadn't seen those eyes flash in quite a while. She was proud of how her mother had aged, flawlessly in her opinion. But menopause and divorce had almost extinguished her mom's spark.

"Go online," Nicki told her. "You're not going to meet many men running an upscale women's clothing boutique, Mom. Men who come into your store already have a woman in their life." Nicki didn't add that Stella's dressing in all black, baggy, shapeless clothes wasn't helping. Maybe she was hiding. Her mom kept saying that her father had "erased" her so maybe she thought it a good idea to continue to be invisible. So unlike the mother who raised her to be bold.

"Stella Maria, come to me," Dibrovna demanded, holding up Stella's signature star necklace. Once something she rarely removed, Stella had stopped wearing it when it had become tight on her thickening neck. "Do not worry, I have put it on a better chain for you. Come."

"Let me just get in front of the fan for a minute, so I can dry off and put on the rest of my makeup." *So attractive to have constant streams of sweat falling from all areas of your body even on the cusp of winter,* Stella thought. She did like the fact there were no more surprise Aunt Flo visits. Aunt Flo had packed her bags and moved to Florida! But the give-backs were soaked bed sheets, heart palpitations, a confused body. Or the most horrifying—looking in your rear-view mirror and seeing random thick black goat hairs sticking out of your chin like the Wicked Witch of the West!

"Okay, ladies, I think this is as good as I get," Stella said, halfheartedly, turning to face them, pinning up the last strand of hair.

Nicki and Dibrovna, sitting on the edge of the bed, beamed. "Mom, you look absolutely breathtaking."

"Oh yes, Stella! And it is so good to see your legs. You should wear more dresses," Dibrovna added with a wink.

As the women descended the stainless steel-framed stairs, they were met with a shrill ear piercing wolf whistle. "See, even Pete thinks you look good, Mom."

Stella almost blurted out that Pete, the African Grey parrot she had inherited from her mom, also whistled like that for food.

They followed her out to the garage and watched as she hesitantly pulled away in her vintage 1963 red Jaguar XK-E, a sixteenth birthday present from her father, given to her before he left for Vietnam.

"Dibrovna, I sure hope this goes well. My mom really needs a boost, something to make her come alive again."

Dibrovna lovingly wrapped her arms around Nicki and squeezed. "I know, dear child. I know."

Chapter Two

—∞—

"**W**elcome back, sir. We will be serving cocktails shortly in the piano bar. Would you care to join us?"

The tall Frenchman just smiled. "Merci, but I have to beg your forgiveness. It's been a very long day for me, and with jet lag, you know," he answered, shrugging his broad shoulders.

"Oh, certainly. We understand. Would monsieur like us to send something up to your room?" the friendly concierge inquired.

"Thank you, but no. I am fine." He was in a hurry to get to his room with his precious package, making it hard to be patient as he waited for the tiny antique elevator to arrive. *What is taking so long,* he pondered as he again pressed the ivory call button. Maybe he should have made a reservation in a more modern hotel. Instead, he opted for the oldest one in San Francisco, reportedly haunted. This is where he had stayed on his first visit, and he was a sentimental sort of man. Also, the European influence in the architecture and design comforted him, made him feel at home. He wanted to keep his vibrations as high as possible at all times now. He could feel chaos churning, especially being on the West Coast, and he wanted to stay protected.

The gilded doors finally opened, allowing its crowded cargo of three guests to disembark. When the elevator emptied, he was glad he had it all to himself. In his excitement, he pushed the third-floor button a few times as if that would make the trip up to his room quicker. Soon, he would be alone. He looked at his reflection in the elevator's filigreed mirror, annoyed by his attractiveness. He knew he should be grateful that he was handsome, but it did make his vocation more complicated. *Finally!* he silently exclaimed, as the elevator jolted to a stop. He hurried down the carpeted hall to his room as he brushed the wayward lock of hair off his brow. Inserting the brass skeleton key into the lock with shaking hands, he quickly closed the door, flipped the dead bolt and laid his prized package on the lumpy four-poster bed.

"Magnifique," he exalted, lifting the enchanting doll out of his shopping bag up towards the antique chandelier, marveling at its beauty. Not only had the exquisite craftsmanship held up after all these years, but he could still detect some magic glistening from under the fullness of the gown's skirt.

"We have been waiting a long time for you, darling Faïence," he said lovingly. When his mother had first asked him to travel to San Francisco to help curate the recently found fashion dolls, with a hope of retrieving this special one, he had been hesitant. He didn't want to disappoint his mother if he was unable to rescue her. After hours spent looking through the numerous boxes of other dolls, he had almost cheered with relief after he found her. Thankfully, his years of training to stifle emotion paid off. He did not betray his joy to the others in the stuffy hotel room where he and his hostesses had gathered for their task.

He kept telling himself he was not stealing, as she belonged to his family. Which was true—to a point. It was evident watching the curators lovingly handle the precious fashion dolls that they, too, were smitten. It would break their hearts when they found out she was gone. But it had to be done.

Both he and his mother Lilli were ready for the next step when they received a letter from the American museum. The curator said they were fortunate enough to acquire most of the exquisite couture fashion dolls from the 1946 international tour of France's Theatre de la Mode as a gift from Mrs. Spreckles. Somehow the dolls had been left behind in the basement of a Union Square department store after their San Francisco appearance. They had been discovered deeply hidden in a corner under the staircase right before the demolition of the now-defunct City of Paris. He smiled at the irony that hell raiser Alma Spreckles, reportedly the model for the Winged Victory goddess in Union Square, had played an unknowing part in the Return of the Divine Feminine.

The dolls had been the idea of the French patriotic charity *Entraide Fransaise* to raise funds for World War II relief. They also wanted to promote French fashion designers and the French fashion industry which had been decimated. He knew they were there, in that basement. Once he had played with them in his youth with *the girl* while his mother worked across the street with the American pattern maker.

He was relieved they had been found, as his mother often assured him they would be. These twenty-seven-inch-high dolls, made of wire, had been dressed and styled with couture designs by some of the greatest designers in history: Balenciaga, Jacques Fath, Schiaparelli, and Dior— fifty-five design houses in all. The dolls were even bejeweled by famous jewelers such as Cartier and Van Cleef & Arpels. Though most of the couture houses had been looted by the Nazis during the Occupation, they were able to utilize remaining hidden jewels and exquisite textiles due to the miniature size of the dolls. San Francisco had been their last U.S. stop of the world tour, displaying the Spring/Summer 1946 Paris collection.

The West Coast museum had acquired the collection and decided to restore the textiles, colors and silhouettes of the gowns. But after years packed in a musty steamer trunk and no luck in finding original photographs, their curators were searching for any assistance to authenticate the originals and help with their restoration. Luckily, a curator had found a faded yet readable manifest tucked into a pocket in one of the trunk's lid, listing Lilli St. Remy Aubert, Dior's assistant, as the packing agent.

Lilli and Christian Dior had, at the time, been employed by designer Lucien Lelong and were responsible for two of the dolls: one dressed in a turquoise white-polka-dotted chiffon gown, elegantly draped with a swirling full skirt; the other, an ivory tulle strapless ball gown, dotted with shiny sequins amid an embroidered gray-blue floral pattern. Also, unbeknownst to the curators, in the voluminous underskirt of the strapless gown was the judicious placement of a star from an ancient textile relic. This was the doll his mother sent him to retrieve: Faïence.

It had been an especially long day spent as they meticulously cataloged the fashion dolls. They had previously sent photographs to Lilli, and she had made notes for her son, Gabriel, to share to help identify which doll was dressed by whom. The curators, mostly older women, had fawned over the handsome Frenchman, telling him how they couldn't have performed their task without him. He tried to be friendly and charming, but female attention always made him nervous. He had been taught not to reciprocate the behavior nor did he want to.

He had his work cut out for him. It would not be easy to pilfer this special doll. The curators had a special obsession with Faïence. "Look at the meticulous embroidery of the gray-blue flowers, weaved in with the white sequins. Why, it almost glows," one curator remarked, drawing a buzzing crowd of the other curators.

Gabriel didn't elaborate that she was named Faïence after the gray-blue porcelain Lelong had collected, or that her red hair was in homage to his own mother Lilli's lovely locks. His duty was to distract them, which he did by pointing out the doll dressed in a bright red organdy gown by Madame Gres.

"But Madame, look at this beauty. See, in her turban? Notice how they used kingfisher feathers, coral beads and rhinestones like a halo around her delicate face?" His mother had versed him well on the other dolls just in case this happened. "Oh, and don't forget about this one," he said, as he led them to the Schiaparelli. "This designer was ahead of her time—always. She even collaborated with Salvador Dali on her famous lobster dress. And this quilted skirt reminds me of Dali's desert paintings." They all flocked to examine the patch-worked skirt more closely, pulling out magnifying glasses, clucking their excitement. He figured right—they all were quilters. It was just the window of time he needed.

Now, as he sat in the antique wing chair, by the hotel's still operating window as the sun set, he closed his eyes as he wandered back to the last time he saw *her*: 1967—that magical summer in San Francisco. The start of the Seven Squares between Uranus and Pluto, ushering in the Age of Aquarius, the Age of Water. The whole world was focused on the "happenings" taking place in the "City by the Bay." An evolutionary and rebellious change in human relationships they called the Summer of Love. A year when it started to feel like the world had become smaller and more accessible, even maybe joined in some way. Soon, the world would watch the American astronaut set foot on another planet and a historical gathering for three days of love and music called Woodstock. After so much bloodshed half a world away, America ached for healing.

And a time, so important to him later in his life's work, when the changes from Vatican II were showing up in a most unexpected and inconvenient way. At least to the top hierarchy of the Church. The Church had no idea what demoting the mother of Jesus Christ, or not revealing the Third Secret, would unleash. But because of life stories passed down through his family as treasured bequeaths, he knew the plan. That plan had consumed the last two decades of his life, starting soon after his last trip to San Francisco. And so had the memories of that trip which still haunted him daily.

He walked over to the intricately carved armoire and removed the small valise he brought just for the doll, pushing his unruly hair out of his eyes. As he lowered the stolen doll into the case, his stomach growled. Satisfied that he had accomplished his goal, he was now ready for the pleasure of a rewarding dinner.

Chapter Three

—∞—

Stella inched her vintage vehicle down the windy steep street, riding her brakes all the way towards Highway 101. The spiciness of the nearby redwoods intermingled with fireplace smoke wafted through her car's vents, tempting her to return to the safety of her wooded hilltop home. She fiddled with the after-market iPod player and found her '60s playlist— a musical touchstone. Maybe memories of a happier time would calm her nerves, bolster her courage, stop her from turning around.

Her stomach hurt. She really wasn't confident that she was ready to dip her toe back into the pool of male-female relationships. Her pain was still raw, but not painful enough to quench her need for male appreciation, maybe even adoration. *When did I become so needy?* She was acting like the newly-single women she and Todd used to avoid. The kind that were never invited again to dinner parties.

Was she acting like this because the love of her life now loved a man? Would it have been less painful to have been left for another woman? She felt so damn betrayed! Cheating is cheating. Frankly, she was also embarrassed. No man had ever left her before; well, if you didn't count the disappearance of her father.

Todd had been her one and only major love affair. Sure, as a child of the '60s she had been *with* other men. But only relationships defined by that era: free love, go with the flow, no commitments. The type of relationship which suited Stella just fine. Not allowing any man to get too close, but still enjoying the spoils of her pursuits. It was part of her DNA. Her widowed mother had taught her well on how to shield her heart and not to let a man hurt you.

Instinctively, she swished her hips from side to side as she chair-danced to *Pretty Woman*. Orbison's growls reminded her that she was once the pretty one, able to walk into any room and have whomever she wanted. Reel one in and then discard the poor lad without a second thought, like a crumbled used tissue.

Probably why I hunted Todd with such bold determination, she thought. The two had become instant friends since sitting down next to each other at the San Francisco State University orientation where both were studying art history. It started as an after-school glass of wine to discuss art, fashion, school, and politics. Easy, comfortable conversation. He didn't act like the others, trying to immediately get her horizontal and unzipped in eight seconds flat like some steer roping contest. In fact, in hindsight, he had been very sexually aloof to her, mainly interested in just being her friend. At the time, she had felt a little puzzled, then dejected. Sometimes it drove her insanely mad. Eventually, she learned to live with it.

Married not long after graduation, they traveled the world before opening their successful art gallery in San Francisco. They had been the ultimate '70s San Francisco society couple, out every night for some event. Plays, movies, and especially disco dancing. They weren't the kind of romantic couple who snuggled in front of the fireplace, watching television. But they couldn't keep up with the pace—and the drugs and drink. As the decade started to come to the end, Stella noticed that Todd was going out more and more without her. It made her nervous when she saw his picture in the *San Francisco Chronicle* society pages with strangers. In an effort to save her marriage and her reputation, she decided it was time to move out of the city and start a family. Todd had been easy to persuade as he was also getting tired of the lifestyle. Too many of his friends lately had been dying.

It had taken longer than expected after moving to Mill Valley and suffering a few miscarriages, but eventually they were blessed with a beautiful honey-haired daughter. They functioned almost normally, with Nicki as their focus. Then Nicki got married—and Todd left. Erased her. Their life together now seemed to be just an apparition.

She wasn't in any hurry to share her space with a man again. The renovations had just been finished—or lack thereof. Todd hadn't fought for their luxury home. He was more than happy to walk away and return to his new life in the city.

First, she had the whole interior of her house painted the starkest white she could find. Only one painting graced her walls. Gone were all of Todd's fussy little knick-knacks, dust-gatherers that occupied every available horizontal space. She wanted this to be her domain, with no reminders of him. She could erase too.

Why the hell am I going on this date? To prove to my daughter and friends that I'm well? We need to rethink marriage, she thought, as she drove through the town center.

Recently, she had read an article about the Mosuo, a community of women in China. The article claimed it was the happiest place on earth. The women had an arrangement called *Sisi*, a walking back and forth. No marriage, just a visiting relationship between lovers. After a young girl came of age, she was allowed to receive male visitors if that was her desire. However, the man could only stay in her room overnight and must return to his mother's house in the morning. If a child was born from the union, he or she remained with the mother. The father had no social or economic responsibility for the child, and the males from the woman's family helped raise it. When the woman found she no longer desired the male, she simply didn't answer her door.

Stella loved that idea. No divorce attorneys, no long drawn out battles over piddly-ass stuff, no ex-husband screaming at her over a glass conference room table that she disgusted him with her plump dimpled thighs and could she please pull her dress over her bulging saggy knees!

As she was about to turn on to U.S. 101 South, she noticed a woman, probably about her age, standing by the freeway exit with a simple hand-written cardboard sign—*Trust the Journey*. Stella quickly avoided looking into the woman's eyes for the fear that could someday be her. *Please God, if you do exist, don't let me end up old, poor and alone,* as if she wasn't half-way there. But it was too late. Their eyes met. A fleeting moment of familiarity. *I've seen those eyes,* she thought. She had a hard time turning her eyes away, as she accelerated into traffic, shaking her shoulders as if she could shake off the sudden chill worming its way into the marrow of her bones. A muffled buzzing tickled her eardrums and made them itch. Maybe a side effect of the Xanax.

Feeling unsettled, she switched off her iPod and tuned into the local NPR station. A reporter was interviewing young French women. Apparently, it was St. Catherine's Day, where French single women celebrated the day by praying to find husbands. "Yeah, be careful what you pray for," she said out loud. "Pray for Sisi, sister—and don't end up like me!"

Muscle memory kicked in as she maneuvered the freeway's curves headed towards Sausalito and through the Waldo tunnel. The fog had just started to roll in through the Golden Gate Bridge. The sparkling gray blanket hugged the top of Mt. Tamalpais, known as the Sleeping Maiden, before it spilled through the suspension cables of the bridge, the wispy tendrils directing her into the sunset-lighted city.

A lot of locals complained about the infamous fog, but not her. The billowing moistness made her want to be enveloped in its cotton candy fluffiness, like the down comforter on her bed. Tonight, if she had been religious she might have likened it to the rapture, watching the setting sun's orange and purple rays saturate the asphalt and steel of the most famous bridge in the world.

God's blanket is what her maternal grandmother, Nema, called it. Nema was a native Northern Californian, born and raised in the Sierra gold country. From the Southern Maidu Nisenan tribe as defined by the white man's definition of her words. Nema just said she was Miwok—"the People" to her ancestors. It was her grandmother's passed-down stories that had introduced Stella to the mysteries of life. She could feel her grandmother's presence now, calming her down. "Just breathe, Morning Star. Stay in your breath." She exhaled loudly, releasing her taut muscles. Breathe through the fear, Nema had taught her, before she had slipped into her old age prison of dementia.

Most of the grandmother's tales she hadn't shared with anyone, not even Todd. She wasn't sure what was a true ancestor's tale and what was an old woman's demented ramblings. Plus, keeping them to herself made them precious. Something special to share with grandchildren one day, perhaps. She believed her Nema's teachings that you couldn't always see everything with the naked eye. She knew in her gut there was more to God than what she had been taught as a child in church.

Traffic wasn't too bad going into the city, she thought after paying the toll. It was only a Wednesday night. A good night for a first date, better than the pressure of a romantic Friday or Saturday date. She drove through the Marina, trying to keep her eyes on the road. The docked bobbing sailboats swayed in unison on the choppy dark water like speared cocktail weenies on a nervous server's tray, hypnotizing her. The Marina is where she used to sail with her father. In an instant, a tear spilled over the bottom rim of her eyes. *Damn menopause—makes me so emotional!*

She drove past Fisherman's Wharf, glad for the distraction of gawking tourists and bright flashing neon lights. Within minutes she pulled into the parking garage near the Embarcadero Center. She appreciated the water's closeness. God's tranquilizer, her dad had told her. She remembered that quote every time she sailed. Probably why Todd had given her the devastating news while sailing out on the Bay. Trying to soften the heart jab, maybe. He told her that he had always loved her and always would, that his love for her wasn't defined by his sexuality.

Hollow words now. In retrospect, it probably was just a gesture to ease his guilt. It was time to be just Stella.

Chapter Four

—∞—

Stella agreed to meet Chet at Mist, the trendy new San Francisco restaurant located not far from the Ferry Building. Rave review in the *Chronicle*, his email said, which contained his unsolicited summary: "One Michelin star young chef, serving an innovative seafood/French fusion menu, using only locally farmed or just-caught ingredients. Stunning Art Deco design including a liquid blue lighted ceiling with a profusion of thick dandelion bouquets artfully dangled from the ceiling. A rosewood bar, lighted by amber copper-clad sconces, with its blush walls, something, something . . . ."

"Sounds lovely," she had responded, thinking he was trying way too hard to impress her. Actually, the review had revved up her appetite, not that she needed any help with that. She did love great food and was a little lonely for dining companionship that required her to get dressed and out of bed. She hoped the amber light from the sconces and low candlelight would have the same effect as a greased-up camera lens did for aging actresses.

She spotted him at the bar, talking on his cell phone as he waved to her. *Time to post a more recent photo*, she thought dismissively. Nicki had warned her about that. "Everyone posts a decade-old photo, Mom," Nicki had advised, "so be prepared and don't look shocked." Still an attractive man, not too fat, too sloppy, not too —she stopped herself. She felt like a black crow feasting on road kill. Once a Virgo, always a Virgo.

She turned a critical eye towards the restaurant. Just the type of place she and Todd used to frequent with wealthy clients in tow. Money well spent to move the expensive art and make them wealthy in the process.

Looking back now, it felt pretentious and predictable. She had become so irritated by the snobbishness of San Francisco's foodies; well, at least with the younger crowd. So impressed with tweezered food on their plates, artfully arranged. Nowadays, she just wanted clean food that you could plop onto your plate and savor. The kind where she knew where it was grown and by whom. Grown and prepared for her with love. Lately, she was lucky because her food came from what Dibrovna had grown and raised on the outskirts of Novato. Dibrovna said the flavor and healing properties of her food had something to do with the marshes being so close. Minerals and such, she had said.

As she walked towards him, her old trick knee wobbled. Damn high heels! She hoped he hadn't noticed as she flashed a dazzling smile, tucked in her tush, sucked in her stomach, pushed back her shoulders and approached him. The runway walk, just as Maggie had taught her years ago at I. Magnin. Her intent was not for Chet to be her forever man—just a starter, like an appetizer.

"Chet? I'm Stella," she said, extending her hand. Their eyes met as he shook her hand in that limp way some men mistakenly think a lady wants to shake hands. Instantly, she recognized the look of disappointment. Her eyebrow flinched. *Just in your mind, let it go*, she tried to convince herself.

"Nice to finally meet you," he said, the corners of his mouth curled up just slightly. He flipped his phone closed and put it in his monogrammed shirt pocket as his eyes followed the cocktail waitress. "How was the 101?"

Her smile slackened. *The 101?* When anyone referred to "the 101" or "the 5," it was a red flag: LA! Southern California! A snobby hangover from her marriage that she didn't mind sharing with the world. Northern California was superior: better educated, better cultured, better everything than shallow Southern California, in her opinion. She was tempted to pivot on her expensive Dior casino heels and march right back to her car, but she stayed so as not to disappoint her daughter. Show her she could, once again, do hard things.

They had emailed back and forth about five times since she had first "winked" at him, then talked briefly on the phone when they had decided it was time to meet. Chet was, according to his profile, a:

> *never married, 56-year-old writer/poet/financial planner, witty, intelligent, 5' 10", average build, salt-and-pepper hair, blue eyes, lives in San Francisco, loves the arts, sailing, cuddling and holding hands in front of a fire while sipping a 2004 Chateau Pontet-Canet French Bordeaux and feeding his lady Belgium chocolates. Fan of both the Giants and the 49ers, and comfortable in both jeans & a tux. Creative but still grounded in the realities of the world. Looking for a woman with a nice smile, intelligent, takes pride in her appearance, has a good sense of humor. Values intimacy, but friendship first. Not into games. Someone who is sensual, non-judgmental, and flexible. Willing to consider marriage with the right woman.*

Sounded good enough to Stella. Never married, so no baggage. Only a date. She was about to find out how drastically dating had changed in the past three decades and the new code words for "danger—stay away." A seasoned online dater would have recognized all the flaming warnings.

The waiter led them to a lovely bay-side table where Chet had paid the waiter to discretely lay down a just-blooming pink tulip on her plate before they were seated.

"Thank you, young man," Chet said, making sure Stella saw him put money into the maître d's hand. Stella was impressed by the flower, as all of Chet's first dates were. "Here, let me get that for you," he said as he pulled out her chair. "I've already ordered some of my favorite French champagne," he whispered into her ear as he pushed in her chair.

His closeness made her blush. Stella couldn't remember the last time a male had been in her personal space. *Oh, what was I worried about?* She knocked up the first impression of him to her nerves. He really seemed to have excellent manners and knew how to treat a woman.

As she scooted closer to the table's edge, she had that unnerving feeling that someone was staring at her. Slowly she turned her head and locked eyes with the dark-haired man in the corner as he jerked his head down, looking intently at his menu while pushing the black wavy lock of hair off his forehead. Something about his masculine beak of a nose, the cleft in his chin and his piercing blue eyes seemed so recognizable, but she couldn't place him. Probably one of the customers from the art gallery, she assured herself, waiting for his trophy wife to join him.

She returned her focus to Chet, catching him doing the "elevator look" as their lovely young waitress approached. His rude behavior was making her increasingly uncomfortable as attested by her reddening chest, fly-speckled with humiliation. Her "fight or flight" survival reflex that had occupied her entire last year started to kick in. *Calm down*, she reassured herself, hoping she could hide her slow but shallow breaths as she studied the menu. *Just be charming to me—at least until the end of appetizers and a drink*, she prayed.

"Hmm, I think . . ." she started to say, strategically holding the menu without twisting her forearm so her aged skin wouldn't look like a wrung-out dish cloth, when Chet interrupted.

"We're ready to order," he said, grabbing the passing waitress's arm, demanding her immediate attention.

Stella was stunned speechless, unsure how to react. Was he just intuitive, knowing what she wanted? Or was she being treated like tonight's chattel?

"We'll start with the chilled smoked lobster soup and organic endive with melted Olema goat cheese, followed by the Mendocino abalone with crisped pork belly and garlic chips, then . . ." He stopped when he noticed Stella's gaping mouth. "We'll order dessert when we get closer to the end of our meal. Thanks, sweetie," he said as he summarily dismissed the hired help, patting her hand.

"Did I do something wrong?" Chet inquired, a puzzled look on his face.

"Why did you order for both of us, without asking me what I wanted?"

"Sorry. Just habit. Truthfully, I usually date younger women, and they enjoy me making choices for them. You know, stepping up and 'being the man' and all. Is that a problem?"

Inside, Stella was screaming. *Yeah, that's a problem. And I don't want you cutting my meat for me either, Daddy!* But instead, as was her nature, she politely replied, "Well, I'm used to having input, especially when someone doesn't know me." She could feel the date was veering off the cliff at super-sonic speed. She, again, was aware of the man in the corner staring at her and glanced in his direction. He smiled slightly, shrugging his shoulders as if sympathetic to her plight but helpless to intervene. Feeling like a trapped rabbit as her breath quickened, she placed her napkin on her lap to hide her shaking hands as the waiter placed the steaming bowl of soup in front of her. She bargained with herself and decided to stay and at least eat.

By the time she had finished her soup, her mouth cramped from the forced smiling. Chet talked non-stop about himself and rarely met her eyes. Twice, he received a call on his cell, which he took without excusing himself. He seemed oblivious to how his constant flirting with the waitress and ogling any female body part within eye shot might not be appropriate. They finished their appetizers and started on the abalone. At least the food was excellent. She just kept eating since Chet obviously had no interest in hearing her talk and finding out more about her. Plus, he was paying.

"That's what I like about mature women. They're never afraid to just eat what they like without a care for calories."

What? she screamed in her head. She couldn't believe what she had just heard—the most stupid, idiotic words you could ever say to a hormonally-challenged midlife woman. Like a wild fire, the red tell-tale flush of rage rose from the tip of her toes, shot up her legs and torso, spreading to every capillary on her chest before the final explosion onto her cheeks. She snapped her head toward the stranger's table and caught his look of pity. *Why won't you help me?* her eyes pleaded as she glared into the stranger's guilt-glazed eyes, mindlessly rubbing her right knee. *Why would I think this man whom I don't know would want to come to my aid?* Confused, she felt like she was caught in between two different worlds; too much like her last year.

She desperately wanted a Xanax, even just half a one. She wanted to grab old Chet around the neck and scream in his face: *you have no right to treat me like this! I have worth. I'm not invisible, not erasable.* Instead, she excused herself and walked hurriedly to the bathroom, using the blade of her hand to fling her mascara-stained tears down onto the wide-planked wooden floor.

"Excuse me," she said as she pushed into the open stall ahead of another woman. She leaned against the Italian marble walls, using the stone's coldness to absorb the heat from her cheeks. She hated that her skin always gave away her feelings. *Maggie, I need you now*, she cried silently. Maggie always looked so sweet on the outside, but could explode like a firecracker, using her words like an African poison dart gun. But not Stella. Never speak in anger, she was taught. Instead, she started to silently tap on her breastbone, unaware her necklace was missing.

After a few minutes, she was composed enough to return to the table. "I'm sorry, but I have a migraine headache. I need to leave now so I can safely drive home."

"Oh, okay." Chet seemed perplexed, but also a little relieved. No sense trying to seem interested—the night was still young. He didn't even stand up to say good bye or offer to walk her to her car.

I'm so out of here, she angrily muttered to herself, her click-clacking heels loudly echoing in the parking garage. She didn't feel even a twinge of guilt as she stepped over the begging homeless man who weakly reached up for any left overs. She couldn't get out of there fast enough. As she backed up her sports car and started for the exit of the parking garage, she caught a glimpse of the stranger, walking in between parked cars. Or she thought she saw someone; maybe just her imagination.

In seconds, she was gunning for the exit, screeching her tires around the curves of each garage level while she bounced her mirrors with the hammering bass of the Animals *Don't Let Me Down*. Oh, perfect song, she screamed as her tears avalanched. She pounded her foot on the floorboard to the beat of the drum so hard the left heel broke off her cherished pumps. All she wanted to do was get out of the city and back into her safe cocoon in Mill Valley.

She shot-gunned the little white pill to the back of her throat and swallowed.

Chapter Five

—∞—

Gabriel's stomach growled loudly, as he stood under the narrow hotel canopy waiting for his taxi to arrive. The hotel concierge had recommended a new place called Mist, which specialized in Mediterranean-style seafood. Sounded perfect, like a piece of his beloved Provencal home right here in San Francisco. In a flash a dented, though relatively clean Yellow Cab swooped up to the curb to fetch its next passenger.

"Where ya going, bro?" the grizzled black cabbie growled, his eyes barely visible under his floppy, pin-studded beret.

"The Mist," Gabriel tried to say, as his head bounced against the back seat before he could click his seatbelt.

"Hey, man—sorry. Rush hour!" the cabbie explained, eyeing Gabriel in the mirror. "Gotta be aggressive in this town," he said as he made an illegal U-turn. He stepped on the gas with so much force, the decorative pins on his hat jingled, while his dashboard chock full of Raiders' and A's bobble heads danced.

"I believe it's down on the Embarcadero," Gabriel offered, securing his seat belt.

"Hey, I know the city by heart, dude. I'll get ya there in a heartbeat."

Gabriel tried to sit back and relax, which was hard as the taxi weaved in and out of traffic like San Francisco 49er Jerry Rice headed for the end zone. Americans moved at such a fast pace, always rushing from one place to another. He had forgotten about that, being around the older women today. The women out of necessity naturally moved at a pace he was used to and savored. Instead, he tried to concentrate on the architecture and the skyline, as much as he possibly could. He rolled down the window so he could feel the refreshing air on his face, delighting in the night's crispness and hoping it would cure his jet lag.

Soon, they were close enough to smell the sea. Gabriel leaned forward. "Sir, could you please let me out here," he asked, just a few short blocks shy of the restaurant. "It is such a beautiful autumn night here in your city. I would like to walk. Merci."

"No prob, Frenchie," the cabbie said, appreciating the generous tip that had been added to the fare.

"Do you have a reservation, sir?" the pretty hostess asked him, when he approached her polished steel podium front and center in the swanky establishment's lobby. She was clearly the appointed gatekeeper.

"Oui, madam. I mean, yes. My hotel called it in for me, I believe. Gabriel Aubert."

His accent wasn't lost on the hostess whose demeanor quickly changed. "Good evening, Mr. Aubert. We are pleased you are joining us this evening. Please follow me," she said, as she touched his forearm for a little longer than was common. She held the abnormally thin, long menu close enough to her hip to accent her curvy silhouette and flipped her long auburn hair over her shoulder. Gabriel was fully aware of her swaying hips, as her conversation with him became more flirtatious. However, he did not respond beyond a cursory smile. His day with the female curators had sharpened his avoidance skills.

He was glad his table was in the corner so he could observe the other diners. He had spent so much of his life doing solitary work that crowds made him uncomfortable. He was trained to observe and pay attention, not only by his employer but by his mother. His stomach rumbled as he perused the menu, causing him to look around hoping no one heard him.

That's when he felt the room change, like an airplane door opening in mid-flight, sucking all contents out into space.

A presence, an energy. No, not just a presence—*her presence.* Looking up, he honed into the energy flow until he found her. She was walking to one of the tables, a little off kilter, slightly favoring her left leg over the right. Guilt overwhelmed him after all these years, seeing her like that still. He remembered that wobbly walk because he had caused it. Quickly he bent his head over the menu, dropping his gaze, as if he had been caught doing something wrong. He knew this had not happened by coincidence. There are no accidents, his mother had taught him.

He tried to concentrate on the menu, but he couldn't keep his head down. She was there with a man. *God, are you testing me?* he asked, as jealousy tightened its grip on his heart. *Act as a priest, not a man,* he reprimanded himself. But he couldn't stop watching, weak against the foreign emotions penetrating his psyche. Emotions that needed action to appease them. The more he watched, the more upset he became with his lack of bravery, disgusted by his weakness. How dare that man humiliate her so openly with his obvious flirting.

Gabriel could sense her distress. When she turned his way, his heart almost exploded. *The face that never left his mind's eye.* Feeling like a schoolboy whose social skills with the opposite sex were sorely lacking, all he could do was just shrug his shoulders. Once again, he'd failed to come to her rescue. He simply did not know how to intrude into her life. The last time he tried to rescue her he had almost killed her, or so he thought.

Returning to his soup, he suddenly felt like he was being buffeted by winds similar to his homeland's mistrals. He knew it was just chaotic energy and jerked his head up. She was walking quickly towards the bathrooms, obviously in distress. He signaled his waitress, waving dollars. *Get to her quickly,* the voice said.

Then she fled. He immediately followed her out to the parking lot, trying to stay hidden in the shadows. He only wanted to make sure she was safe. Actually, he wanted to reach out to her, comfort her, hold her close. Provide her peace before her soul became callused. But she sped out of the garage before he could catch her. He had failed her again.

Chapter Six

—∞—

"How dare you!" she screamed as she pounded the walnut steering wheel with the heel of her hand. Barely able to catch her breath, she was having a difficult time staying within the undulating narrow lanes of Highway 101. Strings of entwined snot and tears dripped off her chin into the crevices of her cleavage as her tires repeatedly clipped the lane markers. Fortunately, after years of commuting she knew the way back home like a homing pigeon.

"Why do men think they can treat me—or any woman—this way," she raged. "I am not some lump of unfeeling flesh, a receptacle for your thoughtless word dumps! I deserve to be treated with respect, you effin' small-dicked moron! I didn't want to go on this goddamned date in the first place!" she cried, her final punctuating whack cracking the vintage steering wheel.

Out of the corner of her puffy eyes, she saw the large Mercedes sedan. Some guy in the next lane, gawking at her. She laid on her horn as she flipped him off, just as he mouthed "nice car." His niceness devastated her, throwing a burning match on her emotional bonfire.

Sausalito, next exit. It was on their last sail out of Sausalito when he told her the truth about himself, his new love and asked her for a divorce.

"We made a vow to be together forever," she yelled. "How dare you leave me to grow old alone! And now I have to date again?" She stomped the gas pedal so hard she fishtailed into the next lane, barely missing the sleek BMW coupe next to her.

She thought of what one of her long-time customers mentioned recently; that over four million women had been married to gay men. *So effin' what!* Was that factoid supposed to ease her pain?

In fact, it did the opposite. Now no longer unique—just common, part of an emerging demographic. Betrayed. Ashamed. *How could I not have known?* There had been signs she had chosen to ignore, like most spouses. The portrait of the perfect sophisticated couple suited her better. She desperately didn't want to end up alone like her mother.

Finally, she reached her exit and pulled off the freeway, managing to navigate to the safety of her garage. *Thank god, for automatic door openers.* She cherished her recluse enabler, pushing its magical button that allowed entrance to her home without any interaction. The small square of plastic-encased electronics had allowed her to conveniently avoid interacting with her neighbors. No more answering any of their prying questions after Todd had left. *Are you okay* or *can we do anything for you?* No, she wanted to scream—just leave me be!

She put the car into park as the garage door softly lowered, unaware of the crack as she laid her forehead against the steering wheel while taking a few slow breaths in gratitude. Home. She tried to raise her head. Stuck. Her white-blond strands were stuck in the crack of the steering wheel making it impossible for her to move. She carefully coaxed out each strand hoping it would not break when something flashy caught her eye. Her star necklace, lying on the floorboard. She hastily grabbed it and threw it into her purse, wondering how it got there.

Quietly walking into the kitchen, she made a beeline to the French doors and Pete's large wrought-iron cage, where he was fast asleep with his head cradled into his chest. Stella tiptoed, her damaged shoes in hand, so as not to give her eight-year-old parrot a startle. She blamed Todd's lingering negative presence in her home for causing her beloved bird night frights. She cooed with the ritual kissing noises that signaled an end to their day and gently covered his cage.

It felt as if her stair steps had doubled since her last ascent as she lugged her exhausted body up. Once on the landing, she unzipped her dress, shrugged her shoulders, and let it drop to the floor as she entered her artic-white bedroom. Hooking the Armani with her unsteady right foot, she slung it into the corner without a concern of its multi-thousand-dollar price tag.

She pried the sweaty Spanx off and slipped into her ratty old black sweats. It amused her that the $20 she had spent at Target was more valuable right now than the $4,887 she priced for the dress carelessly discarded on the floor. *I won't share that with my customers. Must keep up the illusion that money will buy you happiness. Money over honesty to keep the business profitable*, she cynically mused. A seasoned veteran of a wealthy lifestyle, she realized she was also a victim. She was the unhappiest she had been in her entire life. Just a little joy was all she wanted. With that thought, she decided to do what made her most happy—making bread while drinking wine and listening to opera. No sense being miserable over some guy she would have ignored in high school. Seize every moment.

Stella had been introduced to opera by her father. He explained to her that it was more than just music; it was the storytelling. His introduction to opera was during his service in Italy at the very end of WWII, as part of an Allied group that helped rebuild the San Carlo opera house in Naples. Naples had been so beautiful, he said, even after it was decimated by the bombing, all because of the music. Women singing every day in their homes, the music floating out their windows over the rumple in the streets taught him the safety music provided with its comfort. A useful tool for a soldier, he said. *Pay attention to each note. Stay present.*

Now a useful tool for a divorced middle-aged fool of a woman, she thought, as she shuffled in her motley sheepskin-lined slippers over to the kitchen's iPod docking station.

Perfect! Nessun Dorma, Pavarotti. The angelic chorus mixed with the passion and pain of dying for love filled the high-ceiling great room as she wrapped her stained Ralph Lauren apron around her thick waist.

Instinctively, she reached into her kitchen island and pulled out her grandmother's hand-thrown moss green bread bowl, her fingers tracing the rim's banding of waves and stars. She used to see how many times she could circle her finger around the bowl as Nema told her about the women-chiefs of the Star People. It had been a long time since she had made bread, a beloved ritual Nema had taught her so she could cope with being father-less. Nema would play music with a beat, from Big Band to traditional Indian drumming on her Hi-Fi, teaching Stella how to use the music's rhythm to knead the bread. The repetitive movements of pushing, kneading, rolling—a culinary meditation helped clear the Third Eye, Nema had said.

It wasn't her Third Eye she was concerned with right now. She could barely see out of the First and Second, as she squinted her tear-swollen eyes peering through her designer cheaters that rested on her nose. Reaching for the bottle of wine, she luckily didn't need to read the label, as she always kept bottles of her son-in-law's vintage reserve Cabernet Sauvignon on the second shelf of her island. On autopilot, she opened the bottle, poured a glass, and began adding ingredients in the chipped bowl.

It wasn't necessary to consult any cookbook. She knew the recipe by heart for her favorite Tuscan bread. It was just six ingredients that she could eyeball as to the right measurement. Gulping her glass of Cab like it was an ice-cold beer on a blistering hot sunny day, the liquid dribbled out of the corners of her lipstick-stained mouth before landing on the smooth ball of dough. Pushing and pulling, she kneaded the bread as she remembered what Nema had told her in one of her last lucent moments: *Flour and yeast together do not rise and become alive until you touch it. It is the same with man and woman.* She realized now that Nema probably sensed Stella's marriage was in trouble, though she had tried to hide it from her grandmother. Hell, Nema probably knew Todd was gay too.

Tonight, she used her bread making as a release valve, venting her anxiety and pain with each violent slap of the dough on the cold stone counter, flour erupting off the hard surface and raining back down, building to a crescendo of relief. Now was not the time to be immobilized anymore. No more politeness!

Slap, went the dough on the granite counter top in unison to every soaring high C in Pavarotti's aria. By the time Luciano hit his last high note, she had downed her second glass of wine and was pouring another; she had drunk enough wine to bubble her blood. Almost spent, the distaste of her first bite at a new love life had been replaced with the mellow sexiness of the rich red wine and wafting promise of buttery bread melting in her mouth. Comforting yet numbing. The flow of liquid sadness ebbed, replaced by a slight throbbing headache. After she covered the dough to rise, she bent over and laid her head down on the floury counter, hoping the pulsating pain would soon ease.

Bzzzzz. She swatted at her ear as her solace was shattered. Pete began to squawk as he paced rapidly back and forth in his cage. Afraid he might hurt himself, she rushed to comfort him, her flour-dusted face leaving a trail across the high-glossed hemlock floor.

"Ach, pretty lady, ach, pretty lady," he crowed. *What the hell? Never heard him say that before,* she thought, when she witnessed a brilliant flash of light outside on the deck. Suddenly, unreasonably calm, she gently placed her wine glass on the floor, walked past Pete's cage and opened the French doors onto the deck.

Numb to the chilled late November night, she first looked east as a trail of eerily glowing orbs floated towards her in a five-pointed star formation, cresting high above the redwoods. The supernatural orbs came closer, connected and melded before gently morphing into a new form. All the mystical matter blended into an undulating feminine form that drifted towards her, glowing in bright hues of color that emitted harmonic chords. Almost close enough for her to touch, it instantly swirled into a perfect circle before slowly drifting upwards and once again forming into a curvaceous womanly shape. Stella eagerly allowed the unrecognizable force to guide her towards the small grotto's moon garden wedged into corner of her backyard's mossy cliff fence.

Stella felt as if every drop of blood in her veins had been replaced with a euphoric potion that melded her mind, soul and consciousness into oneness with the misty image. Suddenly, her body jerked as if she had been zapped by strings of electricity, dropping her to her knees on the deck, engulfed in an ecstatic trance as she stared at the vision.

Blissful, love-filled energy exploded in every cell of her body as she stared at the ephemeral image in a flowing sheer gown. Any thoughts of that night's trauma no longer existed, no worries of what might happen tomorrow. *Now was now.* Her nostrils filled with a fresh bouquet of roses unlike the overpowering cloying scent of Todd's roses she had ripped out in a drunken rage. She heard the image talk—no, that wasn't true. She *felt* a message emitting from shadowy vapors undulating before her.

Know thyself. Awaken and come to me. Reveal what has been hidden. Know that I am. Love as One.

Swiftly, a super-heated energy blast of pink radiant love erupted in her body, surging through her blood and tingling every nerve ending. She felt as if she were entangled in some kind of cosmic web, connected to everything that ever was and that would ever be. She touched her cheek, surprised to realize she was still crying. But these were tears of sheer heavenly joy. She felt that living long enough to experience this moment made her whole life worth living. Her last thought as her body crumpled into a heap on the deck was *take me with you.*

Chapter Seven

∞

"Monsieur," the flight attendant whispered as she gently nudged his shoulder. "It is time to buckle up and prepare for landing. We will be in Paris shortly."

Unaccustomed to being touched, he automatically snapped his shoulder back in retreat as his eyes popped wide open. He was still dressed as a civilian in his black turtleneck and slacks, so how would she know his occupation necessitated a more delicate approach.

"I'm so sorry for startling you. But I do need you to raise your seat back up. Regulations for your safety, you know."

Wiping the crusty sleep from his eyes, he inquisitively stretched out his long legs, slipping his feet underneath the seat in front of him. Good, the valise was still here. He looked to his right to see if the passenger next to him might be annoyed. He, no doubt, had been snoring during the long flight, deep in a sleep with vivid dreams. During his seminary days, his fellow Jesuit brothers had constantly teased him about his snoring, saying he was "loud at night, silent during the day."

He noticed the neon yellow plugs in the businessman's ears with relief. He had no control over his utterances while asleep and felt assured his secrets were still his. Too much in his mind right now that must not be shared—yet. *Concentrate on your task*, the voice scolded, *you are by no means finished yet.*

The last recollections of his dream before awakening were still vividly lifelike. *If only I could make it through the mist this time, just make the connection once.* That's the way the dream always ended, ever since he first met her in his youth. He still carried the sadness and regret he felt last night, watching her flee the restaurant. When he saw Stella in the parking lot, his immediate response was to provide a safe harbor and comfort as he had been taught in the seminary. But his intentions for her comfort were anything but priestly. She was just as beautiful as the young creature he had met so long ago. To him, she was one of the bravest and confident humans he had ever encountered.

He was eight then, accompanying his mother for his first visit to America to meet his mother's dear friend and long-time colleague. The two women had been friends since 1946 when they prepared the doll exhibition at the de Young Museum in Golden Gate Park. The exhibition had been sponsored by I. Magnin, along with two other department stores, The White House, and the City of Paris. "It was the grandest of all nights. All of San Francisco's society were there, and they gave Dior the key to the city," his mother had told him.

Gabriel adored the man he felt he knew so well, yet had never met— Christian Dior. His mother had been merely a child when she met Dior in Gabriel's home town of Callian. Dior's nanny had a family home in the small hilltop French village and frequently hosted Dior's family on holiday getaways from Paris. Gabriel's grandmother had taught Dior how to garden when he showed up one day on her doorstep, admiring her abundant lilies. With her help the emerging designer had avoided combat and instead was assigned to the village for farm duty during the war. Many nights Gabriel had fallen asleep to Lilli's stories of the magical maestro who "talked to cloth" the way Michelangelo talked to stone. Much more than a dressmaker, his mother said. He was a true visionary whose only wish in life was to make women happy. "And he fulfilled his wish," Lilli would say as she finished the night-time tale, "when he saved my life."

Since that first visit, Lilli traveled twice a year from Paris to San Francisco, training the California pattern maker in European draping and cut so they could reproduce Dior's revolutionary New Look designs to sell more inexpensively in the United States. It was years later when his voice started to lower that he learned his mother was involved in much more than just fashion. A plan dating back centuries. The whole history and real purpose of the fashion dolls. Her continued interest in the sun-kissed California girl was understood more fully by him now—and her part in the plan.

Gabriel remembered feeling so grown up when he was told he would finally accompany his mother to San Francisco. Since his birth, he had always remained with his father during his mother's frequent trips and absences. But as soon as he showed signs of puberty, his mother informed him it was now time to cross the ocean. The small Provence village had a celebration in the town square where they presented him with his first piece of luggage. "Now you can put all the stickers of the world on your valise, just like your maman's," his papa had exclaimed.

"Hurry, maman, let's go," he had urged, dressed in his best suit and rocking to and fro on the bed on his first California morning.

"Soon, son. Be patient and let me finish," she had said.

He knew his mother, like most Frenchwomen, would not go out in public until she was properly coiffed and chicly dressed.

"Now," she said after tying her Dior scarf snugly under her chin, "let's go."

They confidently emerged from their hotel, blending easily with the morning's business crowd that cloudy morning, and walked to catch a cable car to Union Square.

He gasped when he first caught site of what his mother referred to as "The White Lady." The famous I. Magnin department store, constructed of ancient white marble, rose high enough in the sky to reflect majestic shards of sunlight through the thick morning clouds to the dark streets below.

Upon their entering the department store lobby, Gabriel tingled. His eyes darted around the large store, in search of the source of the magnetic energy. He scanned the magnificent murals on the lobby walls, trying not to get lost in the intoxicating beauty of the graphic storytelling. Then, as if divinely guided, his young innocent eyes looked upwards.

Casually leaning against the Art Deco bronze waved railing on the third-floor landing, stood a beautiful blond teenage girl with long tanned legs, her sparkling blue eyes piercing his brain. His heart almost burst through his hairless chest when she smiled at him. Gabriel was welded to the lobby's floor, mesmerized.

"Mom, can I take the boy for ice cream?" the girl asked as she coyly winked at him.

"May I," her mother corrected, never missing an opportunity to do so. "Of course," her mother said, handing her a handful of coins from her dressmaker's apron.

The girl swept down the stairs, grabbed the startled speechless boy and whisked him outside. As soon as they walked into the sunlight, she pushed him up against the store's wall. "If you want to have some fun, you gotta swear you won't tell anyone what we are about to do. Okay? Far out! Let's have some fun."

He had barely finished nodding his agreement, when she grabbed his hand and yanked him across the busy street, past the Goddess of Victory in the square as they headed to her secret playground deep in the basement of the City of Paris department store. They arrived, unseen. He could tell she had done this many times before.

"Wanna play a game?" she teased him. "Okay, chase me and try to catch me. Got it?" she asked as she scurried off to hide amongst the stacked boxes of unpacked clothing, her short skirt ratcheting up her smooth legs. "If you catch me, there's a prize." She didn't elaborate what the prize was, leaving it up to his adolescent imagination.

He had played tag with the young boys of his village before, but this was different. Exciting and dangerous. He liked how it made him feel. He just wanted to catch her, touch her, perhaps even kiss her. Always a fast runner, he took off after her. When he caught her, he blocked her into a corner, trembling with excitement.

But instead of an anticipated kiss, she pointed to the left of a hand-made cardboard stage. "Sit!" she demanded. It slowly dawned on him he had been duped. *This* was her endgame. He watched her in wonderment as she raised the creaking lid of the old trunk, releasing a burst of effervescent particles into the air as she handed him a doll. A vortex of visible circling atoms encased his hands as he held Faïence for the first time. He tried to act like nothing was happening, gazing into the teen girl's face for any clue that she was seeing the same apparition, hearing the buzzing. Nothing.

"We're gonna play 'fashion show,' okay?"

"Okay, oui," he reluctantly agreed. His mother had taken him to many shows during Paris Fashion Week, where he helped the dressers unpack the clothes. He was familiar with back of the house, but unsure how to actually "play" fashion show. The once-visible energy source had dissipated by now, leaving as quickly as it had come. Utterly bewildered by the lightening-quick succession of events, he willingly agreed. Just to be in the presence of this tantalizing creature was his goal.

Entranced, he watched and listened as she orchestrated the impromptu fashion show. Looking back now he didn't remember much of their playing. His mind's eye memories were of her cute dimples when she smiled, the herbal headiness of her freshly shampooed golden hair when she threw her head back in laughter. And the accident.

As he had watched her strut the dolls to and fro, sitting cross-legged across from each other on the floor, he had come up with a plan. He wanted to show her he was much more than just a lanky awkward country boy.

He remembered the movie his father had taken him to in Paris where lots of American boys and girls were laughing and playing in swimsuits on a sun-soaked beach. The handsome dark-haired boy had grabbed the girl and kissed her.

That's it, he brilliantly thought, *that's what I'll do*. He had rocked forward on his knees, his legs still crossed, and tried to place his hands on her cheeks while puckering his lips for the big romantic smooch. Instead, he lost his balance, lurched forward and smacked her nose with his forehead before planting his face smack in her crotch.

Screaming, she had jumped up and started to run up the stairs. She made it half way up before she slipped, falling down a few steps, twisting her knee.

My God, I've killed her! In a panic, he ran to her as she moaned in pain clasping her swelling right knee. He managed to clumsily help her up the stairs and back across the street. Never in his lifetime had he felt such embarrassment. But he also had never experienced such intense pleasure as having his arm around her waist as he helped her hobble back to their mothers. Gabriel had almost fallen himself when she laid her hand on top of his steadying hand. Felt like the most normal thing in the world, having his skin next to hers. He didn't want to disconnect.

In the intervening years, he had relived that moment at least a million times. It was the most intimate moment he had ever shared with another human. When he took his priestly oath, he wondered what would have happened if he had been older, more suave and manly. Would they have kissed? Would he still have become a priest? She was never far from his mind.

Gabriel had secretly hoped that somehow he would see her again during his short visit. However, the chance of bumping into her in this big city would be a miracle. He could see the card in his mind that had arrived at his mother's house in Provence just a year ago, telling them that the girl's mother had died. Lilli had been unable to attend the memorial for her old friend, which was held in the middle of a Napa Valley vineyard. He could picture the moment in the florist's shop when he was ordering an arrangement of flowers, memorizing the address in Mill Valley, California, and wondering why her surname remained the same. Had she never married?

Before his departure while dining in a quiet back street bistro in Paris, he asked his mother that very question. His mother had always been a "seer," a family trait handed down many generations in her family. Raised to not abuse the privilege, he had always been judiciously cautious in asking her to predict the future—his future. But this was one question he needed answered.

At the time, Lilli smiled and chuckled, knowing how Gabriel felt towards this lovely creature. One of the reasons she had counseled him to choose research as a Bollandist, instead of raising in the ranks of the Church. "Yes, she married, but that is no longer true." He started to ask her more, when she raised her bejeweled slender index finger to the middle of her lips and said "that is all that you're to know right now. Be patient. In God time."

He wished he had time to gulp down a cup of coffee before landing, but it was too late. He needed to be alert and quick witted when he landed at

Charles de Gaulle Airport, so he could succinctly respond to his mother's inquiries. Gabriel knew Lilli wished she were strong enough so she could have joined him, but at eighty-three, though still fairly limber and spry from her many years of herbal therapy, she simply no longer had the stamina for long plane flights. It pleased him that he could return her doll to her.

As the plane was landing, Gabriel was jolted back to the present and remembered a question he had for Lilli. He pulled out his ever-present notebook and made a note to ask her about it on the drive back to Callian. Being a Bollandist had made him a meticulous note taker. He had to be to keep track of the apparitions as they rose in number.

He beamed with pride when he caught sight of his beautiful mother waiting at the baggage claim for him. Though no longer natural, she had the most beautiful red hair, with its soft waves loosely pinned up off of her neck. Soft dangling wispy curls framed her face and gracefully caressed the nape of her neck. A proud Frenchwoman, she still carried herself regally on her tall slender frame. As always, she was dressed impeccably, with an air of easy elegance about her, a trait shared by French women her age who knew their value and especially their place in history.

He sensed her impatient eagerness, and nodded his assent that, yes, he had been successful in his mission. No sooner had he placed his valise on the ground, she picked it up and laced her arm through his. "Good, we must now take her to the sacred grotto at Chartres. It is *le calme avant la tempete.*"

They gathered his garment bag and headed to the taxi queue to take them to the train. As he assisted his mother into the cab, she turned his face toward hers and smiled. "You saw the girl again, didn't you?"

Chapter Eight

∞

The blood throbbed at the base of her skull so severely, Maggie could keep count of her heartbeats through her pulsating eyebrows. Slowly, she parted her eyelids and cut her eyes to the right. "No. Not 5:13?" she mumbled, as she squinted at the bright blue electrified numbers on her nightstand. It wasn't the cold Kentucky morning that caused her to shiver as she pulled her knees tight to her chest and tugged her heavy rose-colored comforter snugly under her sharp bony chin. Josh's birthday is May 13th. She tried to ignore the disturbing synchronicity—unsuccessfully.

The pain had wakened her from her dream about him. Since her son's deployment in Iraq, his sixth, nightmares were a frequent occurrence. In this dream, she was galloping out to the horse pasture to join Jim, her recently deceased husband, and Josh. But before she could reach her men, they sprinted at neck-breaking speed away from her.

Slow down, she begged. *Wait for me.* Her thin-as-tin voice went unheard in the frigid morning air. *Danger*, she warned, but they just laughed and dug their heels into horses' flanks deeper. She watched helplessly as they disappeared into the woods, with a pack of black salivating wolves hot on their trail. The dream had disturbed her deeply.

She feared it was an omen, but hoped it was just changing hormones. It wasn't the first time her dreams foretold the future.

Ever since she had started going through the Change, she had trouble sleeping, just like Stella. If it wasn't severe night sweats soaking her linens all the way through to her mattress, it was symptoms sure to be the threat of imminent stroke. Stella had told her to sleep in the nude so she didn't have to get up and change her night clothes. Sleeping in the nude wasn't an option right now. Her skin needed the closeness of clothing.

It had been almost a year since she lost Jim to a drunk driver. She blamed the stress of losing him and having her only child away in a war for throwing her into early menopause. Her mother hadn't gone through the Change until she reached sixty. *Well, at least I have Stella going through this with me,* she thought, *even if it is by long distance phone calls or email.* Stella had been unusually quiet lately. Didn't want to talk on the phone much since last fall.

Her head started throbbing harder, making her nauseous. She reached for the bottle of ibuprofen on the nightstand and fumbled three into her mouth with a slug of last night's stale water. Maggie kept the meds close by now after one too many trips in the dark, stumbling over the resident stacks of books around her bed. One of the work-arounds she had to make in the last year to survive—without him. Jim would have tended to her, comforted her. He had always been so tender and protective, since the day he had rescued her at the Rolling Stones' concert at Altamont Speedway in California. Called her his little wounded bird those rare times she was ill. The type of man who thrived on pleasing his wife.

The thought of even being compared to something as fragile as a little bird made her momentarily grin. Some people wrongly assumed due to her classic Renaissance face with luminescent alabaster skin framed by a bouncing head of fiery copper curls, that she was delicate. She wasn't.

At 5'10", 134 pounds, she was still on the wiry, thin side. The perfect model body which had served her well in her youth. Her perfect posture now was sustained from her daily rides on the ranch. Mucking horse stalls kept her body toned and muscular. Being the only girl in an Irish-American family of five brothers had gifted her a fierce tongue. Being a military daughter, spouse and mother had made her resilient.

That toughness carried her through as she cared for the ranch almost single-handedly since becoming a widow. It had been her childhood dream to own a horse farm, ever since riding her first horse as a young child in the Blue Grass state before her family transferred to California. Just as Jim had promised her when he retired early from the Army, they moved outside of Louisville so she could live her dream.

But it was more than loneliness that was bothering her right now. It was something deeper, like the feeling you get walking in the darkness. Something was seriously wrong—just like that same jumpy, edgy feeling that stormy March day a year ago. Fiddly, never able to stay still, constantly checking out the windows, watching things flying through the air, fixing cups of tea that she left all over the house—untouched.

She thought her uneasiness was due to the threat of a spring tornado. She almost missed the suddenness of a California earthquake so catastrophe could strike and then recovery could begin. Maybe then she could stop holding her breath. She had never liked East Coast weather.

"Can you stop and pick up some food at the grocery store in case we lose our electricity," she had asked Jim right before he left the office that night. She hadn't wanted to ask him. His irritability had her walking on egg shells lately. He seemed unusually tense, but she chalked it up to starting a new job, especially at his age. It was his first non-military job. Her brother Bob advised her that maybe Jim had lost confidence in his abilities. That seemed like a reasonable explanation; he had been working on something very important that he couldn't talk about. Not unusual but he seemed more introspective and stressed than normal.

Jim had started leaving the room to talk in hushed tones when he answered his cell phone. He was distant and seemed to be pulling away from her, which made her nervous after what happened to Stella. However, as a military wife she had gotten used to not being privy to all her spouse's thoughts, especially after their move to Maryland early in his career. She didn't like it, but she respected the necessity of secrecy to keep her country and family safe.

Still she worried. Ever since the vice president had "outed" that CIA Operations Officer, she worried that her husband's past top secret duties would be exposed, putting their family in the crosshairs. This was a different world now. No loyalty to country, just hard-knuckled politics aimed at the next election and lining one's own pocket seemed to rule the day. No loyalty to those in service; elected politicians called soldiers "privileged belligerent."

Right after Fort Campbell boot camp in Kentucky, soon after they had married, they had been transferred to Fort Meade in Maryland. Instead of being shipped to Vietnam, Jim was trained to work as a psychic spy. Of course, Jim couldn't tell Maggie what he was doing. It wasn't until they were watching *NBC News* in the summer of 1976 that the truth came out. NBC aired a story about the Stanford Research Institute and remote viewing. Maggie remembered studying Jim as he ran his left index finger under his nose like a saw. It was one of his tells she had learned long ago when they played Friday night bridge with other military couples. It didn't take much for Maggie to put two and two together. She turned to her sandy-haired husband and asked, "That's what you do, isn't it?"

"Yup," he reluctantly sighed, as he got up to get another beer. After he took a big gulp of his Miller Light, he had explained psychic spying to his librarian wife. First started in the USSR in the early 1960s, he said, using a technique called remote viewing where the "spies" could, using extra-sensory perception, view people and locations miles away and gather information. By the mid-'70s the U.S. had started its own secret program, the Star Gate Project. "And I was the perfect candidate. Somehow, they saw something in me in boot camp."

After many years in the Project, he said he had become very adept in remote viewing, and was among one of the top in the world. He had enjoyed great success in helping locate hostages in Lebanon. During the first Iraq War, his team zeroed in on the whereabouts of SCUD missiles and biological and chemical weapons. "Our team located the elusive mujahedin in the Afghanistan Mountains," he had said.

But then it all changed. Politics. When the Democrats lost control of the Senate in 1994, the Republicans declined funding for the program. The Defense Intelligence Agency transferred the program to the CIA, where it supposedly disintegrated. "That's when I was transferred to the desk job at the Defense Information School," he ended.

Maggie remembered that time. One of the few dark periods of their marriage.

Remorseful for tearing off the scab of the wounds from that painful period, he had tried to change the focus of the conversation. "How about I teach you some of the techniques? I think you might find it amusing."

She had been reluctant to learn at first. Within a short time, however, she became better at it than he was.

And then, like most Americans, their lives changed when the planes hit the twin towers on September 11, 2001. Maggie remembered how enraged Jim had been, violently pitching his just-filled morning cup of coffee against their family room wall with such force the pictures clanged askew.

"Hell, they could have located the terrorists and eliminated them, if they wanted to," he yelled. "It's the goddamn Elites again! Their twisted New World Order plan. Treasonous bastards!" Jim's agitation had started the day before when Defense Secretary Rumsfeld had announced they couldn't track $2.3 trillion in military transactions. "This will change everyone's focus. That's how they work—distraction," he told her. He noted later that Pentagon accountants died on 9/11.

She was afraid of what he might tell her, so she didn't ask him to elaborate on whom the Elites were and what they had to do with such a tragedy. She had been shocked to watch her husband become so angered with his country. She had grabbed a roll of paper towels from the bar area and cleaned up the dripping coffee from the freshly painted terra cotta wall before it dripped on the newly-installed Berber carpet below, giving her time to think.

Nine days later Congress approved $10 billion to fight terrorism, ramping up the terrorism industrial complex. They built a $3,500-million building rivaling the Pentagon to house the newly created Department of Homeland Security, which some insiders said was a candy store without price tags to bureaucrats. Then they created seventy-two fusion centers across the nation to gather intelligence, at a whopping price tag of $420 million. They started keeping information on war protesters, including Catholic nuns, and put their names on terrorists' lists.

The final straw was after Colin Powell's February 5, 2003 speech before the United Nations that convinced her husband it was time to leave service to his country. He and his friend from his Star Gate days, Brent McConnell, had gotten really drunk at a sports bar in downtown Baltimore, watching the Washington Wizards lose again. They started talking about the war.

"Ya know," Brent, drunkenly and too loudly, said "I heard that only six senators had read the frickin' NIE." He and Jim had been discussing the National Intelligence Estimate on Iraq that indicated the yellow cake and WMDs information was dubious. Unfortunately, he was overheard by some of the patrons who felt they weren't patriotic enough.

"Yeah, right," Jim yelled back at them. "You think Congress will send their kids to die?"

Brent got him out of there quickly before a drunken riot started. Maggie had picked them up around the corner where they had tried to hide. She patiently listened to Jim's rant all the way home until he and his buddy passed out before they even reached the ranch.

Two months later, in disgust at the military and the government disbanding something that could have brought real peace to the world, Jim retired and registered as an Independent. Said there were no more elections, just auctions.

Not long after buying the horse ranch on the outskirts of Louisville, out towards Bardstown and the whiskey distilleries, they learned raising and training horses as part of the Derby set was an expensive lifestyle and not maintainable on a government pension.

Brent was aware the Barretts' finances couldn't sustain this new lifestyle. He also knew where Jim could make big bank quickly and then retire for good. Thanks to the Iraq war and lack of a military draft, the private military field was a booming business, like Tech in the '80s.

Brent had planned on retiring after the Star Gate program shut down. However, he changed his mind when approached by GA7 president Lucas Stanchir to come work for his private military firm. After a few years and seeing how Jim's new desk job was making him miserable, he suggested it might be a place for someone with Jim's talents. "We provide services from mercenaries to intelligence gathering and 'public relations,'" Brent had told both Jim and Maggie. "Jim, I think you would be a perfect fit for GA7," he said, encouraging him to apply for a position.

Within a week, Brent and Jim traveled to a huge building in Washington, D.C. that was four stories high, yet ten stories deep. GA7's headquarters, state of the art. Brent had arranged for a gig where Jim could work part-time in Washington and part-time at home so he could still help with the ranch.

At the interview, Lucas Stanchir told Jim this was an opportunity to use his talent and skills to really make a difference in this terrorist-threatened world, to keep his grandkids safe. "As part of the private sector, we aren't limited by government oversight and budgets," Lucas had told him. He didn't volunteer that all their hefty compensation was funneled through black budgets that Americans had no idea about. A blank check to charge the American taxpayer whatever they felt like.

Lucas had offered Jim almost four times his military salary. Jim figured out that if he just worked for another five years, they would be set for life. The money they offered him was too good that he couldn't pass it up so he started work immediately.

The nightmares started about three months into the job. One night Maggie had been awakened by Jim fiercely flaying about in bed, uttering in his sleepy stupor that he wanted out. He whimpered repeatedly, something about a grid as she rocked him in her arms. However, by morning, he refused to discuss the matter, saying it was just a bad dream.

He never made it the five years.

That ominous dark March evening on his way home, he was struck down by a drunk driver, an illegal alien from Spain, in the grocery store parking lot while walking to his car. Maggie could remember the clothes she wore, the smell in the air, the television in the background, two full tea cups on the entry table amidst that day's mail, one still warm and steaming—every little detail about that night, like time had stood still.

She remembered the knock at the door, looking through the peephole and seeing two police officers back lit by flashing red and blue lights. The taller one with a bulbous nose and an acne-scarred face, the other shorter and rotund, with a nervous shoulder tick. She had slowly opened the door but the bullying wind from the storm blasted the door into the wall, leaving a dent. The taller policeman had reached for her shoulder and said "Ma'am, I'm sorry . . . ."

It was then that she had left her body. She remembered listening to herself scream and then watched as her body hit the granite entryway as she fainted. She found the scene all too troubling and floated back up to her room while the police tried to revive her body.

She stayed numb all through the funeral, then the trial, which had been fast-tracked due to the Stanchirs' far-reaching influence. The drunk driver with the port-stained ear was quickly convicted and deported back to his homeland Spain.

Maggie still woke up each morning trying to figure out how to live as a widow. Was she supposed to remove her wedding ring? One thing she never did remove was Jim's old silver water-proof Bulova watch with the domed glassed crystal. She had bought it at the local Rexall's Drug Store and given it to him on their first wedding anniversary. As long as it kept ticking like a heartbeat, she could keep going.

Chapter Nine

∞

I'm alive, Stella rejoiced, turning left onto Highway 29 towards Napa. After months of hibernation in her secure Mill Valley fortress, she was finally ready for an adventure. She hadn't seen Nicki since their brief Christmas visit.

When Nicki called last week with an invitation for a long weekend, she didn't hesitate. It was a new year, 2012, and Stella was buoyed with getting a do-over card, a chance to start living differently. Plus, she needed relief from the isolation and the never-ending "thoughts."

Still unnerved by her "vision" that fall night, she hadn't trusted herself to drive the two hours to St. Helena. Still unsure of what or why it happened, she entertained the idea of it being an alcohol-induced psychotic break. Visiting her daughter who lived at a winery so soon after the incident would not have been a wise choice. Alcohol loosened her tongue, and she didn't want the story of that night to slip out, signaling she might still be damaged. Her ego was still too fragile from all that had happened to her. She fleetingly contemplated, for the thousandth time, cutting back on the pills.

This is what I need. Family and a road trip. Her first Napa Valley trip had been with Maggie's family, all loaded up in a 1957 Ford Fairlane station wagon. Maggie's dad, Big Bob, had folded down the back seat, tossed in an old lumpy pin-striped mattress and with the help of his good-natured wife, Jo, piled in all of his six kids, Stella and the family dog.

"You gotta go to the source for good Dago wine," Maggie's dad chortled above the din of fighting kids on the family's monthly outing. They always packed a big lunch, stuffed tightly into their dented silver Coleman ice chest and headed north to the vineyards, nestled in the Vaca Mountains. In those days, wineries were corrugated metal barns with the barn door opened just enough to accommodate a rough-hewn barn wood plank on top of saw horses, displaying gallon jugs of home-made unlabeled wine. Old Bob loved to haggle on a deal, always insisting on a picnic space in the vineyard as part of the transaction. This was the way she remembered Napa Valley before it became as famous as Disneyland. She wished Maggie was riding shotgun with her today, sharing one of Jo's fried bologna sandwiches slathered with Velveeta, wrapped in wax paper.

The prevailing serenity made her smile as she continued through Napa headed to St. Helena on this chilly bright February day. She had always felt a kind of home-town pride about the Napa Valley, being a kid from Vallejo. Most Northern Californians felt like they were a part of the area, as if somehow connected.

Off on the sides of the road, she noticed the first buds of emerging leaves on the gnarly vine stubs. Swaths of mustard grass appeared like wide landing strips of neon chartreuse, making her smile as they waved in the slight breeze, like skewered lemon drops saying a cheery hello. She focused on the color, wondering if she would see that particular color at Paris Fashion Week which she would be attending in a few weeks. She hoped so. She has always had an innate sense of trends and thought that was the next new big thing.

She looked at the car's clock, impressed on the quickness of her trip. Off season for tourists, as evidenced by the somewhat vacant road. She was grateful. Too many times she'd been stuck in the endless snake of limos and people wandering back and forth across the quaint two-lane roadway, a little unsteady from the grape.

Truth be told, her favorite time for this drive was harvest time when the pungency emitting from the many barn-sized hills of fermented grape waste—lees they called it—would seep through the air vents in her car giving her a contact buzz.

But there really was no bad time to be here. Everything felt so alive, with the abundancy of the lush fields, the slower lifestyle, the fantastic artisan foods, and, of course, the wine. The air smelled cleaner, the sky's light a different hue.

Her love affair with red wines started here, on her first date with Todd. They visited Stag's Leap to see the Foucault Pendulum in the Wine Cave and to taste the best Cabernet Sauvignons in the Valley. Their private tour took them into the caves located below the pendulum, with its swinging sound reverberating through the tunnels, like a heartbeat. "They say it symbolizes that wine continues to live after the grapes leave the vine," the guide had said.

It was just enough woo-woo to start her love affair with the cabernet sauvignon grape. Eventually, it evolved into her passionate hobby of pairing bread and wine. That avocation had helped her make it through this first holiday season as a divorcee. She had gifted all her friends with her favorite vintage wines from her son-in-law's winery, with her signature Tuscan rustic bread. The constant bread making was a credible excuse to spend time closeted away, shut off from everyone. And gave her time to think about *that* night.

Her breath quickened when she saw the fast approaching car in her rear view mirror. A black Audi A4, with its four inter-connected circled grill that ironically reminded her of how her family was once connected. Sweat beaded on her brow, as she struggled to catch her breath. Not now, damn it!

She had been nervous that she might run into Todd and his lover while visiting. *San Francisco's own Oscar Wilde*, as one local newspaper called him. Todd had many art disciples here in the Valley where he curated art auctions. Once upon a time, her adoration mirrored his fans'. Now she just thought he was a snobbish asshole. With that thought in mind, she finally managed to take a deep breath, hold it and then release the panic through clenched teeth.

The black Audi, obviously in a hurry, passed her. She didn't even try to look in the smoked windows to see if it was her ex-husband. She wondered if the driver would exit at Yountville. Maybe dine at the French

Laundry, where they had dined so many times in celebration of their anniversary. Can't change the past. Build a bridge—get over it, Maggie had repeatedly told her. *Let it go*, her gut whispered. *Don't let it be a trigger.*

She still had panic attacks, which had become less seldom since that November evening. She thought about it every day, wondering what happened to her. Dibrovna, as always, had been her saving grace, almost single-handedly taking care of the boutique. Dibrovna also nursed Stella back to health, with at least one of her home-cooked meals a day. "Eat real food, Stella, and fix your brain." And she did. And now she was ready to make this year grand. That had been her New Year's resolution, along with the mystic mission she had been assigned to *"get to know herself."*

First on her agenda was Paris Fashion Week to buy for the boutique and get back into the swing of the fashion world. Stella had really neglected the business and herself for too long. *Maybe I'll ask Maggie if she wants to go,* she thought, making a mental note to call her after arriving at Nicki's.

Thoughts of France oddly brought pictures to her mind's eye of the handsome dark stranger in the parking lot. She had thought about him too—a lot. It bothered her that his identity still eluded her. *Maybe my brain is still not completely healed,* she admitted to herself. She still had not discussed it with anyone, not even Maggie, though she knew that wouldn't last long. Guilt plagued her for keeping this from Maggie. Her dear friend was still grieving the loss of dear Jim and now worrying about Josh's deployment in Iraq. She couldn't burden her with such nonsensical stuff.

Self-preservation also kept her mouth shut, fearing she would be judged as terminally unstable. Maggie would probably tell her it was from drug flashbacks from her hippie days, she thought, amused. Better she kept the secret to herself for the time being. She reached over and shook her handbag, listening for ping-ponging inside the plastic cylinder, signaling she was safe with her pills.

Then she saw it, as she slowly took the corner headed towards St. Helena. Her right eye started twitching as she watched the gathered leaves and debris, cycloning upwards. A wind spout, maybe; her heart started to beat faster. She had longed to be re-visited by whatever it was that fall evening. If only she could feel that bliss once again. Then just as quickly as it had begun, it dissipated, leaving her incredibly disappointed and sad.

Chapter Ten

∞

Laying stiff as a 2x4 as she waited for the pills to kick in, Maggie tried to remember every word of her phone call with Stella last fall. Sometimes her sassy mouth drove her down a bumpy road. She hoped she hadn't offended her best friend. It wasn't like them to not talk. Not for this long anyway.

For almost four decades, Stella was never far from Maggie's thoughts. Not since that first meeting in the bathroom. No ordinary bathroom, the Ladies Dressing Room on the fifth floor of I Magnin's was regal and elegant, decorated with Italian marble walls and floors, the sunlight gleaming off the gold-plated fixtures.

Stella had been perched on the toilet in one of the mirrored-door stalls, smoking and drawing with her No. 3 pencil, trying to capture the delicate gradated nuances of painted silver leaf on the store's murals. Maggie was almost doubled over with cramps and trying to stifle her tears, unsuccessfully, in the next stall.

"You okay?" Stella had softly whispered under the stall wall, leaning her long body towards the expensive shiny floor.

"It's my period."

"Aww, shit. Bummer. I can help you. I always have a stash. Here," she said as she had passed three Midols under the stall, cupped in her nicotine-stained hand.

"My mom works on the ninth floor, as the lead pattern maker in the Custom work room," Stella said as they washed their hands together in the gold-plated wash basin. "We just moved to San Francisco so I could start at San Francisco State. I'm studying art."

"Is that your sketchbook?" Maggie asked, pointing at the dog-eared three-subject, college-ruled notebook.

"Kinda. My mom likes me to come here to help her out in the work room. But I tell her I have homework so I can come in here and sketch these Max Ingrand murals in my school notebook."

It was years later when Maggie found out that Stella had to work to bring in extra money to help buy school supplies and pay their rent. Like most POW families during the Vietnam War, finances were the biggest issue. Even then her dear friend hated being judged as "less than." She finally told Maggie her mother had given her an ultimatum: work or sell her Jaguar. They bonded that day over menstruation. Just like they were bonding nowadays over menopause.

She was still eager to hear the post mortem on Stella's date. Before Jim died and Todd left, they had always shared everything. But Maggie reflected on how she wasn't the same woman she had been just a year ago, so she didn't push Stella. They both had been through too much. The only news so far about the blind date was a short email that it was her first and last date with the guy. She worried that Stella might have had a relapse being all alone in that big cold house and made a mental note to check with Dibrovna before talking again with Stella.

Maybe I should try to meditate, Maggie thought, *and let the answer come to me.* When they spoke in November, their conversation was about the one aspect of menopause they actually enjoyed—sharpened intuition. They had talked about how they could sense things now before they happened, like going to answer the front door before the doorbell rang or feeling a speeding car in your blind spot before you saw it—sometimes good and sometimes bad. Stella said it was called "psychic knowing."

"Really? You don't think it's just women's intuition? Physic knowing sounds pretty New Agey to me, Stella Marie. Or maybe we're just being crazy or something. Thinking we know the future," she said, laughing.

She was about to add that she had changed her mind on the great unknown forces in the Universe, due to Jim's training but caught herself in time. Stella was still in the dark when it came to Jim's remote viewing skills; maybe now was the time to finally spill the beans. But before she could utter another word, Stella had hurriedly said she had to go and hung up. They hadn't talked since.

Was Stella's avoidance due to Maggie's questioning of anything mystical or supernatural? Stella had always been more of the "woo woo" type than Maggie. As a librarian, she tended to be more conservative and needed to see solid scientific proof before believing in anything. She questioned Stella many times on her beliefs, asking for proof. Stella had started to ask Maggie something about visions or ghosts before she flippantly squelched the topic by saying "Never mind. You're Republican now."

It wasn't until she met Jim that she took the plunge and became a Republican. Everything had changed that December day in 1969. She and Stella had hitchhiked to the free concert the Rolling Stones were putting on at the Altamont Speedway, full of anticipation that this would be the West Coast Woodstock. It wasn't long after arriving that she had almost been run over by Hell's Angels, bullying their way down the crowded hill where she and Stella were huddled in the unwashed pot-smoking masses. The young muscled man, dressed in sharply-creased Levi's and closed cropped hair, had pulled her out of the path just a moment before her feet would have been crushed by the roaring thugs on bikes. The same man who coincidentally had tried to flirt with her at Berkeley's People's Park just seven months before.

Maggie knew instantly he was newly-military, with the bright white skin above his ears, exposed by the standard military cut she had just witnessed on one of her own brothers. He pulled her onto his lap and shared his jug of wine with her and Stella. By nightfall, even those far from the stage where a man had just been stabbed to death, could feel the evil wickedness penetrate the snarling crowd. Jim insisted the girls leave immediately with him and his buddy before they could be harmed.

During the drive back to Vallejo in his 1959 Chevrolet Impala, his buddy had tried to console the girls, now disillusioned that the promise of a day of peace and love had just ended with a senseless death. Stella had ranted about how the unending war in Vietnam was to blame for all of today's ugliness. When she finally stopped to take a breath, Jim announced that his Army unit was being shipped to Vietnam in twenty-eight days. Fifteen days later Maggie and Jim said "I do" in a small Reno wedding chapel.

Jim informed Maggie he had come from a long line of Republicans and every generation had been military. As a new, young military wife, she felt it her patriotic duty to belong to the same political party as her husband. Politics never really mattered to her anyway.

Her conversion had not only shocked and displeased Stella, it had also surprised her own family. She had been raised in a typical 1950s Irish Catholic Democrat household, with a stay-at-home mother and a union member father. Although Jim was well liked by her parents, Big Bob wasn't happy at all about his only daughter becoming one of "them." He still held a big grudge from when he had been beaten up by GOP delegates at the Cow Palace when he was reporting on their convention back in 1964. He still limped from his badly healed broken leg.

But she didn't think it was anything about partisan politics that was causing the lapse in their communication. The two friends had formed a truce not to discuss politics long ago when Bush the First was still president. They agreed to disagree and talk about other things, like how to use these "personal computers" everyone was buying at the time and why did they need them.

Rolling over on her back, staring at the ceiling, it came to her. Was Stella's frostiness because she used the "C" word—*crazy*? The thought that she had hurt Stella started her crying. She quickly wiped her eyes when the phone rang. It was Josh's wife, Eva. Before heading out to his second deployment, Josh had moved her and their two boys, Alex and Jason, the lights of Maggie's life, back to Louisville to be closer to family. Jim had even bought two little Shetland ponies so he could teach the boys to ride.

Now with Josh once again deployed, Maggie was helping Eva cope living life as a military wife—a single mother. It was a proud life, a lonely life, and to Maggie, an increasingly false and angry life. She hated the war. She wanted her son home—now.

Chapter Eleven

—∞—

Speeding across the uneven buckled railroad tracks, the Jag almost rocketed across the center line of the narrow two-lane country road. Quickly correcting her steering as she entered St. Helena, Stella caught sight of the beloved weeping willow that graced the yellow farmhouse on the left. She barely slowed, excited to soon be holding her child again. And, of course, visiting her adopted family—the Sanchezes. Not only had her daughter met and married a wonderful man, but joined a strong, fiercely proud family. It felt like a homecoming.

Before divorce jaded her opinion about relationships, Stella often used her daughter's special love story as cocktail party banter. Nicki had met Carlos Sanchez at one of her father's art and wine auctions at the exclusive Meadowood resort a few years before. "If I hadn't tasked her with bidding on the Screaming Eagle Cabernet Sauvignon," Stella loved to add, careful not to mention the vintage so she wouldn't appear gauche, "my daughter would have completely missed meeting her soul mate. She got into a bidding war with this gorgeous Latin man with a mega-watt smile and within six months of that first meeting, they were engaged! Supposedly, Carlos was quite the catch," she would continue under her breath. "You know, they were the first Latino family to move from being laborers to esteemed vintners," she would add, unaware how some found her white privileged liberalism slightly offensive.

Actually, Stella was quite proud of her son-in-law's family. His Mayan grandparents had originally emigrated from Chiapas, Mexico, to escape poverty and starvation. First working in the fields of Imperial Valley, they later migrated north to the Capay Valley almond orchards outside of Sacramento, before finally landing in St. Helena in the 1960s.

"St. Helena, the magical lady," Lupe, Carlos' grandmother, had told Stella, holding up a cluster of grapes out in the orchard on Stella's first visit to the winery, "where the sumptuous nectar of the Goddesses is presented to the mortals in perfectly frosted pearls dangling from crimson leaves, awaiting the loving tender touch of the harvester and the artistry of the winemaker."

"You can tell my grandmother is passionate about wine making. It *is* her calling," Carlos had said, joining the women in the vineyard. "She was the one who insisted that I be the first in my family to go to college. My family worked sixteen hour days to save enough money to buy twenty acres in the late 1970s. Now we own over two hundred acres and are producing award winning Cabernets and Syrahs," he said, opening his arms wide to the vista of row after row of twisted branches peppered with luscious ripe fruit. "Still, most of the raising of the grape crop is still done by Mexicans. But with lots of hard work and sacrifice, we are living the American dream."

As she maneuvered her Jaguar through the quaint downtown of St. Helena, headed for the Sunshine Market, the image of a painting they sold at that Meadowood auction flashed in her mind's eye. It had been a last-minute decision to send it along with the other paintings, spurred by guilt mostly.

At the gallery's closing time as they were finishing packing up the art for the trip north, a woman appeared, struggling to carry her one painting in her left arm. She was wrapped in a traditional African-type sari, vibrant yellow and purple. When she introduced herself, Stella went to shake the artist's right hand.

"I apologize," the African woman said as she carefully placed her lone painting atop the glass display case. "My name is Mary Rose, from

Rwanda. I lost my right hand during the massacre in my country; it was hacked off by a machete." Mary Rose immediately tried to put Stella at ease, accustomed to people's reaction. "Please, I am fine now. I was rescued by French missionaries who taught me how to use my remaining hand to paint so I am quite capable with just one hand."

Stella remembered the fiery reds in the background of the work, but what she was thinking about right now was the ghostly image in the foreground. Almost like the image burned into her mind's eye.

Her daydreaming almost caused an accident as she swerved to avoid hitting the old dented Dodge truck in the grocery store's parking lot. Visibly shaken by the close call, she parked and entered the crowded store to pick up bouquets of flowers for Nicki, her mother-in-law Rosa, and grandmother-in-law Lupe. Normally, she would have brought wine and bread, but how do you gift someone with wine when they own a winery? *Kind of like bringing shoes to a cobbler,* she mused. Plus, she had a gut feeling that something special was going to take place. Just a knowing.

After accepting Nicki's invitation, she had also received a call from Rosa. She said Carlos and some of the ranch hands had just slaughtered one of their pigs for this special dinner celebration.

"Would you like to join the women in the kitchen?"

"Of course! You know I love to cook with you ladies. What's the celebration?"

"Your visit," Rosa replied matter-of-factly, before she recited the menu.

Stella's mouth watered in anticipation of tasting the bold flavors. And, truth be told, she was also looking forward to sipping some of their exquisite tequila, present at every one of their celebrations. *Yep,* she thought, *we "mature women" do like to eat. Bite my fat "mature" ass, Chet!*

"Rosa, I would be honored to join you in the kitchen," Stella had ended, joyfully.

Outside town, she turned right and drove down the long oak-studded driveway into the Bodega Sanchez winery. Not quite closing time, there were still a few cars parked in front of the tasting room and gift shop as she pointed her car towards the back of the property where the mission-style main house and bungalows sat. Like most farmers and ranchers, theirs was a family-operated 24/7 enterprise so all lived here on the property. Carlos

Sr. and Rosa lived in the main house with her mother, Lupe. The bungalow on the left side was where Carlos Jr. and Nicki lived. The remaining bungalow on the right of the property housed his sister, Carmen, her husband, Ricardo, and their three children.

As she parked and turned off the ignition, Nicki came through her front door onto the porch. Stella beamed, a little teary eyed, as her lovely child walked out to greet her. Dressed in dark skinny jeans and wearing her Christmas gift from Stella—an exquisite art-to-wear tunic, one of Stella's own designs embroidered and painted by one of her boutique's local artisans. Nicki had big brown eyes like her father, but favored Stella with her long slender body and silky straight honey blond hair, as well as her husky smoky voice. It was still a toss-up argument as to which parent had contributed to her talent via DNA.

Nicki was an up-and-coming artist, mainly working in large abstracts which sold well to wealthy corporate clients. Stella wondered if it was the healthy living up here or the golden back lighting from the household's warm lights, but Nicki's tawny skin glowed. She knew how happy Nicki and Carlos were and she said a silent thank you of gratitude, adding *please God, let her happiness last.*

"Hey, Mom, you're looking really good. Did you lose some weight?" chirped Nicki as Stella stepped up on the porch.

Please don't, Stella thought. She resisted any compliments from her daughter, afraid they would lead to the stupid dating thing again. After that disastrous blind date, Stella had closed her dating account, ignoring the trickle of winks. She had enough on her plate just acting normal.

"Carlos will be here in a little while, after he gets through with today's pour and can get your bags."

Those simple words made her feel special, again. It was the simple things in life that a husband does that she had taken for granted, like lugging heavy bags, taking out the garbage, making sure the car was serviced. Now she was responsible for those duties and hated it. She knew the Sanchez men took great pride in these tasks, and she wasn't going to stand in the way of their pleasure.

A life-long feminist, she now realized that there was nothing wrong in recognizing that some jobs were done better by certain sexes. Wanting equal rights was not an excuse for bad manners. Opening doors for a woman did not signal that she was too weak to open it herself. It showed respect and reverence for the female species. Breastfeeding—a girl job; lugging heaving bags—a boy job.

Stella climbed the few steps onto the Craftsman porch and hugged her daughter, nuzzling her hair. Since the first time Nicki was put into her arms, she was intoxicated by her scent.

"So, what do you think?" Nicki asked as she stepped back, revealing the cozy bungalow's living room. Having recently sold a three-piece abstract painting for six figures to one of the largest and oldest wineries in the area, she had the luxury of redecorating her house. She had fused Carlos' love of traditional Mexican colors of turquoise and mustard with her penchant for the richness and warmth of soft rose and copper.

"It's lovely," Stella said, as she took off her coat and started to put it in the guest room where she usually stayed.

"Uh, Mom, Rosa and Carlos have set up the guest room for you in the main house."

"Oh, okay, that's fine. But I'll miss having our late-night talks," Stella replied, obviously disappointed.

"Oh, Mom, we'll still talk. It's just that I'm not done with that room, and we all wanted you to be comfortable."

Stella knew something was up. Did they think she needed adult supervision? Oh, please, just let it go, build the damn bridge! At least she wouldn't have to traipse across the gravel drive in impractical shoes in the cold late evening hours after imbibing.

"Why don't we go ahead and go over to the main house now, so we can help Rosa with the preparations?" asked Nicki, as she swiftly maneuvered Stella out the door.

"Sure, I'm looking forward to it," smiled Stella, still suspicious.

"I'll just text Carlos that we'll meet him there."

Texting—another thing Stella wasn't comfortable with. Nicki had tried to teach her, and she grudgingly gave it a try. Maybe, she just needed to practice. She mentally added it to her list of New Year Resolutions—text more.

Chapter Twelve

Her migraine having subsided, Maggie was finally able to get out of bed. As was her waking habit, she walked to the bay window facing the front of her property and opened the drapes to greet the day. It tugged at her heart looking at the empty dusty crystal vase, sitting on the round occasional table in front of the window. It used to contain weekly fresh flowers from her husband; she quickly looked up, and focused on the mound of kudzu consuming the ranch's sturdy white fence instead, knitting itself around the fence posts that outlined the front of her property. Her grief was like that kudzu—hack it back so you can't see it, but it just kept coming back.

She opened the gallon-sized ziplocked baggie that lived on the seat of the wing chair. It was stuffed with a neatly folded threadbare T-shirt. She took a deep whiff. Each day his scent became fainter. But still there was enough dust, sweat and his essence to fill her nostrils.

She watched the plain white boxy American-made car slowing making its way down her long drive from the main road. The voice in her head urged her: *Go ahead! Just grab the T-shirt, go back to bed. You can hide under the comforter. No one will know you're home.* But duty made her body move down the stairs. She lovingly placed Jim's bagged T-shirt back on the chair.

Maggie stood at the closed front door, listening to the crunching footsteps coming up her driveway, getting louder and closer. Her body was rigid, the tip of her nose almost touching the red oak of the door, her chassis ramrod straight. They started knocking.

If this time I don't open the door, then I won't have to go through the loss and pain again. She was impressed by this clever thought, as though inspired by genius. If she didn't open the door, then it wouldn't be real. No observer effect, like Jim had told her about. If you don't see it, it doesn't exist. Maybe if she used her thoughts, like Stella had tried to teach her once, she could "intend" them to go away.

She looked out the peep hole and saw the familiar green uniforms. Strangers stoically stared right back at her. They knew she was there. Maybe they were using their thoughts too—to get her to open the door. Jim had told her about that technique—remote influencing. How long had she been standing here? Had her feet rooted into the lovely granite slabs that Josh had helped his dad install?

Okay, I'll just put my hand on the door knob. It felt hot in her hand, searing and soldering her flesh onto the brass. She couldn't pull her hand away.

"Mrs. Barrett? We need to talk to you. May we come in?"

She watched in horror as someone's hand—maybe hers—started to twist the knob. The door opened just enough to allow a wisp of frosty February morning air mixed with the strong smell of horse dung to saunter into the warm house. This time, she vowed, you are not allowed to hurt me.

She angrily pushed past the Army casualty assistant and the female Army chaplain, stomped out of her house to the corner of her garage, took down her American Flag, and flung it to the ground. She walked back to the front door, with her thin worn chenille pink bathrobe flapping in the morning's wind, exposing her clinging flannel pajamas underneath, still wet with last night's sweat. She slammed shut the door in their faces, grabbed the crystal carafe of Kentucky bourbon from the bar and the picture off the hallway wall of her once-happy family and marched upstairs to take a bubble bath. "Fuck you!" she yelled from the top of the stairs.

Chapter Thirteen

—∞—

"Stella Marie, I'm so happy you are here!" She had barely walked through the kitchen door when Nicki's mother-in-law Rosa grabbed Stella's waist and gave her a big squeeze. The two women had connected instantly when they first met, fitting together like puzzle pieces. Rosa was a slight, short woman with close-cropped salt-and-pepper hair and an enormous electric personality evidenced by the same mega-watt smile as her son, Carlos.

Stella had to stifle her emotions. It was so easy for her to cry these days, especially in the face of such kindness that was the staple of the Sanchez family. Still deeply feeling the loss of her own mother, she really treasured her relationships with women as she was getting older. Relationships built on honesty, true friendship, less judgment.

"My Stella—come sit with me, my dear," Lupe, Rosa's mother, said as she patted the padded kitchen chair next to her wheelchair. Sweet Lupe reminded Stella of Nema. Her visits to Nema in the nursing home had lessened lately. It was rough because she felt her beloved grandmother was already gone. She missed her wise counsel and longed to hear her stories once more. She wished she felt healthy enough to have her Nema live with her. Maybe she could find a way.

Fortunately, Lupe was still mentally sharp and, as always, strongly opinionated. It was her body that had finally given out from the many years of working long days in the fields. She could walk if needed to, but found it so much easier and less painful to get around in a wheelchair.

"What a lovely coat, Stella," Rosa said as she helped her take off the knee-length, winter-white cashmere coat. "Here, go sit with mama. And try this, Stella. Carlos Sr. brought this up especially for you, my sister friend. It's some of our estate reserve 2006 Syrah," she added, bursting with pride as she cupped Stella's hand around the glass of claret-colored wine.

Stella swirled the wine to oxygenate it, and then sniffed. "Good *piernas*" she said, using her limited Spanish to compliment the wine. She marveled at the ruby liquid as it slid sensually down the sides of the glass as she held it up to the mission-style wall sconce. She walked over and sat down with Lupe, welcoming the wine's warmth trickle down her throat. Gently grasping Lupe's hand in hers, Stella asked her how she was doing.

"Life is good, my child," Lupe said as she loving stroked Stella's face and fiddled with her long bangs between her swollen knuckles. Still smiling, the old woman studied Stella's eyes. "But you, my child, something is on your mind, yes?"

Startled by the elderly woman's astute observation, her immediate reaction was to pull back, shut down, disconnect physically from Lupe. "No, I'm just a little tired from the long drive," stammered Stella, pushing her hair behind her ear as she tried to recapture her composure. But she could tell from the steely look in Lupe's eyes that this wise woman wasn't fooled at all by the clichéd excuse.

Lupe slowly nodded. "Fine, fine," she said as she patted Stella's hand with a knowing look.

Stella knew that the conversation wasn't over, just postponed.

Rosa scampered back into the kitchen, grabbed an apron and handed it to Stella. "I have the pork shoulder simmering, getting nice and crusty just the way you like for your tacos. So juicy and tender, Stella! Makes my mouth water. Nicki is going to make the palm salad, the *cocido* is already on the stove, and Mama and Carmen will make the *chiles rellenos de Sardinas.* The men are just finishing up closing for the day and should be here shortly. How do you like our Syrah?"

Stella took another sip and sighed, "Rosa, it's divine. A gift from the Goddesses, no doubt." Rosa beamed as if she had birthed the grapes herself.

"Thanks to Our Lady who blesses us every day," Rosa said, raising her glass of wine to the holy picture on the wall.

Stella turned her head and looked at the religious painting. Growing up in California she had seen pictures of the Lady of Guadalupe thousands of times on candles in convenience store visits when she was still smoking, but never really looked carefully at her. The brown-skinned Virgin Mary was dressed in a rose-tinged embroidered dress, her dark hair covered with a star-studded turquoise shawl held with a crown on her bowed head, cascading almost down to her feet. Her hands were in prayer as she stood on a crescent moon held up by an angel, with a gold and orange fiery halo circling her body in light. Not like the Virgin Mary she grew up with—the more white one. She didn't know much about the icon's story but wondered how she had never noticed her embellished costume, similar to her own artwork with cloth.

"I hate to say this, but I really don't know the story of Our Lady of Guadalupe," Stella sheepishly admitted. She had been a good student at after-school catechism, but Bible stories never resonated with her.

Rosa turned from the stove, stunned that someone in her family, even if by marriage, did not know the story, and started to open her mouth, when Lupe commandingly raised her thin wiry arms. "Let me tell you the story then. Come, Nicki, you should hear also about our Lady."

Nicki wiped her hands on her sturdy cotton apron and sat down, snuggling up to her mother on the banquet seat at the small round kitchen table. Lupe took a sip of her wine, then wiped the corners of her mouth with her crumpled napkin, and once sure her audience was ready, recited the story:

"On December 9th 1531, a man named Juan Diego was walking from his village to the city when he saw a vision of a young girl of about fourteen or sixteen, surrounded by light at the top of a hill in Tepeyac, Mexico. He said the Lady—that's what he called her—spoke to him and asked for a church to be built on that very spot in her honor. Juan Diego told his bishop of this vision and her wish. But the bishop did not believe him. He demanded Juan Diego bring him a miraculous sign to prove his claim.

"On December 12th, the Lady appeared again. She asked him to gather some flowers at the top of the hill even though it was winter, and they were not blooming. Magically, the Castilian roses started blooming," Lupe said, throwing her arms up to the heavens in a flourish to liven up her storytelling.

"He quickly gathered them in his cape made of cactus—a tilma is what they called it. The Lady rearranged the flowers in his tilma and sent him back to the bishop. When Juan opened his tilma to the bishop, the image of the Virgin of Guadalupe appeared inside the cape, exactly as you see in the picture hanging there on the wall.

"Now, almost 500 years later, the tilma, which has been burned, bombed, even spilled with acid, is in perfect condition. They say you can look in Her eyes and see an image of everyone in the room the day Juan Diego revealed the tilma to the bishop. They have analyzed the paint and said that it is not from any known earthly source. Said it appears as if it was painted in one stroke.

"Some say she is the Mexican Goddess Tonantzin or Coatlicue, an Aztec Goddess also known as Mother Earth. But to most of us, she is the mother of Jesus, our Lady who protects and keeps our family strong. Either way, she unites us Mexicans as the 'Mama of the Mexicans.'"

Not to be outdone, Rosa added "In the Book of Revelation, Chapter 12, it states: 'And there appeared a great wonder in heaven; a woman clothed with the sun, and the moon under her feet, and upon her head a crown of twelve stars.' This is Our Lady of Guadalupe."

Stella swirled her wine and stared as the ripples widened. *Was the feminine misty figure that night "The Lady?" No, stop chasing that thought!* Seeing the Virgin Mary or Jesus in toast was for religious fanatics—not her.

"Thank you, Lupe, for educating me. I will never look at the Virgin Mary without thinking of you." Stella gripped the elder woman's hands in hers, hoping her gesture showed how much she loved her.

Loudly, all the men began falling into the kitchen. "Stella," both Carlos, Jr. and Sr. rang out in unison, rushing to see who could hug her first. With great affection, they felt it their duty to protect her now that she had no man in her life.

After hugs all around, she and Rosa quickly attended to the rolling out of the tortillas, flipping them back and forth on the flat top of Rosa's industrial-sized stove to a light-brown doneness.

"I would really love to have a stove like this," said Stella.

"It's a necessity when you have so many to cook for," Rosa said with mock martyrdom. Rosa's family was her life, and she looked forward to it growing with more marriages and grandchildren.

As everyone gathered and sat, Stella attempted to help Lupe out of her wheelchair, but the elderly woman swatted her hand away. "I'm a *Mexican*, not a *Mexican't*. Now stand back and let me get to the table." Lupe's walk bounced with joy as she joined the noisy room.

After all the steaming and sizzling platters of food had been set out on the Mission-style wooden table, Carlos Sr. asked for everyone to bow their heads and say grace. What was once awkward for Stella, bringing back memories of the same ritual before her dad disappeared, now gave her comfort. With the last amen, he stood and held his glass up and asked everyone to join him in a toast to his son Carlos Jr. and daughter-in-law Nicki.

A toast? Stella questioned, as she shot a flinty glance at Nicki. Nicki averted her eyes towards her husband, beaming as they stood up.

Carlos, Jr., with glassy wet eyes, lovingly placed his hand in the small of Nicki's back while tenderly rubbing her stomach and announced "we are blessed with child." The room erupted with tears flowing, chair legs scratching the old wooden floor as cheers rang out among the hugging crowd.

Carlos' brother Sergio brought a tray of shot glasses and the finest tequila made, Herradura Seleccion Suprema, reserved for special occasions. Everyone, except Carmen's children, and, of course, Nicki, raised their glasses, drank and welcomed the news. It was news Stella had hoped to hear soon. She felt as close to blissful as when she laid on her deck that night last fall.

She always envied Maggie when she talked about her grandchildren, and now she would be able to join in on the conversation. Stella was so excited about becoming a grandmother and the only one she wanted to share the news with was Maggie. But it was already almost midnight Eastern Coast time, too late to call. Everyone knows you only get bad news when the phone wakes you, and she wasn't going to add to Maggie's anxiety.

It pleased her that she received the good news before Todd. She knew it would irk him to be in second place. They had talked at times about being grandparents someday; discussed which museum to take the child to for his or her first experience with art. Reminded her that plans don't always work out the way you want them to. At least the new baby would have Rosa and Carlos, Sr. Maybe someday she would find a grandpa for her grandchild. One that wouldn't leave them. But she wasn't going to plan on it—just in case.

Well, I guess this is a good time to make good on one of my New Year's Resolutions, Stella thought as she turned on her cell phone after retiring to her room. She struggled, but managed to text Maggie with the news. When she laid her head on the pillow, she thought she would never be able to sleep. She thought back to how she and Maggie had been pregnant at about the same time, both struggling with fertility problems. They each had become godparents to the other's child, and she thought it would be a nice touch if their children carried on the same tradition.

Tipsy from the wine, the tequila toasts and the hearty meal, with thoughts of how she would make this a better world for her grandchild, she fell into deep sleep within fifteen minutes.

* * *

At 5 a.m. Stella woke up to a vibrating sound on her nightstand. Still fuzzy from the alcohol last night, she wasn't sure what the sound was. It was her cell phone. *Why isn't it ringing,* she thought, as she picked it up. It was then that she saw something on the screen—an incoming text message. She fumbled around the night table for her reading glasses and read the message.

She couldn't breathe. Her mouth and body contorted as she emitted only a forlorn, guttural moan. She fell back onto the bed, dropping the phone on the floor.

Frightened awake, Rosa ran down the hall into Stella's room, with Carlos Sr. right behind. Rosa grabbed the wailing Stella and held her tight, while Carlos picked up the phone: "They killed Josh."

Chapter Fourteen

—∞—

Stella put her Geranium Birkin bag on her lap and pulled out the fuzzy photo Maggie's brother Bob had emailed her to refresh her memory. It was Brent McConnell, the former co-worker and friend of Maggie's late husband, who was picking her up from the airport. Maggie said Brent had really been a godsend, helping her with the funeral arrangements for Jim, and now he was helping with Josh.

She remembered meeting him at Jim's funeral, but not fondly. She had an immediate gut check when introduced, a distinct distrust of him. An oily, hard-bitten man, a Republican war hawk, no doubt. If she remembered the story right, it was Brent who had urged Jim to go to work at GA7.

"You ever notice he never looks at someone straight in the eyes, but rather with his head turned to one side, eyes peeking out through thin slits like a lizard? I might not have the best Gaydar," she said, referring to her marriage, "but I do know when something's just not right. My gut is telling me not to trust this guy," she told Maggie once on the phone.

Maggie had been instantly ticked off by Stella's comment and defended him fiercely. She sang his praises as a loyal friend, very involved with his church and a patriot and veteran—a real stand-up guy.

Stella backed off and apologized. "Wow, sorry, just voicing my gut reaction." They dropped the subject. The less said, the sooner mend.

Brent had volunteered to pick up Stella from the Louisville International Airport, knowing Maggie wasn't in any shape to drive. *I guess I should give him a chance to show me who he is,* she thought as she popped another Tums into her mouth. She didn't know if it was anxiety of being alone with him in a car, or just the fact this was her second trip in a year to Kentucky, both for funerals, or just the combination of it all—but she just couldn't get rid of her heartburn. Drinking cheap red wine on the plane probably didn't help. Plus, eating crappy peanuts and some kind of chemical concoction that was supposed to be cheese and salami was tearing at her insides. She could have used her accumulated miles for First Class seating, but wanted to save it for Paris Fashion Week. She was regretting that decision.

Think positive, she chided herself. Instantly, she thought of her coming grandbaby. She had hardly enough time to savor the news when she learned that Josh had been killed in Iraq. The news of the how and when of his death were still sketchy, as was Maggie's message that "they" killed him. *Odd,* Stella thought, *usually, you would say "so and so is dead."* She wasn't about to press Maggie on the details right now. Maybe it was better not to know. Deal with it later.

It helped to close her eyes and remember all the happy times in her life with her godson. Taking Nicki and Josh to the Exploratorium with a picnic on the lawn by the Palace of the Fine Arts. Nicki and Josh's first trip to the zoo and being more interested in the flocks of pigeons than the caged animals. Kite flying on the windy stormy beach at Dillon Beach. The kids losing their first tooth within days of each other. Dating. Graduation. His wedding. Nicki's wedding. His children. Nicki's unborn child Josh would never know.

Now she knew what people were talking about when they said their lives were replayed like a movie. That's all she had left now of Josh. She wiped the splashed tears off her age-spotted hands and looked out the plane's window, wondering how much pain and change people are equipped to handle.

As she studied the mottled hues of grey in the sky, she shuddered with a chill. She was already missing the warm California sun. CNN reported tornadoes here yesterday. She hoped Maggie's place had been spared. And that they were done with any more bad news. Time for a break from chaos.

Glancing at the network of steel across the Ohio River, she remembered the time not long ago when they watched fireworks spilling over the bridge. It made her think of happier times, when she and Todd visited right after Maggie and Jim had bought the horse ranch. They came for the ten-day celebration for the Kentucky Derby. Parades, big outrageous hats, sweet mint juleps, loud happy crowds, and, of course, the horses. It was a magical time. Both Todd and Stella agreed that if they ever thought of leaving their beloved California, this is where they would come.

She thought of her and Maggie playing "bride" as teenagers on sleepovers at each other's house, with half-slips on their heads, regally marching down an imaginary aisle to their grooms, with ratty nylon hair brushes standing in for the bridal bouquets. The reminiscing immediately turned to anger and disappointment. It wasn't supposed to work out this way, dammit! *How goddamned innocent we were then*, Stella fumed. *Now what do we do?* She thought "the Change" was just when her period would stop, not that her life would turn upside down, caught in some kind of frantic Twilight Zone revolving door, spitting people out of her life lickity split, as Maggie would say.

She wondered if Maggie would want to stay here. Maybe she'd ask Maggie to come back to California for a while so she could take care of her and give her a chance to ponder what to do next. Maggie would probably laugh, since she was the one who usually took care of everyone. And now Stella was going to step up to the plate? Change, indeed. They had never played "fiftyish and single."

Stella straightened her clothes from her Economy class-induced dishevelment, and started to make her way down the concourse to the baggage claim where she was supposed to meet Brent.

"Ma'am, would you allow me to give you a ride to the end of this here Concourse?" the man in the electric cart drawled, pulling up slowly beside her.

She gladly hopped into the cart. What was she thinking, wearing her four-inch Louboutin boots when she needed to walk in airports? She had just been so excited that she could wear them again, recently having lost weight from eating Dibrovna's "real" food, she couldn't resist. *I guess old habits die hard*, she reflected.

Back when she first started flying, one dressed up for the occasion. Now they stupidly made you take off your shoes because of one idiot with matches in his soles. It made her want to scream at the utter lack of common sense and critical thinking in the War on Terror.

Just one more reason for her to be angry at the government. Well, two—the Iraq war that had just ripped out part of her heart and soul. She felt as angry now as when she was a teen protesting the Vietnam War. When would this insanity of killing others in some pissing contest end? Wars had taken her father, now her godson. Since she received the horrific news of Josh's death, her rage grew like an oily, festering pimple about to burst. This shit had to end!

The cart stopped at the foot of the escalator. Stella smiled and thanked the cart driver as he lent her his arm to aid her disembarkment from his cart. She walked down the stairs to the baggage claim, and she spotted him. *Handsome, I guess, as old redneck men go*, but *definitely not someone she would ever get naked with*, she thought, amusing herself. "Ha!" she said out loud, catching herself. There I go again, no filter. She tended to voice aloud her thoughts a lot lately, since living alone. A very bad habit, or audio remnants of a misfiring brain?

As she walked towards Brent she had to admit she had a soft spot for this city, Louisville. Some of the kindest people she had ever met came from here. Hopefully, she and Maggie could rely heavily on that southern comfort for the next few days to get through this personal hell they had been thrust into.

A lot of strong people grew up here, like Mohammad Ali, whose pictures were everywhere. Maybe they could channel some of his strength and bravery.

She admired "The Champ" not only for his boxing ability but for his courage to stand up and not go to Vietnam. He had refused to go 10,000 miles away and drop bombs on other brown people while people of color in his own country were denied simple human rights. He bravely stood up, knowing he would lose millions of dollars and eventually serve time in jail. He had said it was time for these evils to come to an end. A true patriot in her eyes.

As Brent got closer, Stella tried to get a read on him: light blue jeans, pressed with a sharp crease down the middle, a crisp and clean oxford shirt under his puffy nylon Army-green bomber jacket. Good hair, recently cut and coiffed with lots of product so it wouldn't move. Strong jaw, broad shoulders, small waist, obviously a man who worked out. *Probably a gym rat or just a good old Dudley Do-right*, she thought. Reminded her of a sinister Kevin Costner.

"Stella," Brent yelled out, waving his hand. She pasted on a smile and allowed herself to become emotionally opaque. He grabbed her carry on and walked with her to the baggage claim.

"Nice flight? Hope it wasn't too bumpy for you."

"Under the circumstances, it was okay," she replied somewhat icily. The thought of having to make small talk on the one-hour ride to Bardstown made her head ache. *Stop being so rude*, she scolded herself. After all, this guy volunteered to drive you so you didn't have to rent a car and take a chance in case the roads were slippery. *Relax and be nice*, she told herself; *stop being such a bitch. Give the guy a chance to show you who he is*, a voice schooled her.

Brent grabbed her garment bag from the luggage carousel and escorted her to his shiny red American-made SUV, parked curbside. He hurried to open her car door, making sure she was settled in the warmed vehicle before placing her bags in the back. *That was a nice gesture*, she admitted, and she liked red cars, so maybe he wasn't all bad. Nothing in his rough exterior had suggested such kindness. Maybe it was just a southern gentlemanly way of treating a woman.

After some awkward small talk as they headed towards Nashville on I-65 South, Brent inquired about how she met Maggie and Jim. Thinking it was none of his business, Stella gave him the abbreviated version of their I. Magnin days and Maggie meeting Jim at a free concert.

They continued this uncomfortable game of Brent asking and Stella reluctantly answering for about thirty minutes before he asked a very strange question: "How much did you know about the work Jim was doing?"

The skin on her skull tightened, like freshly laundered yoga pants. Maggie and Jim had always been very close-lipped about Jim's work, only that he worked for a special program with the Army. Frankly, Stella had been too involved with her own life to care what Jim did professionally.

"I'm sorry, I really don't know about Jim's professional life. I doubt Jim knew much about my ex-husband's taste in art, either," she replied with a dash of venomous sarcasm, hoping to end this inquisition.

"Did Jim ever talk to your ex about his work?" Brent continued to pry.

"I guess you would have to ask him. Do you want his number at his boyfriend's house?" she cuttingly replied, impressing herself at her newly-found sharp tongue.

"I'm sorry. I didn't mean to pry. I was just making conversation," he defensively stated, leaning his left shoulder on the driver's window.

Not damn likely, Stella thought. She was going to keep a sharp eye on this one. She trusted her gut, and it screamed danger. And forget that he drove a red car—he drove a gas guzzling, planet destroying SUV!

"Do you mind if I turn on some music?" Brent asked, not waiting for her reply as he turned the volume to mid-level. "Surprised?" he asked when he heard Stella's intake of breath. "Yeah, most people don't peg me for an opera lover, but there's something about Pavarotti's Nessun Dorma."

Stella stared at the road while she twiddled her handbag's handles, never once letting go.

They finally turned on Clermont Road, heading towards downtown Bardstown. As they started to drive down 3rd Street, she saw a historical marker stating "First Diocese in the West." She wondered if they had their own version of Virgin Mary worship, southern style. Our Lady of Whiskey, maybe. Now she knew for sure she was going to hell. That is, if she even believed in hell.

Slowly, they wound their way through the streets lined with old brick houses, some built over two hundred years ago with slave labor. Outside the shops lining the streets, Stella noticed lots of American flags snapping crisply in the winter air, strung from the light posts. *Is this normal*, she wondered, *or maybe something special for a hometown boy—Josh?* She had read somewhere that small towns always came out to show their support for fallen soldiers, while big cities barely took notice. Pity that. She knew she would never look at a flag or a soldier in the same way ever again. She was proud of Josh and his service, but hate was mounting inside of her for the people who rushed her country into this never-ending war.

Stella missed feeling patriotic. She used to tear up when she saw a flag, especially if she was holding her father's hand. But now she felt like the flag didn't matter anymore. Didn't matter who you voted for anymore. It was all about money. She wanted to feel good about her country again. One that didn't sacrifice the lives of its military all in the name of profit.

They wouldn't even honor the dead by showing their coffins when they returned home. Sneaked them back into dark military terminals with no fanfare. Just processing incoming freight.

"If women ran this country, war would end," she, again, blurted out, forgetting someone else could hear her.

"You hate our country?" Brent asked with just the slightest hint of indignation.

"I don't want to talk about," she said, turning her body facing the car door, heart facing the flags. She knew which side he was on. In fact, it was her deep love for her country which fueled her rage. Despite their pact, she and Maggie had had many arguments about this war. Stella felt that she was more patriotic because she didn't support the war. Maggie disagreed.

Stella had been a real firebrand back in the day. She would spout very provocative almost-anarchist opinions but was given a lot of leeway because of her looks and charm. However, that didn't work for her anymore. She still felt very strongly about justice, but kept her opinions mostly to herself. She wondered where Maggie's allegiances were now, but knew this was not the time to find out. Her priority now was to support Maggie. Her best friend had sacrificed enough for her country.

They were almost at Maggie's ranch. Stella thought of the shot of Kentucky bourbon she planned on downing as soon as possible. She wished she could just curl into a ball and cover herself with a blanket.

How was she going to help her best friend bury her only child? She imagined the cracks in their entangled hearts must look like a spider's web by now, sticky and catching every drop of pain.

Feeling a little dizzy, she saw the grotto image flash quickly in and out of her mind's eye. "*Can't think about that right now*," she thought, feeling an overwhelming urge to sneak a pill before having the shot.

Chapter Fifteen

—∞—

Passing the Old Kentucky Home State Park as they headed out of town, the tension in the car was as solid as cold lard stored on a back porch in winter. Maggie's place was half way between Bardstown proper and all the bourbon barns, as she liked to call them.

As they approached the Barretts' ranch, Brent slowed and turned right towards the main house at the end of the long winding frozen driveway. They crunched past the old black barn that had originally been used for tobacco drying.

Stella's gut clenched at the thought of seeing Maggie once again shattered by grief. *Please let me be strong for her*, she prayed to no one in particular.

Brent backed up his rig, parking beside the other cars already assembled in front of the Barretts' large gravel parking lot.

Good, Stella thought, there's a lot of other people here. She hoped all of Maggie's five brothers had arrived. This was a time for family to gather and stand strong for each other. As she walked up the front walk, she noticed the big black ribbon loosely tangling from a flag pole. She thought it odd, as she knocked on the front door, that it wasn't tied in a pretty bow. Resembled some kind of abstract noose, something one of her Bay Area artists would do as a protest piece.

Silently, the door opened and what she first believed was a minister motioned her to come in. The person introduced himself as the Army chaplain. Shaking his hand, she watched a blueish cloud ghostly dance over Maggie's head from the far corner of the family room. A mixture of cigarette smoke and dust flotsam marked the spot where she was burrowed deep in the sectional sofa, the cigarette almost burned down to her fingertips. Maggie sat still, staring straight ahead. *I guess she had a relapse*, Stella thought. Maggie had quit smoking when she got pregnant with Josh.

Stella sat down beside her on the sofa and laid her hand on Maggie's sharp bony knee as her friend slowly turned her head in Stella's direction, her neck bone protruding as sharp as an executioner's blade. Stella tried to stifle her shock as the sadness rose in her throat, threatening to choke her words. "Maggie, I'm here." No response.

This is just Maggie's body in front of me. Where's my Mags? she wanted to scream. She looked into Maggie's eyes, devoid of recognition or joy to see her best friend. The once glowing gold flecks that reflected her inner spark now were rusty and dulled. The grittiest person she had ever known had vanished.

"Here, sweetie, let's put this out," she said as she gently helped Maggie stub out the smoldering cigarette filter that had now browned her fingertips. She lovingly took her friend in her arms. "Mags, I'm here. And I'm not leaving."

A faint recognition registered in Maggie's eyes as her rail-thin sharp body crumpled into Stella's arms. Nuzzled safely into the soft shoulder of Stella's cashmere sweater, Maggie whimpered, like a sick kitten. They sat like that for the next six hours.

Chapter Sixteen

——∞——

Stella rolled gently over to check on Maggie. They hadn't slept in the same bed for almost thirty years. Stella had hugged her, sang to her, rocked her—all in an effort to keep them both safe and sane until the morning light. That's what friends do, she told Maggie. "Would you like a cup of tea, sweetie?" Stella whispered.

Maggie's head lolled to one side as she looked blankly at Stella. "Put a shot in it." Not a good way to start what promised to be a long day.

How is Maggie going to handle going back to the same cemetery where Jim was buried? she worried. Maggie had never been back to visit Jim's grave, saying she didn't need to visit his "vessel."

"He will never leave me. You know that, right? Our souls never die, they just find another form." It was so all matter-of-fact, like describing how summer turns to fall. "But I knew he would die before me. Just had a knowing. I guess like the kind you and Jim used to talk about back in the day—just a knowing."

She returned with Maggie's tea and started a bubble bath for her. As she looked around the replica of the I. Magnin bathroom, she longed for the simplicity of their youth. They had never discussed how this part of their lives would play out. It was a conversation they would need to have eventually, but not today.

As Maggie shuffled into the ornate bathroom, Stella helped her disrobe. "Maggie, I love you and would do anything for you. You know that. Except you need to get into this tub by yourself. Our asses are way too big to fit in that bath together." It was the first time Stella saw a flash of her Mags since she had arrived. Just slight hints of the corners of her mouth lifting upwards. But her eyes remained clouded. Like someone had taken her index finger and thumb and—bam—flicked the gold flakes right out of her irises.

Stella brought in the desk chair from the bedroom. She told Maggie that it was so she could hold her tea cup for her but it was just a way of making sure Maggie didn't take a deep dive into the tub to drown herself. The whiff of bourbon was certainly jarring this early in the morning, causing Stella's gag reflex to kick in. The smell mixed with her recently-returned acid reflux was almost more than she could handle. She placed the delicate cup with its loaded contents on the marble floor, using her foot to push the offensive smelling cup as far away as she could.

Maggie leaned back in the tub, staring at nothing in particular, her tears plunking into the bathwater like a leaky faucet. "Promise me no dirt will fall on my baby." Like a magpie, Maggie pleaded over and over not to get dirt on the coffin. It had been so long since Stella had played with Josh, she forgot how he had been so fastidious about cleanliness; Nicki loved to roll in the dirt.

"I'll make sure. Don't worry," Stella assured her. "I'll be right back."

She quickly went downstairs into the kitchen where Bob, Maggie's oldest brother, was pouring himself a cup of coffee. "Bob, you gotta go to the cemetery and make sure they move the dirt away from the grave," she blurted.

"What?"

"Maggie is worried that dirt will get on Josh. I know it sounds crazy, but it's just a small thing. Make sure the mound of dirt they dug up is moved out of her sight. Please." She hoped her request wouldn't get some kind of rebuttal or a request for more information. Maggie came from a family of verbal jousters. But not this time.

Bob's eyes started to well up, and he simply answered, "Anything my sis wants, I'll do. Tell the rest I'll be back shortly." Stella hugged Bob and hurried back upstairs.

Stella was so glad Maggie's brothers had been able to come out. They had always taken care of their little sister, and this time was no exception. At Maggie's request, her five brothers had gone, with Josh's wife and children, out to the airport to pick up his returning body. Maggie had been informed that the casket would be met by the Army's honor guard, a general and a chaplain for transport to the funeral home. She knew she would only have enough tolerance for military pomp and circumstance at the funeral, so she stayed home. Maggie wasn't ready to see her boy in a box.

Stella gasped as she entered the bathroom. Maggie was lying trance-like with her head back against the tub's rim in the same position since Stella's absence. Her pallor was a light mousy gray which made her dusting of freckles pop. She looked dead. Maggie, startled by Stella's gasp, abruptly sat up. "What the Sam Hill are you trying to do? Scare me crazy?"

"Sorry, sorry, I didn't . . . "

"Oh, never mind. Honey, can ya help me with my hair? I'm just laying up in this tub with no get up and go," she slurred. The empty tea cup was laying on its side, under the claw-footed tub, far from where Stella had left it.

"Sure, of course." Stella, still unnerved, grabbed the empty tea cup and rinsed it out in the sink so she could use it to wet Maggie's hair. She tried to take off her rings so they wouldn't get caught in Maggie's curls, but she was still bloated from flying. "Okay, I'm trying not to get caught in your hair. So don't yell at me again, okay."

Maggie reached back and patted her best friend's hand and nodded her agreement. She shampooed Maggie's hair in silence, hypnotized by the soapy water cascading into rivulets through Maggie's curls. It was a ritual from their younger days—shampooing each other's hair.

Stella remembered the first time, right after the first Zodiac killing in Vallejo on the Fourth of July. Maggie was so unhinged by fear she tearfully begged Stella to spend the night. They talked for hours but still Maggie wasn't calm enough to sleep. That's when Stella remembered how much it calmed her when her Nema washed her hair. That's how their ritual started.

Suddenly, a loud rumbling emanated from the cast iron tub, causing Stella to jump. It was Maggie—farting. Something that would have had them both howling in laughter any other time, still managed to bring a smile to Stella, which she tried to hide.

"Mags, do you need to use the toilet?" she asked wondering if Maggie had a secret stash of bourbon somewhere in the bathroom; she hadn't put *that* much in the tea to cause Maggie's apparent drunkenness.

"I'm fine. Just let me toot, okay."

"Not a problem," she said leaving the odorous bathroom. "I'll go get your clothes ready." She pulled out the clothes she had hung last night: an ink-black Calvin Klein jersey column dress with bracelet-length sleeves and a Chanel silk wool blazer, size eight. Maggie had told her all she had to wear nowadays were her riding clothes. Dibrovna, still painfully aware of the pain of losing loved ones to war, without being asked, had immediately pulled the items from the store and brought them to Stella's house.

Stella was wearing the same black dress she wore on her blind date and to Jim's funeral. She wondered what kind of statement that made. She made a mental note to pack something new and colorful to wear in Paris. Maybe her red vintage Dior New Look dress, handed down by her mother. It might fit now.

Stella decided they should both wear their star necklaces. A show of sisterly unity and connection. The necklaces had been presents from Stella's mother's French friend. Her grandmother's face had brightened the first time she saw the lovely stars. "Those are magical talismans. Never forget that and cherish them always," Nema advised.

"Sis, the limo is here," Matthew, Maggie's youngest brother, yelled up the stairs. Maggie grabbed Stella's hands, with pleading teary eyes. "We'll make it through this day, Mags. I swear. But we have to go." *Just another pockmark on our heavily scarred hearts*, Stella thought.

She zipped up Maggie's dress. Not one to fuss about her appearance, as soon as the zipper of the dress reached her neck, Maggie gave a nod of her head, straightened her spine, and proceeded to the stairs. It was obvious her years as a military wife would come in handy for her today. Stiff upper lip and all. Love your country, right or wrong.

Chapter Seventeen

—∞—

Josh had been dressed in his Class-A uniform, though no one would know. His young wife, upon advice from Josh's commanding officer, had decided to have a closed casket to spare the family the reality of his injuries. Death must have been a blessing for the young soldier. His flag-draped coffin with the stars strategically placed over his heart took center stage at the church.

"Follow me, sweetie. We're sitting up front with the boys and Eva," Stella said, trying her hardest to be brave.

Maggie made sure not to catch a glimpse of her grandsons' eyes as they scooted into the hard-worn wooden pew, eyes focused on the simple altar. Feeling their pain along with her own was more than she could bear. She had lost her son, but they had lost their father.

Stella admired Maggie's courage and bravery. All she could feel right now was deep guilt over her apathy. *Why didn't I do more to oppose this stupid war?* she thought. She felt she had been bullied into silence. She knew in her gut that Iraq had nothing to do with 9/11 but voicing that opinion was viewed as "unpatriotic." The president went on TV and let everyone know you were either "for us or against us," and just go shop to please the corporatocracy.

She vowed then and there if given another chance, she would prove her loyalty to truth and justice. She would stand up, not be silently appeasing. War should never be casual business as usual. She felt true patriotism was making sure that war was the last resort—always.

Stella looked down and recognized the initials carved into the pew's bench. Same spot where she and Maggie sat only eleven months ago, in the same Unitarian church Brent had arranged for Jim's funeral. Fortunately for Stella, it wasn't Brent's Catholic Church. She remembered that Maggie had allowed Brent to pick the church, telling him "Our family worships God differently. Our church is being out in nature, riding our horses and smelling the wild sage." Since no one in Maggie's immediate family were active church goers, Brent's choice sufficed for the funeral and also satisfied his wish to ensure God's blessing on this fallen soldier.

Stella was grateful he hadn't picked one of the "Six Flags over Jesus" churches where they bussed you in on Sunday, espoused some twisted view of what Jesus said to support their own political views, collected the money, and bussed you right back to your car.

Soon everyone had settled down into the pews, and the music was cued. The minister entered from a side door, walked towards a chalice which he lit while chanting "In our time of grief, we light a flame of sharing, the flame of ongoing life."

Stella tried to pay attention, but her mind drifted as she intently stared at the flame. She vaguely heard a solider eulogizing Josh; a prayer by his Uncle Bob. She blinked hard and shook her head a little as she tried to focus on the minister's words.

"Josh served his country well, with dreams of peace and freedom for all citizens of the world. He now has tasked us with carrying on his mission. Let us remember what the Prince of Peace said from the Gospel of Thomas:

> *The Kingdom of God is inside and within you, and all*
> *about you, not in buildings or mansions of wood and stone.*
> *Split a piece of wood and I am there, lift a stone and you*
> *will find me.*

He then called for insight and knowledge, choosing a hymn from the Secret Book of John:

I am the forethought of pure light, I am the thought of the virgin spirit, who raises you to a place of honor, Arise, remember that you have heard, and trace your root, which is I, the compassionate. Guard yourself against the angels of misery, the demons of chaos, and all who entrap you, and beware of deep sleep and the trap in the bowels of the underworld.

The mention of the virgin spirit caught Stella's attention. She listened more intently as his words resonated deep within her soul. This sure wasn't like any Catholic service she had ever attended. And definitely not one of the Southern ministers who preached killing and torturing "others" as a moral and patriotic duty.

She could never understand how anyone who believed in God could support war. Just didn't make sense. *Had they heard what Jesus had said? If we truly believed and felt God's love*, she thought, *our military would roam our lands, looking to clothe, shelter, and feed our fellow humans. We would strive for harmony every day, not conquest.* She picked at a hole in the wooden floor with the pointed toe of her expensive high heel, angrily chipping away at it.

The priest finished with "When our hearts are broken, the crevices welcome in light and love. Our compassion grows from these pockets of love, like trees growing from granite."

Everyone rose as Eddie, a fellow soldier and Josh's best man at his wedding, escorted the flag-draped coffin down the aisle to load into the hearse. All the mourners dutifully followed and climbed into their cars for the procession to the cemetery.

As the limos and other cars followed behind the hearse slowly going down the flag-draped frozen streets of Bardstown, they were greeted by veterans lining the streets, red-nosed and teary-eyed from the biting cold. Even the cook from the Shoo Fly Pie restaurant, with his food-stained apron straining tightly against his bulging belly, came out and stood at attention. Stella hadn't felt so patriotic in years, if ever. Josh would have been so honored. And Jim would have been one proud father.

They pulled into the Cave Hill Cemetery in Louisville, circling past Victorian-era statues and monuments that highlighted the historic garden cemetery. Stella could feel Maggie's anxiety as they drove up the incline and passed the lake to the burial spot, next to his father's. Off to the side, a van load of honor guards had arrived from Fort Knox, sharply dressed in green uniforms with berets. They had their M16s ready with three rounds for a military salute. One soldier was off to the side, holding his trumpet.

Their limo was greeted inside the cemetery gates by a civilian group of motorcyclists called the Patriot Guard Riders. They were a group of men and women from different walks of American life. They had banded together to make sure to always be there to honor both the family and the fallen soldier. They huddled around their parked motorcycles, drinking their *7-11* coffee, with words of small talk, patiently waiting to express their condolences and gratitude.

As the long line of cars came to a halt, the soldiers removed the casket from the hearse and laid it on the scissored gurney next to the open grave. Brent had made sure that the burial hole was lined with a burial vault, called the Iraqi Operation Freedom vault. It was etched with scenes from Iraq, including the falling statue of Saddam. Maggie's brothers thought it was a good idea. Eva and Maggie were too numb to care, just wanting him to stay clean.

The graveside service was brief. *Hallelujah* was sung by a high school classmate. Then the priest read Ecclesiastes III 3:1-3:8 "to everything there is a season . . . the love that we shared, and the memories that remain with us still."

Then came the signal.

Seven soldiers in line shot the first volley, then quickly the second and the third, in perfect unison. Maggie's body violently jolted back and forth with each volley, as if taking each shot. She remained ramrod straight in her folding chair, with her quivering hands folded limply in her lap. She avoided looking at the casket, instead staring off into the distance with vacant, dull eyes that were as dry as an ancient bone.

The lone solider to the side, raised his gleaming trumpet and began playing mournful taps to accompany the spreading sadness. The other soldiers returned to the open vault to fold the flag, first lengthwise twice, then in thirteen triangular folds. Before the second fold, one solider inserted three of the spent shells from the salute, polished and clean, which were intended to never leave the folded flag. The flag was then passed on to the officer who had been randomly assigned to attend the funeral on behalf of the Army.

Today, it was fifty-four-year-old Brigadier General Betty Paulson, who was flown in specifically from Washington, D.C. Paulson tenderly placed the folded flag into Eva's hand as the young widow raised her watery eyes and immediately clutched the flag to her chest, lest anyone take more from her. "This flag is presented on behalf of a grateful nation and the United States Army in appreciation of your loved one's honorable and faithful service."

Stella was struck by the kind demeanor of this government representative who couldn't hide her own tears. She was glad that a woman was the one chosen to comfort them. It made a difference. Though exchanging a flag stuffed with spent bullet shells for a life wasn't much of a bargain.

As the soldiers returned to their van, they collectively exhaled. One of the young baby-faced soldiers started uncontrollably sobbing as his comrades pulled him into the van, hoping no one had noticed. Witnessing the bravery of these young men, some barely more than boys, Maggie grabbed Stella's hand. "Please, I need to walk—now."

Stella, at first stunned by the forceful tone of Maggie's plea, jumped up. *Oh, God, of course, she can't watch her son being covered with dirt. Why didn't I think of an exit plan earlier?* Swiftly, they started walking, with no destination in mind, leaving the other mourners to finish the ceremony, worried about Maggie's sudden departure.

Finally, out of earshot of the others, Maggie started crying. She raised her fists to the sky and shouted, "God, why do you hate me so much? Why am I being punished? Why, god dammit? What kind of God wants his child killed before he'll forgive their sins? What kind of God is that?" The spittle from her angry tirade became foamy, mixed with salty tears and mucus.

Fearing Maggie was about to collapse, Stella maneuvered her to a nearby stone bench that faced a huge deep cave. *I hope the kids can't hear her,* Stella thought, as she tried to avoid a scene. Then just as suddenly, she didn't care. She just wanted to help Maggie excise her overpowering toxic grief. Let her pour out the poison of such unbearable pain, stop the rotting of revenge inside, preserve her soulful goodness. Stella held Maggie on the frozen bench, allowing her to scream and curse at God, the military, even the damn cold weather.

It felt like they had been there for hours, though it had been less than an hour. As the sky turned to dusk, Stella was still formulating how to approach the now-spent Maggie and gracefully guide her back to the warmth of the waiting limo. Their clothes were damp from the late afternoon fog, and Stella was trying to figure out the right thing to say to Maggie, without sounding selfish and uncaring for the want of leaving the darkening cemetery.

She first noticed the wave of warm air on her stocking-clad legs before it embraced her entire body. She turned to Maggie, to see if she had noticed. But before either could utter a word, in unison their heads were snapped towards the frozen spring leading into the cave. Arching electrified misty fingers of fog slowly made their way towards the cave's interior. Stella instantly recognized it. That, and the smell of roses.

Stella's breathing quickened as she watched in anticipation as the mystical fog twirled upwards into the now very recognizable feminine form. Their heads jerked upwards towards the sudden burst of bright white light inside the mouth of the cave. Caught instantly in an ecstatic trance, they smiled as a lady spoke to them:

> *I am you and you are I. Wherever you are, I am there, I am sown in all, and you gather me from wherever you wish. But when you gather me, you gather yourself. Gather the women.*

And as quickly as the mysterious vision had appeared, it vanished.

Stunned into silence, Maggie and Stella gripped each other's hand as they slowly rose and made their way back to the car. There was no need for conversation.

Stella noticed as they passed Josh's grave that it had already been marked with a temporary shiny metal nameplate: Sgt. Josh Barrett, 1981-2012. She stepped up her pace as they walked to the waiting limo, anxious for its warmness unaware their once-wet clothes were now completely dry.

As Stella started to enter the car, something caught her eye. She turned and looked around, noticing a man in the shadows of a bronze memorial statue. She watched as he slowly jogged out of the cemetery towards the shiny red SUV, his breath rising in frozen puffs from words spoken into his cell phone.

Chapter Eighteen

—∞—

"Time to pump the brakes, sister! Why didn't you tell me what you saw?" Maggie slammed the front door so hard it bounced back open. She turned on Stella, the veins visibly throbbing in her long, slender neck. "I'm your damn best friend!" They hadn't been inside Maggie's house more than thirty seconds when Stella told Maggie she had experienced something similar last November.

"How could I tell you? It happened when I thought I was finally recovered from 'cracking open.' I didn't know if it was the meds my pill-happy doctor keeps pushing on me or the copious amounts of wine I drank that night. I question my sanity every day now, ya know. If I had told you I thought I saw some kind of ghost or vision, would you have thought I lost my mind?"

"Well maybe it's time to cut back on the meds, honey! And while you're at it, submit your resignation from the Itty Bitty Shitty Committee of her Lady of Self Doubt," Maggie screamed.

"Why are we fighting?" Stella pleaded. "I'm so sorry. I was fragile and thought you might think I was friggin' nuts, like I was having flashbacks or something." She had learned to be cautious when it came to Maggie's conservative judgments about her lifestyle, especially now during this historic election season. Even with their long-standing pact to never discuss politics, it was a subject hard to avoid. It started every Americans daily conversation, obsessed over the first Black president being re-elected. Plus, she still wasn't convinced she wasn't losing her mind. Right now she just wanted privacy so she could pop a Xanax.

She thought she had been so successful putting space between her and that fall evening. She believed that what you focused your thoughts on made a difference in your life. Conflicted with fear of completely going over the cliff versus the best feeling she had ever experienced, she did what was now second-nature—shutdown. It had been a turning point in her life that she still wasn't sure of what it meant or why it happened. Or maybe if she shared her experience, it might make it not real. Not a chance she was willing to take.

"Oh, please, Stella, give me more credit than that," Maggie shouted out as she kept circling and flapping her long wiry arms around her thin body, trying to bang the chill from her body. "What just happened to us? What was that?" Maggie tearfully pleaded. "Do you know?" She noticed someone had been kind enough to build a fire for her before they all left for the services, and walked over and lit it. Babying the flames gave her time to try to regain control of her emotions.

Stella tried to avoid Maggie's eyes, still flamed with desperation. "Well, no, I'm not totally sure, but I may have an idea," Stella offered. "Please, promise not to laugh or scream at me. Be patient and let me tell you a story first." Not getting any lip, she motioned for Maggie to sit down in the opposite wing chair flanking the fieldstone fireplace.

"Let me start this story in my own way and in my own words. But you must promise to be quiet and listen. No interruptions." Maggie agreed with just a blink of her eye. That was sufficient for Stella. She stretched her shoulders upward, exhaled and began.

"Before I tell you what happened to me, let me tell you a story I was told just last week." She proceeded to tell Maggie the story of the Lady of Guadalupe, as told to her by Lupe just a scant seven days ago.

When she finished, Maggie stood up and glared at Stella, half questioning, half unnerved. "You mean, this is something like the Song of Bernadette?" Maggie said, her voice steadily rising. "You're scaring me crazy right about now! Do you honestly believe in that crap? That the Virgin Mary talks to people?"

"See, I asked you not to yell at me. Damn!" Stella quickly stood up and turned her back, pouting like a seven-year-old.

"Sorry for being salty and all, darlin', but I've just had the worst damn day any mother can have so give me a little leeway to get my head wrapped around this, okay?" Maggie said, as she walked over to the glass-doored liquor cabinet. Pulling out the Waterford crystal carafe with two matching glasses, her fifteenth-year anniversary gift, she poured both Stella and herself three fingers of Maker's Mark. Droplets of the amber liquid dripped down the outside of the glasses from her jerky attempt.

She turned and looked at Stella and instinctively added another finger for good measure. "So, this happened in your back yard, right? You heard a voice?" she said, taking a dangerously large gulp of the Kentucky bourbon. "I don't know if I'm ready but my gut says I need to know what you heard. Tell me everything—please!" She again started walking in circles, reeling from the day.

"Sit," Stella ordered. For a few moments, they silently sat and sipped their drinks as they watched the flames dance in the firebox. Stella parsed together in her mind how best to tell the story.

She cleared her throat and nervously began. "First, I heard a buzzing right above my left ear, like a fly or that sound you hear when you're underneath a power line, ya know." She edited out the part about lying face down among the flour-encrusted granite counter top, heavily under the influence of wine and pity. "Then Pete started getting agitated in his cage and squawking 'pretty lady, pretty lady.'

"Remember, this was after a two-hour crying jag, so I may be a little blurry on some of the details. I do remember that Ave Maria by Pavarotti was playing, because I later thought that was a bit coincidental or something. You know I love to listen to Pavarotti while I make bread." Stella could tell by Maggie's familiar head tilt and twisted mouth that her patience was growing thin. She needed to stop digressing and get to the point.

"Anyway, I opened the French doors onto the deck because I felt a storm was coming in, and I wanted to bring in some houseplants. Suddenly, the sky lit up with a brilliant flash of bright almost blue light.

Brighter than any light I have ever seen in my life. But it didn't hurt my eyes. That's when I noticed the mist moving along the floor of the deck. It started from the left and moved towards the grotto in the back corner of the yard. I thought it was just the nightly fog, but it was moving too fast. It almost had a character or a mind of its own. It had an ethereal sparkle to it, a body to it. I can't explain it. I just felt it! And it did the same thing as what happened today. The mist started spiraling up towards the sky until it became a form, like a woman. Then slowly, I started to make out a face, a flowing gown, something over her head, with her hands pressed together like she was praying. And the wildest thing was the smell of roses. You don't smell roses in Marin in the middle of November!

"Then she smiled at me. Maggie, I have never felt so loved in my life," Stella whispered, tears now rolling down her cheeks. "There was an energy field I had never felt before. I couldn't move, I couldn't talk—and I didn't want to! I just wanted to stay there, looking at her, being with her. Then, without moving her lips, I heard *Know thyself. Awaken and come to me. Reveal what has been hidden. Know that I am. Love as One.'* Then she just dissipated into the air, as quickly as she had come. I think I passed out or something, because the next thing I knew I was waking up on the deck, shivering like a wet dog. I got up, went inside, ran upstairs and stayed under the covers for the next twenty-four hours.

"Maggie, I didn't trust myself to know if I had seen something or not. Was it an alien? Was I just drunk and seeing something like the proverbial 'pink elephant?' I mean, I was still recovering from the horrible date I had been on. Please, don't look at me like that. I sometimes don't trust that I *do know* myself."

Maggie, obviously hurt and trying to understand Stella's behavior, simply stated, "I wish you had called me. Sweetie, I will always be in your corner, no matter what. But I must be able to trust you. I trusted Jim so much I never even asked him where he was going or when he was coming back. We gave each other space and freedom because we trusted each other. You don't keep secrets."

Her sincerity gripped Stella's heart like a vise.

"But remember this. Nothing is what it seems. Jim taught me that. And it's true. Just pay attention to patterns, he told me. So, let's just keep an open mind here, okay. Too early to make assumptions."

Maggie took a sip of her bourbon and looked out the plate glass window, wondering what was out there in the dark black night. The sweetness in her eyes just a moment ago, when she re-vowed her loyalty to Stella quickly reverted to a quiet panic of never feeling normal again, of exposing the gaping hole in her chest where she held her family for so long. Images of her son being lowered into the ground started to emerge. Swiftly, she snapped back, switching her mind to something else.

"Okay, time to build a bridge and get over it," Maggie clipped. "Do you think it was the Virgin Mary?"

Stella was a bit stunned by her brusqueness. "Do I think we just saw Christ's mother? Who died, I don't know, almost 2,000 years ago?" Stella said, flabbergasted. "Seriously, Mags, how the hell do I know? I barely even know the story of her. Remember, when I was going to church, everything was still in Latin. I don't have a clue about Mary. You probably know more about her than I do. What do you think?" She couldn't believe they were having this conversation.

"Well, I don't think it was an alien in that cave today," Maggie said fiercely. "I doubt aliens come smelling like roses. And you said, it was just like what you saw, except she said something different. Do I think she looked like Mary? I don't know, maybe. Do I believe in seeing visions of the Virgin? I don't think so! Stella, what I do know is I need to do some research on this."

Maggie was not only a talented librarian, but a problem-solver. When she needed answers, she jumped at the opportunity to use her head for something other than a hat rack, as her dad used to tell her when she had a problem. Also, it was a good tactic to stall the discussion.

Books were her portal into other worlds, the words her keys to treasures. Using her above-average memory for facts, she would read and read then weave everything together to come to her conclusions on any matter. Even though she hadn't been employed as a research librarian for almost a decade, she kept up her membership with the American Library Association, and frequently worked with both the Louisville library system and with Josh's old schools. She was a fierce believer in the power of words. Maybe that was why she parsed them out so judiciously like valued treasure, knowing their emotional impact before freely releasing them from her lips. She had just told Stella no more secrets, yet hadn't divulged all of hers—yet.

Chapter Nineteen

—∞—

Stella thought she detected a lively spark in Maggie's eyes, or was it just the glow from the laptop? She finished her drink, unsuccessfully trying to hide her jaw-breaking yawn.

"Mags, I'm sorry, I need to go up and finish packing," she said as she walked to the kitchen and gently placed her empty glass in the sink. "My flight leaves early, and I need to get back to the shop. I leave in less than two weeks for Paris Fashion Week. I would love for you to come with me. You know what they say: two carrying a load can lighten the burden. Let's stick together and get through this. It might help to get away." Again, Stella's filter had failed her.

Maggie looked up from the computer, stunned and angry by Stella's comment. Was losing a child a burden? No, it was a gaping wound that would ooze emotional puss for the rest of her life. But she softened as her inner voice guided her to treat Stella with kindness; she, too, had just lost someone she loved like her own child.

Still grieving the loss of their husbands, and now Josh, this wasn't the time to squabble. It was a time to hang on to each other for life. Being away from Stella for so long, she just needed to acclimate herself to her friend's bluntness which might translate as uncaring to a stranger. After all, she had been raised by a mother who taught her daughter how to shut down and not let people get close. Maggie thought maybe the distraction of a trip would help her remove the searing red-hot poker lodged deep in her heart. Not going wouldn't bring her men back to life.

"I'll sleep on it and let you know," Maggie said, turning back to her search results, allowing her anger to dissipate.

"I've saved my frequent flier miles so I could fly first class, but I wouldn't mind exchanging them for two tickets. I really want you to go with me," Stella said as an enticement. The thought of the two of them in Paris brought back the memories of when they were young. She felt guilty thinking of the fun they might have.

"Darlin', I'm bereaved, not bankrupt. We'll talk in the morning."

* * *

Stella's eyes sprung open by the sudden jolt. Instinctively, she was half way out of the bed running to a door frame to shelter herself from the anticipated earthquake. Maggie, wild of hair and eyes, scampered into the bed beside her, clutching a huge splayed stack of papers in her hand. She waved the documents like a Las Vegas drunk with a winning poker hand. Some of her papers slipped to the floor, as her red curls bounced to and fro like sprung springs.

"Stella, you are not going to believe what I found," she excitedly said as she spread the papers around on the bedspread. "Here, look at this," she said, as she pointed to a printed article entitled *Marian Apparitions in the 20th Century.* "See, it's not only us, honey. The Virgin Mary has been showing up all over the goddamned place!"

"What? Maggie, did you sleep at all last night?" To say she was a little frightened by Maggie's manic behavior was an understatement. She was glad to see Maggie with some life in her, but she couldn't tell if this turn in behavior was a good thing or something that may need medicating. Her heart was still racing from the fear that everything was about to crumble onto her head. Satisfied that it was just Maggie and not the "Big One," she climbed back into bed.

"Oh, maybe an hour or two. Never mind that—here, read this," she said as she shoved more paper in Stella's face. She had been up most of the night on the internet, doing her best to ignore her previous churchification judgments on heaven and hell. She concentrated on educating herself, clicking here and there, and hoping the blanket she placed on top of the printer muffled the constant whirring as it spit out page after page. After too much caffeine and the events of the last twenty-four hours, she felt like one frayed nerve, waving in the air like an unmanned fire hose. Being able to throw her mind into research was the lifesaver she needed right now to get her through from hour to hour, still intact.

Stella flung the covers back and said "First, I'm going to use the bathroom, then I'll read it."

"Well, here—just take it with you. You know, multitask," Maggie insisted as she presented the now balled-up pages to Stella. "And pay close attention to the story about the Third Secret!"

Stella grabbed the articles and shuffled into the bathroom, as she struggled to get vertical. Sometimes, she felt like a slow-motion depiction for the evolution of man, from an ape bent over dragging its knuckles, morphing into an upright homo sapien. She longed for the days when she could spring out of bed, with vim and vigor. Some days she felt like her bones were as calloused as her heels—rough, cracking, in need of lubrication. Right now, she just prayed her bladder would behave itself until she could reach the throne. Relieved, she sat and started reading. By the second paragraph, the hairs on the back of her neck started to rise.

"Oh my God! I think we've been visited by the Virgin Mary," she yelled from the toilet. "But why me? You? Us? And why now?" Her recessed Catholic guilt whispered in her ear: "You sinner, you married a homosexual! You're going to hell!" *No, that's not it at all,* her inner voice told her. This was something far greater. She knew with a certainty that this was bigger than her and Maggie. For whatever reason, they had been chosen to participate.

By the time she returned to the bed, Maggie had brought her a nice big mug of steaming coffee with her favorite hazelnut creamer and placed it on the bed's nightstand. Stella sat on the side of the bed, enjoying the creamy hot liquid as its warmth woke up her body.

Bounce! Maggie was back on the bed, flapping another piece of paper—her one-way airline ticket to SFO.

Stella bunched up the one-thousand thread count sheet to wipe away the spilled coffee on her thighs. "What the . . . ?"

"I'm almost packed—started last night. I'm going to California for a while with you. And I'm also going to Paris—First Class! You think they only give frequent flier miles to Stella St. James? What's your flight number so I can book it now?" Stella sensed danger in this increasingly manic behavior of Maggie's, but who was she to question how others dealt with their own personal grief.

"Did you read the article about the Third Secret?" Maggie frantically asked, shoving random items of clothing into her suitcase, layered on top of the treasured ziplocked bag containing Jim's T-shirt.

"I skimmed it. Something about a dancing moon, and the 'Lady,'" she answered, realizing her desire for calmness was as elusive right now as the image she had witnessed. Their lives would never be the same, and change was coming so quickly she now just desired a moment's peace.

She wondered if now was a good time to discuss her medications. Maggie may need one—or two.

Chapter Twenty

_____∞_____

"**D**o you think pain brings you closer to God? Like that's its purpose or something? I feel like what I imagine Mary felt when her son was killed." It was Maggie's first utterance since boarding the plane almost fifteen minutes earlier.

Stella put her tray down and slowly unwrapped their airport deli sandwiches, trying to think of a response. "Let's order some beverages while I think about that," Stella said, trying to buy time so she could scrutinize her thoughts about God and religion first. She had spent a good amount of time thinking about those two subjects lately. But now her world was changing rapidly, not allowing the luxury of deep reflection.

"To me, I just can't get behind the image of some old man with long white hair and a beard, sitting on a throne in the sky passing judgment and having wrath," Stella responded as the attendant handed her a glass of champagne and a Bloody Maria to Maggie. "To me I see God when I look at the redwoods in my back yard. In the waterfalls, smelling jasmine-perfumed June evenings, random kindness—that's God. But I do believe Mary existed and birthed a prophet named Jesus." Stella hoped her views weren't offensive to Maggie. Wasn't a subject they much talked about before this happened.

"I remember my mom told me that Jesus' first miracle, turning the water into wine at that wedding, was because his mother told him to do it," Maggie said. "I told Josh I didn't want him to go back on another stinkin' tour. But he felt it was his duty to go. He wouldn't listen to me."

"We didn't listen to our mothers either, did we?" Stella asked. "Why, oh why, don't we give our elders more respect for their wisdom? Nema warned me many times to pay attention to her words."

"I guess we all need to learn our own lessons," Maggie replied, as she started in on her food. After a few bites, she decided this might be the right time to inform Stella of the upcoming appointment she had made. Maggie casually laid her hand on top of Stella's in an effort to keep her calm.

"I found a woman, an ex-nun in San Francisco, who seems to be an expert on Marian Apparitions. I was referred to her by a friend who's Catholic. We have an appointment with her day after tomorrow." She didn't let it slip that she had called Brent after Stella had retired for the evening; a little drunk from the bourbon and emotionally exhausted, she told him what had happened. He was her "Catholic friend," and she already knew how Stella felt about *him.* Some things are better kept to yourself, she rationalized. Especially, since this ex-nun also happened to be Brent's cousin. Her lips were sealed. Stella didn't need to know that. It wasn't a secret really—only a teensy omission.

"Are you crazy?" Stella hissed under her breath. She didn't want to cause a ruckus and have air marshals escorting them off the plane, their pictures plastered across the evening news. She never thought it necessary to promise to keep the knowledge of the incident to themselves. She was livid. "What did you tell her?" she asked, afraid their secret was now exposed. Her hand shook as she pulled it away from Maggie and placed it securely in her own lap.

"Stella, now don't go drowning in a cup of water, okay. You know it's always been my way that when you want to know the facts, go to the experts. This woman is an ex-nun and a supposed expert on the subject. Even studied at the Vatican under the supervision of the pope's assistant. Don't you want to know more about what happened?"

"I don't know what I want at this point, except not to be considered a fringed lunatic, some kind of fundamentalist 'born-again' nut case. I just wish you would talk to me first before you make 'appointments.' Let's agree that we not share this information with anyone else without consulting each other first."

"Deal," Maggie agreed and shook Stella's hand. Though it had been a long time and she no longer owned a rosary, she silently said a prayer to Mother Mary: *please help and guide us.* This was a friendship that had to be strong, never break. Had to be worked on just like a marriage.

Just then the flight attendant delivered a blanket Maggie had requested, casually mentioning the weather and wondering if they would have an early spring. "Do you know if the groundhog saw his shadow this year?" the attendant cheerily asked, making familiar February small talk.

"Well, of course, he did, darlin'. If you had that many damn lights glarin' on you, you'd see your shadow too!" Maggie sarcastically drawled. Stella jokingly elbowed Maggie in the side, and tried her best not to spit out her mouthful of wine. "You know I'm just playin' with you, right?" Maggie asked the young attendant, hoping she hadn't hurt her feelings. They all three broke out in laughter.

Stella and Maggie gripped each other's hand in an unspoken effort to cement this humorous moment into their neural traces forever. You never knew when you might need to have a replay cued in your consciousness to help you take another step on your journey.

Chapter Twenty-One

_∞_

She studied her appointment book for the day, tapping the eraser end of her pencil on the two o'clock appointment slot where she had penciled in "Maggie and Stella" in her neat, yet pinched writing. Kathleen Brady puckered her lips as if she were sucking on some nasty foul morsel of rancid food and winced. Today was her meeting with the two women her cousin Brent had called her about. Brent had warned her about the blond—Stella.

"She may be trouble. Be prepared for a quick education in Church dogma regarding Marian Apparitions before she takes Maggie too far afield. Both of them were raised in the Catholic faith, but for whatever reason, neither attends mass anymore or takes communion. Oh, and the blond? Well, . . . she's from Marin County. Could be a real troublemaker."

Kathleen silently practiced her routine lecture about the Virgin Mary and the various reported historic sightings of Her. By now, after her exile to the Vatican for re-training, she knew by rote what to teach. She had been quizzed repeatedly by her teacher: the pope's personal assistant, newly ordained Cardinal Gustav Muench.

She walked over to check her appearance in the plain wooden framed mirror, hanging on the wall beside her hollow-core door. She had never been mistaken for an attractive woman, even when younger. Now, sixtyish, with crispy gray hair cut severely short, topped off with a thick rasher of sharp bangs that obscured the deep crevices between her bespectacled beady eyes, she just looked mean.

She had always known that she would be a nun from the time she first attended mass. Growing up in County Cork, Ireland, it was expected that someone in the family would serve God in a formal way. She was from a family of ten children, with only seven reaching adulthood. It had been a very rough life. Being the plain one, it was just assumed that she had been God's pick of this generation's litter to devote her life to the Church. Someone had to if you were Irish. At least for those who hadn't yet immigrated to America.

Her father had been very strict, treating her with humiliation and degradation—his version of tough love. She obeyed her father's daily reminders: "We are all sinners and must repent if we want to go to Heaven."

To prove her devotion and love to him and to Jesus with all her heart, she would ask her father to spank her when she did something wrong. She desperately wanted to join Jesus in heaven and strived to be free of sin. With every smack of her father's hand on her naked buttocks, she felt closer to God and his mother, the Blessed Virgin. She would imagine the painful tears dropping from her eyes with each beating to be the dissolved waste of her sins.

When she was told by an elderly nun at her church that once you entered the convent you no longer were allowed phone calls from your family and that their letters were limited to one a week, it appeared to be the answer to her prayers.

Now in the twilight of her life, her life was lived in devotion to the Queen of Heaven. She prayed continuously to the Virgin during the horrible trial and eventual child abuse conviction for her disciplinary style while working in the Sisters of Mercy orphanage. The court agreed due to her age and her bishop's plea that she be sent to America to "rest and recover," with reassurances that she would never be attending to children again. However, the outcry from the victims had been so fierce, the bishop had no alternative but to ask her to leave her Order and the Church. They both understood that you always protect the Church first.

She had tried to accept her fate as God's will, but the resentment continued to build inside her. How dare they denounce her for doing her duty—God's work. She had pledged obedience to the needy, especially women and children. But those girls had been "dirty" sinners and deserved their punishment, especially if *they* wanted to get into heaven. Couldn't they see how she was just trying to help them?

It was unfortunate that the one girl had lost two teeth when she stumbled into the wall, unable to see after Kathleen had wrapped the girl's head with her urine-soaked underwear. That's how you cure bed wetting, Kathleen firmly believed. That, and wrapping the irresponsible girls in their own wet bed sheets. *That will teach them,* she thought, as her lips straightened into their usual tense flat line. She knew what was best to please her God. No weak emotions, just discipline and hard work. That was her credo. She did not believe in coddling; it made you too soft and weak to temptation. It displeased God to be weak.

As she returned to her desk to apply some lip balm to her cracked, dried lips, she reflected on the phone call she received just two days ago. It had been difficult to hear the muffled call from her cousin, asking her if she could help him.

"I'm at the cemetery. My buddy's wife just buried their son. Something weird happened. She got up and took off with her friend before her son was even lowered into the ground. I was worried, so I followed them. Then it happened. Something not of this world."

As a devout Catholic who was now working on a secret project for the Vatican, her cousin Brent knew how important it was to the Church to quickly contain the re-telling of these visions.

The next morning Brent called Kathleen again. "She called me last night. I think she was drunk. Said she thought she saw the Virgin Mary. I convinced her not to jump to conclusions. Maybe go to California, get some sun and rest. But I insisted she meet with you. It was an order."

Due to the time difference, Kathleen knew she was still within the time frame to successfully influence the observer before they started to form their own opinion. That was how the Church had handled apparitions since the first documented sighting in 358 A.D., a scant three decades after Constantine's Council of Nicaea. A wealthy childless couple on a hilltop in Rome reported being visited by a spirit—a woman. It was hundreds of years before documentation of the next sighting. However, the pace of today's 21st century apparitions simply exhausted her. The rapidness of how fast rumors could spread on social media made her life very stressful. Hard to contain secrets now.

"It is my duty and responsibility that I have all the details, cousin dear. You need to keep an eye on your friends. How closely can you monitor?" the ex-nun asked.

"I'll see what I can do. Luckily, I have access to everything."

Lost in thought as she prepared for the women, she jumped when her intercom rang, causing her balmed finger to slip and jab her cheek. The receptionist loudly announced the arrival of her two o'clock appointment.

"Please show them into the conference room," she said, as professionally as possible. She knew the visitors could hear her in the lobby. The school's receptionist lazily refused to pick up the handset to call and always used the speaker phone. It irritated Kathleen to no end. In her biased opinion, young girls of color were lazy and sometimes beyond helping.

She again approached the mirror and ran her hands through her hair in an unsuccessful attempt to fluff up her sparse lifeless hair, while she thought of apt punishment for the rude behavior of the receptionist. Rapidly rolling her clothes with one of her ever-present lint brushes, she deemed herself presentable and proceeded to walk down the musty hall to the conference room that also doubled as an office supply storage room.

She had sent many memos to management complaining about the unprofessional impression the staff and premises gave visitors, but always received a boilerplate response about budgets. She had indeed been spoiled by the formality and opulence of the Vatican.

That was when she thought it an apt opportunity to raise the matter with Cardinal Muench. She would tell him she either had to have a bigger budget or a new assignment if he wanted her to keep her end of the bargain.

Chapter Twenty-Two

—∞—

"**D**o you still wish to be a Bride of Jesus?" Cardinal Muench quizzed the nun, leaning towards the speaker phone as he stroked his obese Persian cat nestled in his just-as-large lap. Delivered slowly in a deep measured voice, he knew his question had sufficiently bullied the ousted nun back in her place. "Please keep to the plan until further notice, Sister. We'll be in touch shortly."

He wasn't happy her phone call had interrupted his monitoring of the visiting French Bollandist on his laptop. It had taken a long period of time, but they now had state-of-the-art 24/7 surveillance on all Mother Mary's statues throughout Europe, especially in Vatican City. The Shift was coming, and they were prepared to defend. He wasn't surprised the priest was in the grotto. It was an exact duplicate of the Lourdes grotto, donated to the Holy See by the French priest's family. He was anxious to speak to his knowledgeable visitor more about the Holy Mother at the upcoming meeting in Amsterdam with Lucas Stanchir. Gabriel was the premier expert on Marian Apparitions and might give GA7 and the Church some insight about the recent frequency of visitations.

But first he had to deal with the ever-nagging nun. After years of working closely with the head of the Office of the Congregation for the Doctrine of the Faith, the Cardinal had become adept with moving scandal-plagued members of the church around the world while manipulating them to do his bidding. He counseled his wards that accusations of abuse by the clergy dated back 1,700 years, so the Church understood the sacrifices of serving and had practice in such matters.

Cardinal Muench's skills were legendary. He had decades of experience being covert, from the time he arrived in Rome after World War II and worked his way up the Catholic hierarchy. His ability early in his career to move ex-Nazis to Central America, and his most recent accomplishments keeping sexual predator priests in the workforce and out of jail had cemented his job as cardinal and assistant to the pope. Just as promised when he was first approached decades earlier.

Still, the lowly nun's phone call irritated him more than usual. After all he and the Church had done to start a new life for her, how dare she call and threaten him with her petty demands.

"I know you are quite busy, but I just wanted to bring my concerns to your attention, Your Eminence. I do not want this office to reflect badly on the Church, and I know how quickly you can make things happen," Kathleen had said, trying to be persuasive. Her words impressed him. She obviously had spent enough time with him to understand his ways.

"I will make a note of your concerns and see what we can do," he lied. He hoped his false promises would placate her as he had no intention of pursuing the matter further. He had clicked off without even a civil goodbye and made a mental note to keep watch on her too.

He remembered how she had been when she first arrived in Vatican City. She had no alternatives after ex-communication, no life skills, and a family that considered her a disgrace. She had been so grateful with his invitation, even telling him she was flattered that one of the pope's closest associates would be interested in helping her. She said it was a sign of Jesus' forgiveness.

"We appreciate your dedication and agreement to spread the Vatican's view of these apparitions. This is work that will purify your soul. It helps to somewhat wipe the slate clean. Pray for forgiveness, and you may still be recognized in God's eyes," he sternly told her. It convinced her.

Cardinal Muench started her re-training by explaining the blow-back the Church had experienced after the June 26, 2000, release of the so-called Third Secret of Fatima by the pope. "Apparently, the faithful are questioning whether the pope revealed the real Third Secret," he had remarked as lightly as possible, attempting to raise his tone from bass to tenor. He remembered her reaction as she shrugged and said she didn't quite believe it either. That was not what he wanted to hear.

"But I've had enough trouble with the Church, that I have. If there is a way for me to do penance, I will do whatever you instruct me to do."

He was just about to abort his mission, when her words assured him she was the right candidate. They had been looking for a messenger, and Kathleen appeared to be perfect. Increasingly, people were becoming more curious and aware of the apparitions, especially regarding the Secrets of Fatima. The Church had worked too hard to keep the sightings off the world's radar. They knew time was running out and needed to launch an offense.

After her six months of intense training at the Vatican, he felt she was ready to start her mission. Arrangements were made for her to move to the United States where she stayed with her cousin Brent in Kentucky. While she got acclimated to her new life in America, the cardinal worked on getting her placed in her present job as a teacher at the California Academy of Theology in San Francisco. The Church had wanted to focus its offense on the West Coast—Ground Zero—as soon as possible.

* * *

Kathleen knew Cardinal Gustav, as she called him, well enough to know that he was not pleased with her phone call. However, she had been well schooled on this subject by the Vatican on how to answer inquiries from both the public and her students. She knew better than anyone how valuable her teachings were to the Church, and made sure to stick to the doctrine. She would prove her loyalty still existed, for both the Church and God, by having a successful meeting with the two women and nipping in the bud any further nonsense.

However, part of her still questioned whether the real Secret had really been revealed. She remembered as a child the excitement of her father and mother, waiting for Pope John XXIII to finally open the sealed envelope entrusted to him containing the Third Secret. However, when the pope opened and read the contents of the envelope Aug. 17, 1959, he stated "this prophecy does not relate to my time" and returned the envelope to the box. Her family, like most Catholics around world, were very disappointed, but had no alternative but to blindly trust in the wisdom of His Holiness' infallible decision.

Then his successor Paul VI read the contents. He also decided to do nothing.

The next pope, John Paul I, read the document. He only lived for thirty four days as pope. Some say he was murdered.

One of the first things Pope John Paul II did upon being elected pope in 1978 was read the document. He also placed it back in the box.

The world had waited almost twenty years. She wondered when the time would come, if ever. It had to be monumentally damaging to the Church if four popes wanted it to stay hidden. She was determined to root out the truth.

During her stay at the Vatican, she happened upon some documents in the Archives which indicated the contents had been revealed to several people on a private basis, including members of the American government. Though not worldly in many ways, she knew something evil was about. So much so she told her cousin about it. He warned her to be extremely careful.

She had questioned Cardinal Gustav during her training about why during Vatican II Mary's significance in the Catholic Church had been lowered. "Why did Mary go from 'Queen of Heaven' to Mary, just a housewife?" she asked.

"Just a little dogmatic housecleaning," the Cardinal replied, as if discussing the day's weather.

That didn't satisfy her, but she kept her mouth shut. Did dogmatic housecleaning include removing statues of Mary overnight and stopping the singing of Marian hymns? Then yanking Salve Regina, which had been recited at the end of mass for centuries? She just filed away the information in her memory, ready for a time when she may need this as currency for her own salvation.

Her suspicions that something was being hidden increased when she overheard some nuns in the local Vatican City grocery store discussing how when Sister Lucia, the one who had written down the Third Secret, died at a convent on February 13, 2005, the Church immediately sealed her room and confiscated her diaries. Cardinal Gustav singularly packed and moved the sister's belongings to the Vatican, they said, and he ordered them to be sealed in an underground lead crypt. Kathleen had requested to view those diaries during her studies, but had been denied. She had decided to continue with her assignment, be a good Catholic and bide her time.

Chapter Twenty-Three

—∞—

"Hello, my name is Kathleen Brady," she said as she awkwardly thrust her hand outward to the redhead.

"A pleasure to meet you. I'm Maggie Barrett. This is my friend, Stella St. James."

Stella extended her hand reluctantly. This woman might not be wearing a nun's habit, but she reminded Stella of every nun who had swatted her knuckles at catechism. Stella quickly shook hands and then jammed her hand into her protective jacket pocket.

"Welcome to our school, ladies. Now let's get right to the subject, shall we. When you rang me, Mrs. Barrett, you said you had just experienced something unusual which you thought may have been a Marian Apparition, a vision of Mary. Am I right about that?"

"Yes, ma'am," Maggie said warily, not sure how to address this woman. *Should I call an ex-nun Sister?* she wondered. She despised unnecessary rudeness and didn't want to be offensive. But she figured the ex-nun's demeanor was direct, getting right to the point. *I'm sure she'll let me know.*

Sensing Maggie's unease, Kathleen offered: "please call me Kathleen." She really didn't like being addressed so informally, but she had learned that was how one conducted oneself in the United States, especially in California. In her opinion, that was why the young were so uncontrollable today—lack of formality and respect. But she had learned her lessons the hard way and wasn't willing to jeopardize her new career by forcing her views onto others—as least not yet.

She quickly assessed the redheaded woman as one of those who probably did yoga, judging from her slim physique. She agreed with the pope who was against such practice, calling it the Cult of Body. It would only lead to deviant sexual practices masquerading as spiritual experiences, in her opinion.

"Kathleen it is then. Yes, as I told you on the phone, my friend Stella and I thought we saw something in a cave at the cemetery where my son was being buried." Maggie gulped for air after saying those words, tears welling up in her eyes. She wondered if she would ever get used to saying that, or was there comfort in knowing it would always be painful. She wished she had something to drink, her mouth was so parched. There had been no offer of beverages. Apparently, no Southern hospitality here.

Stella instinctively reached over and grabbed Maggie's hand while taking over the conversation. She wasn't sure how much Maggie had told this woman, so she decided not to include her first experience.

"We had walked over and sat on a bench in front of this cave that had a spring flowing into it. Well, we think the spring *would have* flowed into the cave, except it was frozen at the time. We saw a mist move across the ground and then spiral into a ghostly feminine figure in front of the cave." She wasn't going to tell Kathleen what they heard and especially not what they both had felt. She was going to play this as close to her chest as possible. Let the nun talk first, before deciding on sharing more.

"Interesting. Have you heard the story of Sister Bernadette? No doubt you've seen the movie with Jennifer Jones, but let me refresh your memory," Kathleen started, just the way she usually did. "In February 1858 in Lourdes, France, a young girl about fourteen years old named Bernadette Soubirous was gathering firewood with her sister and a friend in the remote Grotto of Massabielle, when a beautiful young lady appeared to her in a grotto. Neither of the other girls saw the lady—only Bernadette.

"She said she heard a noise like a gust of wind. She noticed a rosebush at the mouth of the grotto was moving as if it were windy. But it was not. A golden-colored cloud appeared inside the grotto, which then materialized into 'The Lady,' as she called her. She said the lady was lovelier than anything that she had ever seen. Dressed in a white dress cinched with a blue belt and a white veil on her head, the Lady had a yellow rose on each foot.

"The Lady, smiling, motioned for Bernadette to move closer, which she did. Feeling no fear, she fell to her knees and began praying the Rosary with the Lady. As soon as they finished the prayer, the Lady withdrew inside the grotto and disappeared. Does this sound familiar?"

Both Maggie and Stella, stunned speechless, just nodded their heads. Kathleen continued.

"Over the next six months, Bernadette experienced eighteen visitations from the Lady, never knowing who the Lady was until the last apparition. She said she was continually drawn to the grotto by an inner voice. During the ninth apparition, the Lady instructed Bernadette to dig a hole in the ground, then drink and bathe in it. The hole later turned into a spring of water which the Lady promised would be a healing spring for all who came to use its waters.

"The Lady also asked Bernadette to tell the local pastor that she wanted a chapel built in honor of her appearances there. However, the pastor did not believe Bernadette. He told her before he could undergo such a project, the Lady would need to perform a miracle by making the rosebush in the grotto bloom. But the rosebush failed to bloom, dooming the church. On March 25th, the Feast of Annunciation, the Lady announced to Bernadette 'I am the Immaculate Conception.'"

Kathleen did not add how this announcement had been quite surprising as Bernadette had only received a rudimentary religious education cland was deemed mentally slow. It is doubtful that she knew that the pope had declared Mary as the Immaculate Conception as official Catholic Church doctrine just four years earlier. As schooled, she stuck to the official script. No need to invite speculation.

"The apparitions were declared authentic in 1862, and Lourdes rapidly became one of the world's major pilgrimage sites, with over five million visitors a year. It is said that thousands have been cured from a variety of illnesses, both physical and spiritual, as evidenced by the stacks of crutches left behind.

"Bernadette became one of the Sisters of Notre Dame in Nevers and died there in 1879 at age thirty-five after a long and painful illness. She was declared a saint in 1933, not because of the apparitions, but because of her dedication to a life of simplicity and service to our Lord. They dug up her grave in 1909 and then again in 1919, and found her to be totally incorrupt, which means her body had not decayed. She now lies in a coffin of gold and glass at the mother house in Nevers, France."

Stella found that last fact about Bernadette's body both interesting and a little bit unsettling. *Why did they decide to dig her up—twice? What were they looking for?*

Maggie was taking notes as fast as she could. She saw Kathleen relax her shoulders, signaling her job was done. "I've done some research, and I'm interested in hearing about Fatima."

Oh Lordy, here we go, Kathleen thought. Brent had warned her about the blond. Might be time to get his picker fixed; he might be surprised to know that the redhead was just as dangerous.

"Yes, Fatima. I assume your research is from the internet?"

Maggie nodded her head in assent.

"Right. I was afraid of that," Kathleen said, pursing her thin lips in disdain. "There is so much disinformation about the truly holy events that happened in Portugal in 1917. May I give you a correct brief history of what happened?" She didn't wait as she launched into Part Two of the script.

"On May 13, 1917, right in the middle of the First World War, three shepherd children: Lucia, the oldest at ten, and her cousins, Jacinta, age seven, and Francisco, age nine, were in the hills above Fatima, Portugal. While the sheep grazed, the children played. Suddenly, there was a flash of light far over the tops of the trees, moving over the valley from east to west, coming in their direction."

Maggie and Stella fought the urge to look at each other to acknowledge the familiarity of the tale.

"Startled that a storm was coming, the children started to gather the sheep when there came a second flash. And in front of them was a lady of dazzling light, brilliant and beautiful, with the scent of roses in the air."

Stella tried to keep her best poker face on and not show any reaction to the last fact about the roses, but her eyebrow was twitching like an electrocuted frog. Maggie's eyes just got bigger with her gold flecks flashing like strobe lights as her gulped saliva visibly bubbled down her throat.

"The Lady said 'I am from Heaven.' Lucia asked 'What do you want of us?' to which the Lady replied that she wanted them to come to the same spot on the thirteenth day of each month for the next six months.

"The Lady then asked 'Do you wish to offer yourselves to God, to endure all the suffering that He may please to send you, as an act of reparation for the sins by which He is offended and to ask for the conversion of sinners?' The obedient children replied 'yes, we do.' 'Then you will have much to suffer. But the grace of God will be your comfort.' She asked them to daily recite the Rosary before she rose in a cloud of light and glided away into the eastern sky.

"This so frightened the children because the government of Portugal was heavily opposed to religion at that time. But being children, it was hard for them to keep a secret. That is, it was for the younger children.

"The first secret shown them by Mother Mary was of a terrifying vision of hell, with visions of twisted burning bodies and souls. The second secret involved the future of Russia. Mother Mary indicated that the war would soon end, which it did the following year, but that it would be followed by a second world war if God was still offended and if Russia did not consecrate to the Immaculate Heart and convert. Many believe this was a direct warning about the spread of communism.

"There was also a Third Secret which was only revealed to Lucia with express instructions to keep it secret, which she did. Her cousins both died in the Great Flu Epidemic shortly thereafter.

"Lucia became a nun and kept her promise not to reveal the Third Secret for twenty-seven years until forced to finally write it down on January 9, 1944, by the order of Bishop Silva. She had suffered a grave illness, and the bishop did not want her to die without the secret being revealed. However, Sister Lucia was adamant that the secret remain sealed until 1960, as specifically instructed by the Lady.

"Through God's divine guidance and wisdom given to our popes, the Third Secret was not revealed until June 26, 2000. Though there was much speculation, the Third Secret seemed to only prophesy the assassination attempt on John Paul II and warn against evil. It also reinforced that we must pray for the salvation of our souls and repent for our sins."

That doesn't seem right, thought Stella. "A warning of an assassination attempt is kept secret? Wouldn't you want this warning if it was you?" she asked, incredulously.

Kathleen had been asked this same question many times and her standard reply was "the popes read it, they were warned, and they felt it would just be an obstacle to their service to mankind if this prophecy was revealed and sensationalized. Thanks to the Blessed Mother, it was an assassination attempt that the pope survived," she said. "Maybe they felt the message would have more of an impact on the faithful after the act, to further the importance of prayer and repentance."

Maggie gripped Stella's hand and abruptly stood. "Thank you so much for your time you have been very helpful we do so much appreciate your graciousness," in one single breath as she pulled Stella along.

Kathleen clumsily stood, grabbing a chair back to steady herself, stunned by her visitors' hasty retreat. She watched helplessly as the visitors stormed down the hall and out through the lobby.

While quickly walking down the hallway, Maggie snatched the small handbill she had seen on her way in, tacked up on the bulletin board. Stella just caught the headline of "Miracle of Mary in Rwanda, a UC Berkeley Global Series Event" as she stumbled behind Maggie trying to figure out what had just happened.

Chapter Twenty-Four

—∞—

Briskly marching back to her office, Kathleen closed the door and tried to get herself sorted. Standing at her desk, she snapped the hem of her skirt downward taut against her spindly thighs before she sat down and unlocked her top desk drawer. She opened her address book to the paper-clipped page and dialed the secure number, starting with the international code of 011 then 39.

Cardinal Gustav had instructed her on her last day at the Vatican that he wanted to avoid the nuns of the Pious Disciples of the Master who manned the Vatican switchboard twenty-four hours a day. "I know they are dedicated souls, but they have a tendency to gossip. If you need to contact me, use this number."

It was a phone number that even the Vatican switchboard didn't know existed. Only a handful of people could reach the pope and also had the secure number Kathleen was dialing to report of the visit with the women. It was imperative to alert the Vatican with every new claim of a Marian vision. Her telephone call was brief, as were the instructions.

"It's a sorry thing that you'd be disrespecting me, lasses," she thought smugly, as she snapped the latex gloves snug over her wrinkled liver-spotted hands as she retrieved two new lint rollers from her safe and proceeded to the conference room. She was careful to use just one roller per vacated chair, dropping each tool into the properly marked zip lock bags she had stowed in her pocket. Once inside her office she carefully plucked the hairs with tweezers from the rollers, careful not to contaminate the specimens and inserted them into a clean vial from her storage cabinet. She marked them for a next-day delivery to Vatican City, c/o Lucas Stanchir, Vatican Lab.

Chapter Twenty-Five

—∞—

He concentrated on his hot breath as its fog appeared and disappeared on the cold wavy window. To the casual stroller along the Oude Delft looking up into the historic Amsterdam hotel's luxury suite, the slight, balding, blond fifty-five-year-old man, standing rigid at the window might appear to be just another anxious waiting lover.

He did not notice the walkers along the waterway. His laser focus was on the ancient glass, visualizing his atoms merging with the sand particles of the glass as they quantum danced with the water molecules below, imbuing the rushing water with his DNA. Thinking about the water. It was always about the water.

His decades-long meditation practice had started at Stanford University after hanging out with the remote viewers at Stanford Research Institute ("SRI"). Now that his father had passed, he had ramped up to twice daily. Tonight, he needed the power of the water below to center him for his big speech.

Lucas Stanchir, newly appointed president and CEO of the world's largest private military firm, GA7, would be the keynote speaker. In celebration of the Liberty Group's Golden Anniversary, he planned to recite the Group's enormous success in molding global policies to keep the world at peace, while diplomatically maintaining each member's agenda, of course.

But more importantly he wanted to memorialize his late father, Elliott Stanchir, the only keynote speaker the group had ever heard. His father had been one of the founding members of the international group and always opened each year's meeting.

Lucas had specifically requested this room. It had been lucky for him once, he thought, reflecting on the last time he had been here. It was cold then too—almost Christmas. Just a mere week after he orchestrated the Elite's coup d'état of the White House.

That night he and his family's life-long friend, Cardinal Muench, had conducted a conference call with three of the largest international corporations and some Washington politicos. They discussed the specifics of the delivery of the final payment for their help with the Supreme Court decision. It had been a most challenging assignment, a bit messy—but they had succeeded. Secure in their allegiance, he had lowered the hammer.

"Cancel the funding for the UN Population fund," Lucas had ordered matter-of-factly.

"That's not possible," the president-elect's liaison had stuttered, shocked. "The funding has already been approved by both houses of Congress."

"Was it possible that nine justices could overrule the votes of fifty-one million people? Do it!" He hung up, annoyed at the man's whining. The funding was canceled not long after.

Elliot had taught his son that it was vital to GA7's bottom line to keep producing "units" as he preferred to call them. Young, economically struggling people, mostly of color, to join up for wars. Wars made GA7 rich and, most importantly, kept them in power.

The cardinal and he both held little regard for women and their rights. Such a lesser species, Lucas thought, as he fingered the rusted bottle cap in his pants pocket. Weak and best used as breeders. Pathetic, how the first to sign up to fight for America were usually the ones who had received the least as citizens.

Cardinal Muench used his contacts with the fundamentalist Christians in the United States to help feed the rage. He encouraged them to preach the evils of abortion and birth control every chance they got. Pushed the pride of loyalty by declaring themselves red states, good; blue states, bad. That started their plan.

Some accused his group of behaving like a shadow world government because of their attendees. Each year's attendance included most of the world's top politicians, electronic and print media owners, corporate CEOs and even some royalty. But as always, it was closed to outsiders and enforced by state-of-the-art security.

For a long time, no one knew of the group. It helped to keep out of the press when you included most of the top media owners in the world as valued members of your group. The Liberty Group had effectively turned journalists into their lackeys.

Lucas was a master at media manipulation. On his sixteenth birthday, his father had given him his own well-worn copy of *The News Twisters*. It was a "how to" on how to doctor evidence and influence the media.

Using propaganda techniques mastered during World War II, Lucas' first job with his father was in the early '80s. That's when they instituted the dog whistle that giving money to the poor created more poor, making poverty a "behavioral" condition, a subtle way of race-baiting. Effortlessly, it still worked like a charm to this day.

The group's agenda was to bring back the Gilded Age–21st Century style. His group members understood the difference between pro-business versus pro-market. Their interests lie in enriching themselves, not starting new businesses and sharing wealth.

The Liberty Group's leadership had its challenges. GA7's problems had begun in the 1960s when President Kennedy went off the Vatican-approved script and asked people to join together for their country. His June 19, 1963 commencement speech at the American University in Washington, D.C., dubbed *A Strategy of Peace* had sealed his fate. The Group's Plan did not include connection.

It didn't help that the president's speech came on the heels of *Pacem in Terris* from Vatican II, Pope John XXIII's effort two months before his death to join the world in peace. The papal encyclical was addressed to all men of goodwill, not just the Catholics. His reference to politics sent up a red flag that the pope might reveal the Third Secret. He had to be stopped. The Group could no longer count solely on their mole in the Church to control the papacy's message and keep the Secret hidden.

That's when they started grooming "the actor" from California who had the Irish gift of gab. His march from the California governor's office to the Oval Office was designed to make the denial of compassion not only acceptable, but respectful, even patriotic. With GA7's help they made the '80s the "Me Generation." Shaming the actual victims of their greed created a scarcity culture, making everyone believe they didn't have enough and the poor, the working women and the dark-colored immigrants were to blame.

"If you want to retain power, create a culture of fear using racism and sexism. Superiority is a great divider," Elliot told his son. "But before fear and hate, you must have ignorance!" The group's political members made sure to slash education funds and then funneled the funds into defense spending.

Lucas was a quick student, learning how masterfully Elliot worked the media to keep creating crises to fatigue the population. The fatigue manufactured apathy, keeping the downtrodden home—frustrated and away from the voting booth.

His father had beamed with pride at how Lucas had handled the cowboy president and his bully of a vice president when they decided it was time to invade Iraq. The Liberties had at first been outraged by the whole Iraq debacle. But the Stanchirs had planned for such an event when the group ushered them into office. He and his father convinced the group how much more money would roll in. Lucas insisted that the president snarl at the cameras and say "you're either for us or against us." The American public lapped it up like vanilla pudding and had caved like a house of cards.

Nothing happened in this world by chance. It was all orchestrated. And after tonight, it would be time to ramp up the next phase.

Chapter Twenty-Six

—∞—

Cranking furiously to lower the window while she gripped her cigarette between her crimson feathered lips, Maggie exploded. "Skippity dippity dee! What stinkin' bullshit! Does that dried-up prune really think we would believe three shepherd children—dirt poor and illiterate to boot—would even be able to pronounce the word 'consecrate?' This is why I left the Church. Total! Bullshit! Dogma!" she said as she manically punched the outside air with the fire-end of her Virginia Slim, wayward ashes fluttering down to the car's mint condition coco mats.

"Should have known something wasn't right when she was so unpleasant. Didn't even have the good manners to offer us something to drink? How do you *not* offer guests a beverage? So unbecoming!" she exclaimed, wagging her long index finger in shame.

Stella turned towards Maggie, about to ask if skippity dippity dee was Maggie's way of saying fuck. It did sound more ladylike and refined, she guessed. She knew to watch out when Maggie started wagging that finger. No ambiguity with that gesture! No absence of subtlety—she meant business.

She hated Maggie smoking in her car, sullying her never-used pristine ashtray but was willing to overlook it right now. Crossing Maggie might prove dangerous and more than she could handle at the moment. She could always get a new one.

Stella didn't know if it was the intoxicating nicotine she still missed to this day, twenty-five years later, or the overwhelming information and emotions, but she was seriously dizzy. Something fluttered in her side vision, and she wondered if the fog was rolling in. She could see sparkling floaters in the air, like water bugs stroking across a pond.

She nervously anticipated the curves ahead, as they drove past Golden Gate Park towards the Golden Gate Bridge. She eased a bit off the accelerator as she rubbed her left temple.

"You alright to drive?" Maggie asked.

"I'm fine, just overwhelmed and confused. Before you found that article on the web, had you heard about Fatima before? About this Third Secret?

"I remember watching that old movie, *The Song of Bernadette*, once when I was babysitting a neighbor's kids. I paid more attention to Jennifer Jones' cheekbones than the fact she was seeing the Virgin Mary. But I don't ever remember any stories about Our Lady of Guadalupe or Fatima or Mary showing a young girl visions of hell when I went to church. Maggie, how could I grow up Catholic and not even know these stories?"

Stella felt guilty, blaming her ignorance on her constant flirting and self-interest. Maybe she would have learned more if she had paid attention in after-school catechism. Actually, she found her Nema's Indian stories more fascinating. Nema's version of God or the Great Spirit was a lot more entertaining, with stories of coyotes, chipmunks and snakes. Besides she could never accept a young girl having a baby without sex. Too many of her friends in high school had to go to a "special school" after having sex.

"Darlin', it was all in Latin, and in our day girls weren't taught Latin. All I remember from catechism was coloring Jesus each week in my coloring book. Most of my religious knowledge is from watching *Jeopardy*. But Stella, my gut is buzzing," Maggie said, rubbing her slightly pouchy abdomen.

"Remember how Nema always said there were no accidents? Think about that, Stella. Something is going on here, and it appears you and I are somehow a part of it. We need to go to this seminar tonight and see what they have to say," she said as she stubbed out her long skinny cigarette. Stella winced and quickly averted her eyes, trying not to gag.

She stopped at the traffic light, grateful for a chance to take a breath and get her bearings. She could feel someone staring at her from in the park. Stella turned to look.

"Oh my god, Mags, there she is again!"

"Who again?" Maggie asked as she frantically jerked her head in the direction of Stella's gaze.

"The homeless woman I saw at the freeway exit the night of my damn blind date! She looks at me like she knows me. Oh God, I sound crazy, huh?" They both stared at the woman with her hand over her heart and the other hand pointing up into the sky. Leaning against her body was a huge plywood sign that read in neon orange spray paint:

> *It's not a conflict between good and evil, but between ignorance and enlightenment. BEWARE OF THOSE WHO HOLD THE SECRET*

"Oh yeah, that was a coincidence! Damn, Stella. First, San Francisco ain't that big, so no surprise you might recognize someone. Second, I know you can't be surprised that crazy people are standing with signs in Golden Gate Park. It's just coincidence. But 'beware of those who hold the secret?' That's not an accident. This is some grandma-in-the-attic crazy shit we're dealing with."

Stella took the corner a little too fast, screeching her tires, almost causing a tear in the stolen flyer as Maggie gently smoothed the slightly crumpled handbill on her lap. "Miracle of Mary in Rwanda Seminar, a U.C. Berkeley Global Series Event—a Gathering of the Women."

The event's description said that the speaker was a woman who survived the genocide in Rwanda with the Virgin Mary's help. After the presentation, there would be an opportunity for questions and answers. Maggie wondered if Stella would want to participate or just keep quiet about everything. She hoped it wouldn't be an audience of Bible thumpers. Didn't have patience for that right now. She was kinda pissed off at God, to tell the honest truth.

"Rwanda, huh?" Stella asked. "I kid you not, I was just thinking of a Rwandan artist we exhibited at the gallery once. She lost her hand in the war, but was taught to paint with the other. She told me her country's genocide had been fueled by the media. Said the troubles first started when the newspapers printed stories against one tribe, then the radio joined in, whipping the other tribe into a murdering frenzy. Over a million people had been slaughtered with machetes in less than one hundred days. Her right hand had been hacked off with a machete by a schoolmate who had been a visitor in her home many times. She couldn't believe how the rest of the world ignored the story.

"Her paintings were very red, frenetic, haunting," Stella continued but not mentioning the ghostly image. "I vividly remember she said she had been inspired by watching *The Power of Myth* with Joseph Campbell on PBS. Said he believed the poets and artists will change society, that they are magical helpers. I believe that's true. Said we should pay attention to propaganda, that we weren't immune to something similar happening in our country. Of course, we doubted anything like that could happen in our country." She stopped and caught herself before ranting on about the war, knowing Maggie needed no reminders of Josh's death right now. *Damn Republicans,* she smugly thought.

"I remember watching that woman who survived by hiding in a bathroom for some ninety days on Oprah," Maggie replied. "But I don't remember anything being said about Mary. But what could happen here in America? We don't have tribes."

"Really? Wanna talk about the ongoing race wars or what they did to my ancestors? Your ancestors?"

"Point taken. I sometimes open my mouth without engaging my brain." Maggie figured it was better to focus on their similarities than their differences right now. As they crossed the bridge under a newly emerging blue sky, Maggie looked out on the shimmering bay. "Did you know that female sperm whales travel in groups with their young and if they are being attacked, they circle their young to keep them safe? We should have stopped them, you know."

Stella didn't need to ask who "they" were. She knew. The ones who sent their children to war. They needed to take action to save their children, their grandchildren, and she knew it was imperative for them to go to Berkeley tonight.

"We have enough time to swing by the house, change and grab a quick bite before driving across the bay to Berkeley. Wanna go, Mags?"

"Let's hit the dirt, girl," Maggie said as she slid down in her seat, relaxing against the rolled head rest.

Reading Maggie's body language, Stella believed the invitation accepted. She accelerated, leaving the sparkling bay and orange girders in the rear-view mirror.

Chapter Twenty-Seven

_∞_

Tucking his speech notes into his inside tuxedo pocket, Lucas reflected on his last conversation with his father, less than a month ago.

"Never forget why this all was created," the frail and dying senior Stanchir mumbled, as he gripped his only son's hand. "You must promise me to carry out the Plan," the old man wheezed, as he struggled to sit up in his hospital bed.

"I promise. I will not let you down." His father had always been disappointed in Lucas' lack of physical stature, blaming it for Lucas' failure to sustain his family's tradition of attending an East Coast Ivy League college. But Elliott placed great store in his son's tenacity and steeliness. He knew his son worked hard to gain his acceptance.

"This is my last chance to tell you the story, so listen carefully, son."

Lucas had grown up with the stories of his father's war-time experiences. Since World War II, GA7 and the Catholic Church had worked closely together. Their entangled relationship had led to the eventual formation of the international Liberty Group. Even though he had heard the story many times, he knew soon he would never hear his father's voice as he listened intently.

"I was what they called a man's man—tall, blond, athletic, and confident. When I graduated from Harvard Law in the late '30s, I had great plans on using my legal skills to make America great again after the Depression. Right after my Valedictorian speech about God, country, and personal responsibility, I was hired by one of the premier Wall Street firms. I made partner in five years!" With the last exclamation, Elliott started to violently cough and gasp for breath.

"Father, please, rest. I know the story."

"I want to tell it again, dammit!" he sputtered. However, so close to death, he was spent. The once formidable man closed his eyes and fell into a deep slumber.

It had pained Lucas greatly to watch his hero as he faded into death. He hoped his words tonight would tell of his father's great place in history.

His father's rise on Wall Street had not gone unnoticed in Washington, where many politicians were his clients. Elliott Stanchir, a young Republican and staunch Catholic, was a true believer, just the type of leader needed as it became clear that America would soon be joining the Second World War.

The newly formed Office of Strategic Services, the OSS and precursor of the CIA, was looking for educated smart men with a lot of patriotism and the burning desire to do well. They recruited the young Elliott, compelling him to enlist in the Army's bomber pilot training. After he put pen to paper, they told him his real duty would be as a spy. He was not disappointed.

At the time, the OSS needed help with the Jedburghs, a team of American and British commandos who worked with the French Resistance. Jedburghs received special intense training to provide crucial communications and intelligence. The group provided a link between the Allied command and the guerrillas. Together with the French Resistance, they were responsible for the majority of the war-time sabotage.

Stanchir's first directive was to form a close American alliance with the Italian Christian Democrats, the political party of the Catholic Church. Although not Italian Catholic, he knew how to talk to God-fearing people of faith.

Elliott had worked closely with the Christian Democrats in the fight against communism in Europe. Using the OSS propaganda program, they produced films depicting Communists thrashing Catholic churches that were projected on building walls as makeshift outdoor cinemas in Italian towns and villages.

"He who controls the message, controls the world." Elliott had told his son. "OSS knew that the Church was expert in mass message mind control, ever since the days when the Roman Emperor Constantine supervised the writing of the New Testament. Together, we are unbeatable."

The Catholic Church propaganda program against Communism was just the start, Elliott had said. This was a quest for world dominance. America recognized the Church's vast wealth and political influence in regards to global politics. Of special interest were the Vatican archives. The world's greatest repository of raw intelligence—and the world's secrets. A spy's and blackmailer's gold mine.

To monitor developments in the Holy See, they needed a "mole." Someone under their control on the inside of the Vatican.

Elliott's nephew, Matthew Stanchir, a Jesuit priest in Rome during the war, had been tasked with the effort to replenish the membership of the Society of the Jesuits from among the young German prisoner of war soldiers, many of whom were now homeless orphans. That was how the Stanchirs' alliance with the young German, Gustav Muench, had started.

Father Matthew deftly convinced the young teenager he had a new mission—as a soldier for Christ. The priest's message was short and persuasive: "God saved you. He has a plan for you." It was exactly what these young, forever-damaged soldiers, searching for hope and answers to why a God would allow such atrocities of war to happen, wanted to hear. They now had a purpose, especially the lumbering redheaded teen, who followed the young priest around like a puppy. Father Matthew always made sure his charge was allowed a second helping at meals. Little did the orphaned teen know that he was about to became the unknowing pawn in the New World Order.

Satisfied with his performance in Italy, the OSS stationed Elliott in France to join the Jedburghs, where he could utilize both his spying skills and his pilot training. However, not long after arriving during a reconnaissance flight to bring new paratroopers into the south of France, Elliott's plane suffered engine trouble, forcing him to bail out of his plane. He landed in a lavender field, not far from a country chateau—battered, bruised but alive. His crash landing had been noticed by the group whose mission was to watch the sky in case of such incidents.

The rescuers were members of the French Resistance's Comet Line—all women. They had kept him safe from the Germans by sheltering and nursing him in the southern chateau on the outskirt of Lourdes. When he was well enough, the women arranged his trip over the border to Spain, with instructions to join the pilgrimage on the Camino de Santiago for a safe route out of Portugal on his journey home.

Elliott had become a war hero before hitting stateside. He told his son he enjoyed his celebrity of heroism, but he was hungry for much more. One of the Comet Line's members, a pretty French woman had told him stories, shared secrets. Told him it was no accident that they had met.

Elliott was quickly tapped to head the OSS, with a promise to be an architect of real world power. To achieve the ultimate mission to make the United States the dominant super power, the agency started its metamorphosis from OSS to the CIA—the Central Intelligence Agency.

By 1948, when the OSS became the CIA, the logical choice was to appoint Elliott as its first leader. The CIA had been formed through necessity of war to be America's "eyes and ears."

Though Elliott had enjoyed the power being head of the CIA, postwar he could see all the money that was being made by civilians. He wanted a piece of the action and decided to leave the government and returned to his Wall Street law firm.

Elliott quickly became one of the original Global Elite Wise Men, and they decided to form the Liberty Group. The Group had decided to hold its inaugural meeting in Amsterdam.

Ironically, on the morning of the group's inaugural meeting the Amsterdam newspaper's headline read in bold twenty-point type: "**I ASSURE YOU THAT THE WORLD WILL CHANGE.**" Allegedly, the reporter wrote, this phrase was uttered by the Virgin Mary to a twelve-year-old Amsterdam girl named Ida Peerdeman that very morning.

Remembering the Frenchwoman's story and the information he forced from the Portuguese nun, he rapidly scribbled a plan.

Elliott had read a one-page document in the Portugal convent on his way home from the European theater. Written in the hand of the middle-aged nun who had witnessed "the Lady," he said they called it the "Third Secret."

Elliott knew he had to act quickly with the Church's American allies to contain and manage these messages. He was smart enough to figure out how to not only gain world power but to profit immensely with what he had been told. GA7, God's Army of the Seven Continents, was born, the Grand Plan was formed and the seeds planted.

The Church had been GA7's first client. And, the old man had stressed many times, if they were not successful with the present mission, it would be their last.

However, money was not the topic on Lucas' mind. After tonight's speech and celebration, there would be a secret meeting with the pope's personal secretary, the newly promoted Cardinal Gustav Muench. The meeting was due to begin sharply after the clock dinged for the twelfth time. The Shift was rapidly approaching and timing was critical. It was now up to Lucas to finish what his father had started.

Chapter Twenty-Eight

—∞—

"'Allo, this is Gabriel."

"Good afternoon, Father. I am pleased to finally have located you. You did not tell me you were departing the Vatican. I trust you are well," the Cardinal inquired, his tone insincere. He did not like it when his minions failed to keep him aware of their whereabouts. He intentionally dampened his temper because he could not afford to jeopardize Gabriel's alliance. Elliott Stanchir had taught him well on the art of manipulation.

"I'm so sorry, Your Excellence. I had a family emergency and did not have time to contact you. I am now with my elderly mother, back in France. Is there something you need me to do?"

"Are you able to meet me in Amsterdam by tomorrow? I have a very important meeting and may need your advice on a delicate subject. Your Marian research is very essential to our discussion."

"But, of course."

"Excellent. You may call for your ticket at the airport, along with the directions to our meeting. I look forward to seeing you."

Cardinal Gustav felt comforted knowing he would have one of his own along for his meeting with Lucas Stanchir. This would be his first

GA7 meeting since the death of Elliott, and he was nervous about Lucas' abilities to continue on course.

He felt as if he had lost his own father, whom he never knew, when Elliott Stanchir passed. They first met the spring after the end of the war when Elliott had been invited to return to Rome. To recognize and celebrate his outstanding service as a war hero standing against communism, Elliott was awarded the Grand Cross of the Order of Saint Sylvester, the oldest and most prestigious of papal knighthoods by the Vatican. Only one hundred of these awards have been given out in the Church's history. This act of supreme respect from the Holy See paved the future relationship with Rome, the Stanchirs and, more importantly, GA7.

It was years later when Elliott revealed why he had chosen Gustav to be part of his Plan. "I knew instantly you were a soldier for Jesus. Your erect posture, strong jaw, glaring intensity in your eyes as you clutched your Bible to your chest impressed me immediately. I would never doubt your unyielding devotion to the Church and to my nephew," Elliott had told him.

"I knew with some nurturing and mentoring you could be very instrumental in making history and saving the Church. Father Matthew was correct. Your life had been saved for a reason. And this is the reason."

The pouring of affection and attention on Gustav proved effective. A troubled child, raised by a no-nonsense mother, by the time he reached the prisoner of war camp in Northern Germany he was informed his only family member was dead. Because of the crime of having a red-haired child, it was decided by the SS that his mother needed to be sterilized. She died in surgery.

Father Matthew saw special potential in this tall, bushy-haired German. The priest had rescued the young man from sterilization while a POW. Gustav had been labeled feeble-minded and a possible homosexual. Father Matthew took the orphan under his wing and brought him to Vatican City to begin his seminary studies, but not before the thirteen-year-old had raped and impregnated one of female prisoners at the camp in a vain effort to prove his manhood. He was whisked off to Rome, never knowing if his off-spring survived or not.

Gustav was a quick study, and soon became Father Matthew's assistant, almost his shadow. Gustav looked to Father Matthew as his one chance to make something of his life, vowing to even lay down his life if necessary in his service to Father Matthew, Jesus and the Catholic Church.

Not long after Gustav finished his seminary training, he started secretly working with Elliott and the CIA as an undercover operative in the Vatican. His first assignment was to spy on liberal churchmen on the pope's staff who might challenge Church decisions that were advantageous to the United States' positions—and to the Stanchirs'.

Within twenty years, he quickly advanced through the ranks of the Catholic hierarchy. Mostly lobbying members of the Curia in the Vatican government, they eventually used Gustav to pass large sums of money to other priests and bishops who became witting partners in CIA covert operations.

Gustav had been warned by the elder Stanchir of the fine line they needed to walk. Especially if they were both to stay in power.

"Nothing is more hazardous than trying to separate politics from religion. If both are to survive, there must not be any wedge in between. It gives order to power to effectively rule civilization. It's necessary to sacrifice a percentage for the greater good. Fear and salvation are the grease to our wheel," Elliott gleefully stated. "We must ease into this carefully, and not set off any alarms."

As a reward for his critical assistance during Vatican II, now a bishop, Gustav had been entrusted by the pope to assist with the Vatican's Intelligence Service's merger with the Jesuit espionage network. The mole was now firmly entrenched, with full access to all the secrets.

But it was the one big secret that would be the focus of his meeting with Lucas.

Episode Two

~

The Reveal

"The world is a dangerous place to live, not because of the people who are evil, but because of the people who don't do anything about it."
~ Albert Einstein

Chapter Twenty-Nine

∞

"I have hemorrhoids."

"What the baby Jesus are you talking about?"

"I have hemorrhoids. I've never told anyone that, not Todd, not even my general practioner at Muir Hospital. You said we should have no secrets, so—there you go. We both know I have hemorrhoids. They are disgusting, and I don't want to talk about it. Let's talk about Paris now," Stella said, holding the steering wheel with one hand while twirling her other. "*Fini!*"

Still stinging from Maggie's disappointment in her for not revealing her first visitation, maybe now she could relax and hope that by exposing her last, darkest and most humiliating secret, at least in her eyes, Maggie would trust her again. Stella wasn't about to jeopardize her friendship with Maggie now, so transparency and honesty were her top priorities.

"Your secret is safe with me, sweetie. Though, honestly? Maybe a tad too much information. But—we're good."

They continued silently on U.S. 101 towards the Richmond-San Rafael Bridge. Within the first mile on the old bridge, their bodies synchronized to the slow rhythmic beat of the bridge's pavement. Da-dum, da-dum, da-dum. They swayed, and their breasts bounced in unison as the car hopped over each groove, lulled into a shared space of silence.

The thought of being back on the U.C. Berkeley campus with her dear friend flooded Stella with memories. The last time they had been on the campus together was at the end of their sophomore year in high school. They had hitchhiked to attend a free concert in People's Park a week before the infamous May 15, 1969 Bloodbath.

Stella had felt it was her moral duty to protest the Vietnam War. She also believed God dealt in a reward point system. Maybe if she got enough God points, they would find her father and bring him home. She never gave up hope, even to this day to at least find out his fate.

As they merged onto Interstate 80, Maggie broke the silence. "Remember that hippie who asked us if we wanted to sell that radical newspaper Berkeley Barb for some spare change the time in high school when we were cut school and came here? I always wondered if we passed as real hippies or if he knew we were posing. I mean, c'mon, we were dressed exactly alike, with our braided leather headbands over our frizzed hair, ponchos and Army Navy Surplus Store sailor pants. What a hoot!"

Stella laughed. She remembered the day well. "And the line of station wagons driving slowly by, taking a picture with their Kodak Brownies of 'real hippies,' like they were at Yellowstone or something. Yeah, Freakstone Park, was more like it. God, that was such a fun day!"

Maggie's sudden sadness was palpable in the small sports car.

"I'm so sorry. You okay?"

"Yeah, I will be," Maggie replied, with a sniffle. "A lot of good memories here. Just remembering how you really didn't like Jim at first. You thought he was so uncool, the straight guy."

How can you fall in love with someone who is on his way to kill innocent women and children? Stella had yelled at Maggie back then. They had a loud fight about it. Maggie married Jim in Reno two weeks later.

Before he left for boot camp, Stella got to know Jim. She softened, and found he had a really old soul. He was kind, thoughtful and very intelligent. Best of all, he adored Maggie.

They had a small party the night before he was to leave, just the three of them in the newlywed Barretts' tiny East Bay apartment, drinking

Spanada out of the bottle and sharing a bucket of original Kentucky Fried Chicken. That night Stella realized how scared he was to go to war.

"Why are you going?" she had asked him.

"I love my country. It's my duty to stand up for freedom," he'd replied.

Stella knew all little boys were raised to be heroes. Going to war for your country was like slaying the dragon. The way to show honor and manhood. That night she was so glad she was a girl. How sad it must be to be a boy.

As she reflected, it dawned on her that he was only eighteen, a kid. She had listened to his story of his family's military history, going all the way back to the Revolutionary War. He had given her a pretty convincing tale of why it's important to serve your country and fight for our freedom. Probably a story that had been passed down through the generations along with the family Bible. It hadn't convinced her that her own family's sacrifice was worth it, though.

Jim's whole family history had revolved around war. A family tradition that had just put his only child into the frozen ground, never to return. *Are we any safer*, she pondered, not feeling safe at all. She wondered if women ruled the world if wars would stop.

But it was something else they discussed that night that she was thinking about now. After Maggie had gone to bed, Jim told her about psychic premonitions and his "gift." He always knew when the phone was going to ring, who was at the door or how someone would answer a question.

"Stella, there is so much we don't understand in this universe. You ever get that feeling someone is staring at you? It's because of morphic resonance and morphic fields. Morphic resonance is the memory in nature that connects all living things, like when birds fly in formation or head south for the winter. It's how your pet knows you're coming home. Our morphic fields are merging all the time. We are all connected, Stella," he had stressed.

Of course! The restaurant; that's what had happened that night when she knew the stranger was starting at her. And the lady in Golden Gate Park. Stella hadn't thought about morphic fields for so long but it sure did explain a lot now.

As they took the Berkeley exit, both women were still silent, deeply lost in thought. Maggie was the first to speak as they made their way down University Avenue towards the campus. "I think that guy was standing right there, smoking that same damn cigarette and holding that same damn protest sign the last time I drove down this street."

They burst out laughing.

"Yep," Stella chuckled "some people loved the '60s so much they made a decision to never leave."

"True," Maggie agreed, wistfully, "but I see the changes, too. It's starting to get that *Any City, U.S.A.* boxy feel, huh? It's not quite the same. Oh, but look!" she excitedly blurted as she noticed The Click Café. "Remember when we used to go there with Jim, and we all ate on $10? Let's stop there on the way home, if we can, okay?"

So much had happened in the last three days, Stella wondered if remembering Jim in a public place was a good idea. But if it made Maggie happy, she'd happily oblige.

"Sure, why not? I'd love to," Stella replied with a smile. She wondered if it was still owned by the same Turkish family.

Chapter Thirty

—∞—

"**E**xcellent! You've arrived just in time, before the cardinal," Lucas cooed to his trusted long-time employee.

"No worries," Brent McConnell replied, in his usual clipped way.

"You brought the blueprints? I want to go over some details and talking points before His Eminence arrives. As you know, he and the Church have been extremely helpful to us during these wars. We may have only one chance to convince him to implement our plan."

"Understood. Here are the renderings," Brent said as he opened up his custom-made titanium tube and slid out the large roll of papers. "Like you instructed, I took the blueprints of the abandoned convent and using all the available specifications from the Army's 1993 lab build-out for the original DNA experiments, I think we're close. Of course, some modifications might have to be made once on-site. We are dealing with a centuries' old building and installing 21st century technology."

"I trust you, Brent. You have never failed to execute your assignments. You were one of my father's most highly regarded employees."

"GA7 has been good to me, too, sir. If you don't mind, I need to use the head."

"Please, be my guest."

Brent sat on the toilet, reflecting on his role today. He was well aware GA7's business plan included world domination. War had changed. Since the draft was discontinued in 1973, the government's All-Volunteer army was mostly from the Bible Belt. An endless supply of boots on the ground. But it took more than that now.

There was a market for mercenaries or "contractors" who provided wartime services that were "deniable, disposable and undetectable"— perfect for secret wars and black-budget operations. The No-Draft policy opened a massive market for private military firms and the weapons industry, just as Elliott Stanchir had planned so long ago. Their government contract had already tripled in income since 2000, and over-all arms sales were up fifty percent.

The U.S. needed trained killers, which just happened to be part of GA7's product line. GA7 was ready with its own army of soldiers of fortune. Brent was one of their best.

He had seen the writing on the wall when the Star Gate Project was in danger of being eliminated. With his high security clearance, he knew the future of war was in the oil-soaked Cradle of Civilization.

His first assignment when he was hired by GA7 was to prepare a report on the cost of outsourcing a war. Those in power had been pushing for Saddam's ouster since as early as 1998. Didn't take a genius to see which way the wind was gonna blow.

Again, Brent knew that had all been planned by the Stanchirs. The War on Terror alone had brought in $150 million a year for surveillance which provided intelligence to both Fortune 500 companies and the CIA. And a lot of the money was in his own bank account now, due to the overturning of Executive Order No. 11905-22 just a day after 9/11. The president declared "America at War" which effectively allowed assassinations as a U.S. foreign policy tool. Brent was given carte blanche to carry on more of his enormously lucrative "wet work" across the globe.

GA7 was profiting handsomely. Outsourcing fault and immune to legal justice, they had won the largest security contract worth $300 million, without having any experience in the region. They won because not only could they provide the required mercenaries, but they had extensive experience with "spin" which would be needed when eventually no weapons of mass destruction would be found.

The current administration was counting on GA7 to push the message that Saddam was a brutal tyrant who had tortured his own people and needed to be taken out. The skill and craft was to keep the American people from asking why we were spending billions to do this, and putting it all on a credit card. It didn't hurt that the president was a born-again Christian who had fired up his base and made the invasion as entertaining as a summer blockbuster action movie.

There was a knock on the door. "Are you almost finished? We really need to go over the material now." Brent was surprised. He detected a slight sound of panic in Lucas' voice. Very unusual. Now he was certain this had to be something big. Lucas hadn't shared what the Plan was, but he had a pretty good idea. Though he hadn't been part of the Army's 1993 DNA experiment, he knew plenty enough about it. Especially after what he and Jim had discovered.

"Coming out now."

Chapter Thirty-One

—∞—

They turned off University Avenue and started the narrow, windy climb up into the foothills of the Berkeley campus. As they got closer, they noticed the crowds of women walking up to Arthur Andersen Auditorium. Not so much surprised that it was mostly women attending the seminar—it was the type of women. Hair various shades of gray, wrinkles of varying depth and number, waists plumbed by wisdom and a life lived. If Stella had to guess, she would swear all post-menopausal women. Sisters of Change.

Maggie turned. "Kinda looks like a forty-year-high school reunion from a girl's school."

"No kidding. Okay, where's my perfect parking space?" Stella asked right as a car backed up to exit the packed parking lot. She swooped the Jaguar into the spot directly across from the entrance.

"Damn, how do you do that? You got skills, girl," Maggie said with a wink.

"Some of us are just gifted, my friend."

They could feel a certain excitement in the air as soon as they joined the crowd climbing the steps. It didn't go without notice that everyone was making eye contact, smiling, chatting getting along. They darted when they saw two open seats near the stage, almost smack in the middle of the audience.

Stella sat next to an exotic tall dark woman who seemed oddly familiar. The woman turned her head and greeted Stella with a nod and a very British hello. She couldn't shake the feeling that they had met before; maybe a customer of her boutique. The woman definitely had style, from her funky vintage Rolling Stones T-shirt under her Brooks Brothers jacket to her skinny jeans and red Converse high tops.

"Fancy how it feels like church, yeah?" the Brit asked.

"It does, I guess. Haven't been to church in a long time. But it's exciting," Stella half-lied. She had been to church—three times in a twelve-month period—but it definitely hadn't been joyful.

Blinking house lights quieted the crowd. The auditorium dimmed into darkness as a lone spotlight fell upon a youngish woman maybe about thirty, short and very thin, with skin the color of cobalt-tinged coal.

"Good evening, my name is Mary Rose Bugato. I stand before you this evening because Mary, the Mother of God, saved me from being murdered," the woman said, waving her handless arm to the crowd. A collective gasp filled the room. But the loudest gasp was Stella's.

"That's the woman who showed at my gallery!"

"Shhh," Maggie said, "we'll talk about this later."

"You see, I was born Tutsi and lived in very small village in southwest Rwanda, next to Lake Kivu, across the border from what is now known as the Democratic Republic of the Congo. To understand the horror of what happened, I must tell you a little of Rwanda's history.

"Rwanda is made up of three tribes: a Hutu majority, a Tutsi minority and a small tribe of forest-dwelling pygmies called Twa. We had lived for centuries in peace and harmony. Then the German colonialists came, followed by the Belgians who converted our social structure into a race-based class system which spawned discrimination and hatred. The Belgians made our people carry ethnic identity cards. This created the rift between the Hutus and the Tutsis.

"In 1959, the Belgians encouraged the Hutus to overthrow the monarchy, leading to the murder of more than 100,000 Tutsis. By 1962, the Hutus were in charge of our country's government, and the Tutsis, like me, became second-class citizens.

"My parents tried to keep us ignorant of this history. They did not want us caught in the cycle of hate. My two brothers and I were raised in a loving, close knit Catholic family. My father was a fisherman while my mother worked our coffee crop with the help of my brothers. We were not rich, but also not poor. Most importantly, we were raised with love and deep faith in God. My parents raised us to always have an open heart to everyone we met.

"But then things started to change. They could no longer keep the true meaning of ethnic balancing from us.

"As a little girl, I remember sitting at the table and discussing the Miracle at Kibeho. Starting in 1981 and lasting exactly seven years, three private school girls said they talked to the Virgin Mary. The girls reported being warned by the 'Mother of the Word' about hell and seeing dead bodies lying about. My mother told us even she had dreams of an impending 'red storm.'

"Many nights my parents would discuss what Mother Mary was trying to tell us through her visits with the Kibeho visionaries, fearing another bloodbath like the 1973 coup. Nightly, we would hold hands and pray to the Holy Mother to keep our family safe. But never, as that innocent young girl could I have imagined what her messages to these girls meant. I now know that was a prophecy, a warning.

"As Easter approached in 1994, after the signing of a peace agreement between the Hutus and Tutsis, the chief leader of the Interahamwe—the government death squad of young thugs—vowed to never make peace with the Tutsis. He promised to return to Rwanda 'to prepare an apocalypse.'

"Using a radio station, they started drumming up hate, calling for 'Hutu Power.' They said the Tutsis were cockroaches who were out to kill Hutus, and take over the government. They said they must be stopped.

"We couldn't believe the government was allowing Hutus to openly threaten the lives of Tutsis. But we had no idea how quickly the seeds of hate can fester into genocide.

"The massacres of my people in my village started the night before Easter. We had heard rumblings in the village that the killers were on their way. We could barely see the sun set through the dust kicked up from the hundreds of machetes being clanked against the dirt roadways on their murderous path. We were finishing our meal, when suddenly my mother stood. It was time to leave, she said.

"For the past few weeks we had discussed nightly our escape plan. My protection plan from danger included my scapular. It had been blessed with the Virgin Mary's promise and a pledge of peace that 'whosoever dies wearing it shall not suffer eternal fire.' I wrapped it around my neck as we quickly grabbed our packed knapsacks by the front door and silently but swiftly headed out to the water's edge. We passed our neighbor's lush green lawns strewn with recently discarded toys amidst hacked up bloody body parts.

"My father planned on getting us out of the country before morning's light on his little fishing boat. However, the boat could only safely hold three people at a time, so he took my mother and youngest brother across the lake first, leaving me on the shore with my older brother, Joseph, hiding under fallen tree branches. That was to be the last time I saw my family together.

"Before my father could make it back, the Interahamwe started coming towards us, dragging their machetes along the dusty wheat colored road, sparks flying when their weapons struck rocks. They chanted *kill the cockroaches*. No longer able to see my father's boat, my brother and I started digging into the mushy bog digging a hole big enough for us to hide in. As the killers came closer, we jumped in the hole and covered ourselves with the branches.

"We stayed hidden like that for over two months, only coming out at night and creeping along the shore on our bellies, looking for any kind of food we could eat. We survived on berries, ants and worms, slowly starving to death. We would gather more leaves to lay in our hole to soak up the urine and sweat. During the day, we could hear the screams and cries of the slaughter of innocent Tutsis by the Hutus. Insects would crawl over our bodies, into our ears—but we would not flinch. We would sleep during the day, with one eye open.

"One day, Joseph started to cough. I tried to muffle his coughs with my hands wrapped in the remnants of my scapular. My dear brother tried so hard to keep silent, with silent tears streaming down his face as he held his breath. He knew his cough would be our death knell.

"It was not long before we could hear the death squads coming, with their chants of hate and death and the ever-clanking of their machetes. Joseph pushed me out of the hole with all his oldest brother authority he could muster and told me to run—run as fast as you can to the shore and jump in, he urged.

"I jumped out of the hole, trying not to cry and ready to run for my life. But after laying in the hole for so long, my muscles had withered and couldn't carry me upright. I could almost feel the breath of the thugs on the back of my neck. Hot urine ran down my leg as I kept running; I was so afraid they would catch me.

"We had heard the stories of what they did to the women and girls they caught. They would first gang rape them and then slowly insert their machetes into each woman's vagina, cutting her from the inside out, and torture her until her last breath.

"Then I heard the weakened scream of my brother. I knew they had killed him. All I could think was *run, run, run*, but my legs did not obey. I tripped over a stone on the rocky path to the shore, just feet away from the water. I knew it was now my time to die. Time to join my family. I grabbed the remnants of my scapular and held it to my lips and prayed for Mary's mercy on my soul.

"As I watched the death squad approach me down the path, I started to roll on the ground. A young neighbor boy, maybe eleven or twelve, swung his machete and cut off my hand. I rolled over and looked into his eyes as he raised his machete once more, only to be distracted by a swirling sparkling mist that rose up from the water and rapidly moved towards me.

"I had never seen or felt such beauty in my life. I thought maybe I was already in Heaven. The mist then covered my bleeding, filth-encrusted body. I saw her face; the most beautiful face I had ever seen. I have never felt such love in my life. As I watched the blood thirsty thugs running down to the shore, I realized they could no longer see me. I do not know how long I lied on the dirt, protected by Our Lady.

"The next thing I remember was a nun approaching me with soldiers whose uniforms I did not recognize. As one soldier approached me, I realized the bleeding from my missing hand had stopped. This solider swiftly lifted me up and within minutes we were in a boat on Lake Kivu, headed towards Zaire. Operation Turquoise had begun. Soldiers from several French-speaking countries had set up camp near Lake Kivu and had begun rescuing the few Tutsis left.

"I stayed in the refugee camp for the next year until I was able to come to this country, America. While in the camp, I was taught how to paint with my remaining hand.

"I have never found out what happened to my parents and younger brother. I fear they were slaughtered as was my older brother Most of the people from my village were killed. Lives full of promise were cut short because of the evil of unchecked power and bigotry.

"Half a million Tutsi women were raped, then shunned and shamed by their own men and left mentally and physically broken. Today, a woman or a child is raped every minute in the Congo. Rape is now a weapon of war.

"The reason I am here today to tell you my story is so you can understand what fear and hate can do to people. Today, in Rwanda, women now top the world with the highest rankings of women—forty-nine percent—in parliament. We have a place at the peace table. Our sense of community is what helped us recover quickly from the horrible genocide.

"I believe that is why Mother Mary saved my life, so I could speak to the women of the world and urge you all to stand up and help put an end to war. Mary has taught me that when you have hope and love in your life, you lose your hate and anger towards others. I know that's why I was saved because of what I heard Mary tell me: 'gather the women.'"

Gut punched, Stella went rigid as she gripped Maggie's hand. She felt a light hand touch her thigh.

"You too, lovey?"

Stella warily turned and nodded her head.

"If you and your friend would like to join us for a drink and a nosh to talk about it, you're more than welcome. Do you know The Click Café?"

Chapter Thirty-Two

—∞—

As he studied the plans, Lucas was both impressed and worried. Such a simple set-up for such a colossal impact on the world. Almost too simple. "This is adequate?" he asked.

"I brought all the data from our beta site in the States, if you'd like to review it. But we achieved the results you wanted. You remember the effect on the Marin woman? We could have made it even more bare bones, but you said the Cardinal would be more impressed with lots of bells and whistles."

"Yes, he is a man swayed by extravagance. And, yes, I very well remember the results on her," he said, twirling the bottle cap around in his pants pocket. "You must forgive me. My grief, mixed with the anxiety of this meeting, have dulled my mind."

"Understood. I'm very sorry about the loss of your father."

Lucas nodded, accepting Brent's sympathies, as he tried to again focus on the blueprints and layout. There was no time for grieving now; work had to be done. It would be what his father expected. Always business first.

They had a small window of time with no second chance due to the rapid time acceleration leading up to the Shift. The Plan had to be carried out with clockwork precision.

Each morning Lucas was briefed on activity from GA7's world-wide monitors. The Magneto Sphere reports lately were showing increased rips, allowing for radical increases in consciousness. Not surprisingly, there was an alarming upsurge in reports of Marian Apparitions throughout the world.

But what concerned him lately were the Random Number Generators or RNGs. GA7 had installed them globally to monitor changes in the consciousness right before the 1998 Milky Way Alignment which had created a new magnetic field. Every time there was any kind of significant world event such as the death of Princess Diana, the 2000 tsunamis, even Christmas, the randomness of the numbers would change.

The generators normally produced "1s" fifty percent of the time and "0s" the other fifty percent of the time. But they stopped being orderly right before significant world events. Three hours before the September 11th attack, as early as 4:30 a.m. Eastern Standard Time, they had started generating wildly random numbers. Now they were starting to see indications of randomness the closer the Milky Way got to aligning with the axis of the Earth. The so-called "end times of December 21, 2012."

The Plan was necessitated if what the elderly Portuguese nun wrote was true. His father had first told him about the Third Secret when he was a teen, but it wasn't until his days at Stanford in the early 1970s, studying quantum physics that the genius solution to stop the prophecy was hatched. They couldn't allow the prophecy to come true. Simply not good for business.

His inspiration was Max Planck's 1944 identification of an energy field. Heart coherence. The Matrix. And how GA7 could disrupt the field.

The next war would not be fought with guns and bombs. Information and psychic energy were the new weapons. But the game changer was DNA. Human emotion could change DNA without even touching it. That was the future. The use of psychotropic weapons, quantum war.

Lucas looked up from the table at Brent. "Fear is indeed a powerful tool. Did you know that only one child has ever died from Halloween candy being poisoned? Just one. And he was poisoned by his own father. You keep repeating a lie long enough it will become truth. Look at how fearful parents are now on Halloween.

"My father paid close attention to Franklin D. Roosevelt's first inaugural speech in 1933 about nothing to fear but fear itself," Lucas added. "At Harvard, he learned that the language of consciousness is the language of emotions. He knew if you wanted power over the masses, use emotion. Especially fear. Create a 'culture of fear' and you control emotions and soon you are entangled with the collective consciousness.

"Fear makes it so easy to lead the public. My grandfather learned that when he volunteered with almost 75,000 other men to be the first 'four minute men,' created by President Wilson during the First World War," Lucas said. "Wilson had hired a Missouri newsman to create a long propaganda campaign in its truest form: 'propagation of faith' to sway the American public that war was good.

"These 'four minute men' would talk up the patriotism of war for about four minutes in social settings like movie theaters, churches, even cocktail parties—the typical attention span of the listener. They even censored all news stories to keep the war effort on a positive note. We are only carrying on that tradition, on a much larger scale, of course," Lucas finished with a gleam in his eye.

With a sharp rap on his door, the strategically planned meeting was about to begin. Lucas had always thought it would be his father as the conductor and story teller when this phase was put into motion. But God appeared to have a different plan. The man who was once one of the six most important men on the planet was gone. The last words Elliott Stanchir heard before the brilliant white light engulfed him was his son, Lucas, assuring him that he was ready to take the helm.

Lucas powerfully strode to the door, as much as he could with his knock-knees brushing together. His demeanor changed during his short stride from the blueprints to the door as he prepared to present himself as the alpha male dog. His moves were somewhat graceful from his years of martial arts training, the one sport he was good at. He possessed the ability to move swiftly, to snap a man's neck with the swift slice of his hand.

He confidently opened the twelve-foot gold baroque doors of his Amsterdam grand suite, allowing them to swing inwards as they had for the last five centuries, slowing revealing the breathtaking view outside the adjacent bay of fourteen-foot windows behind him.

"Your Eminence, please come in."

Cardinal Gustav Muench greeted his old friend with a genuinely warm hug and smile, as he entered the decorative Renaissance suite, wired with 22nd Century technology. Walking behind the obese elderly cardinal was a strikingly handsome priest, who brushed back an unruly lock of hair from his forehead, while he extended the other hand.

"My pleasure to meet you," he said in English with the lyrical lilt of a French accent.

"You must be the Bollandist. The cardinal says you are the premier expert on the Virgin Mary, including the apparitions." Lucas had been eagerly waiting to meet this man, his connection to any missing pieces of information the cleric researcher may provide.

"This is Father Gabriel Aubert, Lucas. And I need no introduction to this man," the cardinal said, shaking Brent's hand. "I hope your cousin is well," he added, not letting on he had spoken with her less than twenty-four hours ago.

"My pleasure. Please sit. First, I would like to thank you for coming here at this late hour. I hope you don't mind if I get right to the point."

"Not at all, Lucas. Please proceed," the holy man said.

"GA7 has obtained some information that could have grave repercussions on the Church. If not remedied, the beginning of the dissolution of the Catholic Church as we know it could begin."

That caught their attention, Lucas thought. Just as planned.

"We have global monitors that started reporting a sharp uptick in web traffic regarding the International Day of Prayer of the Lady and Mother of All Nations, coming up May 31 right here in Amsterdam. Last year the event attracted thousands of people from seventy countries and six continents, all converging to honor the Lady of all Nations. This year city officials expect that number to double."

"Yes, the attendance at such sites as Lourdes, Fatima, and even the so-called Mary's House in Turkey have also increased," Gabriel said. He paid close attention to every word said, every gesture of all in attendance.

"It is not so much the increase in numbers, but the increase of Catholic clergy at this event. Scores of priests, bishops and cardinals were expected to attend and oversee services; we believe this could be dangerous if allowed to continue. The concern is the common thread of each message. A message of unity, connection of all religions. A very unprofitable message for GA7. I fear for your Church also."

At the mention of money, the cardinal seemed to perk up. The pope would be disappointed in both the loss of control over his flock and on world affairs. No other religious leader was allowed on the floor of the United Nations as if he were an elected official. He had worked with the Stanchirs for enough years to understand the political and business need of divisiveness.

"As my father discussed with you prior to his passing, we think we have a way to disrupt the clergies' message. But we will need the Church's vital assistance," Lucas said directly towards the cardinal.

"I now understand your father's instructions on the collections we've been performing. Let me assure you we have taken the utmost care of the samples. We have employed the same protocol as we use for our most priceless relics in our archives. As for the lab, you know I have worked with the pope over many years, and he trusts me. The building is vacant, we have the money, and I see no barrier to completing the project within your proposed time frame. We *must* finish it. We must make certain the Church continues. It is our duty."

"I knew we could count on you, Your Eminence. If you don't mind, I would like to have some time to chat with Father Auber—alone."

"Of course," the cardinal replied, though not at all comfortable with being excluded from the conversation. However, it did give him the opportunity he needed to alert Brent.

He leaned in close enough to Brent to whisper, "I have unfortunate news from your cousin. We have a problem."

Chapter Thirty-Three

—∞—

"Cheers, ladies. I'm Sophia and this is my charming beautiful wife, Sarah. Will this table do?" the British woman asked, scooting into the rounded corner booth. "Me mum would say: you can't change the world if you sit in the corners of a round room!"

They all settled into the red Naugahyde booth as a young, twitchy waitress handed them menus. Stella smiled at the lithe girl, shackled in layers of tie-dyed thrift store clothing, her nest of dreads chaotically bobbing on her head. Stella studied the braids, hoping nothing unpleasant would leap out and land on her. She mentally gave the young girl a makeover.

"I'm an anthropologist and a professor here at Berkeley, and Sarah is a therapist specializing in NDEs. You know, *near-death experiences.*" They reached across the wobbly table to shake hands.

Glancing over the menu, Stella was comforted that the menu had changed little over the years. She raised her head up, sensing Maggie. They shared a smile.

"I was going to order some wine. Would you like me to order a bottle?" Stella asked.

"A bottle is a good place to start," Sophia piped in, boisterously. "Blood-red wine, please. I got red blood!" Sophia said with fluttering jazz hands.

Stella just smiled, puzzled by Sophia's word choice. Maybe a British thing.

"And maybe some soup?" Maggie suggested, looking around the table. "They're famous for their French Onion soup. It was my husband's favorite," she mentioned, twirling her watch.

"French onion soup, some blood-red wine with some freshly-baked bread would be properly perfect, my dear," Sophia said to the waitress, pushing the menus across the table. There was no pretense—she wanted the waitress gone.

Again, Stella found Sophia's conversational style odd, but enjoyed her accent. She studied the couple, marveling at how opposite they seemed to be.

Sophia was a bold noticeable person with her dark-burnished mahogany skin stretched tautly on her tall, kinetic body. She kept pushing up her jacket sleeves to her elbows when she tried to get her point across, as if to punctuate her opinions.

Sarah, on the other hand, was petite and reserved, with closely cropped spiky silver hair that suggested a refinement, an elegance. She looked more like an art buyer than a therapist, Stella thought, evaluating the expensive gray cashmere sweater and pant ensemble that looked like Calvin Klein. She lusted after the woman's exquisite chunky abstract silver jewelry—not too much, not too little.

As she was eying Sarah's jewelry, their eyes caught. Sarah's irises, spirals of gray mixed with blue, reminded Stella of a famous abstract expressionism painter, Marta Rothman. In fact, Stella happened to have one of her paintings hanging in her own living room. It was part of her divorce settlement proceeds from the art gallery. It was the only piece of art in her ruthlessly stark house.

"I hope I'm not being too bold," Sophia said, "but I felt a connection with you two, especially when the young women mentioned 'gather the women.' By your reaction, I take it you have heard this phrase somewhere?"

Both Stella and Maggie hesitated to respond, not yet fully trusting strangers.

"Crikey, I know it's scary, ladies! Letting people in on your secret and all. Sarah and I have both been there. We know midlife women are marginalized enough without having people think we see spooky spirits too, yah? I thought we both might be barking mad when it happened to us."

"Yeah, seems like a lot of that going around," Stella added sarcastically.

"Most of the women in that room tonight, I suspect, have been visited by something they assume is the Virgin Mary. No doubt they all have experienced some kind of vision, but aren't sure what or who it was," Sarah said.

"For us, it happened while we were walking the Camino de Santiago Compostela in Spain," Sophia interjected, finishing her wife's thought. "We had just finished a late night dinner in a small town after a pretty exhausting day walking the Camino. We decided to take our pitcher of sangria down to the town square fountain and sip under the stars of the Milky Way.

"Sarah noticed it first. The air was thick with roses, like me Nan's knickers' drawer. We looked around but no rose bushes—anywhere! We actually weren't too surprised. Lots of unexplained things had already happened in the last thirteen days of our five-hundred-mile journey. But nothing like what happened next.

"Standing in front of us was this glowing orb, throbbing. It was opaque at first, then shiny like a crystal. It pulled us towards it like a magnet. It didn't really have any kind identifiable shape, but it kinda felt female to us, ya know. Strange, right? Anyway, then she 'told' us things; telepathically, I mean. And she ended with a message to 'gather the women.' Then poof—she was gone. As was the rose smell, thank goodness.

"Neither of us was raised Catholic—Sarah is Jewish—but we both agree that the vision appeared to be similar to what others have reported as the Virgin Mary.

"Well, Mary was Jewish, don't forget," Sarah said.

"Quite true, lovey. We've been obsessed since then, performing months of research as to what it may have been. Now we're connected to a world-wide group of other women who have experienced the same thing. One even said that Edgar Cayce, the sleeping prophet back in the early 1900s, had visions of a woman of radiant light who assured him his prayers to help the sick had been heard and would come true. Crazy, yah?"

The young waitress returned with glasses and the wine, and a busboy that hastily dropped off a basket of bread, almost dumping its contents onto the Indian-bedspread tablecloth. Maggie leaned over the basket and deeply inhaled. "My god, heaven," she said as she pulled a chunk of still-steaming bread out of the basket and slathered it with butter.

The waitress poured them all a glass of wine, and then reached behind Stella to adjust something on the window sill, continuing to annoy her.

"I've been doing a bit of research also," Maggie added. "I'd be interested to hear what you found."

"In our talks with these women around the world, it appears that visions of Mary are becoming more and more frequent, especially to older women. As you probably know from your research, the most famous reported visions have usually been to young girls. Due to some interesting stories Sarah uncovered in her research in NDEs, we decided to consult other sources beyond the religious press.

"Because my background is in Central American anthropology, I started with the Mayans. You may have heard about 2012," she asked, noting their body language. "Aw hell, let me guess? You've heard the world is going to catastrophically end in a horrific ball of fire, yah?" Both Maggie and Stella nodded their heads.

"No! Not the end of the world, loves. Wankers! The Global Elite have cranked up the disinformation machine, making everyone afraid. It's been pretty effective, don't you think? Look how easy it was to unilaterally invade and bomb another country. Little proof, just fear of the 'smoking gun turning into a mushroom cloud.'

"No, it may just be the end of an *era of time*, a Long Count. Did you know we are only the sixth generation of humans to experience a new cycle of time? That may be why we know so little about what the Mayans were trying to tell us."

Rocking forward, Maggie said "We are very ignorant of all First People beliefs. Did you know that our own Constitution is based on the

Iroquois Constitution, where it was decided that the chiefs would be chosen by the women of the tribe? They reasoned that only women truly knew what it felt like to have grown a child in their bodies and birthed, nurtured and cared for this precious soul only to lose them in a senseless bloodbath called war." Maggie's tears fell from her eyes like a fully opened spigot, as her rocking quickened.

"I'm so sorry. I didn't mean to start crying. It's just that it seems up to us women to remind humanity: don't forget our brothers and sisters. Maybe that's why Mary is here," Maggie said, embarrassed by her weakness.

Stella put her arm around Maggie and softly said, "She just lost her son in Iraq. He was buried a week ago."

"Oh lovey, I can't imagine the pain you must be feeling. I'm so bloody sorry," Sophia said, tears welling and holding her hands over her heart as if her own heart was breaking.

"Thank you for your kind words," Maggie managed to say. "You would have no way of knowing. But what I say is true. If mothers ran the world, I know we would have fewer wars, if any. Did you know that man's inhumanity to its fellow humans in the 20th century was the worst in all recorded history with a loss of almost 175,000,000 lives? Why do you think that is?"

"Chaos before change, I suspect," Sophia said. Noticing the confusion on everyone's faces, she added. "Let me tell you some facts from my work. Then you can decide if it makes any sense to you.

"Let's go back to the 1998 Winter Equinox, shall we? Called the Galactic-Plane Ecliptic Crossing or The Great Alignment when the Earth supposedly aligned with the center of the Milky Way, our Universe, and the Sun. According to Egyptian lore, this center of the universe symbolizes Isis, the goddess of the Milky Way. Some believe this alignment started the return of the Goddess, an energy that will psychically alter the field of consciousness on our planet. What some call the Return of the Divine Feminine.

"About 2,500 years ago, the first Mayan suddenly appeared with advanced technological skills in the Yucatan Peninsula of Mexico. They had an unsurpassed talent and obsession for calculations of cosmic cycles and time. Their precise system of galactic time was correct for over twenty-five centuries.

"They tracked the upcoming rare celestial alignment of our solar system, our Sun and Earth with the center of our galaxy. An alignment that won't happen again for 2,600 years. Their calendar appears to end on December 12, 2012, hence all the apocalyptic rantings.

"The Mayans believed we must finish this 'darkness' age before we can enter the 'light' of the next cycle. We are going from the Age of Pisces, with its symbol of fish swimming in opposite directions, a separation and divisiveness, to the Age of Aquarius—the age of water, unity, connection and community.

"This is also causing the sun to go through a magnetic shift which will affect all life. Studies show how our magnetosphere affects many species, from whales and dolphins to ducks and bees who navigate this magnetic 'superhighway' to arrive at their feeding and mating grounds. It's the science called emergence.

"Scientists are now realizing that humans also rely on this magnetosphere. The human brain contains millions of tiny magnetic particles which connects us similar to other species. The human heart generates the strongest magnetic field in our bodies, radiating three feet around our bodies. So when you hear that we are all 'connected' it's a scientific fact, not just some woo-woo stuff."

Stella giggled. "That's what Maggie calls me—woo-woo. Sorry for the interruption. Please continue."

"You're not getting tiddly, are you?" Sophia queried, squinting hard at Stella before she continued.

"That's why we decided to walk the Santiago de Camino from France to Spain. It's a mystical pilgrimage that follows the magnetic lei lines of the Milky Way or what some call the 'Mother's Way.' There's been reports 2012 will change the global magnetic fields. It is believed that the alignment will cause the magnetic fields to decline, creating change everywhere.

"Weaker magnetic fields are good. They cause people to be more open, creative, hence the shift. There is a zero magnetic contour line parallel to the West Coast, from southern California to northern

Washington. However, the places where the magnetic field is stronger, like in the middle of America, people have a tendency to become fundamentalists, deeply rooted in tradition and fearing change. Why the difference? Water!"

"I actually wondered if what we saw had anything to do with changing energy," Stella offered. "I studied art, and the spiral naturally occurs everywhere, in sea shells, sunflowers and the Milky Way. It's the Fibonacci spiral. And I've heard it said that the 'shape of time' is 'spiral energy.'

"Could we actually be witnessing the energy changing? Does it appear as a swirling energy orb that may or may not resemble Jesus' mother?" asked Stella, hoping with every fiber of her body this was the answer.

"Could be," Sophia shrugged. "You know, the church in Santiago de Compostela, at the ocean's end of the Camino, was the first Christian church, built by one of Jesus's apostles, St. James. And its symbol is the seashell, used to mark the whole path. That's why I commissioned this piece for my wife," she added, pointing at Sarah's necklace. "I love your ladies' necklaces," she said, pointing at the best friends' stars.

"If you don't mind, Sophia, I think this is a good time to tell them about my NDE research," Sarah said, pouring herself some more wine.

"I first got interested in NDE research after my mother, an artist, attempted suicide. She was declared clinically dead for almost seven minutes. After she left the hospital, she told me during that seven-minute period she spoke with light beings who told her a new world age was coming. That was back in 1987.

"Recently, I treated a man who once worked as an assassin for the government. He said he had been shot and was declared clinically dead on the operating table. But he wasn't. He felt very much alive as he floated above his body, engulfed in bright white light. Through a mist, he was approached by radiant silver form. He, too, said it was the most joyous feeling he had ever experienced.

"Then he mentioned 2012; that caught my interest. The 'being' told him that an energy system that had existed a long time ago was now returning to Earth. An electromagnetic polar shift that would present humankind with a new consciousness, a new spirituality. Multi-dimensional intelligence would be available to all.

"Another scientist thinks that when the galactic center is rising on the horizon, that psychic ability in humans increases exponentially, with an explosion in synchronicities. I think we are seeing great evidence of that right now. Do you think it was luck that you happened to get two seats right in the middle up front tonight? It's all synchronicity, ladies."

"We are women of a certain vintage, meant to meet," Sophia added. "It is time for another revolution, similar to the '60s and again led by women. You know, the world thinks it was The Beatles who led the change but actually it was us baby-boomer women. If we hadn't been there screaming, no one would even remember 'the lads' today," she laughed.

Sarah joined in. "The women we've been communicating with are all planning on meeting in France. There is a special celebration in Lourdes, marking the anniversary of the first time Bernadette saw the 'Lady,' February 11th. We're not sure if that's where we are supposed to 'gather the women,' but it's where we are starting. We started our walk on the Camino from there—magical place."

"Talk about synchronicity! We're both about to leave on a buying trip to France for my clothing boutique. I think we might be able to arrange a side trip. What do you think, Maggie?"

Before Maggie could answer, Stella knocked over her wine, soaking the bread basket. All the women jumped up to avoid the swiftly spreading red spill. The young waitress with her dreads unleashed rushed to the table and threw her stained service towel on the moving liquid.

She grabbed Stella's wrist, trying to blot any trace of wine off Stella's cuff. What Stella failed to realize was the hippie chick had applied a 'paper ant' to her blouse. A gig proffered by the mean gray-haired lady only moments ago before these women arrived. It would dissolve in forty-eight hours. The target would never know it was there.

The waitress reached back towards the window during the chaos and retrieved the small silver voice-activated recorder. In the commotion no one saw her walk outside and hand the recorder to the irritated stern woman in the shadows.

Chapter Thirty-Four

—∞—

"Okay if I make a fire?" she yelled at Stella, who was busy making breakfast.

"Sounds good to me. Thanks."

Maggie wasn't use to Bay Area fog; seemed wetter than the Kentucky kind. The moisture had seeped into her bones last night as she walked to the car; she hadn't stopped shivering since. Maybe a combination of weather and circumstances, she contemplated, studying the kindling's architecture. She was glad Jim had taught her how to make a fire, among other things.

She placed the kindling in a teepee fashion over her tightly crushed newspaper nuggets with enough oxygen to feed the fire. She struck the match on the hearth. *Matches, kind of like soldiers. Very useful and necessary, but after their usefulness, they are disposable*, she thought flicking the small burnt stick into the blue flames.

She stepped back, coffee cup in hand, enjoying the jumping flames' heat as it chased the morning chill upwards towards the living room's cathedral ceilings. Stella's new aesthetic of total white gave one the feeling of frosty detachment, as did the dead Boston fern by the Eames chairs, now freckled with brown curls of once-vibrant green leaves.

Stella had said her house was now decorated in mid-century style. Maggie had hooted when she heard that. "What the flip does that mean? You mean that Danish crap from our childhood? Does that mean we're now mid-century?" she had laughed. She wondered if Jim Morrison was alive if he'd pen an update to his song *20th Century Fox* to *Mid-Century Fox*. Marin pretentiousness. She missed her ranch.

As she watched the fire grow, she went over all the questions in her mind. Things were happening way too fast. She worried about how Stella might be dealing with the information overload. She seemed okay this morning, as evidenced by the aroma coming out of the kitchen. Everything for now was alright in her world, especially with Stella's homemade breads.

Maggie studied the large abstract painting of blue and gray swirls above the mantel. "Is this painting new?" she asked Stella, as she walked towards the kitchen for a refill.

"Yeah, it's my one big extravagance from the divorce," Stella yelled, as she pulled the cinnamon rolls from the oven.

"This might sound weird but it kinda reminds me of Sarah's eyes. Didn't she say her mother was an artist?"

Stella froze. She wiped her hands on her striped apron and rounded the corner. "Oh my god, Maggie, you're right. I think this is a painting by her mother! How odd is that?"

"Ah, cheese and crackers, Stella! It's that synchronicity thing, like Sophia and Sarah were talking about. I'm texting Sarah right now to see if this is by her mother."

The rarely used doorbell rang, startling Stella. No one ever came to her door—and that's the way she liked it. Her heart raced as she opened the right side of the double front door. A woman in a chauffer's uniform stood before her in a perfectly professional stance and handed her an envelope. "Special delivery for Stella St. James, ma'am."

"I'm Ms. St. James," she said as she reached for the envelope. She hated to be called ma'am, but knew her days of being a Miss were, sadly, behind her, just as surely were her days of being a Mrs.

"Please sign here," the delivery woman said, pointing to her clear Lucite clipboard. Stella did as instructed. Awkwardly, she realized she should tip the person.

"Uh, please, wait a second while . . ."

"That won't be necessary," the delivery woman said as she smoothly turned about face and walked away.

Puzzled and a bit frightened, Stella slowly closed the door, intrigued by the unexpected package. Never had a limo delivery before.

"What is it?" Maggie asked.

"Don't know. Looks expensive. It appears to be an invitation or something," she said as she pulled out an elegantly monogrammed card, with three large, extravagantly intertwined letters, SRA, over a five-pointed star.

"It appears to be an invitation."

> *Lillian Juliette de St. Remy Aubert graciously invites you to the premier of "Dior's Dolls" at Paris Fashion Week.*
>
> *The House of Dior will debut its Spring Couture collection inspired by the Theatre de la Mode fashion dolls of 1945.*
>
> *Reception at The Ritz Hotel to immediately follow.*

Also enclosed were a personal note and a photograph: "My darling Stella. It has been a very long time since I last saw you. Gabriel and I would be honored if you could join us for this special occasion. Since it's been so long since we've seen each other, I've enclosed a picture of me with my son. We hope to see you at the fashion show."

The photo shook in Stella's hand.

"What's wrong?" Maggie yelled, rushing to Stella's side.

"It's him. The man at the restaurant!"

"What man?" Maggie said, alarmed. "The blind date creep?"

"No. Well, uh, I didn't tell you everything that happened that night," Stella said weakly, hunching slightly as if Maggie was going to let loose with a round-house punch.

Maggie pursed her lips and crossed her arms with such disgust her mass of curls jiggled. She was bracing for the next unending wave of revelations.

"Oh good," Maggie said. "You can tell me about your damn hemorrhoids but not about some mystery man? What's next?"

"I was going to tell you, but there's been a lot of stuff happening lately, ya know. That night—at the restaurant, on the blind date from hell—there was a man there who was watching me."

The hairs raised on the back of Maggie's neck, fearing for what she might hear next.

"When I left the restaurant in tears, I saw him in the parking lot."

"Did he try to hurt you?" Maggie barked, readying for a fight to protect her best friend.

"Actually, quite the opposite. I could tell by his expression that he wanted to help me, comfort me, but he couldn't approach me. I could feel his compassion."

"Wait a minute, Stella. Isn't this that geeky French kid who visited you and your mom back when we were in high school?"

"It would appear so." Stella marveled at how geekdom looked so much more appealing in adulthood.

"This woman—Lilli—was my mother's closest friend," Stella uttered. She felt a pang of pity, remembering her mother's mostly friendless adult life. Stella's father had been her mother's best friend. Her mother had spent most of her waking hours, working hard, dressing rich women—none of which were her friends. Stella quickly walked over and hugged Maggie. "I'm so grateful you're here."

Her mother's physical image hadn't changed much through the years after her father's disappearance, but something had changed. After the devastating news, Stella sometimes wouldn't even notice her mother had entered the room—her energy was so dim.

She had not only lost her father forever, but also her mother. She felt like an orphan before the fact. Yet when Lilli visited, her mother would perk up, come alive again as she must have been once upon a time.

She had prayed really hard for her mom to stay happy. And, of course, her prayers had not been answered, proving there was no God.

"Wow, a personal invitation to a Dior show. Even I know that's big. We are going, right?" Maggie asked a little apprehensively.

"I think we have to go, at least to honor my mother's memory," Stella said, wiping a tear while she checked her face and hair in the mirror by the front door. Since the Change, she felt like a dim light herself, unable to shine. She half-hoped the handsome Frenchman would find her attractive. But she wasn't going to bet on it. *What the hell*, she thought, *I'm going to a couture Paris fashion show.*

"I'll send out an RSVP today in the mail. Now, let's have one of those cinnamon buns and get ready to go to the shop."

Chapter Thirty-Five

—∞—

"They plan on meeting at Lourdes for the anniversary?" Gustav said into the speaker phone after listening to the recording Kathleen played for him.

"It appears so, Your Eminence. I told you those two were troublemakers. What shall we do?" she asked, hoping this tidbit of news would ease her entrance into Gustav's good graces after her last demanding call.

"What do you think is causing all these women to blasphemy the Virgin Mary?" she asked, not without a little bit of self-serving curiosity as to his opinion.

She knew the cardinal was ambitious, hoping one day to become pope. She wanted to know more about what was really going on. After her questioning the cardinal about the Church's downplaying Mary's importance and her power, she had a renewed interest in the Third Secret. She suspected it wasn't by accident that sightings were becoming more frequent.

"My dear Sister," Gustav started, knowing she yearned to be called that again, as if she could go back in time and redeem herself, "that is not for us to answer. We must pray and reflect. With Jesus' mercy, we will know the answer. Thank you for your diligence. It will not go unnoticed." He clicked off.

Today was not a good day to get into such a conversation with *that* woman. He really found her offensive, as he found most women, but especially her. He had worked diligently to appease all after her damage to the children. It had cost the Church millions. He didn't mind paying that for the priests, but to give out money for the sins of what he thought was a radical feminist lesbian was beyond generous.

His power lay in knowing she would do anything to get back into the Church's favor. She could prove to be quite useful if utilized correctly.

He was still unnerved since his meeting with Lucas Stanchir. Stanchir appeared to be overly concerned about the coming galactic alignment in December 2012, predicting the alignment would cause a shift in consciousness that jeopardized the present industry of war. He had repeatedly insisted they had to be prepared with a counter attack. Gustav felt personally threatened when Lucas mentioned the staggering costs of paying off the sexual abuse cases. He reminded the cardinal that with the closure of so many churches in the United States, ending war was not a profitable solution for the Vatican either.

The Vatican had hired GA7 to launch shaming campaigns against the victims of the sexual assaults. By exhausting the victims daily with published "leaks" about prior behavior, they were too busy defending themselves leaving no time or energy to join forces. The Church had handled this in-house for years, but with more and more publicity about the molesting priests, they needed outside professional help to mold the message. It was critical for the Church to go along with GA7's plan if they were to survive. On the Church's behalf, he had no choice but to agree with Lucas' plan on generating fear in the world.

Surprisingly, he felt slightly remorseful when he had signed the lease on the old convent. He tried to remember when his commitment to the poor, his compassion for the downtrodden, had ebbed. Attending to the needs of the less fortunate in the beginning of his clerical career had been so rewarding.

Maybe it all changed for him in the 1960s. First, when he had read the Third Secret, then Vatican II. So much turmoil; the world was changing too quickly. He hated seeing women clamoring for power, especially in the church. Sister Lucia's hand written message was ominous.

He still bore the scars of his upbringing which had formed both his fear and loathing of women. His mother believed beating the young boy would make him love God more, make him God-fearing and all.

In the company of men, he felt comfort. Them he understood. Having spent so much time among them every day had intensified his dislike of women even more. He didn't trust them. They had powers men would never possess.

That was why the Church had to silence those who referred to God as Mother, such as Pope John Paul I and Francis of Assisi. That's why they had to regulate the vision stories of Mary. Keep her a virgin, untouched and without sin, even if Jesus had never taught that sex was sinful. He didn't care. Facts were for fools. Time to weight the scales for their side.

Shortly, Lucas would be in possession of the lab technician's report. It centered on the volume of rapidly rising chatter and spikes on the random number generators. Chatter focused on the hot subjects like the Virgin Mary, Third Secret, 2012.

Lourdes was really spiking.

He picked up the phone and pressed redial. "We need you here—now!"

Chapter Thirty-Six

—∞—

"**W**ow, this place is hopping, Stella. Been so long since I shopped, I forgot that women actually enjoy doing this. Personally, I'd rather go horse riding. That's my therapy."

"Shhh, I'm trying to make a living here, if you don't mind. Remember all the 'For Lease' signs we saw coming from the airport? Please, let's not add my store to the inventory. I've got to sell those couture Dior pieces in the window before I can buy more. Extremely overpriced and very expensive."

Even in the affluent Bay Area, Stella's shop the Third Act had not been immune from the recent global crash of the economy. Fortunately, Dibrovna's daughter, Sylvania, was a creative genius when it came to knowing the store's market. She had recently launched a social media campaign and had added all the goddess books by the local author, Jean Shinoda Bolen. If your customers are Juicy Crones, why not celebrate them? she had asked Stella. Now business was starting to boom. Especially when they started selling Stella's One-Off Tops: small abstract art motifs Stella sketched, inspired by Joan Miro, Kandinsky, even the quilts of Gee's Bend, and then hired hand-beaders and embroiderers to embellish the designs onto her bias-cut tunics. Each one an original and numbered.

Dibrovna was showing some new arrivals to one of their loyal customers when she saw the pair. "Maggie, my dear child. Excuse me, please," she said, wriggling between the circular racks, as she reached her arms out to Maggie.

Though she was not quite five years older than the two friends, her life experiences as a war refugee made her seem much older and wiser. The news of Maggie's son's death had devastated her whole family. She had lost both a son and her adoptive father in the Bosnian war. A never-ending pain, only dulled with the passage of time.

"So good to see you two together again," Dibrovna exclaimed, her smile lighting up her wrinkled face.

Maggie stiffened in Dibrovna's arms, her pain too close to the surface. They shared a special bond now: mothers who lost children in unnecessary wars. It wasn't a club she had ever wanted to join.

Dibrovna had opened their eyes since she answered the gallery's Craig's List ad. She and her refugee family had recently been brought to San Francisco by a human rights group. Dibrovna, still in a semi-robotic state then, had told Stella being around art was helping her to block the images of war. Images such as digging up a parsnip in the thawed soft garden soil only to find it wrapped in a finger bone from the burials the winter before. Dibrovna said, other than losing her family members, the worst loss were her friendships.

It was Dibrovna who had comforted Stella in her small home in Novato after Todd's leaving. "Family stays with loved ones in their times of trouble—not turn their backs," she said as she pledged her and her family's undying devotion to Stella.

"It's not depression that is tearing you up," the Bosnian woman said to Stella at the time. "It's the longing to be loved—that's it. That simple. Those pills don't love you. You had a breaking open so you could move into *your* third act."

That's how the plan was hatched for Stella to open her clothing boutique for midlife women in Mill Valley, with Dibrovna as her faithful assistant.

Sylvania was behind the register, finishing up her sale to the local famous red-haired blues musician.

"Wow, it looks like we are doing great business, Dib," Stella said, using her pet name for her assistant.

"You know Stella how the women of Marin are. They are enlightened but they are still rich. They want to look good but also to support others," Dibrovna said. Ten percent of the pre-tax profits of the store went to supporting international women's support groups at Dibrovna's urging. The customers loved donating towards rebuilding women's lives.

"Dibrovna, I need to talk to you about the store. Can we go across the street and get a cup of coffee?" Stella asked.

"Sure. Sylvania, I will be back in a while. If you need me, I have my cell," Dibrovna said, placing it into her trouser pocket.

"I really like those pants, Dibrovna," Maggie said.

"Thank you. They're from one of our regular designers right here in Northern California. Petaluma, I believe is where she is from. I'll show you her line when we come back."

"I'd like that. My wardrobe really needs some help. I don't want to look like a country bumpkin in Paris."

"You are going to Paris, too?" Dibrovna asked. Stella searched her assistant's face, hoping she wasn't hurt by not being invited.

"I'll tell you about it when we sit," Stella quickly added, as the three women crossed Lytton Square in downtown Mill Valley to the Depot Book Store & Café. As always, it was busy. Great food and perfect timing as they luckily found a cozy table off in the corner to talk—Mill Valley prime real estate.

"As you know I'm going on a buying trip to Paris for Fashion Week. Just this morning, I received an invitation to go to the Dior show," Stella said, trying not to show her excitement.

"Good for you, dear!" Dibrovna exclaimed, clapping her hands, happy Stella had something to look forward to and not bothered in the least at not being invited.

"Maggie is going to join me because I've also decided to extend the trip a bit. We are going to be taking a little side trip while in France. We are meeting some women at Lourdes," she hurriedly said, hoping her swiftness of speech hid what she said.

The conversation immediately changed in tone. Dibrovna lowered her head, staring at her employer over her thick glasses. She would rather walk on broken glass than to wound Stella. But Stella needed to be informed.

"I know how you feel about the church," Dibrovna said to Stella, holding up her hand to ward off an argument. "Let me talk, please. Thank you. You must know that Lourdes is a very sacred site, true?" Dibrovna asked, eyeing Stella carefully.

"I'm aware of that," Stella said defensively, "but something has come up . . ."

"Have you seen Her?" Dibrovna bravely interrupted.

Stunned, Stella stammered.

"Stella—have you seen 'Her'? The Virgin?"

Seeing how flustered Stella was becoming, Dibrovna lightened her tone and grabbed Stella's hand. "Your face says yes. I have seen this look many times. Do you know about the Virgin and Medjugorje, my village in my country Bosnia-Herzegovina?"

"Seriously?" Stella looked to Maggie in disbelief at the revelation of yet another Marian Apparition.

Maggie threw her hands up in the air, shrugged and deferred to Dibrovna.

Stella was starting to wonder if she was the last damn woman in the world to not have seen "the vision."

"It started June of 1981. Four teen-aged girls from our small poor village of Medjugorje were taking an evening walk up to a peak outside of town known as the Mountain of Thunder. At the top of the peak was a tall white-washed cross to commemorate the 1,900th anniversary of Christ's crucifixion. It was built to protect Medjugorje from hail, sometimes the size of boiling potatoes that rained down destroying all the crops. Winds would blow hard, starting fires everywhere. But after the cross was built, the storms and the fires almost completely ceased. It was a very sacred place for my people to visit.

"That night these girls said they saw a beautiful lady on top of the hill with a child wrapped in a blanket in her arms. Said she was about twenty years old with blue eyes and black hair, a crown of stars around her head.

The lady smiled at them and sang 'go in the peace with God' and disappeared into the mist, leaving them in ecstasy.

"They returned the next evening, this time with two village boys and saw a big flash of light. The lady had appeared again, except without a child in her arms. All six children climbed the hill in less than two minutes, without any scrapes or cuts from the brambles and rocks. Even the most experienced climber could not make it to the top in less than ten minutes. Something not from our world was going on, I assure you.

"When they returned the following evening, crowds of thousands followed them. Then, three flashes of light, and the lady said 'peace, peace, peace, only peace. Peace must reign between man and God and between all people.'

"Later that summer more than one hundred witnesses said they had looked up to the cross, and it had been replaced with a statue of the Madonna, and they saw in gold letters the word 'mir' meaning peace, in the sky above the mountains. Some of the witnesses observed the sun spinning and pulsating, throwing off giant red, purple and blue bubbles in the sky.

"There was, of course, much argument that the children were possessed with Satan, or they were tricksters. When the children told the local priest the story, they all recited the story in the same exact words.

"Even after all this time, some twenty-plus years later, the Lady still comes to my country, one of the most blood soaked in history," Dibrovna said with a fierce pride, tears in her cloudy eyes.

"Nobody can deny it is Mary, Mother of Jesus. She comes to bring us peace. She comes to the women and children for help. Do you not think that is why we are seeing her everywhere?" As tears trickled down her cheeks, she blotted the moistness with her slightly-used napkin.

"Here, look at my rosary," she said as she pulled it out of her trouser pocket. "It is made of crushed rose petals and aurora borealis crystals. You see these stones? They are from the hill where the Virgin stood. Very sacred, very blessed stones. Here, take this with you, Stella," Dibrovna said as she tried to place the rosary into Stella's hand.

"I can't accept that, Dib. It's too precious."

"No, you are what is precious—to me, my family, your family. You saved us. It took two long years to emigrate but you stood with us all the way after we arrived. And Maggie—all of you women: something is going on here. My gut tells me you need protection. Here," Dibrovna said as she curled Stella's fingers around the warm-to-the-touch worn rose-colored beads.

Stella felt awkward holding the rosary. It had been decades since she had held one and recited decades. She pulled it over her head and tucked it into her sweater. She knew it wasn't jewelry, but wanted it close to her body with her star necklace.

"Are you going to answer me?" Dibrovna demanded, not about to let go of the subject.

"About Mary?" Stella asked. She looked at Maggie, who nodded her assent. In hushed tones, she and Maggie proceeded to tell Dibrovna the abbreviated story of what had happened to them.

"I knew something was going on. It is a sense you learn to develop, to study people closely and pay attention, when you have lived in war. You also learn to know when to keep your mouth shut. You were smart to not repeat these stories. Since Fatima, there has been a lot of aggression from the Church and the powerful to stop these stories. Mostly, the struggle has been about the secrets."

"Secrets?" Maggie asked. "Do you mean the three secrets told at Fatima?"

"Those are not the only ones. The Bosnian children have been told secrets too. And like Sister Lucia, they have been told not to tell anyone. This makes some in the Church very nervous.

"When powerful men get nervous, they get dangerous," she warned.

Chapter Thirty-Seven

—∞—

"I smell funkier than a Tower of Power horn riff. Mind if I take a quick shower, sweetie?"

"Be my guest. I'm going to start dinner. Crab cakes sound good? I've got some excellent wine I'd like you try, too. It'll be here when you're done."

Stella was still puttering in the kitchen when the freshly scrubbed Maggie, cuddled up in one of Stella's expensive robes, leaned against the door frame. "She's right, ya know," Maggie drawled. She accepted the glass of wine Stella handed her, taking a sip as she watched Stella flip the sizzling golden crab cakes in the bubbling butter-filled pan, while simultaneously shaking the cast iron nine-inch skillet where she was roasting pine nuts with rosemary sprigs for their tossed salad of baby greens. She noisily sucked in her saliva before it fell from the corners of her mouth as she marveled at Stella's performance.

"Right about what?" Stella asked as she reached for the open bottle of 1969 Louis M. Martini 'Special Selection' Cabernet Sauvignon to refill her glass.

"Too many secrets make powerful men nervous. I know. Jim had secrets."

"What the hell are you talking about?" Stella asked, afraid she might not want to know. The last few days reminded her of a sliced-up golf ball. Her father loved to cut into one and put it in her hand, laughing at her as the powerful rubber insides started expanding and uncoiling, popping out of her small weak hand. Recent events kept expanding, uncoiling—about to pop, unable to control anything.

"You know that Jim had a high security clearance when he was in the Army, right?"

"Yeah. Todd and I would sometimes play a guessing game about what he did in the military. You know, 007 stuff."

"Well, not far wrong. Jim was a remote viewer."

Stella slowly laid down her knife on the chopping board. "I'm not sure what you are about to tell me. But I think it is not something discussed at my kitchen island. Why don't you go out on the deck, turn on the heaters and start a fire in the pit? I'll be right back," she said, removing the skillets from the burners as she turned to go up the stairs.

Maggie easily started her second fire of the day in the custom-made fire pit. As she turned on the outside propane heaters, she gazed at the grotto nestled darkly in the corner. She looked upward and asked Jim's forgiveness. "Babe, I hope I'm not betraying you, but time has come for me to tell Stella. Please guide me and help keep us safe." She rubbed the rounded face of the old Bulova watch, hanging loosely from her thin wrist.

She jumped at the creak of the French door, as Stella stepped out onto the deck, wine bottle in one hand and a jeweled Cloisonné box in the other.

"Cocktail hour, which now that we are entering the early evening of our lives, appears to be anytime we damn well please," Stella said with a smile, popping the cork on a chilled bottle of Bodega Sanchez Wine, Special Reserve Sauvignon Blanc.

"First, I need a sip—or two. I feel a magical mystery tour coming up. I don't know what a remote viewer is, but my gut tells me I need to be medicated for this latest bit of news." Stella eased herself into one of the newly purchased teak lounge chairs. She patted the lounger next to her.

"Sit—we're going to smoke some pot." She ceremoniously opened the small box, releasing the skunkiness into the night air.

"What!" Maggie's voice bounced off the mountain and into all of Stella's neighbor's backyards. "Sorry."

"Don't worry. Need I remind you—this *is* Marin."

"Where the hell did you get that? And when did you start smoking that stuff again? Hell, I don't think I've even smelled it since I was in high school."

"I've smoked it on and off—mostly off—for years, but after the divorce and seeing *her* for the first time, I went to one of the medical marijuana clinics. It's helped me cope with the anxiety. Plus, it's organic," Stella said as she handed Maggie a delicate painted glass pipe with its pungent smoke drifting from the bowl. "Try it."

Maggie put the glass pipe to her lips while Stella lighted the dark green vegetation, studded with crystals that glimmered in the winter moonlight. She clicked her BBQ lighter and advised Maggie to suck very slowly.

Maggie tried to comply, but failed. She coughed so long and hard she almost peed her pants. A gulp of wine helped halt the spasms. She handed the pipe to Stella and watched as she lit the bowl. As she watched the smoke rise in spirals only to dissipate in the cool darkness of night, she wondered what it was like for Stella that night last fall. *Was she scared, all alone?* Was the story she was about to tell Stella going to make her more afraid, never able to leave her house again? Hard to gauge Stella's fragility, her own intuition obscured from her recent traumas. Maggie took her time. It was the first time she was telling this guarded secret to anyone outside her immediate family.

Stella took another hit of the pipe. "You know, sometimes, after a year or so of sex, male shrimp turn female. Maybe that's what happened to Todd."

"What? That was kinda random, honey. You okay? Oh my god. Let me guess. Don't tell me you think you 'screwed him gay'?" Maggie blurted with laughter trying not to snort out her wine. "Oh my poor, stoned, delusional Stella. For crying out loud! Maybe you should back off that pipe."

"And you better not spill anything on my chairs! They're Smith Hawken! No, listen to me—seriously," Stella insisted while puffing away. "Don't you think human sexuality is like a, I don't know, maybe a gas gauge or something. I adore a great set of breasts—I think they're beautiful. But I don't want them sexually. It doesn't make me want to sleep with a woman. At times, Todd was one of the manliest men I knew. I acknowledge my man-meter might differ from yours. I don't regularly hang out with uber masculine men," she ended noticing Maggie was trying her hardest to not start laughing again at her.

"C'mon, I'm hurting here, girlfriend. We had a marriage. I miss his kindness, tenderness, just his companionship. Besides you, he was my best friend. Now, I'm, well, lost. I feel like the last kid picked for dodge ball, like I'm going to die an old maid."

"Too late," Maggie said, blowing out a cloud of smoke. "You can't die an old maid once you've married, honey," she said in an effort to lighten the conversation. "You know, I bet you could be woo-wooed all day long and be gloriously happy, huh? Man, this is fun!"

"That's a fact, Jack!" Stella said, giggling. "Try it—you might just like it. And who knows, you could enlighten the whole world," she finished, stretching her open arms to the Universe as if she had just uttered the most profound statement by a human in this lifetime.

"Did you know they used to grow pot—hemp—on my property back in the '40s to use for the war? They made all American farmers watch a government film called Hemp for Victory. All 4-HRs were urged to grow up to two acres!"

"That's hilarious! You know, I bet that's why pot is still illegal," Stella mused. "They say it's about stopping the gateway to hard drugs, but it's not. If people smoked pot, there would be no wars. Period. Stoned people don't fight—they eat, drink and make merry. Then they go to sleep." They both erupted into snorting laughter.

It was good to hear Stella's laugh float off into the dark of the night. *If only you knew*, Maggie thought. She figured now was as good as any time to start some of the conversation that needed to happen.

"Okay, Ms. Hemorrhoids, I want to be honest with you, too. No more secrets from this time forward." Maggie promised as a preamble to what she was about to reveal, as she slung her slim legs to the side of the lounge chair. "It's my time to come clean. Jim was psychic spy."

"A what?"

"A psychic spy or quantum warrior as they call them in the private sector. Since 1975 until the day he died, he would use extra-sensory perception to view people and locations miles away and gather information." She looked at Stella, evaluating if was safe for her to continue.

Stella lit the pipe's bowl and sucked deeply all the way from the tips of her toes.

"They would give the remote viewers global coordinates and then have them do these doodling exercises while they concentrated on the coordinates. Eventually, because of the power of the mind, they could describe colors, buildings, the weather—everything. Just by using their minds.

"Jim was used to locate hostages, SCUD bombs, and even Osama bin Laden. He said it was easy—he tapped into the Grid, as he called it. I remember one cocktail hour when he said 'we are all antennas, just have to turn on the receivers.' He said we all could be telepathic, even said we were designed to be. Just have to turn the damn machine on. 'Can't watch TV with the power off,' he told me.

"You know what Sophia and Sarah said about 2012 in Berkeley last night?" asked Maggie. "It's true. Jim would talk about consciousness and the Grid and how the next war would be fought without bullets. He told me the military had changed. Its purpose used to be valor but now its objective was numbers. Kill as many as possible—and rake in the money for the Elite.

"In Vietnam they started using simulations like video games on shooting and killing. Since the weapons remained the same, they switched to software—changing brains. He said even the Russians had used something called 'Intentional Harming.' A form of warfare where you injure people from afar.

"Jim had told me a lot about the business of war. You know that a lot of our warfare is conducted by private corporations now, like GA7 where Jim worked—all black budget work. The taxpayer has no idea of the billions we spend on this. Not part of the defense budget. They have no governmental oversight so they can do what they want. The only limit is money. Jim used to talk to me about how peace is the last thing any government wants. There's more money to be made with war. At least nowadays. I've been thinking even these visions could be part of a quantum war."

"I'm not surprised," Stella said, not the least bit bothered by Maggie's revelation. "Jim had always been psychic. And our brains are more powerful, we are more powerful, than we realize. He told me that once."

They both leaned back in the lounge chairs, staring off into the night's vast sky, lost deep in thought. Each missing Jim Barrett in her own way.

"*Ham and Cheese.* That's what Jim and I were—ham and cheese. A perfect fit together. You know, I probably have enough tears inside me to cry for every day until I die—and then some. But that doesn't bring my boys back. It's when I smile that they come to me and fill my heart with joy until my heart about bursts. No one can take away my joyful memories."

Stella gazed up into the heavens and patted Maggie's leg. "Yes, let's focus on our joy."

The two good friends sat back, repacked the pipe, and continued their star gazing.

"Hmmm. You ever wonder why we don't grow hair on our palms, and the skin doesn't tan? And look," Maggie said, pushing at her palm with her index finger, "the skin doesn't move. Why is that?"

"Sweetie, time to put the pipe away. Dinner's going to get cold. Let's eat."

They proceeded indoors to enjoy the most wonderful food they had ever eaten—and everything else in the kitchen.

Chapter Thirty-Eight

—∞—

"**I**sn't she still so divine?" Lilli asked her son as she sat on her cushioned stool, carefully examining Faïence's gown. "The cut of this gown is pure perfection."

"But of course, maman. You and *grand-peré* taught him well," Gabriel responded.

"He was such an eager student of all things. *Maestro* had the magic touch, so meticulous in his craft. We recognized his genius as soon as he joined us in the *atelier*. Could tell just by the way his long fingers caressed the fabric. Now, a stitch here and there, and she will shine again. Faïence, our shining star."

"Oui. I think, though, that she needs to go home for a while."

Lilli knew he was talking about Mary's House—Chartres Cathedral. Like she had done with Dior, she had introduced her son to the mysterious Gothic cathedral. During her son's introductory walk on the mystical labyrinth, she told him the story of Dior's first appearance onto the stage of their shared destiny:

"Dior first traveled to Callian from Paris to visit his childhood governess. Before the war, he and his sister would visit occasionally in the summer and help in her garden. They would sometimes help your *grand-me're* sell her herbs along with their produce at the market. And

Dior was always presented with a huge bouquet of lilies, his favorite flower. *Grand-me're* loved how much enjoyment her prized flowers gave him, especially the Star of Bethlehem variety. They had an immediate connection.

"It pleased her to teach him not only the artistic design of the garden, but how to work with nature. She had explained compost, complementary planting by color and height, and how to attract the insects to the ecosystem to sustain balance and health. Taught him the magic of worm composting using was left in the fields to boost the soil of the rocky terrain. She grew the best vegetables in the village, even out of season.

"He and my mother became very good friends, working the soil together, and enjoying the fruits of their labors during frequent meals at our home. I was just entering my teen years, so he was like an uncle to me. Dior was mesmerized watching my father cut and drape, with grunted acknowledgements of why step one was necessary to achieve step five. When war came, his passionate plea convinced the French Army to assign him to our lovely ancient hilltop town on farm duty.

"It was 1941, during World War II, when he told me he once had a dream, as a child growing up in Paris, of a young redheaded French girl. He was convinced it was me in the dream. Said we were destined to meet because he knew I would help him when he grew up and become famous for making women beautiful. But, of course, I knew this the first time I saw him.

"Like most French girls of my generation, we were schooled in sewing and made our own clothes. But I had advanced skills from assisting my father in the atelier after school. I taught Dior how to 'listen' to the cloth and allow it to be what it wanted to be, like I had been taught.

"Before Dior and I walked the labyrinth, he said he had been raised as an 'enlightened' Catholic, who questioned the dogma of the Church. Said his grandmother was quite mystical and believed in destiny, omens, fortune telling and wanted her grandson to also be a believer. All his life he had consulted with clairvoyants for reassurance and clarification.

"One day, we walked into the village center and sat by the town's fountain. I taught him how I could 'see' using the powers of the water.

I went into a trance once and told him: 'you will be very poor, but women will be very lucky for you and bring you success. You will soon earn large sums of money from them and you will have to travel widely.'

"Later that same year, on a family outing to Chartres, I took Dior underground to show him the crypt that once was the main Druidic sanctuary of Gaul. Swearing him to secrecy, it was there, beside the sacred spring that I told him the full story of the goddesses, Mary, The Lady of the Stars, and the future Shift, the Return of the Divine Feminine.

"I told him about the tunic, and gave him a gold five-pointed star with blessed fabric sealed inside, which he carried with him every day until he died. That was the seed of the special doll.

"Soon after he returned to Paris after the war, he found me and requested I work with him as his *premier*, draping his designs. I worked with him until the day he died."

As they reached the end of the labyrinth, Lilli whispered in young Gabriel's ear the story of the Lady of the Stars and his part in it. Gabriel remembered being so filled with rapturous joy he thought he would burst. He vowed to his mother that day with the sunlight streaming through the many multi-colored windows that he would dedicate his life to the Lady. And someday help tell the true story.

"Yes, we should take Faïence to Mary's house. I still have enough of the holy fabric to fix the gown, if need be, but immersion might be needed at this time.

"Son, you and I are the only ones left living who know the power of this doll and her place in history. It's our duty to protect her with our lives. You have seen our ancestor's Lost Painting. Remember what you learned in Amsterdam. Soon the powerful and their war machines will know of the doll. We must act."

Chapter Thirty-Nine

—∞—

"Thank God—or Mary, Jesus, Joseph and Oprah—for first class," Maggie sighed, as she lowered her lanky frame onto the six-foot long luxury flat seat with its own privacy divider, across the aisle from Stella.

"You know the last time—well, the only time—I flew to Europe was in economy class. Jim and I went to Italy to celebrate our 25th wedding anniversary," she said, as the flight attendant picked up her carry-on bag for stowing.

"Not so fast, missy. It's only a small bag. I'm good with it being right her with me," Maggie said, quickly grabbing the bag back, annoyed by the aggressive service.

Stella was already into flight mode. Routines helped her manage her over-the-ocean flight anxiety. First, she checked the contents of her tote bag: magazine tear sheets first in a plastic sleeve, then look books, and finally fashion show schedules in the big pocket, red pens and yellow highlighters in their appropriate slots. It helped her to focus and make prudent decisions before placing an order that had the potential to bankrupt her store. Anxious, both to get off the ground and start her tasks, she arranged the provided cotton duvet over her legs and buckled in.

"We were still living on a military wage and didn't mind giving up the comfort so we could spend money on other things on our trip," Maggie continued. "One of the most romantic times of my life. You know, I almost didn't go. Thought it was too much of an extravagance. But now I'll always have those memories. Life's short, Stella. We need to remember our next breath is not guaranteed."

Maggie tried to look out the airplane's window, but the view was blocked by the thick pea-soup fog as they sat on the tarmac of the San Francisco International airport. The weather increased her feelings of uneasiness. She stroked her star necklace, thinking about how much she missed her grandchildren. All she had ever wanted to be was a mother, wife, grandmother. She was grateful for those blessings. However, thoughts of her family made her think of the depressing state her country and the world faced.

Was this the world her husband and son had fought so hard for? She focused on what Jim had always told her in times of doubt: "Hope is like cherry pie. You just can't ever get enough. So keep hoping."

The flight attendant appeared with offers of champagne.

"That sounds perfect," Stella said. "What shall we toast to?"

"How about to us?" Maggie said, clinking her crystal glass across the aisle.

"This is my first time in Paris without him, you know. We always said it was our city," Stella said draining her glass a little too quickly.

"Oh, yeah—your honeymoon. You sure you're up for this?"

"No. Not sure. But I'm going. I just hope I can avoid all the special spots in the City of Lights that we had enjoyed together."

"You are aware that the Dior show is being held in the Pavilion de Marsan, part of the Louvre, right?" Maggie asked. She knew the Louvre was, of course, Mecca for anyone in the art world.

"Yes, but I won't be alone. Having you along makes all the difference. We can make new memories." Stella didn't add she was also looking forward to the Frenchman being her escort at the show.

Stella had indeed been to the Louvre many times. But she had never been inside the Pavilion de Marsan, a huge wedding cake of a structure on the western corner of the Palace complex where the first Theatre de la Mode had debuted in March 1945, shortly before the end of the war. She thought it a genius location to stage the 65th anniversary of the little dolls' premiere as part of this season's Dior collection. Maybe it would take some of the tarnish off the House from its latest scandal.

She opened the Dior commemorative look book that had been delivered soon after her invitation. There she was. Dazzling in her off the shoulder ivory gown with the sheer overlay of a skirt studded with blue-green glittering stars and leaves. A Lucien Lelong, she believed, but designed by Dior himself. It had been her favorite doll to play with in the basement of the City of Paris department store. Of course, at the time, they were just dolls to her. Maggie's research clued her in to the whole story, including Lilli's part of the historic show.

"Wow, it just dawned on me that our star necklaces were given to us by the same woman who helped designed the stars on the dress of the Lucien Lelong doll. She worked with Dior from his start."

"More synchronicity, heh?" Maggie said, as she stroked the silver star nested in the hollow of her neck.

"I'm a little nervous about seeing her son again, after the whole restaurant fiasco. It's awkward. Do I acknowledge his presence that night? I hate to even think about that night; well, before 'it' happened, I mean."

"Just do what you do, dear Stella. Smile, lower your gaze like you used to do—and keep your big mouth shut!" Maggie advised. "Not a time for conscious cleansing. Play it by ear. His mother is going to be there, right?"

"Yes! I'm so excited to see Lilli again. It's been so many years. Kind of makes me feel like I'm with my mom again. I wish she could see this show." She leaned her head back, closed her eyes, and laid her hand on her chest over her star necklace. "I'm so glad you came, Mags."

Stella rubbed her temples, trying to sort out all that had happened in such a short dizzy time. The Lady of Guadalupe, news of her grandchild, Josh's death, and now a gathering at Lourdes with her new-found friends. She felt like she had been running between raindrops ever since receiving Maggie's fateful text.

"More champagne, mademoiselles?" asked the flight attendant as she held up the just-opened glistening bottle wrapped in a crisp white cotton napkin. Grinning in unison, they nodded an eager *yes*. The attendant smiled. She noticed both women were posed exactly the same way, stroking their necklaces, as if one and the same.

Stella, satisfied with her fashion week organization, closed her notebook and put it in her Birkin. Mentally, she was prepared like a field marshal, ready for battle. It felt good to be functioning again. Recently, there had been a renewed interest in French designers at the store, after the so-called patriotic backlash against the French's refusal to join forces in Iraq. She couldn't believe how pathetic revolution was these days. Renaming French fries Freedom Fries? Oh yeah, that's standing up for your convictions. Like a bunch of friggin' five-year-olds!

The irony of attending an expensive runway show celebrating dolls created specifically to revive the couture French fashion industry and therefore feed its people and rebuild after a devastating war was not lost on her. She remembered Lilli once advising her teen-age self to have patience with her own country, America: "she is still a teenager." *Sometimes a raging hormonal teenager,* Stella thought.

* * *

As they prepared for touchdown, Maggie pulled out her compact to check if her almost twenty-four-hour-old makeup needed to be retouched.

Stella watched out of the corner of her eye. She was shocked when she saw Maggie smile and close the compact.

"How can you smile while looking at yourself in the mirror?" she hissed.

"What do you mean?" Maggie asked, wondering if she had done something wrong.

"I don't think I've looked at myself in the mirror and smiled since, well, since men stopped turning and looking at me."

"Oh, holy moly, Stella! You're still a stunning woman. Of course you don't look like you did twenty or thirty years ago. Nobody does, because you're not supposed to! I wish you knew your worth in the world. You know what I see when I look in the mirror? I see the woman my husband adored, the mom my 6'2" child wanted to snuggle with, the woman who lights up my grandsons' eyes. It's an insult to yourself to not smile. For cryin' out loud! You're just a different kind of beautiful now—riper."

Stella laughed at that, though her image of ripe quickly flashed onto rotting fruit. Definitely not a fruit producer anymore. Maybe Paris and the Frenchman would help improve her opinion of herself.

As they stood up and gathered their things after the long flight, the flight attendant came up with a lint brush. "Please, madames, let me help you freshen."

Maggie waved her off, not wanting anyone touching her. The attendant rolled the lint brush on Stella, placed it on the tray, and returned to her station. In the galley, she carefully placed the brush and Stella's used headphones in separate plastic bags.

As she was returning to place Maggie's headphones in a proper bag, she was interrupted by a woman who needed help with a stroller. She stuffed them quickly in a bag and went to assist the straggling passengers.

Upon return, she stared at the bags on the galley's counter. She couldn't remember which headphone belonged to which woman. She used her women's intuition and hoped she had it right as she dropped them into the outside pocket of her suitcase and prepared to meet her connection by the baggage claim.

So what if the specimens were mingled. Her thoughts were on what she could buy on Avenue des Champs Elysees with the large sum of money she was about to receive.

Chapter Forty

—∞—

"His Eminence is in his study waiting for you, sir." Martha, Cardinal Gustav's housekeeper, caught Lucas' tossed hat and coat as she closed the door.

"Thank you," he clipped, not addressing her by name even though he had known her for decades. After all, she was just a nun, the hired help.

In his heavy heeled stomp employed to keep air between his knocked knees, Lucas strode directly to the guest chair opposite Gustav's desk. They needed to discuss the troubling report and pictures received from the ex-nun in California. He sensed the potential trouble might necessitate a schedule change. Stanchir had no tolerance for such matters. He was a man used to getting his way.

"Good morning, Lucas. Please, be seated. Would you like some coffee and a pastry?" The cardinal was obviously trying to smooth his visitor's ruffled feathers before giving the latest bad news.

"Let's get to the matter at hand, shall we. I still want to visit the lab and check on its progress. What do you have?"

"These are the photos the ex-nun texted to me that I spoke to you about. She believes the blond and the redhead met the other two women at the Rwandan woman's speech. You are no doubt familiar with the Rwandan woman, who is touring the United States now, saying how the Virgin Mary saved her life? Yes, I thought you were," Gustav replied, noticing Lucas' dismissive grimace. Lucas' business was being up to the minute on any news—and keeping it in the correct lane.

"She said this one, the blond, seemed not to be the troublemaker Brent warned us about. Instead, she warned the redhead is the one to watch," Gustav said, brushing crumbs off his protruding belly. The cardinal casually handed the photos to Lucas, watching him place his reading glasses on his sharp nose. He was about to start reading the report out loud to his visitor when he detected a sharp intake of breath.

"Everything okay, Lucas?

"Yes. I am fine," Lucas replied, realizing he had cut his thumb on the old rusted bottle cap in his pocket. He hadn't been prepared for his reaction to seeing her photo. He was shocked that the still-sensuous Stella had a lasting spell over him. Also surprised she had left her house, thinking her still racked in panic from his little experiment. His heart raced with vengeance. The bottle cap was his daily reminder of her rejection.

So she was involved in this drama playing out before him? And it appeared her little friend, his late disloyal employee's widow, was her wing woman. Not quite a game changer, but a definite wrinkle.

"Is Brent still here, Cardinal?"

"Indeed, sir. He has been in the lab, working on setting up the project. Do you want me to have him retrieved?"

"That won't be necessary. I am ready to view the lab now. I can talk to him there."

"By all means." He rang a bell. Martha entered the den silently.

"Yes, Your Eminence?"

"Have the car brought around. We are going to the construction site." He had been very careful not to let her know what was being constructed at the old convent. She had worked with him, at his request, since Pope John Paul I's untimely and suspicious death in 1978, but he still did not trust her. He had learned not to trust anyone.

"Right away, sir."

* * *

"I think you will be pleasantly surprised at our progress, Lucas. In these few short months, we have almost finished. The lab should be up and running within the next seven to ten days," Gustav informed him on the drive to the old abandoned convent, out past Castel Gandolfo, the pope's summer residence.

"Good. Did you use the paper ants as I suggested?"

"Indeed. They were applied at the café to the blond. Unfortunately, she didn't add much to the evening's conversation by the time they expired. But we do know that the women are planning on gathering at Lourdes. I have ordered the ex-nun to immediately come to Vatican City. And as you requested, I have also contacted the Spaniard."

"Good."

"Please drive around to the back, driver. I don't want our car noticed from the road."

Though he hadn't asked for her assistance, Martha had called ahead to warn Brent that the two men were on their way. She liked him, and wanted him to be prepared for their visit.

"Lucas, Cardinal Gustav, welcome. Come on in and let me show you what we got so far." As they walked in the front door, it still appeared to be only an old convent—plain, lichen-encrusted ancient stone walls, nothing special. That completely changed when Brent opened the heavy oak door, ushering them into an electronic anteroom for full body screening. Once cleared, the stainless steel floor turned in a half circle and a state-of-the-art vault door which opened into a pristine, sterile environment.

"For right now, it only recognizes my face for security reasons. While you're here, we can scan you both to give you access also."

"Good," Lucas replied, as he entered the buzzing lab. "What's that humming?"

"Disruption Technology, sir, from the control hub. The pings are when the 'ears' retrieve useful electronic data. All the video screens are in position in the chamber, with electrical monitoring of the manipulation on the samples. We are working on the sequencing now. Come this way."

The chamber was in the tower of the old convent, with its 12th century curved architecture still in place on the outside, untouched, while the interior had been converted into a 21st century war room. All interior surfaces were clad in a special white vinyl that was not only easy to keep sanitary and virus-free, but vibrated constantly to eradicate any left-over DNA fragments or fingerprints.

Lucas, scanning the five rows of jumbo video displays, was elated. This was going to be his own little toy chest soon, he thought, as he watched the floor-to-ceiling checkerboard mass of monitors, each displaying horrendous images of beheadings, bombings, famine, rapes, torture—anything fear based. The wall of monitors faced the metal shelving containing glass vials wired together in a thin steel web of wires, filled with hosting water for the soon-to-be-deposited DNA specimens. Most of the vials were still empty, waiting for war to launch.

"This is where the DNA will be stored, in these tubes. This is simply one room of almost fifty others to accommodate the ten thousand vials necessary to affect the entire planet. This is the main room where we monitor all the alpha targets," Brent said. "The curvature of the building assists us in getting more saturated instant responses, due to constant motion from reflection and containment."

"Impressive. I see you have delivered what you promised. Now, I have another assignment for you."

"Sure. What do you need?"

"I need you to remote view these women and find out their whereabouts—now!" Lucas said, watching Brent's face for any reaction. He knew Brent had been a close friend of the redhead's husband and wanted to make sure he could put that relationship aside and tend to business. He wasn't too worried, because after all, Brent was a retired assassin, a cold-blooded killer. He knew those people genetically lacked the capacity to express empathy or compassion.

Brent kept his poker face. After all his training, he knew never to show emotion. His tools of the trade were to listen carefully and never react.

"Of course. I will need to be alone and prepare myself. Please be seated, and I should have the results in a short while." He left to go into one of the unfinished lab rooms and quickly calmed himself.

What the hell did Lucas want with Maggie? He could have sworn Jim had told him that Maggie knew nothing about what they had discovered together at GA7 about the Plan. Time to switch to the plan he and Jim had talked about—just in case. Now was that time. Brent needed to keep a constant watch on these two men—and to warn Maggie that she was in the cross hairs. Time to finesse his duality, like a championship chess game.

Still he had to give them something. *I need to know where they are too*, he thought. He sat down and dropped instantly into a trance. He had been remote viewing for so long, it was easy to go deep quickly. He loosely started drawing circles, bigger and bigger. Within a minute or so, his pen spiked up and then down in a swoop, four times. He could see lights, lots of lights, then a river. An Arch, a pyramid. Still faint images meaning they weren't quite at their destination yet. No mistaking, they were on their way to Paris. He could have gone longer for more details, but he wasn't ready to show all of his cards to Lucas. Not at this stage.

"Well, Lucas, it appears to me they are on their way to Paris. If you like I can have one of my guys check with the airlines to see if they have arrived."

"Yes. And hurry. We need to keep a close eye on them if our plan is to be successful. Have our operative collectors meet them at the airport. Notify customs and make the usual arrangements for their passports. That will be all." With that he turned and left.

Chapter Forty-One

—∞—

"**B**usiness or pleasure," the aggravated passport clerk barked at Maggie.

"Hopefully, both," she replied, flashing him a wide smile in hopes of a more friendly exchange. It didn't work.

"Where are you going?" His scowl knitted his bushy eyebrows together like a perturbed caterpillar.

"Paris. We are here for fashion week." She knew it was best to say the least right now. Still a little discombobulated from her jet lag, knowing these days the wrong words could get her in deep international trouble.

"Please wait," he instructed after consulting his computer for a few minutes. He turned his back to her, with her passport in his hand. Maggie was getting nervous. She turned and looked at Stella's face. *Is this normal procedure?* she mouthed.

Stella shook her head slightly, as if warning to Maggie to play along. The passport clerk eventually turned around and brusquely pushed her passport across the small podium. "Enjoy your stay, Mrs. Barrett," he said with no hint of sincerity.

"What was that all about?" she asked Stella.

"Not sure. It's obviously not the same traveling anymore since the Towers came down. But the way he treated you? Maybe simply a bad morning for him. But who cares? We're in Paris," Stella said hugging Maggie. "Let's get a taxi."

As they waited in the queue for the hour-long ride into Paris, Stella wrapped her pashmina tighter around her neck. It was a typical February morning in Paris, damp and gray, with slivers of pink rising above the horizon, teasing hints of a sunny day. She tried to look up towards the sun, but only saw water crystals wildly jitterbugging in the sky; too much activity for her tired retinas to sustain the staring. Stella didn't mind. To her it was perfectly Parisian.

All her worries about being back here without Todd disappeared as soon as she inhaled the sweet morning air outside the airport. Paris was intoxicating and inspiring. Even her annoyance with the stern customs desk clerk was soon forgotten by the time they arrived in the taxi queue. Standing behind a Japanese couple, the husband said something that caught her attention.

"The church of our Lady," the Japanese man said, louder each time, stabbing the location on the city map in his hand. The taxi driver was busy loading the couples' luggage, obviously having trouble understanding what the man was saying. As Stella took a step closer and leaned in, trying not to be noticed as she eavesdropped on their conversation, a stately Frenchwoman passing by on the sidewalk stopped to assist. "They want to go to Notre Dame, monsieur."

Of course, Stella thought. Her mind was looking for complexity when it was simple. Stella had momentarily forgotten that Notre Dame was French for Our Lady. Maybe a byproduct of aging. She sure hoped it wasn't post-traumatic stress caused by her long flight. She shook her bag to hear the reassuring jingle of pills.

"'Allo, dear Stella" the Frenchwoman said, her face beaming. "I am Lilli, and here comes my Gabriel."

Stella followed the Lilli's gestures and caught her breath. It *was* the man from the restaurant. Immediately the emotions of that night—embarrassment, humiliation, anger—flooded her mind, causing her right eyebrow to jump. He had witnessed it all. She pleaded as she looked into his eyes to stay silent.

"I didn't know you were planning to pick us up. I thought we had planned to meet at the hotel," Stella said, covering her eyes, as she fumbled in her purse for her sunglasses.

"A change in plans, my dear. The show has been moved to an earlier time. You know how these shows go. We have just enough time to drop off your luggage and change."

Stella was about to respond when the handsome Frenchman entered her personal space. He smiled and reached for her hand. She watched as he gently grasped her hand while cupping his other hand on top of hers. Her shoulders relaxed. She felt safe.

"Ms. St James, it is a pleasure to see you again. Your flight was good, no?"

She could feel her cheeks flush, embarrassed that at her age she responded like a school girl. "Yes, thank you. This is my best friend, Maggie Barrett," she stammered as she pulled her hand away and sucked in her stomach. Now she wished she had spent more time, like Maggie, in front of a mirror. She had planned to freshen up at the hotel.

"Nice to meet you. Sorry, I didn't catch your name."

"My name is Gabriel St. Remy Aubert, and this is my lovely mother, Lilli." He had barely gotten the words out of his mouth, when an unobservant priest walking by tripped, falling into Gabriel's arms. The priest grasped Gabriel's wrists to break his fall, leaving deep scratches. The priest steadied himself, mumbled an excuse and hurried on.

"I apologize for my brother's rudeness. We sometimes forget social niceties living in isolation," Gabriel said, as he pulled out a neatly folded handkerchief from the inside pocket of his sports jacket and wrapped it around his bleeding wrist.

"You're a priest?" Stella asked, her chest flushed red hot.

"Actually, I'm a Bollandist Jesuit. I was first a Jesuit priest, and then became a Bollandist. We perform historical research on saints to determine miracles."

Maggie said, "I've heard of your group. I'm researcher, too—a librarian. I look forward to some fascinating talks with you."

* * *

The "priest" tugged on his latex gloves, then ripped off the stiff white cloth band around his neck as he entered the airport. By the time he met with the American in the airport bathroom, he had discarded his jacket and hat in separate trashcans.

"In here," the American said, nodding towards the handicapped stall. The American popped open his briefcase and settled it across his bended knee.

"Slowly remove the gloves. I don't want any of the sample to become friable." He removed the slim scalpel from its vacuumed sealed pouch and began to meticulously scrape each of the fake priest's fingernails, placing the substance in the sterile small vial.

"That should be enough," he said, throwing a thick band of cash to the common, middle-aged French thug. "Hurry, you damn old fool," the American said, pushing the petty criminal out of the restroom. "I still have to meet the stewardess."

Chapter Forty-Two

—∞—

"S*'il vous plaît, mademoiselles*, this way. The car is right over here," Gabriel said as he walked ahead, pushing the luggage cart full of Louis Vuitton bags, topped with a few mismatched bags he rightly assumed belonged to Stella's friend. "I'm glad I hired a larger car; looks like it was needed," he said, lifting the heavy suitcases into the now-full trunk.

Lilli shot her son a familiar sharp look. He knew the warning well: "watch your words." His mother had warned him that his social awkwardness around women sometimes was perceived as slightly offensive, often misunderstood. He quickly walked over and opened the car doors for the women, trying to gallantly make up for his momentary *faux paus.*

"Stella, please join me," Lilli said as she sat in the sumptuous leather of the back seat, diagonally behind her tall son. Stella tried to remember what Lilli looked like the last time she had seen her. She was still so attractive and chic at her age, which she guessed must be somewhere in her late-70s. Lilli caught her looking.

"I must say you look as lovely as you did the last time I saw you, Mrs. Aubert," Stella stammered.

"Please, *mon chéri*, call me Lilli. We are family. It has been a long time since our last visit, oui?" as if she had read Stella's thoughts. "Thank you very much for the compliment."

"It's more than a compliment. You look as though time has stood still for you." Stella thought about how her mother looked right before she died, after so much chemo. Old enough to be this woman's mother. Maybe losing her looks had been the final insult, pushing her to take her own life.

"Maybe it is because I am French, no? Beautiful French women are not a scarce commodity. We are brought up to expect to be exquisite creatures—we think we are, so we are. Your mother once told me that in America one is led to believe that one woman's beauty doesn't exist unless another woman is ugly. Is this true? Making women compete to see who is more beautiful—what a waste. It is a contest no woman will ever win.

"We believe differently about aging here in my country. Older women should be revered. No one taught us that being older diminishes our beauty. Such nonsense, don't you agree?"

"I do," Stella said, saddened that Americans didn't feel the same way. She wondered why older American women, including herself, accepted youthful beauty as the standard. Her generation was ashamed of the privilege of growing old.

Noticing the sun glinting off of Stella's necklace, Lilli smiled. "I am so pleased you both wore your necklaces. You will see a lot of star references today. It was the Maestro's lucky charm, you know. Always in his pocket."

"We should be arriving shortly in Paris, as we have missed most of the madness of the morning traffic," Gabriel offered as he adjusted his rear view mirror, grinning at Stella when he caught her reflection. "Your hotel is close to the museum, so we should be able to make it just in time."

Stella noticed that when he smiled, his smile lines extended from the corner of his mouth almost to his ears. *A face full of joy*, she thought. *Maybe his love of baby Jesus made him that happy.* She instantly regretted her cynical thought. She and Maggie had already insulted an ex-nun. It might be wise to not continue on that path with this religious man. There was still a small part of her that believed in a vengeful god. Maybe time to stay in God's good graces—just in case.

At the mention of the museum, Stella's excitement morphed into dizziness. Suddenly, the pace of the last few weeks started to hit her like a tranquilizer. Everything was moving too quickly. It had only been a scant two weeks since they had buried Josh.

She wondered if she should talk to this priest about the visions. Her intuition warned her to take her time, wait and see. She and Maggie had promised each other to stay tight lipped. There would be time to discuss that subject when they joined the others in Lourdes, after their whirlwind buying spree for the shop.

From the comfort of the back seat, Stella gazed out at the now-cloudy sky. The pink was gone, overtaken by the gray as it started to drizzle. Though all the trees were mostly bare, some were starting to bud out. A perfect time to see Paris, as the leafless trees allowed her to study the innovative architecture of the Paris she adored.

The smoke-smudged ivory buildings stood close enough to volley raindrops back and forth, washing the two-thousand year old ancient city. The cobbled streets, smoothed and rounded with wear, were becoming crowded with the day's activities. A day filled with the promise of adventure.

As she studied the buildings looming in front of them, she recalled something Lilli had once told her mother about the Golden Mean. She had been sitting in her mother's workroom, sketching while her mother draped a muslin, when the wise Frenchwoman started talking about proportions. She explained how the human body had the same proportions as an oak tree, nature's divine ratio. Sacred geometry or the golden triangle, she called it. That conversation stuck with her all through school and especially when viewing artist's work while deciding whether to buy or not. It was the one absolute rule of art every artist had to understand—proportion.

Lilli told Stella's mother that Dior instructed her to pay attention to the Golden Mean. He said it was the code of nature, connected everything. It was more than fashion, it was the harmonic code that balanced everything.

* * *

As they emerged from the hotel's elevator into the tastefully-appointed lobby, Stella was thrilled at the sight of Lilli's outfit. The modern suit's references to the iconic Bar Suit from Dior's 1947 New Look collection were unmistakable. It was her personal favorite Dior look—next to the one she was wearing, of course. While packing, Maggie had urged her to try on vintage red wool Dior coat dress hanging in the closet. She was stunned that it fit so well. Better than well, it showed her still ample cleavage and the flared skirt gave the illusion of a pre-menopause smallish waist. As she stepped towards the black Mercedes, she hoped the swing of her skirt wouldn't look as if she was trying too hard.

"Today almost feels the same as that day," Lilli said, placing her large satchel on the car's floor next to her kitten-heeled clad feet. "It was bitterly cold, with rain and fog. March 27, 1945. I was so young then. At the time I did not think so. Sadly, war makes you grow up too fast. We had all suffered too much.

"How fortunate for you two lovely ladies to have never experienced the absolute terror of falling bombs, foreign soldiers roaming your streets, breaking into your houses, being brutally assaulted, going days without eating. But on that day, even though the war was not yet over, we could finally see the end in sight. We could feel hopeful again.

"You know, the dolls were Monsieur Dior's idea. We discussed many times how to return to our previous way of life, without war. Once, by the fountain in our village we came up with an idea. I encouraged him to suggest the idea to Monsieur Lelong, with whom we both worked. He was very crafty that way, suggesting something and letting that person think it was his idea. He told me it delighted him to see a smile on my face again, after what I had been through . . . ." Lillie said, quickly changing the conversation to keep the black thoughts of the camp at bay.

"The beauty of the dolls!" she exclaimed. "Everyone was there—the *Tout-Paris* was there, everyone in Paris society. I remember I was wearing one of the first New Look dresses of Monsieur Dior's. I so adored him and he I," she said with a smile as she closed her eyes, obviously missing her old friend.

"During the Occupation, we had to be brave as we thumbed our noses at the Nazi's restrictions on material—we were only allowed enough to make very slim skirts. The Germans tried to break the Parisians' spirit by targeting our fashion. But we wouldn't let them. Take our fabric, we'll use straw. Burn our straw, we'll use paper. My father was a tailor and had hoarded a stash of fabrics, especially blue serge for men's suits. Dior was ecstatic with so much beautiful fabric to drape and create.

"I remember feeling so grand and grown up that night, as we walked up to the Pavillon de Marsan. The uniformed *Garde républicaine* in their shiny helmets, stood regal and proud on the stairs leading up to the Grand Gallery. We entered an enormous room, with massive amounts of luxurious crimson velvet hanging from every wall. All of us walked silently through the exhibit as if we had entered church. Pictures and descriptions of our couture industry hung on the walls. There was even a picture of me with Dior as we were working on our dolls in Lelong's atelier. We raised a million francs that night for war relief."

Stella put her hand on Lilli's, and for the first time noticed Lilli's pin on her lapel—of winged hands, only for the courtiers. True fashion royalty.

Sensing they were almost at their destination, Stella thought it best to start preparing for the show. She checked her bag, satisfied with her organization. She lifted her head and caught Gabriel studying her in the mirror. Flattered at first then confused as she witnessed his smile fade. His focus wasn't on her; it was on what was behind them in traffic.

His worry didn't go unnoticed by Lilli, who had the advantage of not having to look behind to know what or who may be there. Lilli knew they were no longer safe. She quickly started a new conversation.

"Maggie, is this your first time in Paris?" Lilli had noticed that the red-haired woman had been mostly silent since they met.

"Second," Maggie said, steadying her voice. "Thank you so much for inviting me. My husband and I celebrated our 25th anniversary here." Maggie, sensing the changed mood, reverted to librarian chatter as her safe zone. "Is it true that Samuel Morse came here and was so inspired he came up with the idea for his Morse code and the telegraph?"

"That is true. However, he first came here to paint," Lilli added. "In fact, he started right here at the Louvre," she said pointing at the impressive group of buildings as they approached the U-shaped complex of the former French palace.

"He painted *Gallery of the Louvre*, and took it back to New York," Stella added. "But, like most, he couldn't make a living as an artist. However, had he been a successful painter, we might never have had the telegraph."

"Or dare I say, cell phones," Maggie said, triggering her memory. She reached into her purse, and slipped her passport into the protective sleeve she brought just in case.

At the entrance of the Pavilion, their car was met by a handsome, sharply-dressed young man. "Madame Aubert, this way, please," the usher said, extending his arm for the honorary guest as he lifted her valise.

The party of four followed the usher to their front row seats. It appeared they would be sitting front and center. Stella was almost beside herself—her first time in the front row!

Maggie walked in an observant silence, all of her senses on high alert. Stella wrongly assumed Maggie was uncomfortable with the opulence of her surroundings. However, Maggie's senses were amped ever since the incident at the airport.

Like Stella, she did not believe in accidents either. But unlike Stella, she was well aware of how innocent covert action could seem. Gabriel's concern on the drive here did not escape her notice.

The house lights slowly dimmed as the curtain parted. There it was, the original star emblazoned on the backdrop. The street scape windows filled with the dolls, caught in a moment in time in their doll worlds. The runway started to glow, first with two adjacent lights, then two more until the entire runway was lit with small versions of Parisian 1940s street lamps.

The delicate lilt of the little sparrow, Edith Piaf, filled the room as the first model sauntered down the runway in a slim pencil skirt topped with a structured jacket with its broad circular peplum; and, of course, shoes no woman could walk in. Stella recognized the references and also appreciated the updating achieved with custom fabrics. It appeared that Mr. Galliano had been a good student of "listening to fabric." Dior would have been proud.

As each subsequent model entered the theatre, she could see stripes and bias cutting were the main themes of the collection. As soon as she had that thought, the volume of the dresses ballooned. Galliano had recreated the 1945 Enchanted Garden scene, lowering models on swings entwined with ivy down from the rafters. The models were wearing draped gowns á *la* Madame Gres whose biased-cut gowns had originally appeared in the magical set. So long away from the fashion world, Stella had forgotten the thrill of a Paris couture show.

Though Stella was enthralled with the show, Maggie's quietness disturbed her. *Maybe it's too much for her,* she thought. She hoped she hadn't made a wrong decision to invite her. *Was it selfish to have Maggie attend the fashion show so she wouldn't be alone?* Maybe they should have gone on to Lourdes.

Maggie was very still, her eyes fixed on one certain doll. She wondered if she was the only one to notice the sensation of sparks when the doll peered from the window in the backdrop. It was too similar to what she witnessed and felt that day in the cemetery to not notice. Best not to bring it up to Stella right now. She could tell that Stella was in heaven—right back in her element of fashion and art.

The audience was spellbound, lost in the bewitchment of the show's mixture of yesterday and today's fashion fantasy. For the finale, all the models walked out, carrying their mini-me dolls their outfit referenced. When the last model carrying Faïence walked the runway, everyone rose to their feet in wild, ecstatic applause.

Stella looked over and saw Lilli in joyful tears, her son holding her hand and lightly massaging it. She remembered Dibrovna once told her you can tell a lot about a man by the way he treats his mother. She admired the priest and felt a little envious there couldn't be more to their own relationship.

At the reception at the Ritz, Lilli, clutching Faïence, looked around for familiar faces. She quickened her step when she saw the group of women, hunched with age, in a circle chatting. There they were—her sister *la premiers* from all the famous houses. The years just disappeared, as they squealed in delight and hugged each other. What onlookers didn't know is that this group of chic, wonderfully-aged women not only brought back the fashion industry to France and saved its economy, they saved France itself.

Most had been part of the French Resistance. Some even worked on the Comet Line, saving downed pilots. They had sacrificed their own safety during the war. Some knew their story, but most of the world did not. It was a painful topic Lilli rarely talked about.

Chapter Forty-Three

—∞—

"Splendid!" Cardinal Gustav exclaimed into his cell phone, as he and Lucas entered the heart of the Vatican Laboratory. "The DNA capture from the Paris target has been successful. The specimens will be here shortly. I have instructed Dr. Franco to have the vial ready to activate as soon as it arrives." Gustav had alerted Lucas that the women were no longer alone. He didn't know why but the priest and his mother were picking the women up at the airport. Lucas had quickly changed the target.

Gustav was greatly relieved. The Bollandist had started to make him nervous. The priest had been quite evasive during the Amsterdam meeting, triggering suspicions within the cardinal that were not allayed by watching the priest recently in front of the Vatican Gardens' grotto. He had hesitated to approach Lucas with the idea of adding Gabriel's DNA to their exclusive group of unwilling members. He didn't need another public relations fiasco on one of his projects.

The Stanchirs had become very nervous after the big mistake when the cardinal had organized the first Adult Stem Cell conference. After the world-wide outcry about ethics and the Church's involvement in science, it had quickly been canceled. Any links between the Church and GA7 had been carefully scrubbed by the media at the Liberty Group's insistence.

Lucas had been furious that his life's work had almost been revealed and destroyed. *No more mistakes,* he ordered the cardinal. Everything had to be cleared through GA7 first.

Gustav hoped the news, along with this tour, would further assure Lucas the lab was now a secured fortress and ready to be put into operation. With help from the Swiss guards, who had been protecting the pope since 1506, the lab was equipped with the most sophisticated security system. It used nonlocality locks on all entrances that sent photon signals through fiber optics. A pair of photons on one end would be activated by a laser and the photons on the other end "instantly" reacted. Though nothing seemed to move and no energy was expended, the particles shared information. An unbreakable quantum lock.

They meandered past the mammoth circular console in the center of the room. This was the lab's hub, studded with large monitors, transmitting second-by-second results on the test subjects. It was also here where the Church, with GA7's assistance, constantly monitored electronic data from emails, phone conversations, texts—anything that may be useful to them in their efforts to control the electronic landscape and usher in the Plan. The command post was manned with language analysts from all over the world whose collective ears would perk when their monitored targets used an unusual word, especially anything referencing the Virgin Mary or 2012.

Stepping into the chamber, scanning the rack of test tubes, Lucas recognized the newly-arrived curly, coppery strand of hair next to the tube containing the white-blond strand with silver roots.

"Still no change in the responses?" he asked the bespectacled Japanese lab assistant.

"Not yet, sir. But we are increasing the frequency of some of the images, as you instructed."

It frustrated him that the DNA samples collected from the American women by the nun still seemed electrically unchanged. He was puzzled since he had been so successful previously on the object of his obsession. Maybe the arrival of fresh samples from the flight attendant would produce results. Their timetable didn't allow for guessing.

"I want to meet with Dr. Franco. Alert him now." He was sure he was on the right track. Just needed to discuss the situation more thoroughly with his lab supervisor.

He hoped it had nothing to do with the present location. Previously, the lab had been situated underneath the Vatican Observatory, located at Castel Gandolfo. But at his father's urging, soon before his death, both had been moved.

The Observatory was now in the same old convent as the newest addition, commonly referred to as the Quantum Lab, only a few miles away from the papal summer residence. The press release stated the relocation was for reconstruction purposes of the papal residence. However, in reality, the move was necessitated by the lab equipment's requirements to ramp up the DNA lab. It also was more covert, being hidden away in the non-descript convent. But most importantly, it was built over an ancient well. They needed a mineral-rich conductor for their manufactured energy.

Some thought it odd that a church, known for its persecution of scientists, would have a laboratory. But the Catholic Church was not just a religious institution. It was more like a multi-faceted corporation. It was the largest land owner in Italy, next to the government, and a business owner.

It was also one of the biggest financial institutions in the world, due in large part to Bernardino Nogara. He had been appointed by Pope Pius XI in 1929 as the manager and director of the new financial agency—Special Administration of the Holy See. During World War II, Nogara invested in companies that produced such religious-contrary items as bombs, tanks and even contraceptives, with the pope as the one and only stockholder. In 1959, Cardinal Spellman had reportedly said "next to Jesus Christ, the greatest thing that happened to the Church was Bernardino Nogara."

Lucas' father knew the Church's power was not only its financial strength. Elliott had instructed Gustav early on that if the church was going to survive it must keep stressing to all parishioners that salvation is *only* possible through the church and obeying. The elder Stanchir reassured the Church that while at the CIA his Office of Policy Coordination had effectively schooled all the media through the Operation Mockingbird on how to successfully "manufacture consent" by manipulating the news, turning the public into spectators, not participants. "Intelligent manipulation" playing to their irrational emotion, like the Halloween candy story Lucas was so fond of telling.

It was with the Stanchirs' help that the Church had one of the most sophisticated media outlets in the world at its disposal—Vatican Radio. Since the first radio message by Pope Pius XI on February 12, 1931, Vatican Radio now broadcasted in forty different languages. It was said the signal from Vatican Radio was so strong Romans could hear Sunday mass on their electric doorbells.

Then everything changed. First, the 1975 U.S. Congressional Church Committee exposed illegal intelligence gathering by the CIA and media manipulation. The curtain had been drawn back, not only angering the public, but raising their curiosity and suspicions.

Elliot's big concern was the 1998 Global Consciousness Project findings. They proved scientifically that there was a global consciousness. A whole new world. Now they understood what the Third Secret had meant by *look at the pond, not just the fish.*

Entanglement, Lucas told them, is what his SRI friends called it. He had explained something called nonlocal causality, similar to how tuning forks work. When they all tuned to the same frequency, they became linked by bands of electromagnetic fields. The subatomic particles would then start behaving as one. And it could happen in humans. The more they were linked in the same frequency, the more they observed the same things, and that was how you created a certain consciousness.

"This is the future of the information world," Lucas had informed Gustav. "You want to control the message, understand the relationship between DNA and emotions. The relationship can transcend time and space, regardless of distance. There is no 'here' or 'there' or 'then' and 'now.' Here is already there and then has always been now. Heady, mind-boggling stuff—especially when you see it in action."

Lucas had warned his father and the cardinal about the rise in collective consciousness, connection from global DNA and the greater the observers observed, specifically the women, the more influence on what would take place. Keep the women fragmented by preying on their insecurities and the need to be the perfect mother, wife and breadwinner. Convince them they are not worthy, so they will fight and compete with each other. And at all costs, keep them separated!

As for the older women, he knew making them feel invisible was worse than ridicule. He feared their power the most. Because their electromagnetic fields vibrated higher allowing them to receive information first in their hearts then their brains, feeding the field. A field much stronger than just an individual. The Great Gathering, foretold in the Third Secret, must not happen.

Chapter Forty-Four

—∞—

Promising her cherished friends they would get together soon, Lilli turned to her son and their American guests: "A celebration is needed. Such a marvelous show, don't you think?"

"Simply divine. Wished my mother could have been here." Stella's words caught in her throat.

"Oui, Monsieur Dior would have been so pleased to see all the people leaving with such delight on their faces. It displeased him greatly, what he called 'the wicked commerce of unnecessary nastiness.' Though he probably added to it with his own business practices," Lilli added judiciously. "After all, he created the demand for 'labels' with his licensing arrangements."

"Mesdames, may I squire you to dinner tonight?" Gabriel bumbled, attempting to be charming.

Though dog-tired and jet-lagged, Stella was incredibly famished. "French food in Paris at night? A no-brainer for me," hoping they understood her attempt at a cultural reference. "Maggie, you up for dinner?" she asked.

"I'm so hungry, I'd even eat snails. Feed me," Maggie exclaimed, sounding more like her old self.

"Good," Lilli said. "Let's go to one of my favorite places, in the Sixth District, La Bugarach. I used to be a regular at this restaurant for decades. It was right across the street from the rare bookstore where I had met Gabriel's father during the war. You know how to get there, son?"

Gabriel grinned and nodded as he opened the car door for her. He had grown up dining at this restaurant with his parents, like a second home. He knew every crack in the rough heavy-plastered walls and ceiling, had memorized every scratch in the rich cherry wood wainscoting, patiently waiting for the adults to conclude their discussions. He had fond memories of the rich, burgundy leather banquettes which reeked of cigarettes and cognac, listening to the adults talk of the war years, the art of romance and politics. And the art was magnificent! The restaurant had passed from generation to generation, and with it, all the art bought when artists were merely beginning. Mostly art of women.

"Is that Notre Dame?" Maggie asked as they drove past the magnificent church, still ringed with crowds waiting to get in.

"That is correct," Gabriel said. "Did you know that Notre Dame, our lady in your language, was built on an island in the Seine where Paris began during Roman times? *The exact center of Paris!* Maybe that is why the world loves Paris so. The center of this city is a beautiful church built to honor Her. We should be arriving at the restaurant in a few minutes," he said, crossing the famous river.

Nervous with the mention of Mary, Stella wondered if they should talk to Lilli about their experiences before they left for Lourdes. She'd decided to discuss the matter with Maggie later at the hotel, as they had agreed.

Almost to the Jardin du Luxembourg, Lilli simply stated, "Slow down, son. A car is about to pull out." He did as he was told, allowing the car to pull away from the curb.

"Wow, Stella, she's better than you at it," Maggie said, as the elderly woman grinned.

Gabriel expertly maneuvered the car into the small opening. "I hope you ladies do not mind walking a bit." He noted American women wore shoes for fashion, not for function. "This is Paris, an ancient city with not a lot of places to park. But it is a lovely walk to the restaurant. We will *flânerie*, you know, like Balzac wrote: 'Ah! To wander over Paris! What an adorable and delightful existence is that! To saunter is a science; it is the gastronomy of the eye.'"

"*Vivez joyeux*," added Lilli.

"I would love to walk," Stella said, while Maggie looked at Stella's high heels and whispered, "liar, liar, pants on fire."

As they walked through the Jardin du Luxembourg, past the Fontaine Medicis, Lilli told them the fountain was famous as a place for young lovers. The mention of lovers caused Stella to lose her balance slightly on the cobbled path, falling against Gabriel. "I'm so sorry. I have a trick knee, and these shoes aren't helping." Their eyes met as they both remembered how her knee got that way.

"I'm sorry. Here, let me take your arm and guide you. We are almost there."

Lilli and Maggie, walking behind the couple on the narrow path, wittingly smirked at each other.

"You know why the French are so famous for their food?" he asked the Americans. "It was designed that way as a tactic of politics. Napoleon's plan was to provide every Frenchmen with lots of beautiful, sumptuous food to keep the monarchy from returning. *Win their stomachs, win their hearts.*"

"It is true," Lilli said, then sighing "but Paris is changing. The Moderns are taking over. I adore the art of dining. We nearly lost it, you know—during the war. A lot of people starved. But we survived."

Upon entering the regal restaurant, Stella was impressed as they were greeted ceremoniously as royalty. The maître d' took them upstairs to a window-side table overlooking the avenue below.

"Madame Aubert," the genteel man said, swinging his arm wide as he seated Lilli, "your table."

"Thank you, Christo. How is your family?" she asked, genuinely curious.

"Lovely, but not as lovely as you."

The French, Stella thought, *always flirting*. She loved it.

"You see that little storefront across the street? That was my late husband's bookstore. He was a *boîte aux lettres*, an information drop off, during the war. I was part of the French Resistance, helping the other women to liberate our men from the prison camps. That was how we met.

"They did not take my Jean-Luc because he was too old and damaged from the First World War. His lungs, you know. He had been exposed to mustard gas as a child. He could never again breathe normally. He eventually lost his voice," she said softly, remembering her beloved.

"He adored me and gave me books to read about the history of women. He was furious when the Chief of State of Vichy, Phillipe Petain, implemented his *femme au foyer*, 'women-at-home imperative.' Petain was such a coward, utterly spineless. Just surrendered France to Germany without a fight.

"Women were denied the vote, we couldn't even have bank accounts. So we set up shell companies as a front. First, we set out to help the Jewish people with identity papers, food, and clothing. What a fool to think he could keep Frenchwomen down! We knew we had to stand up for ourselves. We were not raised to give up. We had no guns, were not trained warriors. But we knew the power of connection and information.

"We made and distributed fliers and posted them where ever we saw people gathering. We inspired others and our numbers grew," Lilli said, pausing to sip her wine. There was so much more to her story, but now was not the time to tell it. There was value in patience and timing.

"What do you think of the art?" Gabriel asked. "Most of this art here was painted in 4D, that is, in the fourth dimension. In the 4D world, humans act collectively and consciously. Much of what the eye doesn't see was first introduced to us by artists. All the greats painted in 4D— Picasso, Dali, Duchamp. Did you know that Van Gogh was inspired to paint Starry Night after a visit to Chartres Cathedral, not far from here, or so goes the legend."

"I thought he was inspired by his time in the mental hospital," exclaimed Stella. She had been a straight A student in art school. Had she forgotten? Were there now lapses in her brain from her breakdown? Blank neural traces as if someone was purposely erasing chunks of her memories?

"Yes, that is true. He painted it while he was in the hospital in St. Remy where Nostradamus lived, but they say he was truly inspired after walking the labyrinth in the cathedral. That is where he got the swirls and the stars. Have you ever been there?" he asked.

"No. I'm sorry. I haven't been a big church fan for a while. No offense," Stella said as diplomatically as she could. She found no delight in offending others who had different beliefs.

"I have an interesting tidbit, though," Maggie said. "Did you know that Van Gogh was actually the second so named? He happened to be born exactly one year to the day after as his dead brother, the first Vincent Van Gogh. That's enough to make you a little crazy, don't you think?" She quickly looked over at Stella, wishing she hadn't used the *C* word again.

"Maybe yes, but he also wanted to be a minister like his father, but was unable to. He thought he could serve God through his art, but, sadly, no one would buy it. At least not in his lifetime," added Gabriel.

"God time," Lilli stated. "We humans try to make everything happen when we want it. It is so futile. You must wait for God time. If you have time we could take you there, my dear," Lilli added.

"Most people don't realize how art has been used in wars. The Nazis confiscated so much during the war, branding Modern art as degenerate. During the Cold War, your own CIA supported American Abstract Expressionists, such as Pollack, Rothko, and de Kooning. It was a government ploy to prove America's creative and intellectual freedom. The Russians couldn't compete with the art. It was a program run under Propaganda Assets Inventory, which at its peak influenced close to 1,000 newspapers and magazines."

"How do you know so much about this?" asked Maggie.

"Because they tried to get the dolls, especially mine," Lilli said, as she patted her satchel with her beloved Faïence. "They were brutal to Dior because he was French, homosexual and had certain *other* beliefs. They wanted to shift the culture center from France to New York so they could keep closer tabs on the 'lefty liberals' as they called them. Do you think it was an accident that they were hidden in the basement of a store called the City of Paris?"

Maggie was about to add to the conversation when a young waiter came to serve them the *pâté*. She met Lilli's eyes across the table, both carefully watching the sweating young man. *Pay attention*, the voice said. *Details.*

His sleeves seemed too short, the cuffs dingy and frayed. Scuffed shoes, stained shirt, certainly not up to Christo's standards of excellence, judging by the other waiters' attire. Maggie noticed that his eyes were blinking rapidly, a sure tell of deceit Jim had taught her.

Lilli watched as his hand quivered as he placed the unusual smelling *pâté* down in front of her. *Oleander.* A bead of sweat tumbled off his forehead and dropped onto her hand. His DNA had all the information she needed. She peered out the window.

The darkly dressed man she had noticed when she first sat down was still pacing up and down the street. She smiled gently and thanked the young waiter—or whatever he was. As he turned his back, she caught Christo's attention with a slight nod of her head. It set matters in motion.

Out of the corner of her eye, Lilli recognized the man on the sidewalk below. The streetlight glinted off his ear piece. Definitely the clumsy priest from the airport.

"It's time, *mon fils*," Lilli said to Gabriel as she stood up. "Stella, we need to leave—now. Follow me. I will answer questions later."

"Please," said Gabriel, sternly yet quietly as he lifted Stella by her elbow, ushering her in front of him.

"I will take Maggie and meet you there," Lilli said. The two groups of two headed in opposite directions, with Christo following behind Lilli. The young waiter had already been sucker punched in the kitchen, a dirty dish rag stuffed into his mouth. The other waiters ringed around the table where another petty criminal was trying to act outraged at being detained.

Gabriel took Stella down the restaurant hallway towards the hidden elevator. It was tiny, even by European standards. "I apologize for the smallness of space. This was built during the war for spies who worked in the Resistance. This used to be a popular place for both the French and the Nazis. It was no mistake that we decided to dine there, after what happened this morning and at the show."

"You mean the priest that tripped and fell into you? I didn't notice anything at the show," said Stella, pressing her index finger on her jittery eyebrow.

"I'm so sorry for worrying you. Let us meet up with mother and then we can both explain. First, we must escape quickly and get to the cathedral."

Stella tried to navigate the slippery stone streets through the foggy night in heels that dared her knee to go out, worried each wobbly step was destined to be her last. As soon as she had that thought, Gabriel turned to her.

"Again, I'm so sorry. I forgot about your knee. If I may," he said as he lifted and carried her through the dark streets of Paris. Stella was gobsmacked speechless. First, she was surprised that this man, even though sturdily-built, could lift her up. She was also a little embarrassed that he was carrying her like she was a damsel in distress in some romance novel. It was thrilling nonetheless.

They entered the catacombs through the Sixth Arrondissement exit, a plain cinder block building that gave no hint of what was beyond. Except for the sign.

Stop! This is the empire of death.

Stella gasped. She had heard of the catacombs, a 12th-century maze of limestone and gypsum quarries beneath the streets of Paris, some 185 miles of tunnels. Six million skulls of Paris dead had been moved to the catacombs in the late 1770s. Cemeteries had rapidly filled due to spreading disease. She screamed. Gabriel quickly clamped his hand over her mouth.

"Please, close your eyes." He rushed her through the skull-lined walls, her face buried in the crook of his neck. The crunching gravel under his feet was the only sound as they made their way to the one illicit entrance that opened out to the street. Just large enough to hide a van, ready for their use.

Maggie and Lilli were already huddled low in the vehicle, hidden from view. Even in the menace of danger, Gabriel stopped to open Stella's door and assist her into her seat. Stella was too petrified to even utter a thank you. Dust was coming down from the ceiling—bone dust. She breathed shallowly through her clenched lips.

"Get us to the cathedral as quickly as possible, mon fils. Faïence is with us; she will keep us safe," Lilli instructed her son.

Stella didn't know what they were "safe from" or how, but knew now was not the time to ask. She concentrated on the narrowing French roads they were barreling down, with the lights of Paris dimming in the distance.

Chapter Forty-Five

—∞—

The only moving vehicle for miles in the early morning, Stella honed in on the full moon's bright multi-ringed aura taking center stage in the purple and blue starry night. After a few minutes, she had successfully breathed her heart rate back to a normal, steady rhythm. The only sound in the van was the passengers' collective breathing accompanied by the swooshing of the wind-blown, golden wheat in the passing fields. As they crested a hill outside the small, medieval village, she saw two tall, majestic spires jutting high above the noble cypress: Sun Tower and Moon Tower.

She had studied the famous Chartres Cathedral in her Renaissance Art class, but had never visited. The world's largest collection of stained-glass windows, 176 if she remembered correctly. Trying as hard as she could, she tried to remember what had intrigued her so during that class. Something about alchemy, sacred geometry maybe? She remembered that it was the first use of pointed arched windows and ribbed vaults to support the weight of the massive stone church. Her brain was too exhausted; maybe it would come to her soon. She realized she was still gripping Maggie's hand like a vise, and she peeled her fingers away.

Gabriel pulled into the parking lot, extinguishing the headlights. Maggie and Stella huddled together in the back seat, awaiting instructions.

"Wait, *maman,* let me help you out," Gabriel tenderly said as he hurried to assist his mother.

Stella was surprised to see how alert Lilli seemed. It must be hours past midnight and even she yearned to stretch out on a bed sometime soon. Not yet twenty-four hours in France, and her whole world was in chaotic turmoil.

"Thank you, son," Lilli whispered. "Ladies, follow me. Please, we must try to be as indiscreet as possible. Walk lightly. I'll explain more once inside."

Maggie hunched and held her stomach as she exited the vehicle. The unfolding drama and introduction of rich foreign food were gurgling her bowels.

Stella sensed Maggie's distress, grabbed her by the elbow and quickly pulled her along behind the Frenchwoman and her son.

"This way, please. There is a secret passageway that has been opened for us," Lilli said softly.

"Hold on, sweetie. I'll find you a bathroom," Stella said, knowing precisely what Maggie needed and hoping they could get to a toilet in time. They zigged and zagged around massive carved columns through dark passageways lined with sculpted stories embedded in rim of the underground crypt's walls, tiptoeing in their stocking feet until they reached a spiral staircase. At the top of the steps, they emerged into the cavernous Gothic cathedral.

"Welcome to Mary's house. You are safe here," Lilli said. "You will find the toilettes right over there," Lilli said, pointing towards yet another passageway. Maggie almost sprinted.

Stella stepped into the radiant majesty, her mouth agape with awe. Moonlight illuminated the stained-glass windows, bathing the church in heavenly luminescent hues of reds and blues.

Stella turned and walked south towards the window. *Notre Dame de la Belle Verriére*—The Blue Virgin, set in a red background. Now she remembered—the cobalt blue glass. Her professor told them it was invented by obsessed alchemists specifically for this window, but the formula vanished from the earth within one hundred years. No one could recreate the same particular blue.

"You are okay?" Lillie asked. "I know you have many questions. You must be so frightened. Allow me to briefly explain its history while we wait for our attendant.

"At one time this land we are standing on was called the Mound. The Druids built an altar in honor of the goddess, called *Virgo Paritura*, the Black Virgin. For many centuries, pilgrims who believed in the protective goddesses they called The Mothers, came to this goddess sanctuary not only to worship the Black Virgin, but for the miraculous healing from the sacred spring running underneath, fed from the powerful currents of the River Eure. A prophetic spirit told them in 50 B.C. that a virgin would bear a child who would bring joy to the world.

"It has been said that Mary, on her deathbed, asked the apostles to give her clothes to 'an honest widow who had always served her from the time her Son had returned to his Father.' One of the articles of clothing was the *Sancta Camisa* or *tunic*, given to the bishop of Chartres in 876. It is believed that prompted the building of the first Christian church on the Mound in the first century as a temple to house the Virgin's Veil, as it became known. Since that time many cathedrals were built here to replace previous ones that were burnt down."

"What's the Virgin's Veil?" Maggie asked as she rejoined the group, gratefully relieved.

Gabriel turned and smiled at her. "There are many stories. One is that it was given to the cathedral by the king of France, for safe keeping, in the ninth century. A piece of silk cloth, five meters long, it was thought to be worn by the Virgin Mary when she gave birth to Jesus. The monks took it down to the grotto by the well for safe keeping.

"They called it a 'tunic' but in 1712 they deemed the description tunic unsuitable and started to call it 'the veil' of the Virgin, or the *Sancta Camisa*. It was examined by experts in 1927 who dated it to the first century. Royalty believed the veil had magic qualities and would bring clothing of pregnant French queens to touch the veil. The queens would then wear this imbued clothing to make their pregnancies much easier."

Gabriel noticed Stella wasn't listening. As if in a trance, she was walking towards the south ambulatory and the Notre Dame de la Belle Verriére.

"Our Lady of the Beautiful Window, the only original window to have survived the great fire of 1194. Some say it is the most beautiful stained-glass window in the world. Chartres blue, it is called. The color of the most vivid cobalt blue ocean. They say the blue glass does not get dirty like the other colors nor does it ever fade. This window is deemed sacred and an object of devotion to many. Mary is sitting on the throne of wisdom, wearing a crown symbolizing her as the Queen of Heaven. Jesus on her lap symbolizes that he is within her body of wisdom. The angels surrounding her were added in the 13th century. There are 175 images of the Virgin Mary in all of these stained-glass windows alone. And each tells a story."

"And the well?" Stella asked, showing she had indeed been listening to him.

"Not far from where we entered, under the chapel in the crypt. It is still there today as is the Black Madonna. Actually, a replica. There once was a statue which may have been pagan in origin called *Notre Dame Sous Terre*, The Lady of the Underground. She was destroyed in the French Revolution. Many think the original statue was for goddess worship, specifically the cult of Isis. No one truly knows the real story."

"Thanks for the history lesson, Father. So what the hell happened back there at the restaurant?" Maggie boldly asked, figuring they had waited long enough to be considered polite.

"I think they were after my doll," Lilli said. "She has been missing for a very long time."

Stella looked away. She felt guilty, as if it was her fault the doll had been lost for so long in the department store basement. "I'm sorry. I had no idea of her importance when I played with her as a teen. Is she worth a lot of money now?"

"*Money?* No, she is priceless! Faïence is more important to our world than I can tell you right now. First, my son and I have some business to attend to," Lilli said, clutching her satchel close to her body. "We will tell you more when we have reached our home.

"While you wait, there is a rare treat for you both. Remember at the restaurant I told you about Van Gogh and the labyrinth?" she asked. "It is not often that all the chairs have been put away, and you can freely walk it," she said, leading the women towards the taupe and chocolate brown much-walked stone circle in the center of the cathedral. "Many people come from all over the world to partake in this holy ritual.

"It is only six rings, allowing you to take your time. Before you start, it is best to take a long, deep cleansing breath," Lilli instructed the women. "There are powerful earth energies below."

Perfect timing, Stella thought, as her eyebrow had started to twitch again. Once, she had participated in a peace walk on the replica labyrinth at Grace Cathedral in San Francisco. It had been an enlightening experience, thought provoking and, most importantly, peaceful.

"I've walked the labyrinth in San Francisco, and understand the process," Stella said. Stella slowly filled her lungs, expanding her rib cage as it lifted towards the buttresses above.

Maggie, not quite as anxious as her friend to walk in circles, reluctantly followed her lead. What the heck, these two Frenchies had just gotten her out of a very dangerous situation, so no alternative but to trust them. Maybe the walking would clear her mind as she tried to figure out what was going on. She pleasantly realized her stomach no longer bothered her. In fact, she was starting to feel quite pleasant and relaxed.

"It is good to have a thought to contemplate while walking the labyrinth. The walking helps you to focus, allowing divine God energy to flow and unite us all. We will be back shortly," Gabriel said as he walked his mother towards Our Lady of the Pillar, and disappeared beyond a column.

Chapter Forty-Six

—∞—

Dr. Nicholas Franco, chief scientist and lab supervisor for the Quantum Lab, cleared his throat as he carefully removed his headset. The control center told him that Mr. Stanchir wanted to see him immediately. Reporting to the demanding Lucas Stanchir always made him nervous. The Italian, who had previously worked for CERN, the European Organization for Nuclear Research in Geneva, Switzerland, still was insecure communicating in English. Especially when explaining the theories of how the Plan was supposed to work. He kept his explanations on a simple, understandable level without appearing to be condescending— a delicate balance with a powerful man like Lucas Stanchir who fancied himself as one of the world's experts on the subject.

He had come a long way since his first meeting with the GA7 CEO on the heels of his publication: *Body Decomposition Energy Releases Stored in DNA.* Brent McConnell had contacted him, informing Dr. Franco he was a friend of the doctor's cousin. Said they both worked for GA7 in 2008 on a little project for the American government. Franco froze.

He was well aware of the "project." His infamous cousin always came up during any kind of high-security, background clearance. Seems his cousin had infiltrated the Pentagon's server with a virus via a flash drive inserted into a laptop in the Middle East. For a brief time, GA7 had control over America's whole defense system.

The cousin wasn't punished as GA7 had been under contract with the American government. The government wanted to see where the weak links in the hypersphere existed. Because of his cousin's willingness to bend laws, Franco had always been painted with the same brush. He wasn't offended, mostly intrigued on what the caller wanted.

Brent questioned him about parts of the report that concerned the Shroud of Turin and the Virgin Mary's scapular. The report had stated that not only did the cloth articles still contain the original DNA of the wearers, but the decomposed energy also contained the wearer's emotions in the DNA. Within forty-eight hours, Dr. Franco had flown first class to the United States, with a classified dossier for his first meeting at GA7 headquarters.

"Before we start, I am quite familiar with the theory of quantum entanglement, instantaneous communication between atoms, how two particles come into contact, and if one particle's direction changes, the other will follow," Lucas started. "Einstein's spooky action at a distance, string theory, etc.

"What I want to hear from you is this: the *emotional* connection of entanglement. What you referred to in your report as 'intuition' or a 'knowing,' especially between a mother and a child. Is the emotional entanglement you call 'knowing' different in women versus men? And can it be detangled?"

"I would say yes to both, but it depends. You see, men are left-brained, which defines separation. Their psychic abilities aren't as easily developed as a women's. Women are right-brained, the hemisphere of nirvana. They have the ability to see the 'big picture.' Women's intuition is, what do you call it—a euphemism—for increased psychic skills. Their entanglement is deeper and longer-lived, maybe even passed down in their DNA to future generations.

"The ego is not as deeply rooted in women as in men. Now, it is losing its hold more quickly on women than men, making them more open to a shift in consciousness. Due to this loss of ego, it is easier for entanglement to naturally occur in females, especially the older ones. They have a larger capacity for heart coherence, for connecting.

"From what I read in your dossier, your concern is their ability to observe. The Observer Effect," Franco emphasized. "I'm working now on experiments on observer entanglements."

Franco further explained, "The brain has a neuronet where nerve cells fire together and then become wired together. This happens with daily rage, beliefs, fear—you understand what I'm saying. A spider web of emotions. Any information we are exposed to is colored by our experiences, what we associate with that information or emotion. But if you disrupt the nerve cell firing by your response to information or events, the wiring is disconnected. Interrupt the thought process, poke holes in the neuronet. We know how to do that now on a mass scale, by influencing DNA."

Then he dropped the bombshell: "The key is water, hydrogen bonding. Water has memory and it has consciousness. The science community has known this since the 1927 Solvay Conference, where Einstein, Planck and other highly esteemed scientists realized how important water is. They found that bacteria in our water reacts simultaneously with solar flares happening 2.2 million light years away. We've come a long way since then."

Dr. Franco had noticed how closely Lucas was listening, so he continued. "We could make water pure in Africa and allow them to become more than a third-world country—but we won't. We have machines now that can extract water out of the humidity to provide clean water. We've been successful in convincing the world that you can't trust water out of a tap, it must come out of a bottle. And we've been able to take out all of the energy in that water, making it virtually dead. It only irrigates the human body, never hydrates it."

Lucas had suspected water was the key for a long time, and had been waiting for the right person to help him with his plan. Dr. Franco was his man.

"Water is the 'oil' of the future," Lucas had gloated to his soon-to-be-employee. "It will be our chief natural resource. It's one thing you can't live without. Own the water, own the world."

* * *

"Your father warned us, Lucas," Cardinal Gustav said, as they waited for Franco's return. "He said when you put harmonic water, such as blessed water, into your body, peace and harmony follow. And GA7's profits cease to exist. And the Church loses donors. That is why when a nun delivers the holy water to a priest, she is not allowed to speak or think, so as to not change its structure. Maybe we shouldn't have built over the well."

Lucas wondered if this 'holy water' had been damaged by the child-abusing priests, but kept his thoughts to himself. It wasn't on his agenda to care about something like that right now.

The scientist arrived, looking a bit pale. He had been monitoring the results and was also concerned.

"Why are we not seeing results, Dr. Franco?" Lucas asked in a low menacing tone.

"We are accessing everything now. As you know, all we have to do is drop a sufficient amount of tainted DNA into the water that has been exposed to pictures of war, beatings, hateful words—fear in a drop of water goes a very long way," explained the scientist. "Not only does the DNA produce electrical peaks and dips, it can do so simultaneously and sometimes even earlier in anticipation. Just like the random number generators. We are studying the anticipation theory now."

"Didn't you tell me that there is no place where one's body actually ends and no place where it begins? Blood reacts. Hit a man in the shin thousands of miles away, and his vial of blood reacts instantly?" Lucas asked.

"Yes sir, that is a proven fact," the scientist admitted.

Lucas knowingly nodded. He had learned a long time ago that every time we touch something or somebody we leave our DNA in the form of skin cells, linking us. That DNA could then be changed by "coherent emotions," such as quieting the mind, shifting one's awareness to a heart area and focusing on feelings, not thoughts. Introduce fear into the heart and it disrupts the emotional entanglement.

"Do you think the time acceleration is an influencing factor?"

"It may be. Give me a day to test the fresh samples, and I should have an answer."

Time isn't what Lucas had, not with the women gathering at Lourdes. He knew he had to keep the masses fearful and fighting each other, while generating as much revenue as possible for the richest of the rich—the members of the Liberty Group.

He must get the magnetic field above 7.8 hertz if he wanted to stay in the business of violence. The only way to keep the women in line. Especially *her.* She would regret her behavior. He would make sure of that.

Chapter Forty-Seven

—∞—

Gabriel cautiously side-stepped down the damp stone stairs, as he assisted his spry mother's descent into the circular crypt towards the hidden grotto. The trusted custodian had kept the precarious stairway in fairly good repair, as he promised, including providing a chair for Lilli's visits.

The custodian descended from a long line of Chartres workers, including the Masters of the Compasses who built the cathedral. Mysteriously, no record existed of the builders' names, quite unusual for such an important property. Almost as mystifying as how quickly the fifth replacement cathedral had been rebuilt—in less than sixty years. Legend said the architect who rebuilt the burned cathedral after the 1194 fire magically appeared within weeks after the inferno, a search that usually took years.

The custodian once said the cathedral was not built to glorify men's egos, but for Her. He quoted historian Henry Adams, who was descended from President John Adams: "All the steam in the world could not, like the Virgin, build Chartres."

"Do you remember me telling you about the Golden Mean?" the custodian had asked the teen aged Gabriel. "The proportions of the cathedral's floor plan match exactly the proportions of Da Vinci's Vitruvian Man. Rather vice versa. The cathedral came first." Not long after that conversation, the grotto had been officially walled up, with only the Auberts allowed to enter.

"Maman, here, please sit. I will fill the flasks and then we can perform the ritual of 'cleansing' Faïence."

"Merci, son. First, we must immerse grand-pére's scapular." She gently handed her ancestor's centuries-old scarf to him to submerge into the effervescent magical water. Generations of her family had visited this grotto over the centuries. Maybe even before the first cathedral had been built, according to passed-down tales.

This was the source of water her famous ancestor had used for scrying, allowing him to see in between the dimensions to write his quatrains. The water of the goddesses. The same crypt where the monks had taken the tunic to save it from the fire.

"Son, let me have your hand. What fools! Thinking we wouldn't know what they were up to," she said, half exasperated, half amused, as she dabbed her son's scrapped wrist. They both watched as the wound vanished.

"You know they will try to influence you now, right?" she asked. "Be sure to keep your star on you at all times. Has our mole been planted in the Vatican?"

"Yes. Soon we should have a report back," Gabriel assured her. "How much do you think we should tell the women? I think we need to educate them slowly yet gracefully. I don't want to frighten them, though after tonight we may be too late, heh?"

"I know how fond you are of her, my son. You and I have been patient for so long, allowing destiny to unfold. Let's get them back to our home and let them rest for now. They are unaware of their roles. We must delicately reveal this information as they are both wounded and somewhat fragile."

Two stories above, Stella took a deep breath and placed her stocking foot on the light-colored stone. Focusing on just one thought was extremely difficult. She had so many questions. Foremost, she wanted to know about the visions.

Deeply inhaling, she stepped into the opening, going clockwise. By her second step, she felt her feet tingle as she observed the red wool hairs of her dress statically rise and stand at attention. She stood still for a moment as she allowed the earth energy currents to oscillate up her legs and torso, finally lodging in her heart. Images swirled in and out of her mind, as the purging process began. She continued taking slow small mindful steps.

She stopped. Someone's hand was on her left shoulder, pulling her into an embrace. It felt so comforting, like her head resting in Nema's lap on a lazy summer day in the Sierra foothills, watching a parade of puffy white clouds float by in the bright sky.

She took a few more steps. Someone's breath was on her cheek. No, not *someone's* breath. It was *Nema's*, smelling of acorn mush.

> *Think about the ancient ones. Those who knew how to speak the language of the wind and rain, the stars and the sun, the language of God. They are here to guide you. Look to the heavens.*

Stella stopped and looked up to the high double flying buttresses that supported the apse. A silver thread tangled from high above in the church's night-time shadows, wafting to and fro as it slowly lowered closer towards her.

> *Remember the Spider Grandmother of the Hopis. She took the web, full of dew and threw it to the heavens and created the stars. The web is still all around us, connecting us all. Pay attention. Be brave.*

Stunned, Stella stopped in her tracks in the rose-shaped center. Her eyes chased Nema's ghostly image and watched it shatter into minuscule nuggets of still-vibrating matter before vaporizing into the ether. She turned to ask Maggie if she had seen Nema too, unaware of the stream of tears running down her face.

"What's wrong?" Maggie pleaded, hoping Stella wasn't in the grip of a panic attack.

"I just saw Nema. She talked to me. When we left she was still in a coma. You don't think this means she's left us, do you?"

"Mon chéri, what is wrong?" Lilli asked as she hurried into the main cathedral. She held Stella tightly, pressing the wet scarf still in her hand to the back of Stella's neck.

"I'm so sorry. I should have warned you of what could happen. It is a much more mystical journey than what you experienced before. When you first enter, it is like a mirror of our lives in the present time. It has three stages: releasing, receiving and finally returning to spirit. After what we've been through this evening, it must have been frightening. Did you see something?"

"My grandmother appeared to me and was talking about the Spider Grandmother. My grandmother is half Indian, and spent most of her life as a traditional healer."

"I remember your Nema well. I, too, come from a family of healers and have heard the story in many forms before. Remember, child, God is energy. It's all about energy."

What Stella didn't know was that the eye of the labyrinth was over the most powerful point in the world—the chakra of the earth. It vibrated at 18,000 *Bovis*, a cosmic-telluric measurement of subtle energy. Above 12,000 was considered a holy vibration. Powerful magnetic currents were present everywhere in the ancient cathedral.

"You both must be so tired. Hopefully, you can sleep on the long ride to our home. Let us go. I promise to get us there safely," Gabriel assured them.

As they traveled the narrow country roads to Callian, Stella had a hard time falling asleep. Not from jet lag or an inability to sleep in a moving vehicle. It was her water bottle, sitting close on the seat next to Lilli's Dior satchel. It was emitting a strange rainbow hue, as the bottle filled with star-like crystals.

Chapter Forty-Eight

_∞_

"**W**elcome, Sister, my name is Martha. I am the Eminence's housekeeper. Let me show you to your room."

Kathleen almost corrected the woman, to tell her she was no longer a nun, but she couldn't resist hearing her title once again. It had been such a long time. No doubt the housekeeper knew her history before she arrived.

"Thank you. I see you keep an impeccable house, Sister," Kathleen said, knowing all Vatican housekeepers were also sisters of the cloth.

She remembered the first time she had come here, to Vatican City. She had been deposited in Pastor Angelicus House, a rest home for aged women, founded by Mother Pascalina, Pope Pius XII's German-born assistant. *The Popess* they called her when Pius became ill, as she had long acted in the pope's stead. Mother Pascalina had been instrumental in 1950 getting Mary's Assumption to Heaven declared dogma.

Kathleen had been treated as an undesirable then, someone to hide away in shame. Never had been invited to the large regal apartment on Via della Conciliazione. Looking around at the ostentatious furnishings and gilded accessories, she understood why these apartments were so coveted by ambitious clerics.

However, the luxury did not extend to her room. Small and simple, filled with twin beds covered with identical faded raspberry-colored chenille bedspreads, one flat pillow each. Two pictures graced the ivory colored walls: Jesus and the pope, with a crucifix hung in between to complete the trinity.

"You will be sharing this room with me. I'll let you unpack and then we'll go shopping for dinner," Martha said as she turned to walk away.

As they walked to the Annona, the Vatican City supermarket restricted for Vatican employees and residents only, Martha pointed at the large building not far down the same street. "That's where the Vatican Radio is located," Martha said. "It's mostly run by women these days."

Kathleen had noticed the building soon after leaving the cardinal's apartment. Hard to miss, with its huge radio tower raising from the center and rings of satellite dishes. But what caught her attention now were all the women who seemed to be walking in the same direction as they were, all dressed very plainly. Most in just a blouse, sweater, skirt and comfortable shoes.

"Would you mind telling me, Sister, who are all these women?" Kathleen asked curiously.

"They are other nuns, no doubt on their way to the same place as us. It is our ritual, the daily shopping."

"But none appear to be dressed in habits," Kathleen said. She missed being so immediately identifiable in her holy costume, her wedding dress, commanding respect and reverence. Now that she no longer wore a habit, she felt unconnected. Dressed in street clothes, she was just Kathleen—an old Irish woman, nothing special.

"You'll find the more traditionally dressed nuns closer to St. Peters. What you see now are those of us who find that simple clothing suits us better in our daily lives. Our service to God is to take care of the clergy," Martha said, somewhat wearily.

Kathleen thought she noted a slight hint of bitterness in the housekeeper's last comment but let it go. She felt comfortable blending in with the nuns, feeling part of a community once again. She smiled, contented, as they continued their leisurely walk through the lush gardens of Vatican City.

A chorus of *buona seras* greeted them as soon as they entered the brightly lighted supermarket with its selection of specialized shops.

Kathleen realized that tonight's shopping was yet another Italian social peculiarity, similar to their nightly walks and people watching. Martha seemed to know everyone in the supermarket. They slowly made their way from shop to shop, stopping every few feet to talk to someone new.

"This is a new experience for you, no?" Martha asked, her accent more Italian than French after decades living in Vatican City.

"Yes. I knew Vatican City was small, but didn't realize you all know each other."

"This is our gathering place, to meet and catch up. We don't call each other on the phones because all Vatican phones are bugged by the Vigilance, the Vatican security service. Here we are free to discuss our lives and sometimes to gossip. Not like the priests. They are constantly gossiping as they try to advance up to the top job. Always! But for us, there is a purple ceiling—for the time being anyway," Martha said with a touch of defiance. Kathleen had met a kindred spirit.

"That'll be right about that ceiling. The last time I was about," Kathleen said vaguely, "I did some research in the archives. Did you know that ever since the Popess Joan incident early in the church's history, they now check the genitals of the incoming pope to make sure he's got bits?"

"Of course. Not much is secret here, though they would like to think it is."

More secrets here than you know, Kathleen thought. Gustav had told her about the secret archives, adjacent to the Vatican Library. A collection of documents and priceless artifacts, some cloaked in hundreds of years of secrets, all belonging to the pope. So much information, read once or twice, then deposited under lock and key in no particular order. No one really knew everything that was in the archives.

"We have public spaces for accredited researchers, and also private enclaves that only a select few are allowed to enter. You are one of those who are allowed. I trust you value this privilege and will not abuse it," the holy man had told her. She had proved worthy of his trust—as far as she revealed.

Now that she was back in Vatican City, Kathleen was eager to find out more about those secrets, especially the big secret. She could put two and two together. Something was not right about their concern for the two women she had photographed and recorded.

She had felt a change since that day the women visited. Made her look at her life in a different light. She was tired of being a thug, telling lies. It wasn't living a holy life. She could sense danger—not only for them, but for herself. Time to think about strategies and devise a plan of her own.

Chapter Forty-Nine

—∞—

The sun crested the horizon as they entered the small village of Callian. Gabriel automatically downshifted as they came around the village's waterfall as he started the slow circular crawl up to the St. Remy home. He could hear murmuring from the backseat, Maggie and Stella's faces pressed against the windows. No doubt falling in love with the quaint medieval hilltop town.

Gabriel drove into the circular driveway on the now-level ground. As a courtesy, he pulled up as close as he could to the front door to unload his passengers and luggage. He hoped it gave them enough room to easily get out of the van.

Stella emerged from the vehicle, glad to be able to finally stretch her long legs. The fragrant cloud of herbal aromas, especially the rosemary, revived her after the long night's drive. It felt like walking into a secret garden, lavishly in bloom in February.

"Lilli, what a beautiful home," she exclaimed as she surveyed the quaint cottage, terraced into the hill. The cottage's front doors were flanked with heavily-ladened lemon trees, citrus soldiers on guard. The inside perimeter of the property was studded with olive and almond trees. Lavender bushes had been teased and groomed into a braided fence framing the large formal herb garden. But it was the abundant white mounds of Lily of the Valley all along the walkway which impressed Stella the most. She had never witnessed such vibrant whiteness in a bloom. It made her own Mill Valley moon garden resemble a potted plant.

"Thank you, mon chéri. This has been my family's home for centuries. Please come in."

"I'm surprised your lavender is blooming," Stella said, as she clutched her purse to her chest.

"Year round. We are the herb garden to the world, you know. Excellent soil, even by Provence standards. The mistral blows the sky clear, allowing the sun to shine on our little top of the world. That, and a family secret taught to me by my mother. Someday, I will share it with you, if you like."

"Please," she said, as she snapped off a rosemary sprig and sniffed it deep enough to coat her nostrils with the twig's oiliness. She had heard rosemary was good for memory recovery. Wondered how it would work on her fear.

A bee buzzed Stella's head, almost causing her to fall over from the shock. "Whoa! A bee in February? That's beyond odd."

Lilli smiled. "Not in my garden. They tend to stay here. It is a safe haven for them. Peaceful, and they always have pollen." As Stella looked around she now noticed there were bees everywhere. "They, too, have been here for centuries."

They entered the enchanted cottage, followed by Gabriel with their luggage. Maggie wondered how he had managed to get it all from the hotel and into the van. *How did he get into her room?* She still had her room key in her purse. Two and two were not adding up right.

Gabriel sensed her unease and decided to change the focus of the conversation. He pointed towards his mother and Stella by the garden and said, "Did you know bees and ants have eliminated conflict? They are selfless and will sacrifice their lives for the good of the colony. They are motivated by their desire to belong, to be part of a team. It is said ants even perform funerals for their dead and pray."

"Does that include Army ants?" Maggie asked sarcastically, as they entered through the French doors to the kitchen. It was obvious this kitchen was the heart of their home. Maggie loved the yellows and blue sprinkled throughout the room, from the tiles to the tablecloth. Looking at the rough-hewn overhead beams, she wondered exactly how old the house was, its history.

Maggie turned and watched Stella out the kitchen window. Stella was still clutching her purse like a lifesaver. Was she popping pills? If anything was going to trigger a panic attack, running out of a foreign city into the dark of the night with dangerous strangers on their tail and then seeing your comatose grandmother in a church talking to you would pretty much do the trick.

"Please, let me show you to your rooms so you can settle in. Then come down for a cup of tea and some food. No doubt you are still jet lagged," Lilli said as she led Stella inside the kitchen's French doors. "I have a special tea that will easily help you adjust to our time frame, and the altitude too."

"Sure, thanks. I'd love some tea," Maggie said as she grabbed Stella's wrist and led her up the cramped staircase to a rabbit's warren of rooms. Maggie ducked when walking up, though there was plenty of room for her to stand up.

The two women's behavior did not pass unnoticed by Lilli and Gabriel. Neither Stella nor Maggie had been in this cottage before, but acted as if they knew it intimately. Their behavior did not surprise the hosts. The staircase had been remodeled in the last year to allow for more head space, while the house had been sheathed in copper mesh beneath the plaster to thwart any kind of electronic eavesdropping. They had been planning for the women's visit for quite some time. Maybe Maggie was still seeing it in a prior time period. An experience not unusual in the ancient home.

"Please make yourselves comfortable," Lilli said, puffing up the pillows on each bed. "Small, no doubt, compared to your American homes, but suitable, no."

"Perfect," Maggie said as she sat on the twin bed to the right. The perfume of lavender filled the toasty room, making her quite sleepy.

"If you don't mind," she said as she eased off her shoes, noticing Stella was already deeply burrowed in under the puffy duck-feathered comforter. The room's coziness lulled both of the women to sleep in under five minutes.

The glow of the sunset in the guest room greeted Stella as she wakened, along with the smell of fresh bread. She hadn't eaten for almost twenty hours and was ravenous. Maggie was flat on her back, slack-mouthed and snoring. As she was about to nudge her, she thought this was a perfect time to have time alone with her French hosts; maybe more with one than the other.

With that thought she involuntarily tightened her Kegel muscles. She hadn't had that kind of reaction since, well, for so long she hesitated to do the math. *Not dead yet, old girl*, she thought.

The aromas tunneling up the staircase from the simmering pots and pans below made Stella salivate as she stepped into the kitchen. Lilli was stirring a large heavy pot on the stove while her son, still in his black sweater and pants protected by a chef's apron, was at the kitchen sink washing dishes.

"Stella, you're awake," Lilli said as turned to greet her visitor. "Please sit and let me get you a cup of tea. I'm almost finished with our dinner. We usually eat later in the evening, but I knew you two must be famished. The bread has just come out of the oven, and I'm now finishing the braised lentils. I also have spring lamb stew, peas and the potato pancakes finishing up too."

Stella automatically chose the chair against the wall at the kitchen table. Gabriel pulled out the chair opposite her, sat and turned his attention to a wooden bowl, but not before giving her a wide smile. How adorable, Stella thought, as she noticed his hank of wavy hair fall on his forehead as he stirred the bowl's contents. He was mixing up something delicious judging by the dark glistening smoothness clinging to his spoon. *Please let it be chocolate mousse*, she beggingly prayed.

"I could make you a lovely cup of tea, or would you prefer a glass of wine?" he suggested.

Wine sounded heavenly, but not wise on an empty stomach, Stella decided. "I think it's safer if I have some tea first, but thank you so much," she replied, drawing out each syllable with a bit too much emphasis. She heard a creak and turned to see Maggie's shadow on the wall as she descended.

"Good morning, afternoon or whatever time it is, folks," Maggie said rather pertly. "If you don't mind, I'd love a cup of tea also."

The two women settled themselves at the wooden table, already set with fine china. Stella noticed a small bookcase with some very interesting looking books, judging by their spines. "May I?" she asked, as she pulled one out.

"I see you are drawn to my special book, chéri," Lilli said as she continued stirring the stew. "It is a very rare book on botanicals and healing. From many centuries ago. You have seen this type of book, with its hidden picture on the gilded edge? Son, please show Stella the picture."

Gabriel washed his hands and dried them eagerly on his apron. "May I?" he asked, as he leaned in close enough for Stella to smell his essence. He turned the book horizontally in his large hands with the spine facing his chest. Stella tried to pay attention to the book as he bowed it slightly, the fanned pages showing the faint picture of a luscious garden. She was more interested in his manly wrists. She flipped her hair over her shoulder and smiled, lightly touching her breastbone.

"It is called fore-edge painting. That book was a present from my husband. He had to smuggle it under his shirt when he left his store because the Germans wouldn't let him leave with anything when he closed at night. He risked his life so I could have that book," Lilli said. "I was loved that way once," she sighed.

"I love rare books. Mind if I look through them?" Maggie asked, trying not to think of how she, too, had been loved like that once.

"Please, you are our guests. There is no need to ask permission. Our home is your home," Lilli replied. "I see you have picked the *Mysteries of Water Book*. A very rare book Gabriel found. I think you will find it quite interesting."

"One of my favorites," Gabriel said. "It talks about how water has memory, and how our thoughts change the water's structure. One of the reasons we say grace before eating is because it changes the energy of our food in a very positive way."

He walked over to the bookcase and handed her a small thin paperback. "This is not very old, but read this after the first one. It was written by Dr. Masaru Emoto. He took pictures of how water reacted to different music and words. When water was exposed to the word love, it formed the most beautiful crystal stars. Similar to your necklaces, no?"

Chapter Fifty

—∞—

"I'm about to bust wide open. Why did I shovel all that food down my gullet? You must think me an unmannered pig, but everything was so damn delicious, Lilli!" Maggie said, blotting her mouth with the monogrammed linen napkin.

"Merci, my love. It pleases me very much you enjoyed it so. We adore pigs. Many have been our friends. Our village is responsible for all our food, so sooner or later, in some form, you will meet all the animals being raised," Lilli laughed. "You will discover quickly in Provence that every day is a celebration of the circle of life."

"Maman, since the wind is soft tonight, it might be enjoyable to have our dessert outside. Shall I make a fire?"

"Oui, please, son. We will join you in a moment, after we have cleared the table."

Stella watched Gabriel out the window as she dried the dishes. His body, outlined against the night's charcoal darkness, had a bright green aura. She wondered what his naked back looked like, watching his muscles move under his black turtleneck while he effortlessly chopped kindling. She studied him like she would a Rodin sculpture.

After they had returned each plate to its home, Stella excused herself. Moments later, she returned dressed in a plunging cowled gray sweater dress. The drape of the soft neckline dipped into the cleavage of her nicely aged bosom. She had decided to take Dibrovna's advice and show off her legs.

The abrupt change in costume did not escape Maggie's notice. Many times in her youth she had been witness to her friend's seduction tactics. This girl was not playing. Stella was back. *Hallelujah.* If she had been home, she would have popped popcorn to munch and watch the drama unfold. She watched Stella approach the priest, her hips wiggling like a bucket of worms.

Stella, her shimmering silver blond locks pinned up into a modern French twist, shined with confidence as she walked out to the terrace. The glow of the patio's twinkling lights, wrapped around the cypress trees, mixed with the purple-tinged smoke from the village's evening fires wafting up intensified the Golden Hour glow.

"These stones on your terrace are very unique," Stella observed as Lilli handed her a plate of warm fig tarts with a small earthen jug of warm cream.

"You have a good eye, dear. This house has stood for a very long time. Those stones," Lilli said, pointing to the flat large cobble-stones "are from the Bastille prison from the French Revolution. A constant reminder how precious freedom is."

Gabriel came through the French doors, carrying a bottle of wine. Stella cocked her ear, listening to the melody coming from inside the cottage. She closed her eyes and smiled. *The Very Thought of You* by Frank Sinatra floated into the night air. When she opened her eyes, she caught Gabriel whistling along to the tune. He winked at her as he pulled the cork from the bottle.

Maggie was amused by their display of attraction. "My God, that priest is infatuated with you," she hissed at Stella.

"And I'm supposed to feel bad about that?"

"Don't get salty with me, missy. Might want to consider if the juice on that one is worth the squeeze. Darling, dare I say, you *do* have a pattern with unobtainable men."

Stella was silenced. Her high of a few moments before—gone. She took a big gulp of wine. For a moment, she had been full with promises of more. She had been willing to forget he was a priest. Small talk about the weather helped mask her disappointment.

"You seem so wise and confident about things in the world. Is it your faith?" Stella asked Lilli.

"My faith? You think I'm Catholic because my son is a priest? Logical assumption, but no. I was actually raised Jewish, as all the women in my family were. My ancestors were forced to convert from the Jewish faith to Catholicism back in the early 1500s by Louis XII or leave France.

"First to be baptized into the Catholic faith was my brave ten-times great-grandfather, Michel de Nostradame. He sacrificed his faith so our family could stay in France. The women continued to practice Judaism." Lilli knew that would catch their attention. She tried to be obscure about her ancestor, but sensed she would have to tell the whole story sooner than later. She held hope it would be on her timetable.

"You are wondering about my great-grandfather's name, oui? Yes, it does translate as Michael of Our Lady. And you know him as Nostradamus." A thunder clap couldn't have been louder to her visitors' ears.

Stunned and astonished, Stella feebly mumbled, "Really?" Maggie stared at the Frenchwoman, wide-eyed, fully alert.

"I come from a long line of Jewish doctors, herbalists and astrologers. And seers," Lilli continued, "but none as famous as Nostradamus.

"During the Black Plague which lasted one hundred years, half of all Europeans died. My great-grandfather administered to the sick and dying, but couldn't save his family. He was a broken man and, like many others, he flocked to church trying to find a meaning to what seemed God's wrath upon humanity.

"Unsatisfied and unfulfilled, he decided to take the pilgrimage on the Camino de Santiago, following the Milky Way all the way to the sea at St. James Cathedral. On his way back, he kept walking until he came to Chartres. It was there in the same grotto we visited last night that he first began to 'read the water.' He returned to St. Remy and, for the next four years, he wrote his quatrains.

"Because of all the people turning to the church for answers or comfort from their grief, the Catholic Church became very powerful.

Nostradamus visited many other churches and saw many things," Lilli finished, discrete in her omissions.

She nodded to her handsome son, signaling need for his assistance. Even all these years since France's Liberation, discussing the war was difficult. Rarely, did she discuss her own two years of incarceration in *Ravensbruck*, a prisoner-of-war camp. She had almost starved to death. Raped repeatedly by the German guards, her mother and her only sister did not survive the camp.

"Our ancestor and his work stayed private for many centuries, as it was intended," Gabriel said. "Then came Hitler. The wife of Josef Goebbels, Hitler's minister of propaganda, showed her husband a book of Nostradamus' predictions, alerting him to a prediction of Hitler's rise. Immediately, the Third Reich saw the power value of propaganda. They employed a Swiss astrologer, Karl Krafft, to write interpretations of Nostradamus' predictions, making them favorable to the Third Reich, of course. Goebbels once said *I can make a triangle into a square, if I just repeat it enough.*

"Soon the British started making up fake quatrains, which they dropped from airplanes into Germany. The more negative the prediction, the more readily it was accepted. Nostradamus knew this—*negative is always more interesting.* It's why he hid his biggest prophecy amidst 'doom and gloom.'"

Stella remembered the warning the women had heard at the seminar in Berkeley. Not only was negative more interesting, it was deadly. One-million-dead-in-ninety-days deadly. The negative tide rising in America since 9/11, with what was once considered unacceptable or impolite conversation was now blasted daily from radio and television. She shivered, thinking of what kind of America her grandchild would be born into.

"Haven't lots of politicians used psychics?" Stella asked. "They said Nancy Reagan used an astrologer."

"More than the public knows," Gabriel continued.

"But they don't always stay in favor. By 1941, the same year Sister Lucia wrote her fourth memoir, the Nazis arrested Krafft as part of a Nazi sweep of astrologers and occultists. He died in 1945, being sent to the Nazi death camp of Buchenwald. Ironic, heh?"

Maggie kicked Stella in the ankle. Stella sat stone faced, avoiding Maggie's eyes. They hadn't yet discussed whether to share their story with their guests. Yet—no accidents.

"Son, remember by the time Sister Lucia wrote down the first two secrets, by force of her bishop, we were already involved in war. She grew up in wartime. Don't you think if she knew something that could have averted another world war, she would have said something?" Lilli asked, even though she already knew the answer. She had once asked the infamous sister this very same question.

Her guests sat quietly, sipping their wine and star gazing. Efforts to get the Americans to talk about their visitations went wanting.

"Our ancestor predicted the Great Alignment of 1998 would occur during the Winter Solstice. He predicted because of the planetary alignment there would be monumental earth changes. He believed with the new awareness of western civilization and the accelerated rate of the shift and conjunction of the planets, war *might* be avoided. The degree to which it happens will depend on the awareness people have mentally and spiritually.

"He believed women, who he referred to as "sisters," have a clear perception of multidimensional mental messages and can most easily receive revelation if they unite and refuse to be divided by the dictates of lower interests." Gabriel watched Stella squirm, bursting to tell her story.

"You know, Maggie, Nostradamus stared into a pool of water for his visions. He 'looked between the drops.' Is that similar to how you and your husband were able to see?" asked Lilli, going for the closer.

"What?" Stella almost screamed, her voice echoing off the rocky hillside. "You know about him?"

"Jim and I both used that method," Maggie said, calmly parsing her words on what she would reveal. She wasn't surprised that Lilli knew this about her and Jim. She had been around enough "naturals" as Jim called them to recognize one. Now the cards were on the table.

"My husband was taught to activate his seeing by scribbling on a piece of paper, somewhat like automatic writing. Jim explained it to me this way: there is an ether, the fifth element the Greeks called "air breathed by Gods" where all information resides."

"That is true," Gabriel said. "There have been other references to the same phenomenon throughout history. It was called the Net of God Indra by Buddhists and the web by the Spider Grandmother in American Indian folklore."

Stella shuddered.

"Are you cold? Would you like me to get you a blanket?" Gabriel asked.

"How do you know about the Spider Grandmother?"

"It's my job. As a Bollandist, I research all day, every day. Through my recent research on the Divine Feminine, I have learned many things," Gabriel added.

"My research even involves quantum theory. The Church has tried to keep religion and science divided, but it is not possible. After all, we are all just atoms constantly in motion. A quantum is simply a discrete quantity of electromagnetic energy. Brief tiny bursts of light are quanta. They happen so quickly together to create uninterrupted action, similar to how a movie is frame by frame. Both Einstein and Max Plank said this was the fourth dimension, the fourth world."

Stella's wine glass fell from her hands and crashed to the stone patio. "I'm so sorry! That's what my grandmother told me about when I was walking the labyrinth—the Spider Grandmother and the fourth world."

"Is this what people are actually seeing when they say they see ghosts?" Stella asked, though she really meant visions of Her.

"I'm not completely sure," Gabriel told her. "There is something called holographic consciousness. They say the prayer we make already exists with our prayed-for loved ones exactly at the same time."

"We are masters of connecting, we French," Lilli added. "Some say it is because we are artistic. You see, when you create art your mind is in a meditative state of consciousness. It changes the electromagnetic field around you, allowing you to see more clearly."

"I know," Maggie inserted. "When Jim was first teaching me, I was frustrated at my results. He then suggested I take piano lessons. After that, it was a snap."

"So that's why they are probably cutting arts in school, right? To keep the psychics down?" Stella added sarcastically.

"Yes," Lilli said, seriously. "A very easy thing to do to keep power, don't you think?"

Chapter Fifty-One

—∞—

"You lost them?" Lucas roared, releasing the speaker button and grabbing the handset. It was rare for him to lose control of his emotions, especially in the presence of others. He was livid. At himself, mostly.

When he had received the news yesterday of the successful capture, he had been so pleased their hasty plan had worked that he hired the airport duo again. Of course, he should have known better. But they had to scramble at the last minute after Brent remote viewed the invitation.

The two women were in Paris at the invitation of the French woman and her priest son. That changed the whole scenario. Gustav had been right about the Bollandist; he couldn't be trusted. The duo had been successful all day tracking the foursome through Paris, so he negligently agreed to use the French thug's nephew at the restaurant instead of one of his trained operatives.

He could hear his father's stern voice in his head, chastising him for such an amateur mistake. *Beware the ego, son, as it will lull you into complacency*, Elliott had said to him many times. His mind had been so preoccupied with the lack of DNA results on the women's hair, he hadn't followed his standard operating procedure. He was consumed on getting final revenge on the uppity Ms. St. James.

"Get Cardinal Muench here, pronto!" he ordered his assistant. Lucas was furious that the cardinal had brought someone to such an important meeting in Amsterdam without a thorough background search. *Who was the mother?* They could not allow anything like this to happen again.

"And Franco too!" he said, slamming down the phone's handset.

Within five minutes, his assistant was at his door with a report. "Sir, it appears the priest's mother is Lilli Juliette de St. Remy Aubert. She lives in Callian, in southern France. She's a retired la premier for Dior. Her dossier says she was also in the French Resistance."

Lucas slammed his hand against the desk. "Give it to me!" he demanded, snatching the report from her hand. "You can leave."

Not one accustomed to making mistakes, he wanted to know why the cardinal didn't mention the mother. He had been caught off guard, not knowing the priest's mother was the infamous Lilli St. Remy Aubert, his father's rescuer that dark night in the French countryside. The one who told his father about the Third Secret. He called his assistant again. "Get me the Spaniard on the phone. And make sure it's a secure line."

Of course, a former French Resistance fighter would have an escape route out of Paris. If he had used professionals, all escape routes would have been covered. No more mistakes.

"We've lost precious time," Lucas snarled as Cardinal Gustav and Dr. Franco entered his office. "Soon, the women will be gathering at Lourdes. Why isn't our Plan working?"

"Heart coherence, sir," the scientist said softly, not wanting to further inflame his boss. "I advised you about this previously, that this was a high possibility because of their recent hardships. They appear to have connected on a very deep emotional level; their entangled fields are almost impenetrable.

"Almost. If they get to the water in Lourdes with the most powerful water in the world, it may be too powerful to counteract ours, sir. This could be the Great Gathering you were warned about. We must break the connection immediately before it is too late," the scientist warned.

Lucas did not react to this news. He calmly thanked the two men and excused them as the phone rang. After he was sure the men were safely out of earshot, he picked up the phone to speak to the Spaniard.

"I need you to go to Lourdes. Shortly, the targets' information packet will arrive via courier. I need you to start tracking the targets. We have enabled scanning of the RFIDs in their passports, but at this time cannot locate them. Find them and eliminate. Conventional is okay, just make it discreet and quiet. I don't want any witnesses *this* time."

Lucas' assistant entered the room. "Sir, we have received more intelligence on the targets. One has a daughter, lives on a very successful Northern California winery. Her only daughter. She's pregnant."

"Interesting, very valuable."

"Indeed, sir," the young blond woman replied, one of only two women in his whole operation.

Lucas remembered what his father once told him. "That is one thing most men don't quite understand. A woman has *bullet love* for their children, more so than a man. A man will still shill for a golden coin. But a woman? She will jump in front of a flying bullet before she lets her child die."

"Thank you for the information. Let's start following the daughter. Knead the dough, so to speak."

Chapter Fifty-Two

—∞—

Stella stretched as far as she could out the bedroom window, trying to get some bars on her cell phone. She shook her phone. Still nothing. She shook it again. A habit left over from her father's preferred method of fixing electronics.

Her nightgown was still damp from last night's dream. Nicki was in trouble. Maybe her dream was only anxiety, but she didn't want to take any chances. Too many unexplainable things happening since she arrived on French soil. Not the time to take chances with her child and grandchild. No resting until she knew if they were safe or not.

Frustrated and not knowing if it was technology or the thick early morning fog causing the lack of service, she dressed quickly and descended the stairs. She really didn't want to talk to her daughter here in the small cottage. No privacy. Maybe Maggie would go with her down to the local café so she could use the phone there.

"Good morning, ladies," she said, as she stepped down into the kitchen.

Maggie and Lilli, heads so close their reddish curls corkscrewed together, were deep in discussion at the kitchen table. The women's hushed intimacy greatly intimated her.

Knock it off, Stella, she chided herself. Paranoia and anxiety, perfect partners like Fred and Ginger. She contemplated taking just half a pill to ease her jittery fear.

Maggie straightened up and smiled "Good mornin', sweetie. I dare say you appear a little prickly. What's up?"

"I'm trying to reach Nicki and can't seem to get reception on my cell."

Lilli's face didn't betray the reason. Their efforts in warding off electronic intrusions were obviously successful.

"I'm so sorry, mon chéri. I would offer our phone, but Gabriel is waiting for a very important call."

"I know. He mentioned something about that last night. That's okay, I think I'll walk down to the village café and use the phone there. I won't be long," she added when Maggie started to rise. Feeling like an outsider, she didn't want to intrude on the women's conversation.

For once, she had chosen somewhat sensible shoes for the downhill trek. However, the going was treacherous. The mossy cobblestones in the winding alleyways to the village center were still in the morning shadow. The cloudless blue sky had yet to thaw the crunchy dew on the ground, making traction chancy. She walked sideways to steady her steps, exactly like Nema had taught her when they hiked through the Marin Headlands.

"Hi, mom. God, it's so good to hear from you," Nicki said, her voice hesitant with tears. "I really miss you."

"I miss you, too, honey. How's the baby?" she asked, suddenly coming to tears herself. She felt a need to be with her daughter, to hold her, protect her. She turned her back to the village strollers so no one could see her cry.

"I'm fine, and the baby's fine. Still don't know what sex yet, but will soon. We haven't decided whether to tell people though."

Just that one sentence brought back the pain Stella had endured through her three miscarriages before finally having Nicki. She hoped it wasn't a genetic trait she had passed to her only child. They idly chatted about family before Nicki dropped the bomb.

"Mom, I don't know how to tell you this, or if I should even mention it. But, well, I think someone's been reading my emails. And I think someone's been watching me. A man. A plain man—in a plain car. I think he wants me to know that he's watching. He came to the tasting room yesterday."

Stella felt her knees buckle, her chest tighten. She tried to hold the phone with her shoulder as she rummaged through her purse for the familiar plastic bottle.

"Mom? Mom, are you there?"

"Yeah, hold on, trying to pay for something" she lied. She didn't want to disappoint Nicki or alarm her.

"Listen to what I'm telling you right now. Go buy a pay-as-you-go phone. Do not call me on my cell! I'll get more instructions to you soon. Say nothing else and have Carlos or one of his brothers with you at all times. I will be in contact shortly. I love you." She hung up.

She rummaged through her bag, relieved to find the old crumbled business card from her recent St. Helena visit. "Hello, I'm calling from France. May I please talk to Wayne, the wine manager?" Thank god for small communities, she thought, as she gave him the information to relay to the Sanchez family.

And thank god for Law & Order! During her many sleepless nights after the cracking open, she had watched the show endlessly. It was her sanity touchstone. They always tracked people down using cell phone GPS. She walked into the *boulangerie* and asked for a favor; she popped a Xanax on her way out.

By the time she climbed to Lilli's house, her face was beet red; drenched in sweat, even on this chilly February day. It was more than exertion that colored her cheeks. She was mother-bear pissed!

Chapter Fifty-Three

—∞—

"**W**hat the hell happened? You okay?" Maggie asked as she knelt beside the wing chair and grabbed Stella's trembling hand. Lilli rushed from the kitchen to Stella's side and wiped her brow with a cold scented cloth.

"Lilli, I don't know who's after us or what is going on, but my daughter is being followed and her emails are being read! What the hell is going on?" Stella almost screeched, her voice cracking as she sat up.

"Those men who chased us out of Paris—who the hell are they? If this is about a doll, why are they following my daughter?" she pleaded to Lilli. Hearing the commotion, Gabriel hurried into the room from his study.

"What is going on?" he asked, his brow deeply creased. He could see that the American women were upset, but more troubling so was his usually unflappable mother.

"We must get them to Lourdes!" Lilli ordered in her most commanding voice. "You have both seen Her, no?" Lilli boomed, knowing full well the answer.

"I'm not sure what you are asking us," Maggie stammered.

"Please, we do not have time. I know you both have been visited. Please do not be fearful," the older woman said, rubbing Stella's forearm to comfort her. Within seconds of Lilli's touch, Stella muscles slackened.

"Son, please bring me the jar."

Gabriel removed the silver lid as he handed the decorative small jar to his mother. Lilli dipped her fingertips in and scooped out a dab of the exotic herbal paste inside.

"Oh, that smells divine," Stella remarked with a slight smile, her psyche already responding to the magic mixture. Her thoughts were of her favorite comfort food—a warm croissant smothered with creamy butter. Lilli rubbed more of the paste on Stella's forearm.

Maggie looked the French woman in the eyes. "Yes, we have been 'visited' as you call it. Do you think it was a Marian Apparition?" Maggie asked boldly.

"That is not for me to answer as I was not there. But I am very familiar with the stories. Is this not why you are 'gathering the women' at Lourdes?" she asked, hoping not to alarm the women.

"You know about our gathering?" Stella gasped. Her muscles sluggishly reacted; first, her chest tightened before her breath quickened. She looked at the clock wondering how long it would take for her Xanax to fully kick in.

Lilli added another dollop onto Stella's other forearm.

"Maggie?" Stella asked, "I think it's time to have the talk."

"I agree. Lilli, we weren't completely honest about our trip to Lourdes. We weren't trying to deceive you, just with everything happening . . . ."

"I understand. I know about the women gathering at Lourdes, the visits worldwide. You are all staying at the chateau. There are no accidents," Lilli said.

"That is true," Gabriel said. "Lourdes has a long history with Mary. Long before Bernadette," Gabriel said. "In the 8th century the Castle of Lourdes was invaded by Arabs who refused to surrender until Christian King Charlemagne convinced them to lay down their arms in Mary's honor. For the next 1,000 years, the people of Lourdes believed they were protected by the Virgin Mary until the French Revolution in 1789. However, by the middle of the 19th century, faith in Mary was being challenged by science.

"I think you know what happened next to the young French girl? By the ninth time Bernadette saw the lady in white, she had discovered the sparkling stream. There are mentions of healing shrines in the New Testament—in ancient Egypt, a miraculous pool in Jerusalem that heals when the water ripples and sparkles as if angels stirred the water," Gabriel finished.

"Have you finished your reading, Maggie?" Lilli inquired.

"Not yet, but if you don't mind I would like to take the books with me. I will guard them with my life."

"Yes, take them. I trust you. Also, remember this. Pay attention to your thoughts. If a thought makes you uncomfortable, change it immediately. *Do not forget this.* Think thoughts that make you smile. And *always* wear your necklaces. Now go! Gabriel will take you. I believe the other women are already arriving," Lilli said as she lifted Stella from her chair and lovingly held her face.

"There is no time to waste! You have experienced your harshest winter, Stella. Now is the time for your most shining spring."

Chapter Fifty-Four

—∞—

"**Y**ou've been to this chateau before?" Stella asked, her weakened arms braced on the dashboard of the gray blue Renault Dauphine as it slowly moved down the still-icy, steep road into the lush valley below.

"Oui, many times. My family goes back many lifetimes with the owners," Gabriel said. "It's right outside of Lourdes, in the Pyrenees National Forest. Many gatherings of women have happened there over the years."

Stella was about to ask more when she noticed birds flying low in a circle, following their voyage.

"Look, Maggie. See those birds following us? Aren't they the most beautiful creatures you ever saw?"

Gabriel, keenly aware that Stella was feeling the effects of his mother's salve, slouched down to look out the windshield. "Those are magpies. How many of them do you see?"

"I'm not sure. They seem to be melting into the sky."

Maggie pulled out her phone and quickly snapped a picture of the flock. "Sweet darlin', let me help you. I see one, two . . . seven, maybe. You want to tell us, Gabriel, why that's important?"

"There is a belief in many cultures that magpies are an omen of impending death—or birth. My father taught me this old English rhyme:

> '*One for sorrow, two for joy,*
> *three for a girl, four for a boy,*
> *five for silver, six for gold,*
> *seven for a secret never to be told.*'"

Stella turned in her bucket seat to look at Maggie, eyebrows raised over her now-bloodshot eyes. Even in her drug-induced state there was no mistaking that *here we go down the damn rabbit hole again* expression in her best friend's brown eyes. By the time she turned back to the front, her reptilian brain was shocked sober and whirling like a hamster on meth.

The thick topaz fog continued to hug the hilltops above as their car wound its way down through the sunny rolling plains filled with olive groves and vineyards. On one side of the road was rocky sandstone land, wildly studded with pine trees and mounds of juniper. While across the same road were miles of perfectly spaced rows of both lavender and grapes. Stella studied the vineyards and fretted over what might be happening that very moment back in California.

Secrets indeed. How did Lilli and Gabriel know so much about her, about the visits? Why was someone looking to harm her and her family? What was the connection? She and Maggie had pledged no more secrets, and it was time to shine the light. *A candle flame has no shadow, no dark*, Nema had taught her.

The three continued, each lost in thought, for hours along the Plane tree-lined roads, passing a peloton of racing bicyclists who thought sharing the walled narrow roads with speeding masses of lethal metal was a good health choice.

Worrying about Nicki's safety wouldn't change anything; she needed action. The main theme of Dibrovna's war stories of survival was always keeping her children safe by being prepared, having a strategy. She marveled at that woman's bravery and courage, wondering how Dibrovna could have kept going. Now she knew. You just did.

When it came to your children, you have no other choice. She knew Dibrovna would never let anything happen to Nicki, and neither would Nicki's husband and in-laws. She hoped the message she had sent via the small market's wine manager would arrive in time.

Suddenly, Stella started to feel drowsy, her head bobbing against the window. She wanted to have a conversation with Gabriel about the vision but was unsure if she was a little too high from the pill coupled with the special salve. Didn't want to embarrass herself by slurring. But true to form, her frontal lobe filter failed again.

"So why aren't you a priest with a congregation? Is it because of all the sex scandals?" She could feel Maggie's eyes bore into the back of her head. Her question was not only inappropriate, the tone was accusatory.

Gabriel stiffened.

Ah damn, Stella thought. Her intent hadn't been to make him defensive. She wished she could take back her words. Obviously, not the right time to discuss such a delicate subject. Clumsy and inappropriate. She worried if she would ever recover the art of conversation or was she becoming a cranky, obnoxious old lady. The kind that squirted kids with a garden hose when they teasingly stepped on her lawn.

"No, certainly not," Gabriel quickly, yet loudly, replied. He looked in the rear view mirror at Maggie, when he felt her kick his car seat. "I'm sorry I did not mean to scare you by yelling."

"Oh no, I'm fine. Cool as the other side of a pillow in July. Just a little startled," Maggie lied. She was still staring at her bird photos.

Seven birds, seven orbs of brilliant light. She twirled Jim's watch around her wrist, wondering if souls indeed drifted in an ether she couldn't see. She continued taking pictures of the countryside.

"I grew up as a very curious little boy, loving research. My father instilled in me a life-long love affair of books. I found I could serve God better through my work as a Bollandist than as a priest," he finished, a partial truth.

"History is important. It tells us who we are, and documents lessons learned. My work puts life in prospective. I am constantly searching for miracles, for saints to be recognized. Lately, most of them have been women, especially nuns.

"Their work reminds me it is better to be compassionate than obedient. We all have a responsibility to humankind to advocate for peace. Sometimes that responsibility gets muddled when living a privileged existence, don't you think?

"As for the Church's handling of these sex scandals, it appears they would rather chase gold than protect the flock. I do not approve. However, maybe we can discuss this more at a later time," he said as he spotted the thick grove of Italian Cypresses over the crest. "We're almost to the chateau."

Gabriel drove cautiously across the crushed stone driveway to avoid any unnecessary noise and dust. As if by clockwork, the famous welcoming gaggle of geese approached the car to officially guide them in. He followed the trimmed, boxwood hedges towards the open courtyard, parking in front of the star-shaped fountain with a goddess statue.

"Oh, my—it's gorgeous," Stella exclaimed.

Maggie wriggled her thin frame forward to get a good look. "Looks to me like they confused Versailles with Hansel's and Gretel's house.

"There's magic in this house, isn't there, Gabriel?" she asked, as her necklace vibrated against her collarbone. "I can feel the energy from here. C'mon Alice, we're hopping down the damn hole."

Chapter Fifty-Five

—∞—

"**I** know that statue," Maggie pointed, unfurling herself from the cramped back seat. "Washington, top of the U.S. Capitol Dome. She's called Lady of Freedom, constructed during the Civil War. People thought she represented a Roman goddess because she was sculpted by an American while in Rome. Not me. Always reminded me of Mary, with those stars around her head." She turned to Stella to continue her story but her friend was staggering closely behind the Frenchmen in a beeline towards the chateau's entrance.

Stella was paying more attention to Gabriel's walk than what would be characterized as appropriate as he carried their luggage into the lobby. She stifled her giddiness when she deduced that he possessed deeply indented posterior cheeks—her favorite. Stella reached for Gabriel's backside.

"What the hell are you doing?" Stella asked as Maggie swiftly swooped and blocked Stella by straddling the doorway.

"Just checking the ambiance. Your necklace been vibrating at all? There's something I want to show you when we get checked in. Right now—no worries, we're okay," Maggie said, assured she had stopped Stella from making a fool of herself with the priest.

"Oh, that's weird. I thought the vibrations were menopausal heart palpitations," Stella said, craning her head as she searched for Gabriel's whereabouts in the sea of women all trying to check in at the same time.

"Gabriel! We didn't know you were coming this year," the athletic brunette Frenchwoman said. "Where is your mother?" she asked as she reached to embrace him.

"'Allo, Danette! As lovely as ever," he said, as he kissed her cheeks. "Mother is not with me this time, and I'm only here to drop off my American friends: Ms. Stella St. James and Mrs. Maggie Barnett.

"Ladies, may I introduce you to the Baudin sisters—Bernadette, Danette, Suzette and Nanette. They have been coming here a long time," he said, pulling Maggie and Stella into the circle. "My dear friends, may I present *the delightful Ettes.*"

"We have been coming here ever since Suzette was blinded by her cancer as a child," the elderly white-haired nun, Bernadette, replied. "You can see she has been healed. I'm hoping someday I will be able to leave my wheelchair here along with the others who have experienced the miracle that is Lourdes."

"This is Sister Bernadette," he said as he introduced the wheelchair-bound nun, the eldest sister. She seemed almost impish, with her mop of snowy-white hair and twinkling, happy cornflower-blue eyes.

"Pleased to meet you," the sister said, sounding more American than French.

"This is Danette. Watch out for her. She'll enchant you with her wit but can be very bossy at times." The large-boned women with the obviously dyed brown hair, fiercely grabbed and shook the Americans' hands, ignoring Gabriel's assessment of her.

"Next is Suzette," he said, pointing towards the tall and willowy blond. "She is also the quietest."

"And the baby—Nanette," indicating the self-appointed worrier and caretaker of her oldest sister.

"It is a pleasure to meet you," Stella said, bending down to shake the nun's hand. Before she could greet the other sisters, an unmistakable British accent boomed loudly in the lobby.

"*Stella*!" It was Sophia, doing her best Marlon Brando impression from *A Streetcar Named Desire*. "Rock and roll, lovey! How the hell are ya?" she squealed, scooping Stella up and twirling her in a circle.

Two steps behind her was her wife, Sarah, beaming with bliss to be back with her friends. The lobby soon filled with new arrivals, everyone introducing themselves to the others. Gabriel was the only man amidst the mirthful crowd of women.

"Ladies, this is my cue to take my leave. Enjoy your stay. I will call you in two days," he said to Stella, their heads almost touching.

"Well, look at that, will ya? Someone has an admirer. Well done, missy. Handsome bloke, I must admit even though *it's not my thing*, ya know," Sophia exclaimed, eyeing the Frenchman's back as he swiftly vanished out the door.

"Did you know he is a priest?" Stella asked, defensively.

"And what? Don't give me some deluded tosh that something like a celibacy vow is going to stop you, lovey. I'm not daft. Not bloody likely! That man is besotted with you!" Sophia chortled.

"Time to pop up to our room, get sorted out and meet you all back here for cocktails. I can't wait to hear what life has been giving you lately."

* * *

"Oh my, these are wonderful," Stella said, snatching another luscious, candied violet from one of the silver platters being passed around by a well-choreographed army of highly experienced white-haired female servers.

"And it's *real* champagne, from France," Sarah exclaimed, wrinkling her smallish nose as she sipped.

"Have you tried the *foie gras* on the rosemary crostinis? Absolutely to die for!" exclaimed Sophia. "Look at all of these women. I had no idea there would be so many! Let's mingle. My god, it looks like the bloody United Nations in here. I guess I was expecting just Americans. And Christians, at that. But look—women in saris, burkas, African tribal clothing. Ladies, do you have a feeling something incredibly big is about to happen?"

"Something is going on alright," Maggie said. "We still haven't caught our breath since running out of Paris."

"What? Paris? I can't wait to hear, but hold that thought. I know that woman over there. Come, Sarah dear. Ladies, follow me."

Chapter Fifty-Six

—∞—

The humming congregation of women funneled smoothly into the cavernous dining room. Even with its twenty-foot beamed ceilings, Stella felt a tad claustrophobic. Not since Berkeley had she had been around so many people at one time. Once upon a time she would have commanded a room such as this like a maestro conductor. A skill not completely foreign, just rusty.

She snaked behind Maggie towards the familiar faces—the Ettes. The sisters had managed to snag a large oak table in the far back corner, along with some African women, judging by their brightly colored garb. The Ettes eagerly waved them over to the reserved four chairs.

"Stella, Maggie! Please, join us," Bernadette said, raising her voice over the cacophony of enthusiastic attendees.

"We just met these two inspirational women from Liberia. They were telling us a story of a young man who told his teacher he wanted to be vice president. His teacher asked him why he didn't want to be president. *Because that is a woman's job*, he said. Isn't that the most delightful thing you've ever heard?"

"It's true. In our country we now have a woman president, because of the women."

"Don't forget our peace movement," the Liberian woman clothed in brilliant orange and hot pink said, her big matching hair bow bouncing with obvious pride. "The Women of Liberia Mass Action for Peace. We ended our war in 2003." She appeared to be a woman who was unquestionably confident in who she was.

"Christian and Muslim women banded together. We said *does a bullet pick and choose? Does a bullet know the difference between Christians and Muslims?* Of course not! We started by occupying the fish markets, all dressed in white for peace, praying and singing. Still the men fought.

"But the tide turned when we denied sex to our men. They were very upset and displeased, yet *still* the fighting didn't stop.

"So we stripped ourselves naked. Ha! It's a curse in Africa to see your mother naked. That changed *everything*. We had our cease fire and disarmament. We are juicy, juicy crones!" The women erupted in loud, mirthful laughter, high fiving around the circular table.

"We should have done that. Now it's too late for some of us," Maggie choked.

"She just lost her son in Iraq," Sophia explained, as she and Sarah sat down.

"Our condolences, dear heart," Bernadette said, reaching for Maggie's trembling hand from her wheelchair. "We French all know someone who has lost a loved one to war. It's a pain that you never get over." The elderly woman reverently bowed her head, moving her rosary swiftly through her fingertips.

Maggie took another sip of her champagne. "Time has come for women, mothers, to think and act like y'all did. Put an end to war. You understood how to use the enemy's beliefs to defeat them and make change. No bloodshed. My dad preached *war always starts with the mind*."

"Like we talked about in Berkeley that night. Control the message, control the mind," Sophia added. "My pops once told me about Operation Bodyguard, a disinformation campaign in WWII where England and the Allies deceived the Nazis about the invasion of Normandy. They used German double agents for their deception by giving them only fragments of messages. Made the dirty, stinkin' Krauts believe the invasion was at later dates in a different places. Like Churchill famously said, *it's deception that wins, not military might.*

"Mind games—that's all it takes. Keep in mind it only takes *one thought* for a man to get an erection. Just one thought! It can happen without the slightest stimulation."

"Think what women could do with one thought?" Sarah added, gleefully pouring herself another glass of champagne.

The mention of an erection made the French sisters giggle.

"Seriously. What if all women believed a man couldn't get an erection in times of war? What if we said it enough to make it true? What would happen then? Reality only happens when we choose which possibility is real. The brain doesn't know the difference between what it sees and what it remembers," Sarah argued.

"So if we women, all of a sudden, believe that no man can get an erection, will that stop rape?" Sophia asked, awash in the realm of possibility.

"Who knows?" Sarah answered, clinking her glass gleefully with her wife's at the pleasant thought.

"Do you think we chose to believe it was the Virgin Mary who visited us, so we made it a reality?" Stella asked, changing the tone of the conversation. Again, her filter had been perforated by alcohol, like buckshot in a rabbit's rump.

"Have you been visited too?" Danette asked.

Maggie took a big gulp of her wine, trying to get used to the *normalization* of visions. "What do you mean 'too?'"

"Most of the women in this room have been visited, from hearing their conversations," Sophia declared. "I told you I had been in contact with a lot of women around the world. Most are here tonight. Gather the women, remember?"

"Do you think we're seeing the Virgin Mary? Is that the reality we are choosing? It's not some mass energy from the collective consciousness. Did we all choose Mary?" Maggie asked.

"I think there's more than that going on here," Sarah asserted.

"Remember the man I told you two about at the Click Café? The hired assassin who had the near-death experience and spoke about 2012?

Well, he apparently wasn't the only one. Since we last met, many of my new NDE patients reference 2012. They all pretty much say the same thing: this is the start of a new era, a shift in consciousness, a global rebirth. But here's the kicker. That patient also told me about a vision he had of circles of women standing before a body of water, holding hands with radiant, vivid colors filling the sky. He thought this might be in Lourdes, France."

"One hundred monkeys, that's what's happening," Sophia added too loudly, her mouth too full to be considered polite. She wiped her crème-fraiche-smeared fingers on her black jeans as she licked her lips. "Japanese scientists watched a few monkeys on an island who started washing their sweet potatoes. Gradually, all the monkeys were doing this. Not so unusual, heh?

"But wait. Then monkeys on a complete different island with no exposure to the potato-washing monkeys started doing it too! It was out there in the collective consciousness, right? I wondered if maybe the greater number of women experiencing these apparitions exponentially creates more of the experiences. You know, expanding in the ether."

"So you are saying we women are monkeys?" Sister Bernadette asked, a little perturbed.

"I'm saying *how* we focus our awareness can create a new reality. It's from the Many Worlds Theory of having the possibility to create a quantum bridge to jump from one reality to another. Called Choice Points, windows of opportunity to change an outcome just by changing our focus, our beliefs.

"I think that's what's coming—a big old cosmic Choice Point to change our world," Sophia exclaimed. "These visits by Mary have something to do with it. She's using us."

"If I follow you correctly," Stella said, "you think we're all being visited by the Virgin Mary to help change the world in 2012?"

"Somethin' like that," Sophia said, chomping on a cucumber canape topped with shrimp. "Women have always been conduits for the spiritual world. I'm sure you have heard talk of the Return to the Divine Feminine. I told you about Isis and the Milky Way that first night.

"Men have not always been in power. Five thousand years ago, we were ruled by goddesses. During that time, we rarely had wars! Know why? Because women are hardwired to protect life—not end it. I'm about to visit Goddess Ground Zero—Catalhöyük, Turkey—after our trip here."

"Have you heard of a French priest, Pierre Teilhard de Chardin?" the elderly French nun asked. "He believed the world's destiny was a collective spiritual awakening he termed the *Omega Point*. He said we would all connect not only our minds and bodies, but our hearts. The birth of Christ consciousness."

"Christogenesis," Maggie added.

Stella turned, impressed with Maggie's knowledge.

"I told you I had found a lot of interesting things that night," Maggie added smugly, proud of herself. "And, Sister, wait till you see my photos!"

Chapter Fifty-Seven

"C'mon, girlie girl! Let's go," Maggie said, banging on Stella's door. "I wanna get a good seat in front so I can take good pictures along the way." She still hadn't shown Stella the photographed orbs yet. Maybe tonight.

"I'm ready," Stella said as she turned around to lock her room door.

"What the hell is going on?" she yelled when she saw Maggie. Both were dressed in identical winter white Chanel pantsuits, with black leather Gucci flats.

"This is what Dibrovna packed for my visit here," Maggie told her. "She said it was only proper when visiting such a holy place."

"Dammit. I'm not going anywhere dressed as twins!" Stella hissed, slamming the hotel room door back open. When she returned to the hallway, she had her fuchsia pashmina draped around her shoulders. "I guess this will do."

The shuttle bus, *LOURDES TOURS* emblazoned on its side in big, dark-blue letters, was parked in front of the chateau as they descended the wide curved walnut stairs leading to the double doored entrance. Sophia and Sarah were with the French sisters, waiting, all eager to board on the crisp, sunny morning.

"You two are nicely done up today, lovey. I hope you're not planning on 'peacocking,'" Sophia teased.

"It appears my assistant has either a very twisted sense of humor or an agenda. Don't know which, but this was not our plan." Stella wondered if she had time to change, maybe switch to black pants.

A stocky woman dressed in a stiff driver's uniform with a bullhorn announced last call.

"Relax. No one will notice," Sarah replied. The Ettes smiled and nodded in agreement, trying hard not to snicker.

As they motored to Lourdes the bus tour guide told the story of Bernadette and Lourdes. Sister Bernadette was not satisfied with the canned story about the Lady calling herself the Immaculate Conception and decided to educate the women herself.

She whispered to the women, "Did you know that it was the pope in 1854 who declared it the doctrine of the church that Mary was conceived and born without sin, hence the Immaculate Conception? It is true. Magically made her mother a virgin almost eighteen hundred years after Mary's birth. There's so much more I could tell you, but look—here we are."

Stella was unprepared for the throngs of people as far as the eye could see. Gabriel had told her Lourdes was "The Capital of Prayer," with 2,500 reported healings so far; though the Church only recognized 65. There were hundreds, if not thousands, of wheelchairs being pushed by young men dressed in cobalt blue, with yellow kerchiefs around their thin necks. There were also some women, with white kerchiefs. She wondered what the difference in costume meant.

"It feels like champagne in the air," Sophia remarked, wiggling her nose.

"It's because of the effervescence of the bubbling waters everywhere," Nanette informed her.

It wasn't the bubbles that caught Stella's attention. Roses. She was almost overcome with the familiar cloying scent.

"Would you mind pushing me?" Sister Bernadette asked Maggie. Usually her younger sister Nanette pushed her wheelchair. "I would love to be able to chat more with you."

"My pleasure," Maggie said. It felt good to be of use. Knowing it would be a long day, she welcomed using the wheelchair as a walker, too.

Nanette was reluctant, not trusting someone else with her charge. Her older sister lightly tapped her wrist. A small gesture but enough to assure the young woman she was safe in Maggie's care.

Stella tried to keep from stumbling while walking in the crowd with her group. The volume of pain from the ill, almost lifeless people on gurneys and in wheelchairs was humbling. She had previously entertained the thought of visiting the grotto so she could use some of the sacred water on her knee. Now that seemed so trivial and selfish.

These people were fighting for their lives. They all had such strong faith, more evident as they went from event to event, touring the grounds. It was especially emotional to her and her group when they saw the large group of Wounded Warriors—some with obvious physical injuries such as missing limbs; some injuries not so visible.

"Did we tell you what happened the first time we came here?" Sister Bernadette asked. "My sister, Suzette, was just a child. She had had many operations for the cancer in her brain that had left her blind." Suzette, silent as always, tilted her head and stared straight ahead, obviously uncomfortable by her past memories.

"We came with our parents. They were poor and could not afford any more operations. The doctors had informed us another operation probably would not help. We knew about the miracles that had happened here. They say it's the water. A life force that mirrors the soul. It listens to all sounds, especially prayers. It is said this water heals because it is densely filled with feelings of appreciation and love for the Virgin Mary.

"It happened our first night. We were walking the procession, like we are about to do now. Thousands upon thousands of candles were lit. Everyone was silent, calmly walking in unison and peace, while listening to Ave Maria on the speakers everywhere.

"Without any warning, a group of nuns encircled our family. They immediately made their way to Suzette in her wheelchair. We could hear them praying together, shoulder to shoulder, tightly huddled. Suzette then started laughing.

"*I see the lights, maman,* she said as she stood. A miracle had taken place and healed our sister. That was the day I pledged myself to become a nun," she finished. "And how we met Father Gabriel. He is trying to get it declared a miracle."

Stella looked down at the nun's water bottle hanging from her wheelchair. It was glowing, emitting the same rainbow hue she had witnessed that morning on the way to Lilli's. She wondered if Maggie had noticed. She reached for Maggie's shoulder to nudge her when suddenly the water went ink black.

Sister Bernadette gripped Maggie's hand. "*It is the anti-Christ!*" the sister gasped, cautiously pointing with a jerk of her head, terrified he would see her.

Maggie looked in the direction of the sister's head nod–and almost fainted. *It was him!* The man with the port-stained ear who had killed her husband. *What was he doing here?*

The nun jerked on Maggie's sleeve so hard she tripped and fell into Stella. Maggie leaned down and listened as the nun said: "He *is* the anti-Christ. He is the one I had to train to be a priest, who was the lover of the bishop! The man who had me ousted from my beloved church!"

Maggie grabbed Stella's pashmina and waved it high above her head.

"REDCON 1! REDCON 1!" she screamed. In less than sixty seconds, her group was surrounded by the Wounded Warriors.

A man dressed in uniform, obviously accustomed to giving orders, barked to the others *Diamond Formation!* Without saying a word, the soldiers encircled Maggie and the wheelchair-bound nun—Stella in front, Danette behind. They made their way swiftly through the crowd, closely on the Spaniard's heels.

They were making good progress when they were halted by a large delegation of eastern Indian women. Each group was a wall of immovable bodies. Seconds ticked by with neither budging an inch.

Stella watched as Jim's killer escaped, sandwiched between two women accomplices.

Frustrated and furious, she yelled at the Indian women. "What the hell are *you* doing here? Do you have any idea what *you* just did?" She wanted to lash out and punish them, these brown women who had stood in the way of justice.

The Indian women did not push back. In fact, they had no understanding why this white woman was so angry with them.

An elderly Indian woman turned and said "I see you need help. What can I do?"

Stella knew it was too late to catch the fleeing criminals.

Chapter Fifty-Eight

—∞—

"**W**e are from Vailankanni—The Lourdes of the East in India," the fiftyish Indian woman said, as she cautiously lowered herself in the chair across from Maggie upon their return to the chateau.

"It's true," Giselle, the chateau owner, told the women as they started to gather in the Great Room. "They are part of a delegation that comes here every year to celebrate Mary."

"Our group consists of Hindu, Muslim, Sikh or other Indian religions. Most Christians find that surprising.

"A tradition started almost 400 years ago, when a young shepherd boy from Vailankanni was wakened by a 'lady', a celestial beauty holding a child in her arms. She had asked for some milk from his jar for the child. The boy gave her milk. Later, when he reported the shortage to his employer, the can was overflowing.

"All in Vailankanni were overjoyed, as we are now, that the Holy Mother visited our village. To this day, during the Feast of Mary, celebrating her birthday, people come by foot from as far away as 200 miles.

"They carry food on their heads, singing Ave Maria while pulling vibrantly colored and lighted floats. Mary is glorified, not Jesus. Only a small fraction of those that celebrate Her are Christian."

"I'm so sorry for yelling at you. It's just that man—he killed my best friend's husband. Ran him down in a parking lot in cold blood. We know those women who were with the killer, too. Well, sort of. We only met the one. The other one, well, let's just say we've *seen* her before."

"Oh, crikey! Giselle—we need drinks—now!" Sophia yelled, amid the increasingly chaotic atmosphere.

"Double martini for me," Maggie spat through gritted teeth, still visibly shaking with rage fused with fear.

"I'm telling you, Stella. I'll take that stained bastard out before he takes me out," Maggie sputtered in a drawl. "He has no idea who he's messin' with. Southern women still have a lot of whoop ass left in our DNA on account of that little war we lost!" Maggie said loudly, slugging down her martini in two gulps.

"More!" she said, thrusting her glass tight under Stella's nose, demanding a refill.

"Maggie, we will get justice. They'll find him," Stella assured her as she handed her another slightly warm martini. Giselle hadn't planned on so many Americans' thirst this evening, hence the two ice-cube limit.

"Well, ain't that just hunky dory?! Problem is, justice doesn't hold me tenderly in the wee hours of the night! Justice doesn't cook dinner with me on the first barbecue of the year. Or wink and smile at me for no reason at all while covered in shit from the horse stalls. Justice doesn't give me my Jim back!" she drunkenly sobbed.

Stella hoped she was done. The vodka had shot like a chemical bullet to Maggie's brain, making it impossible to speak without slurring. She didn't want Maggie to embarrass herself—or her.

"Who do these little playground, dime store cowboy wannabes think they are? *Bring it on?* Oh, that was brilliant! Egg on the terrorists and then send my one and only child to fight your fucking battle while you send your child to Yale for a job on Wall Street. We all knew it was a lie—Iraq didn't attack us on 9/11. But who are you gonna tell? The Vatican? The

GA7s of the world? They're not gonna step in and stop it—way too much money to be made.

"Give me five minutes in a room alone with that wimp Bush and his evil-doer pal Cheney! I think they need to *get up close and personal* with a real cowgirl! I'd shred their balls!

"They killed Josh, ya know," she yelled, her olive sloshing over the edge of her glass and bouncing from the chair's hard seat to the floor. "They bullied the American people into this never-ending war. Played the media like a damn fiddle! Let's send their children there! Let them come home in a box! Oh yeah, but let's not show that returning coffin on TV! Televise *Shock and Awe* to entertain us but don't honor those that gave their lives. We let them make us spectators, not citizens."

Stella's eyes darted around the room, as she tried to figure out how she could get Maggie upstairs. She had never seen Maggie like this, like a cornered wounded animal. It scared the hell out of her.

"And another thing: I'm sick and tired of the whole "Support our Troops" crap. If Americans really wanted to support their troops, they'd get off their fat, lazy asses and elect people who are smart enough to keep us out of wars. That's how you support the troops!"

"I hate that our soldiers died for nothing," Sophia said, clearly disgusted and angry at the war too.

"*Nothing*!? Don't tell me my only child died for nothing!" Maggie screamed, standing up on her chair, her martini glass slipping through her hand to the floor. She held out her arms as she drunkenly addressed the crowd.

"What America doesn't understand is how much both of my men stood up for their country—right or wrong. They were loyal. They were patriotic! They loved America!

"It was their fucking country that was disloyal. Politicians squirmed out of any kind of military service—lily-livered cowards! It's all about power and money. My country left the wounded on the field. You know why? We were fed a diet of 'did the latest Hollywood starlet go out to effin' dinner with no panties?' Who fucking cares?

"That's what passed as 'the news'. My daddy was right. He said journalists were just a bunch of note takers now, just re-printing whatever they were fed by the Elite. Nowadays Watergate would never be exposed. Bunch of spineless wimps. They allowed this war to happen! News now is public relations. No patience for a story's truth to be told. Want it as fast as their damn cheeseburgers!

"They used my husband and my son as their pieces of silver. Why didn't we take to the streets like in the '60s and stop this war? Because we let them make us feel like we were traitors, betraying our country. *NO! They betrayed us.* I will not let their deaths be in vain. Never will I let someone bully me into silence again. It's up to us women to stop this insanity."

Stella, inspired by Maggie's bravery to speak her heart and mind, stood up. "There's no bravery or courage involved in dropping bombs on people, especially civilians. I know bravery. I see it every time my best friend here has the courage to get out of bed and get dressed. She keeps going. And that's what we will do too! We will make the end justify the means."

"We will stop war. We will have peace. We are the only ones who can change this world now," Maggie said, spent. "You all felt it tonight, right? The connection. You don't think we all are here by accident, do you? A wise woman taught me and my friend that there are no accidents. We need to focus," Maggie finished, with a resounding seriousness. Releasing her anger had sobered her up.

The small brown-skinned woman, sitting unnoticed at the edge of the room, her head shrouded with a veil under the golden light of the hanging chandelier, stood up.

"He should have held my baby. Your president, your leaders— everyone in your country who treated war like some kind of sporting competition. They should have held my baby, looked into his beautiful eyes and imagined what his purpose in life was supposed to be. And then had the courage, right then and there, to rip away his last breath. Instead, you all bowed to some kind of perverted patriotism.

"Almost a million Iraqi women are widows now. Four and half million of my people lost their homes. Your soldiers did not kill soldiers, they killed civilians. Why did you not stand up and say no?

"I never did anything to Americans, yet you came and bombed my family. Killed them all. Robbed my children of their laughter and their nighttime dreams of a future.

"And you left me like this," she said, pulling the veil's corner and allowing it to slide off of her head. She knew the revulsion they would all feel when they saw her half-melted face. The sunken socket where her right eye once was. Her face was a map of light pink ridges of raised flesh once occupied by smooth almond skin. It looked as if someone had held a match to her face, bubbling her skin until she was left with just one nostril, coagulated reminders of anger and hate.

Maggie barely heard the women's last words as she ran from the room, trying not to vomit. Stella followed as fast as she could.

"I will not hide anymore. You," the Iraqi said, pointing to Maggie's retreating back, "need to tell all about losing your child. We cannot stay silent anymore. We owe our children a chance at a peaceful world."

Chapter Fifty-Nine

—∞—

"Come sit, dear hearts" Sister Bernadette said, waving her age-stained lace handkerchief at Stella and Maggie as they returned. "Your emotional words were not lost on us."

It had taken Stella a while to calm Maggie down and convince her to return to the gathering downstairs. Maggie was sure her drunken rant might have permanently ostracized her. "Remember," Stella told her as she sat beside her on the bed, "we can do hard things." Stella had scrubbed Maggie's mascara-streaked face as best she could. She guided Maggie by the shoulders to the large round table, Maggie's vision tunneled by tear-swollen eyelids. They were both greeted with warm smiles and open hearts.

"I'm so very sorry. I shouldn't have said some of the things I said," Maggie said tearfully as she sat down, holding Jim's bagged T-shirt to her chest. She noticed the Iraqi woman had joined their group.

"Please, no need to apologize. We are no longer isolated women from war-torn countries, suffering alone with our own horrific story. We are now gathered—together," said the softly spoken, dark-skinned woman named Adara.

"We have been discussing Marian Apparitions, specifically the Third Secret. We know we were all brought her for a reason. We must do what we are good at—talking and sharing information."

"Go ahead, dear, continue," Sister Bernadette said, reassuringly.

"Thank you. As I was saying, ironically, the village where 'the Lady' appeared to the three Portuguese children, Fatima, was named for the daughter of the prophet Muhammad, the founder of Islam. She was a Muslim, raised mostly by her father. He wrote after her death, 'Thou shalt be the most blessed of women in Paradise after Mary.' She is the most venerated women in our religion."

"It's true," the French nun added. "Muslims occupied Portugal for centuries. The story goes that a Catholic boy fell in love with her. Fatimah not only stayed behind when the Muslims were run out of the country, but became a Christian. They married and her husband changed the name of the town where he lived to Fatima as a testament to his undying love for her.

"Are you aware that there are approximately forty-one verses on Jesus and Mary in the Quran? Yet I'm told Mary is barely mentioned in the Bible. Many Muslims make pilgrimages to Fatima and Lourdes. Over half of the visitors to Mary's House in Ephesus, Turkey, are Muslims," Adara added.

Stella was dumbfounded, as were most of the other women at the table, but for a different reason. She had gotten used to all the propaganda against Muslims and Islam since 9/11, as evil women-haters. To hear about Mary being dismissed in the Christian Bible while celebrated in the Quran was enlightening, though quite disturbing. However, it was the mention of Mary's House—this time in Turkey. She was confused.

"First, you must understand that the New Testament was not written until 312 AD, when Roman Emperor Constantine, a very nasty man," Bernadette said "decided to unify people of faith for the political purpose of controlling them.

"During the Council of Nicaea in Ephesus in 325, Bishop Eusebius of Caesarea gathered together all of the various gospels. I think it numbered in the hundreds if memory serves correctly. There were also other early Christian writings. The Council then chose what best fit the new Catholic Church's purpose to compile the New Testament. Out of all that documentation, they chose only four. *Just four gospels.*"

"Sister, do you believe that the Third Secret has been revealed?" Stella asked, hoping her tone wouldn't seem defiant or disruptive. The nun's response surprised her.

"No, I do not." Feeling some unease among the women at the table, the nun felt compelled to tell her story.

"First, please understand that I am not betraying my church. You see, I am not recognized as a Holy Sister anymore. I was kicked out for being a whistle blower.

"And please, I beg you to remember the problem is not Catholics. It's the 'seeking of the purple', power and royalty, that has damaged our church," she continued sadly.

"It was man that created the Vatican, man who declared the pope infallible. It was man who came up with the concept of original sin. None of these things were what Jesus taught.

"At my parish in the States, my priest embezzled money and molested many children. He was a follower of the Legionaries of Christ, whose leader even raped his own illegitimate children. I filed complaint after complaint with our Diocese, but nothing happened. Then a young Spanish man came to our parish, as his lover. The man with the port-stained ear." The women gasped.

"I could no longer look the other way. I contacted the local newspaper. Life became hell. The pope deemed me a sinner, and I was left without a job, penniless. The offending priest was moved to an Italian villa and is living on a $10,000 monthly pension. I should have known what would happen. As we all witnessed tonight, the Spaniard is still walking free, destroying lives."

"You know my husband's killer?" Maggie asked, trembling.

"Once upon a time. He is Godless. Absolutely no moral compass!"

Maggie turned her back as she sent a furious text.

A Japanese woman at the end of the table stated, "I just don't *feel* like what the pope told us is the Third Secret is true."

Sister Bernadette turned to her. "Trust your feelings, my dear. Our oldest language is emotions.

"Keep in mind Sister Lucia specifically told her bishop, when forced to reveal the Third Secret, it was not to be unsealed and read by the pope until 1960. It was deemed it would be more understood at that time. Then Pope John XXIII reads it at the appointed time, but won't reveal its message? Again, it was not for our times? Perspective of the time is important here. Three very important things happened soon thereafter.

"First, in 1961 James Mellaart, an archaeologist, found Catalhöyük and Hacilar, and the Natural Religion of Goddess Worship going back almost to 7,000 BC. He had discovered maybe the first civilization; some even say it was the lost Garden of Eden. However, his work was soon halted in 1965 on the grounds that further work would only yield repetitive results of no great scientific value. Excavation finally resumed in 1993.

"Two years after that, April 11, 1963, the pope, disturbed by the separation among people and nations, proclaimed that there would be peace on earth, *Pacem in Terris*. It was a very radical, highly liberal encyclical. He argued against wars, nuclear weapons, declared laws that govern man are different that the laws governing the universe. He talked about consciousness.

"He stressed the need for a worldwide community providing inalienable rights, such as food, clothing, shelter, medical care and the need for all of us to care for one another without judgment. Then he proclaimed women were increasingly aware of this natural human dignity, and were no longer satisfied with a passive role.

"This was radical for the Church. I believe he came to this conclusion after reading the Third Secret. They were afraid of something. He said it was a 'sign of the times' that disputes would be resolved by negotiation and agreement, not fighting and killing. When he warned about propaganda, they called him a socialist, a communist. He died two months later.

"But what happened on December 8, 1965, at the closing of Vatican II is truly prophetic: Pope Paul VI's *Address to Women*." Sister

Bernadette pulled a fragile square of crackled paper from her Bible under the folds of her blanket, carefully unfolding it so as not to tear it:

> *But the hour is coming . . . in fact has come. Women of the entire universe, whether Christian or non-believing, you to whom life is entrusted at this grave moment in history, it is for you to save the peace of the world.*

"Now remember, this is the same Vatican II where they demoted Mary, yet the pope ends with talking about women and peace? Even addresses non-Christians? So do I think the Third Secret, about an assassination attempt on Pope John Paul II, is true? Do you?"

Sarah, a trained listener, had sat patiently. Allowing this new information to marinate in her thought process, she suggested: "I wonder if maybe there was only one vision—*ever*. What if what we all experienced was only one experience in time, but being viewed now by the many? The Observers are seeing, and in our rapid digital world and maybe changing dimensions, we are viewing the Virgin Mary at different times in *our* life? Her message is the same, so maybe she's only appeared once. You listen to enough recitals of near-death experiences, like I have, and you know there are more than the three dimensions we humans see." Though her addition to the community discussion was simple, its effect was not.

"Some herbal tea and hot chocolate for you," Giselle offered, placing the tempting tray of steaming cups, along with some freshly baked-almond macaroons and madeleines on the old oak table. The women eagerly partook of the much-appreciated refreshments while they mulled where the conversation would veer to next.

"I don't think it's an accident all of us are here, do you?" Sarah now stood and asked.

The floodgates opened. Pent up stories about the absurd, the divine, the unexplained, the coincidences. Among the clamorous chatter, the one consistent phrase heard around the room was "gather the women."

"So why do you think Mary wanted us all here?" one of the women asked. "I feel we are all being called. But for what? The Third Secret?"

Sister Bernadette then made a statement that quieted the entire dining room. "You do understand that 'resurrection' involves a shift in consciousness? It is so silly how people interpret the Bible so literally. Need more poetry in this world to understand the nuances. Like your former president; he had no depth with which to truly understand scripture. But he did manufacture myths to sell the war."

"I totally agree, sister. He filtered everything more through a *See Jane Run* level, if you get my meaning," said Stella.

"They feared Mary and the Gnostics. Gnostics believed that the ultimate mystery is One, a united consciousness, a self-awareness. Their teachings were potentially adverse to the church because it taught that everyone had access to God without the need for priests and bishops—and money."

"What makes me the saddest is for people who believe in a vengeful God. God does not punish. God is perfect. He didn't create you to be ashamed of yourself. Why do we apologize for being human? You think the mighty oak apologizes if it doesn't produce the right amount of acorns? Stop beating yourself up because God hears that as a prayer. Let your light shine. Sparkle! *Le mots juste!*"

Stella stood. "I've been shaping my future by living in what happened in my past. I need a new story. We all need a new story.

"Ladies, it's time to start planning. Now tell me, Bernadette, more about Mary's House."

Chapter Sixty

—∞—

"Mary's House," the nun began, taking a sip of her lukewarm cocoa, "is a humble stone house in Ephesus, Turkey. We only know of it because of another vision. A French nun, Sister Marie de Mandat-Grancey, had read *The Life of the Blessed Virgin Mary*, an early 19th century book by German mystic and Marian visionary, Anne Catherine Emmerich.

"The book spoke of Anne Catherine's visions of a house where Mary lived after she fled her son's crucifixion with St. John the Evangelist. John had promised Jesus to keep his mother safe. According to the story, no one believed Sister Marie that the house existed, but she was persistent. Finally, after much excavation it was found July 29, 1891 by Father Julien Gouyet of Paris. Rome was none too happy about the find."

"Sister Marie? I think one of her ancestors, the 12th century Abbott of Cluny, was the first person to translate the Quran," Adara said, the unlikely connection not lost on her. "It was decided that to stop warring, they needed to study and understand the Islam faith. I've been to Mary's House, as have many of my relatives. When I told my mother that I was coming here, she reminded me that *Lourdes heals the wounds of the body, but Mary's House heals the wounds between religions*. I think this is true."

"I've been to Ephesus, too" Sophia stated. "Mind you, this was bloody well before our vision," she added, hooking her thumb at Sarah and herself. "I was there as part of an archaeological venture to study the temples of the goddesses.

"There's a rich history of goddess worship in Ephesus, you know. That's where the Temple of Isis is, mother of Horus. The temple was once a sanctuary for those fleeing persecution, promising protection by the goddess.

"No wonder Mary sought refuge there after they killed her son. A land founded by the legendary Amazons. Diana's Temple is there too, also known as the Temple of Artemis. One of the Seven Wonders of the Ancient World, though not much is left now," Sophia said, sadly. The loss of art and genius pained her, but also compelled her to study ruins and educate people what it may have been once and more specifically, why.

"Sarah, remember our tour guide? Intense woman, I must say. Told us the story of Mary and Jesus was just a rehashing of Isis and Horus. It was such a long time ago, but I remember she fiercely said the world would one day realize *this is the land of women where civilization began.*"

"I do remember. That and the souvenir you bought me. It was a replica of The Lady of Ephesus, the Light Bearer. Her plump body was encrusted with 'eggs' or 'breasts,' supposedly symbolizing fertility. Maybe it's really a symbol of the calling to all women, hence the many breasts? You told me Artemis was replaced in worship with the Virgin Mary."

"That's right," Sophia said. "The Bee Goddess, Artemis, ruler of all the elements of earth, sea and air and birth. To honor her birth and celebrate springtime and resurrection, great festivals are held. In fact it's almost time for Artemision, the annual dance for the fertility goddess. It used to last a month, with people flocking in from all four corners of the known world.

"Sister, you just mentioned resurrection. This could be significant. Do you think this is where we are supposed to gather the women? It's obviously an ancient gathering place for women," Stella asked.

"There's a great theater there. The site dates back to the Bronze Age."

"We could re-create the Maharishi Effect," Adara added. "Create peace in our bodies to reflect it back into the world. My mother participated in the Washington D.C. 1993 mass meditation using that principle. They believed that it only took the square root of one percent of the population to make significant change. Their efforts significantly reduced crime, even car accidents, in more than twenty-four cities. There are at least seventy-five of us here who have been visited. I think they are many more. We must gather them all and go. But how?"

"I have an idea," Stella said, feeling stronger that she had for years. "From what I know there's nothing like social media and a message to band people together. What do they call it? A Twitter blast?" she added, feeling proud of herself that she actually remembered something Dibrovna's daughter, Sylvania, had told her about technology.

"Interesting. Might be time to use our own brand of deception to gather all the women. We could start by sending a fake video to CNN's iReport and Fox News. They never check their sources anymore," Maggie grumbled.

Sophia started to laugh: "Oh, this is good! You know how to connect the women? Send out a cryptic tweet with the hashtag #hotflashes. Men will ignore it because they really don't want anything to do with our lady parts, especially not old, dry ones," she hooted.

"And then send them to a website where it'll take a membership to access the info—gotta make it long. We all know no man will spend his time filling out a form," Maggie snorted, delighting in her own wittiness.

"Don't forget, dear hearts," Sister Bernadette said, "breast your cards."

Sophia cocked her head at her, puzzled.

"You know," the sister added, patting her chest, "keep your plans close."

"Brilliant, Stella. Let's discuss this more over breakfast. I think we've had quite a day," Sophia added, as she got up to head to her room.

As the women were leaving the dining room and heading up the stairs to their rooms, Stella got a text from Nicki: "On bed rest, not to worry. Just had a little bleeding."

"Ladies, may I ask a big favor before you retire. Adara just told us about the power of the Maharishi Effect. Could you join me around the fountain outside to pray for my daughter and her unborn child?"

She realized later it was the first time in decades she had prayed with a group. Her opinions about God and the power of women had changed. She *felt* God everywhere.

* * *

Stella hadn't felt so charged up in years. Almost like her protest days against Vietnam, standing up for peace not war. Justice was as vital as oxygen. But now, it was personal. She now had a grandchild coming, a business that supported her war-refugee family, a grief-stricken best friend who needed healing. Time to bring justice. And stop a killer.

As she readied for bed, she noticed it was unseasonably warm for early spring. She couldn't stop sweating. Her necklace was constricting on her neck. Even with the new chain, she wanted her necklace off—now. With every move of her head against the pillow, it chafed her neck leaving her red and itchy. Lilli's warnings to never take it off rang in her ears.

The one time she had taken it off, she felt like one of those old-fashioned divers with the huge round air helmet whose air cord had been slashed—unconnected. She tried to lie down, deep breath and put herself to sleep, but still it nagged her.

She took it off and wrapped it around her wrist. Quickly falling asleep, she never noticed it had slithered off of her wrist and fallen to the floor, next to a meticulously-neat, handwritten note: "I adore the scent of you. G"

Episode Three

~

The Great Gathering

Man did not weave the web of life—he is merely a strand in it. Whatever he does to the web, he does to himself
~ *Chief Seattle*, "A Message to Washington"

Chapter Sixty-One

_∞_

"I am extremely disappointed!" Cardinal Gustav stated as he fiercely glared at the two mercenaries standing at attention in front of his massive carved desk; Lucas, arms crossed defensively against his chest, watched from the shadows where he was tucked into the far corner. "You both are highly trained in this work. Millions of dollars have been spent so mistakes like this don't happen. This is inexcusable!" he coughed, his face now as scarlet red as his zucchetto atop his head.

"Your Eminence, Lucas, our apologies. It was well planned and well executed. Unfortunately, we were spotted before we could access the target. This happens," Brent explained, evenly.

He had volunteered to be the lookout since the women knew him. But it had also been a ruse so he could telepathically invade the wheelchair-bound nun's morphic field, to alert her of the assassin's presence among the thousands in the crowd. Being spotted was no accident—at least not this time. Brent knew it would soon get dicey, playing both sides of this deadly game.

Brent had seen an opening for his plan to avenge Jim's death but it had required scrambling at the last minute after the Paris debacle. He was successfully able to lure the Spaniard into the failed mission, knowing what the consequences might be. He stood closely to the assassin so he could deeply inhale and enjoy the killer's fragrant fear as the hopes of a new Vatican assignment quickly evaporated. The Spaniard had been lucky once, when the Church and the Stanchirs whisked him out of the United States after the hit-and-run trial. That was then. Brent knew you don't get a second chance with the Stanchirs.

"So, you not only failed to take out the target, you were seen. Is that correct?" Lucas inquired in an icy monotone, giving each of his cuffs a sharp swift tug as he emerged from the corner and walked towards the men.

"Si, sir. But we did not deviate from our plan. It was the nasty old nun, sir. We did not know she was going to be there. You know her, dear Eminence," he said, nervously addressing Cardinal Gustav, as he agitatedly rubbed his fingers and thumbs together. "That woman is evil! You remember the damage and lies she told about her priest."

"I do not need to be reminded of *that* incidence. Your behavior cost the Church greatly!"

"Did you not have the opportunity to 'remove' Mrs. Barrett when you knew you had been spotted?" Lucas asked, not changing his tone one decibel, slowly circling the Spaniard. "I think you forgot the first rule of being an assassin—always look and act like you belong. You flinched and you put me, our mission, the Church—everything at risk. This cannot be tolerated."

Lucas stopped circling as he centered on the Spaniard's spine, sprung his switchblade and quickly slit the fidgeting man's throat to the bone. Crumbling to the floor with arms and legs askew, blood started pooling in his port-stained ear.

Cardinal Gustav knew that Lucas was a man not to be crossed, but an execution? Horrified, he clutched the volume of his pristine cassock close to his body so as not soil it with his putrid, oily vomit as he retched into his lacquered wastebasket.

The cleric's mind was spinning with concern about Kathleen and Martha who had accompanied the Spaniard. They had been the first to report back to him that Stella and Maggie may have seen them at Lourdes, as they sprinted the "assassin" to safety. Not fond of either woman, still *he was a priest* and not an advocate for the sin of murder.

He abhorred violence so closely carried out. Gustav felt there was no reason he should have to be a witness.

"Clean this up before the women get back. You know what to do," Lucas said to Brent, as if referring to a pile of dirty dishes.

"Done. You and the cardinal need to leave—now!"

Fools, Brent thought as he watched the two men exit the room. He had figured his plan would shorten the Spaniard's lifespan, as he removed today's newspaper's front page from his jacket's inside pocket and hastily tossed it next to the bloody corpse. He snapped pictures of the body and the surrounding room with his cell phone before rolling up the deceased in the expensive Persian carpet, the hand-twisted pile now so saturated with sticky blood, it bonded tightly against the stiffening body creating a gruesome paper maché effect.

"Lucas, you never should have started screwing with my benefits," Brent fumed, ripping at the duct tape with his teeth as he wrapped the carpet like a mummy. *Never leave traces of carnage, and always hedge your bets.*

Like GA7 couldn't afford my health care, give me a raise or a bonus? Just because I won't kill for them anymore. Bad, bad choice, you greedy bastard, Lucas!

Brent thought of the short terse conversation he had with Jim during their last Super Bowl together. GA7 had recently reduced their pay after cutting them to back to four days a week, and after a few beers he had started to rant. Jim had abruptly hushed him telepathically with a message to meet him in the woods outside Louisville.

"I found something," Jim had told him. "During one of my routine viewing sessions, something flickered in so I chased it. You won't believe what that son of a bitch Lucas is up to."

Brent was positive that was why Jim was dead. Somehow Lucas had found out and had him killed. And it was all his fault. The big money he had been raking in made him flabby and careless, lulled into a self-centered normalcy. Biggest mistake he made was not adequately planning for the evil he knew Lucas was capable of carrying out.

He pegged Lucas as a bad seed when GA7 hired him with the caveat of his first agreeing to "wet work," a hired assassin. He had been quite good at it until being shot in Chile and surviving his near-death experience.

Many sleepless nights he had indulged reliving his encounter with that other world, knowing he would never be the same, nor did he want to be. Brent first had to devise his escape from GA7, which included building his own covert team. He started by playing up to Lucas' ego and insecurities when he was most vulnerable—on the elder Stanchir's death watch. First, he offered words of sympathy accompanied with comments on how Elliot Stanchir had been a "man's man." Suggesting to Lucas that he could help "beef up" the workforce. Worked like a charm; soon Lucas looked to Brent to suggest new hires, new revenue streams. That was how he got Jim hired as a psychic spy to successfully carry out GA7's planned quantum war.

Jim's death had plunged him into the deepest depression he had ever experienced. At his NDE therapist's urging, he started meditating. She thought that meditation would help to maximize his spiritual hormone, DMT. Then everything started changing. That's when he heard God—from within.

Make the peace you want.

It brought him to tears, his transformation complete in his sixth decade. His whole life had been about war, killing and destruction. Now he only wanted to make peace, not grief.

Maybe we should never fully heal from war, Brent thought. *You heal—you forget.* Maybe before a president decides to go to war, they should spend one night with a veteran who will never know the sanctuary of sleep, without the intrusions of unmitigated terror. Then, give that president a gun and helmet with a 500-foot head start before *you* start shooting. Or maybe, have a president encounter a child standing next to a suicide bomber. *What will you do now, sir? Still think sending a million of America's children to war is a great idea? Want to stick the bear with the pointed stick again?*

As he finished with his grisly chore, he thought about his cousin Kathleen's close-up report on the women at Lourdes. She and the cardinal's housekeeper reported seeing Maggie and Stella at Lourdes among many more women, yet something was missing. It didn't fit his vision of the gathered women. The numbers were too low. The water was not right. The sound not as harmonic as he had briefly heard.

Lourdes could not have been the place Lucas had warned Cardinal Gustav about that night in Amsterdam. The consequences meant that Spider Sweep would now be amped up. He feared for his cousin's life, but also Maggie's. Sadly, Jim had been the Plan's first casualty; Brent knew there was a high probability he could be next.

You don't leave a man on the field, and you certainly don't leave his loved ones in harm's way. It was time to reveal himself and warn them all.

Chapter Sixty-Two

Finally! Maggie picked up her phone, hoping it was a response to her text after last night's fleeing from Lourdes. It was.

"Danger! Leave now!"

Brent's text didn't frighten nor surprise her—the presence of her husband's killer was enough to tell her they were in imminent danger. Still her heart bucked forcefully against her sternum. Finally feeling safe, cocooned in all the sisterhood around her, she didn't want to leave. But she knew when warned of danger not to second-guess the warning. Brent had access to highly classified information and knew more than she. No matter how Stella felt, she trusted Brent and leapt into action.

"Who is it?" Stella yelled, when Maggie pounded on her door.

"Me. We gotta go."

"What the hell are you talking about?" Stella said, opening the door to let her friend enter, her hair flatly matted to the back of her head, dried saliva scabbed on her lips.

"Just got a text from Brent," Maggie said as Stella winced, slumping her shoulders. "Yeah, I know how you feel about him. You don't know the whole story, sweetie.

"He was there last night. And that nun, in San Francisco—she's his cousin. He's watching out for us. We need to get back to Lilli's pronto! Finish packing. Giselle is getting us a taxi and arranging for a car for our journey back." Maggie studied Stella, noticing her eye twitching, her lips quivering. In the ongoing chaos she had completely forgotten about Stella's text from Nicki, a mere ten hours ago.

"Where's your necklace, honey? Lilli told us not to take them off."

"Sorry, I took it off last night. Don't worry. I wrapped it around my wrist," Stella replied, as she held up her naked arm.

"Well, it's not around your wrist now, is it? Dammit!" Maggie frantically started tossing the blankets high up in the air, flinging pillows to the floor in her search.

"Wait! It's gotta be here somewhere. There it is! Under the bed," Stella said, the morning sun glinting off the edge of the star. "Let me just jump in the shower . . ."

"We don't have time! Throw your shit in your suitcase and let's giddy up! Stick your necklace in your pocket. I'll be downstairs in the taxi waiting. Ten minutes, ya got it? Chop-chop, honey!"

* * *

"Finally, here she is," Maggie said, anxiously twisting her Bulova watch. Stella's ten minutes ended up more like twenty.

"Pop the trunk, Frenchie. Just toss in the bags and put the petal to the metal!"

Maggie stood by the taxi's back door and looked Stella up and down. Make-up! Of course, Stella would get all dolled up because the French priest would be waiting for them. Oh Lordy! Does a leopard ever change its spots?

"Okay, pretty ladies, hold on. I will get us there, *tout suite.* No, I don't need directions," he said, waving his hand. "I know this land like I know my own children's angelic faces." With that, he fish-tailed out of the gravel drive, the acceleration compressing his passengers tightly together like a human panini.

"Well, you did tell him put the petal to the metal, Maggie," Stella whispered as she struggled against gravity to open up some personal space. "What about the others?"

"Giselle will let them know we had to leave. We'll be in contact with them tomorrow. Let me see your phone," she said quietly, leaning against Stella's shoulder. "I have burner phones Giselle gave me. We need to put in some of our contacts, and then we'll stash our cells in the taxi to throw off anyone who's tracking us."

"Maggie, I'm frightened. Do you think that man was there last night to kill you too? Jim's death wasn't an accident, was it?"

"Mighty suspicious; looks like that dog don't hunt. I think Brent can help fill us in. Right now we just have to get back to Lilli's. We'll be safer there. Something tells me there's more to *her* story," Maggie said, as she swiveled from window to window, surveying the countryside for snipers.

"Here we are, demoiselles. There is sweet Renee now. She'll take care of you."

"Merci," Maggie said, as she pushed a pile of crumbled euros into his hand and quickly scrambled out of the vehicle. "Now I want you to drive as far north as this fare will take you. Don't pull over anywhere—just drive."

"Bonne, understood. Be safe," he said, as he sat down the last suitcase and got back in behind the wheel.

The two women cautiously walked up to the old hunched-over woman as she slowly emerged from the darkness of her overgrown, dilapidated farm house tucked deep into the damp forest. "Follow me," she said, without introduction as she waddled down the rutted muddy path to her barn, the tall ferns smacking her fleshy thighs with dew-wetted fronds.

"As pretty as Giselle said you would be," the chubby French woman said with a big grin, her remaining teeth poking up like rotted fence slats behind her thin lips.

"Did she tell you how we saved France during the war? America, too! We worked on the Comet Line with Lilli to assist the downed pilots over the border into Spain, using the Camino up into the Pyrenees," she said, as she pointed somewhere up in the sky. It was obvious that she was thrilled to have an audience for her stories after so long.

"Lilli worked with Underground guides to get the pilots train tickets into Spain. She would smuggle them from Paris to either my or Gisele's house. Lilli had a nose for smelling 'rats.' Filthy German spies were always trying to infiltrate our group. I even had to shoot one once—a woman.

"We once saved one of yours, you know—an American pilot. Funny, he almost got caught. He insisted at the train station on walking curbside with Lilli, as he was taught by his mother. Ah, you see, that is not French etiquette. I heard he became a war hero, became very rich and powerful.

"I told the American when we hid him in this very barn, that it was his president who inspired me to join the Resistance and fight the war. Told him I found a 'tract,' a piece of paper, dropped by an English plane right out there in the clearing," Renee said pointing out the barn door to massive brambles of blackberry bushes. "It was a speech by your President Roosevelt about the creation of a world founded upon just four essential freedoms: speech, worship, from want and, most importantly, freedom from fear," she said as she counted them off on her plump, age-curled hand.

"One thing about living a life of fear during war—it never disappoints. I kept that tract, and to this day it is still in my jewelry box," she said, her voice starting to fade in and out.

After some silent reflection, she got back to the business at hand. "Hurry, my son has prepared the car for you," she said, as she shooed them into the clutch of chickens running around, feathers flying everywhere before permanently sticking to one of the many fresh polka dots of poop.

Maggie wondered where the son was. Unaccounted for people made her nervous.

"Citroën, nice," Stella said, not minding its resemblance to an Alexander Calder sculpture—abstract pieces of metal joined into a family with bits of wire. She was more concerned if the mass of metal could at least get her back to Callian—and Gabriel. She missed the gentle priest's kindness—and his mother's calming salves.

"I think one of you should put this on your head," Renee said, handing Maggie a scarf. Stella recognized it as a vintage Hermès and was delighted that even French country women appreciated quality and style.

"French men love beautiful women, so we must disguise you so you won't be noticed. Though that might not help, eh? French men simply love women. You see me? Rotten teeth, goat whiskers, and my body lumpy with age, but still *hubba hubba*! You will get nods and smiles, maybe invitations," she purred. "Just smile like a sweet little kitten—but keep moving with your claws ready! Do not stop, no matter what!

"This is so exciting! I haven't been part of such subterfuge since I was a virgin," she exclaimed, jiggling with delight. "It is time for us women to gather once again. Godspeed to you two. *Viva la feminique*!" Renee punched the air with her fists.

Maggie took over the driver's seat, which suited Stella fine.

"You okay?" Maggie asked. "You seem a little out of sorts, sweetie."

"I didn't sleep well last night. Night sweats, tossing and turning and all."

"Don't you have any nighty-night pills in that big suitcase you call a purse?" Maggie asked, trying to be helpful.

"I'm trying really hard not to take pills right now. I think I need to be as fully conscious as possible, don't you?" Stella snapped.

Their sisterly bickering as they prepared to drive away kept them from noticing the old woman vaporizing, as she rounded the corner of the old ramshackle barn. What once was Renee were now small opalescent twinkling orbs, floating upwards to rejoin the ethereal masses.

Chapter Sixty-Three

—∞—

"A world of trouble we're in, Martha," Kathleen huffed, sidling close to the zaftig, authoritative nun as they marched to the market for that night's shopping.

"I swear I had no idea we were being sent to Lourdes to harm those women. My cousin said he would tell me more later, but he's already told me the Spaniard was sent there to kill the redheaded American. You know I want nothing more than to be a sister again, but not at that price. I should have known. I saw documents the last time I was here that chilled my blood, that they did.

"The cardinal left me alone in the Vatican library for hours on end. I found World War II documents stashed everywhere." She didn't let on that the documents had been sealed. Sealed documents had never stopped her before, as she studied volumes of documents about Marian apparitions in the library. Her talent lay in her ability to read a page at a glance and memorize it, word for word, and understand the contents. Eidetic or photographic memory her Irish teachers had called it.

Cardinal Gustav had foolishly underestimated her thirst for revenge. Didn't he realize bullies never change? They only get older and craftier?

She read everything she could to fill her armory of information against the Church.

"I found detailed logs of war criminals the Vatican had housed in convents. They dressed them as nuns before transporting them to other countries after the war. *The Ratline* is what they called it. The Vatican charged the fleeing Nazis almost half their life's worth for assistance. Helped almost 30,000 rotten Nazis to escape justice. Why do you think they'd do that?" Kathleen asked, watching Martha's expression to gauge if maybe she had revealed too much.

Martha eyed Kathleen, weighing how much to divulge. She knew both had just entered a different kind of sisterhood—one of need. They, no doubt, were now in the cross-hairs of the cardinal and had no choice but to trust each other. She wasn't new to this type of menace. She had endured years of abuse by the cardinal. That enemy she knew.

"We both know the Church has committed heinous crimes over the centuries. So, let's be blunt," she said, as they turned the last corner, almost to the market. "I don't want others to hear us talk, so let's slow our pace. My entry into the church was not pleasant. Pregnant by rape at the end of the war, I was sent to a convent boarding school where I was taught by my Mother Superior that I needed to shed blood as Jesus did so my loved ones would be spared from purgatory. When they ripped my child from my arms right after his first breath, I threatened to go to the newspaper.

"To avoid controversy and keep me quiet after I took the coveted black veil, the Vatican sent me to work in the household of Pope John Paul I. This is an assignment not many young nuns receive," Martha said, knowing Kathleen was sufficiently impressed. "He was such a gentle soul. He trusted *only me* to serve him his breakfast, which he enjoyed along with his assistant, a young priest named Gabriel.

"It was I who found his Holiness dead in his bed that morning, with Gabriel following right behind me," Martha said haltingly, the pain still evident after all these years. "We both knew the pope had been murdered when the embalmers arrived shortly thereafter. There was no autopsy, no death certificate.

"By 6 p.m. that very night, Gustav had made sure that everything ever touched by the pope was gone. It was as if he had never entered the Papal Apartment."

"Gustav? You mean Cardinal Muench?"

"Gustav! I only call him cardinal when I have to. He is vile. No more than a common guttersnipe. But silence now, we are almost here," Martha said as they neared the grocery store's well-lighted entrance.

"Let's hurry with our shopping, and I'll tell you more on the way back. We can take our time and stop in one of the parks. Gustav is dining with the pope tonight."

* * *

"It was Gabriel who arranged for me to become Gustav's housekeeper so I could keep an eye on him. Gabriel was so devastated by our pope's death, he left the active priesthood to join the Bollandists," Martha said as they both sat on the park bench.

"Gabriel had been an instrumental informant to Pope John Paul I about the corruption in the Vatican Bank. John Paul had ordered an audit of the bank to expose those in the Curia who were part of this deception right before he was poisoned."

"Poisoned? Sister, how can you say such a thing?"

"John Paul had just passed a physical three weeks before. He was in perfect health, but they tried to say he had a heart attack. Then they said he had committed suicide by overdosing on his blood pressure medicine. Ludicrous! Who overdoses on a once-daily pill? He was of no mind to kill himself, to commit a sin against God. The Vatican rushed to have him embalmed yet not one drop of his blood was drained!

"Gabriel and I both suspect it had something to do with the Third Secret. His Holiness had read it no less than forty-eight hours before his death. Then he requested a copy of the December 8, 1965 Vatican II speech on women that very night.

"I have listened many times to Gustav and the Stanchirs talk by putting my ear up to the heating vent next to Gustav's study. They've had many discussions through the years on women, similar to how generals talk when planning battles. Said they had to promote the message that women must stay young to be valued. Extremely important that older women be devalued to 'diffuse their power,' the older Stanchir had insisted, time after time."

Kathleen nodded her head, knowing from personal experience if you kept women insecure about their worth based on their beauty, they would waste valuable energy that could have been better spent on serving humankind and God.

"I think there's something in the Third Secret about women, maybe even older women. They are too interested, almost to obsession, with those two American women. Then there's the project they've been working on."

"What project? With my cousin and the Spaniard?"

"No. Bigger. They've converted the old convent out by Castel Gandolfo into some kind of lab. Your cousin is involved, as is the American Government. I have kept all of Gustav's calendars. They show him meeting with American presidents, with notations like 'funding,' 'black $$,' 'DNA.' I can show you when we get back to the apartment."

* * *

"Are you sure the cardinal won't come back and surprise us?" Kathleen asked.

Martha had shut the door to the sparse bedroom then proceeded to retrieve the tied-up package from under the floor boards.

"If he does, he won't come in here. It's too private. He likes to be visible, just in case he needs an alibi."

Kathleen wasn't sure of Martha's meaning, but before she could investigate further her eyes caught something that took her breath away. As Martha opened the large manila envelope and removed the calendars, the word *RAPE* jumped off the page. She thought maybe it was a notation to discuss the recent sex scandals all over the world involving priests, but soon found out it wasn't.

"Yes—that," Martha said, pointing to the hand-written entry in red. "My mind has grown too callused, being around such filth for so long. I forget how horrendous this all is. That was for the meeting they had about using rape as a tool of war. A meeting with the pope. They said since the Book of Judges glorified the gang rape of a young virgin offered up by her father to a drunken mob, then they must obey God's word. Men wrote that, not God."

Any remaining loyalty Kathleen had for the Catholic Church dissipated.

It reminded her of what the pope had said when confronted by his failure to defrock the priest who had abused 200 deaf children. "Faith allows one not to be intimated by the petty gossip of the dominant."

"How dare they kick me out of my marriage to Jesus when they advocate raping women and children. Please, I need to make copies of these documents to insure our lives. Let me take the originals to the house where I once stayed. They have a copier in the library that I can use. Tell Gustav that I decided to visit my old friends for the evening if he asks about me."

Martha hesitated for a fraction of a moment and then handed the originals to Kathleen. "Here, put on one of my old habits, so you can hide them underneath. Please be careful. We both know what they are capable of doing."

As she hurried from the apartment, she failed to notice the minuscule red camera light perched above on the bedroom's door frame, filming her departure.

Chapter Sixty-Four

—∞—

"Did I tell you that Josh was on Ambien? You know, the sleeping pill? Said most of his troop was. Either that or anti-depressants." Maggie whipped around each corner of the winding country road as if on a mogul course, taking out her anger through acceleration.

"That boy never had a problem sleeping before; in fact, it was his favorite thing to do. Said his problem started right after a particular exercise at boot camp. They were being trained to sing songs about killing 'ragheads.' The 'Hajji,' they called them.

> *Kill them on their way to prayer*
> *Ring the bell inside the schoolhouse*
> *Watch those kiddies gather 'round*
> *And lock and load and mow those little motherfuckers*
> *down.*

"Maggie, that's horrible!" Stella howled, clutching her churning stomach. The images of randomly shooting innocent children in a schoolyard brought the remainder of last night's pastries up to her lips.

Maggie downshifted to third as she tried to stay on her side, taking the sharp corner over a stone bridge much too fast.

"Jim told me the military knew that soldiers, humans really, had an inherent resistance to not kill their own kind. That's the way we're made. So the government had to come up with a technique that makes killing a conditioned reflex. You know, like violent video games. I think that's why all of our soldiers are killing themselves, Stella. With this war, they had no mission, no purpose like my dad did in WWII, trying to stop Hitler and the spread of Nazism and fascism. But our kids now—because, believe you me that's who's fighting these damn wars—aren't soldiers killing soldiers to be the victor. It's soldiers shooting children, pregnant women, old men, families.

"Most of these soldiers are lower middle class, looking for a job, not a career. They're loyal, too. I used to be . . . ." Maggie ranted on, not noticing Stella's head lobbing back and forth.

Stella fought the high fever-induced stupor, barely hearing Maggie. She listlessly tried to get Maggie's attention, her weakened hands falling back into her lap.

"Did you know that every year there is enough ammunition produced to shoot everyone in the world *twice*? Is that the most insane thing you've ever heard? Dammit, Stella, I think our own government killed Jim!" exclaimed Maggie, narrowly missing a cow beside the road.

"I know it. Just don't know why yet. I should have known they would go after our own people after all went scot-free when they outed that blond undercover CIA agent. Only didn't believe murder would be part of the package."

Stella again tried to respond to Maggie's outrage, but her voice was broken—silenced. She felt absolutely helpless as she collapsed against the car's door.

Maggie continued, eyes focused only on the road, "You know, you Lefties are right. It's the Global Elite who have no loyalty to anyone or any country. Did you know that the State Department ordered our own diplomats to gather credit card information and DNA samples from

United Nations bureaucrats, making our diplomats spies at every embassy?" she said, her voice rising to a high pitch.

"You know why France was opposed to the war? Jim said they did their jobs and cross-checked Colin Powell's speech. The facts weren't there to support it. We just acted like effin' sheep, because they questioned our patriotism if we didn't go along. We never should have been in Iraq in the first place," she said, slapping the dashboard, tears of rage welling in her eyes.

"I think we need to pull over," said Stella, panting and holding her hand over her mouth.

"What? The old woman warned us not to stop," Maggie yelled.

"Sorry. Now! Pull over!"

Maggie slammed on the brakes and skidded to the side of the narrow country road, plowing under a stretch of new white Snowdrops, recently emerged from the spring mud.

Stella was doubled over with vicious cramping as she gripped her stomach, soaked in flop sweat. Maggie had barely opened the door before Stella violently threw up, retching so hard she wet herself.

"Maggie . . . something's . . . wrong," she gasped while spilling out her stomach contents as she stumbled into the grassy pasture.

"Stella, did you have any water with your breakfast?" quizzed Maggie.

Jim told her only days before he died of GA7's water experiment using DNA to remotely influence people. He had volunteered to be part of the experiment early on, suffering debilitating stomach pain and loss of control. Like what was happening to Stella. Maggie's brain raced, trying to figure out how they had gotten Stella's DNA. Jim had told her they tried to use collected DNA within thirty days for maximum effect.

Holding Stella's hair in a ponytail as she dry heaved, bent over the delicate spring flowers, Maggie knew it had to be freshly taken. *That obnoxious French flight attendant trying to use a lint roller on her!* They must have gotten some of Stella's hair. This was serious; her mind raced, searching for solutions. She knew Stella's life was in danger. No time to waste.

Maggie grabbed Stella's arm, trying to steady her as she teetered like a unicyclist in a wind storm back to the car in her high-heeled boots.

Probably to make her ass look great for the Frenchman, Maggie seethed, as she still gently guided Stella into the small back seat.

"Dare I say woman, do you ever put on the appropriate goddamned footwear?" Maggie fumed, as she jammed the gear shift into first, and stood on the gas pedal.

Impatiently shifting gears, she drove as fast as she could back to Lilli's house. She tried to switch into third gear; it wouldn't budge. Fourth gear—same thing.

"Oh, for cryin' out loud, we only have two gears left," she hollered above the loud whirring of the battered transmission.

Maggie was so focused on maneuvering along the twisting country roadway, she failed to notice the glint of the shiny star lying by the side of the road, atop an unread message.

Chapter Sixty-Five

—∞—

"Now you know," Brent said, stirring more sugar into his already syrupy coffee as he studied his cousin's face for her reaction. She had arrived that morning to his luxury hotel on the outskirts of Vatican City, her heart full of revenge after the revelation of Cardinal Gustav's and GA7's greedy evil intents.

"Jim and I thought something was fishy about all the papal visits by our president. Especially when he personally went to Andrews Air Force in Washington to meet with the pope. Doesn't happen. American presidents never meet a world leader at the airport. Always wait at the White House to receive his visitor; that's the protocol. Something didn't smell right. So we started spying on them."

He was glad that Kathleen had found out through other channels first about the Church's deep involvement in a New World Order; he didn't want to be the one to expose the ugliness and break his cousin's heart or destroy her faith. When she delivered the voluminous copies of the documents to him at his hotel that morning, he made her promise him not to lose her love for God.

"These men are the sinners, not you."

Her teary reaction showed her appreciation. Ex-communication hadn't lessened her undying commitment to Jesus.

He looked around the room, noticing hot spots by the slight humming most people could not hear. He knew his room was probably bugged; if not now, then soon. Standard Operating Procedure, even if they still trusted him. From experience he knew it best to pick a noisy place to discuss the next step of his plan with his cousin and her new roommate. Kathleen mentioned that Gustav had met with the pope last night and was supposed to meet him again tonight.

"Good. Go back to the house, and I'll meet you and Martha there later tonight. Tell Martha we need to go to someplace where we can talk, somewhere loud but also safe. I'm sure she has connections."

* * *

Brent arrived shortly before the official car picked up the red-flocked priest, precisely at 8:45 p.m., curbside. News had broken that morning that the pope, for the first time in history, was retiring. He knew Gustav would be occupied in meetings for the rest of the night, jockeying for position.

Rome was now overrun with cable news networks' vans everywhere—and cameras. That was the reason he wore his dark aviator glasses, his face shielded by a stylish fedora. He blended seamlessly, simply another chic Italian, out for a night-time stroll. Not a retired assassin who was about to turn the tables on his employer and possibly destroy the Catholic Church. First order of business was telling his cousin and the cardinal's housekeeper the whole incredible story in public, concisely. No time to waste. Must put *his plan* in motion.

"Did he see you?" Martha rasped, her brow furrowed in fear, thinking Brent had arrived too soon after Gustav's departure. She grasped his jacket sleeve and yanked him in through the front door.

"No. He should be arriving at the Vatican right now. One thing you learn in my business is where and when not to be noticed. It worked in Lourdes, didn't it?"

"Si, si. Okay, let's go. I don't want to talk here," she said, pulling on her plain cloth coat as both she and Kathleen quickly joined Brent in the cool night air.

"I made reservations at Eau Vive for 9:00," Martha said. "It's a French restaurant on the left bank of the Tiber."

"Sounds great. I'm ready for a break from all this Italian food," Brent said, uncomfortable in his now too-tight jeans. The irony of eating at a restaurant whose name translated into "long live water" did not escape him. He wondered how much Martha already knew. Maybe it was just a coincidence, though he no longer believed in such things.

"Aren't you worried? Shouldn't we be *dog wide*, Brent?" Kathleen asked, nervously looking around. She was surprised that Brent seemed so relaxed as they walked, considering what he had revealed about the Spaniard's fate. From what she knew so far, her own cousin could soon be on the "slit list."

"Nope, not worried. You learn after many missions to stay calm and carry on, as the Brits say. Look around at all the beauty of the gardens here. Take a deep breath of the deeply perfumed night air. Each flower planted with a purpose. Open your ears to the nightly singing of Ave Maria. Concentrate on that; it'll keep you safer. Let us not worry about what may happen. Let's go enjoy a nice meal. I have a story for you.

"Have you been to this restaurant before, Martha?" he asked in an effort to keep the conversation neutral as long as possible.

"A few times," Martha responded. "It is a meeting place for those of the church and the laypeople. It's operated by the Missionary Women Workers of the Immaculate Virgin. I know many of their members."

"Well, I like the sounds of that, I do," Kathleen clucked, as they entered the plush restaurant.

The moon's reflection from the Tiber right outside the massive wall of windows complemented the warmth from the restaurant's candle lights. The serenity from the moon glow was broken as the host approached them, his mouth twisted to one side.

"Scusi, Sister Martha, I thought the reservation was for His Eminence," he said, flustered by the cardinal's absence. He worried if he should seat her and her friends at the cardinal's table. There were certain protocols in his restaurant that must be followed.

"No, it's for me and my friends, Giorgio, who are also friends of the cardinal's. He is dining with Il Papa tonight." That was all the reassurance the polished yet sensible Italian needed. He could work with that.

"This way, please," he bowed, as Martha smiled, satisfied with her ruse. "Shall I bring you some wine?" he asked, once again his charming self as he pulled out her chair.

"We will let you know," Martha replied. Once he was out of earshot, she leaned in to her companions. "They are all terrified of Gustav. Everyone knows what a wretched hog he is. But I'm not afraid of him anymore. I am immune to his violence.

"You know, Brent, I started out as la perpetua to Pope John Paul I. After he died, I was assigned to Gustav to keep an eye on him. The rapes started immediately. He always bends me over the kitchen table, to ram me from behind, defiling my work space. Anything he can do to humiliate me. But I am strong, and I know God is using me," she finished, knowing full well her guests would be repulsed by her revelation.

"Why do you stay?" Brent asked her, shivered by her ongoing horror and its obvious numbing effect on the woman. He had always disliked Cardinal Muench. Could never understand how a priest could sexually abuse anyone.

"We are not only brides of Christ, but la perpetua, housekeepers. It's an everlasting relationship. I will stay with him until one of us dies—or he ends up in prison where he belongs!" She ended her sentence with such force, Brent felt spittle on his cheek.

"I could feel evil always coming from that one. I'm so sorry, dear heart," Kathleen said, deeply saddened by her sister's pain.

"Okay, let's order as if everything is just a normal night out. Then as we eat, I'll let you know as much as I know," Brent said, as he opened his napkin onto his lap, scanning the room. He laid his customized hybrid cell phone on the table. The flashing icon on its screen indicated the surveillance app was active.

"Will you first tell us about your own involvement, Brent? I have listened to Gustav's and Lucas' conversations many times, and I know they have mentioned you. Please do not try to fool me," Martha warned, her old shrewd eyes drilling fiercely into his.

Brent eyed her carefully—unflinching, stoic, unemotional—tells of someone who has surrendered with nothing left to lose. No wonder she revealed her cards so early in the evening. No doubt after the years of abuse, she was ready for her pound of flesh. He had no reason to lie to her.

"Yes," he replied, looking over at his cousin. "I'm sorry Kathleen, but it's time you too knew the whole filthy mess. When I started with GA7 after leaving the Army, I did 'wet work.' That's what they call us hired killers. In fact, the Spaniard and I have worked together many times. That was the kind of man I was then. Until Chile. I was shot while on an assignment there and nearly died. Actually, I did die—for a short time. I had what they call a Near Death Experience or NDE. That's when I saw Her."

"Her?" Kathleen asked, stunned. "Are you talking about Our Lady?"

"I believe so. I'm sorry I couldn't tell you when you stayed with me, telling me tales of our home land, your studies at the Vatican and especially Our Lady of Knock. But it was for good reason. Because right after the NDE, I convinced my buddy from the Army to come to work at GA7.

"I told you we were spies, this morning. What I didn't tell you was we both worked as psychic spies." He could tell they had no idea what he was talking about. "We used telepathy to 'see things.' I know it sounds like a science fiction movie. And if it doesn't sound like that now, it will by dessert. You see, Jim found out something at work while using his 'abilities.' Something called Spider Sweep. A global vibrational poverty plan.

"GA7, along with Cardinal Gustav and maybe all the way to the top of the Vatican too, have a plan to use DNA to remotely influence all world leaders to keep the world in fear and chaos. They know that if the world is kept in constant agitation using 'Shock Events,' the population will eventually become exhausted into apathy and therefore unable to fight for freedom.

"The plan is for a global master/slave race. It's already been very effective in getting people to fight each other. Look at how many Americans are killing other Americans under the guise of constitutional right. They don't even realize they are in a war in their own homeland.

"That's how the rich got so filthy rich. We were all so busy fighting each other over politics that we stopped paying attention. Now they are targeting the minds of everyday people. That what's going on in the lab, our little project on the outskirts of Rome.

"But there's potentially a big glitch in Spider Sweep. It has to be completed before December, 2012, when we enter a new era, an evolution in consciousness. Something about the women. That's what's in the Third Secret—a warning."

"Why are you telling us now?" Martha asked. "You came with us and the Spaniard. Were you not there to kill also?"

"Yes. And no. My agenda was to make sure no one got killed. You see, the woman, the redheaded American? She was my buddy's wife. GA7 must have found out that her husband discovered Spider Sweep— and they killed him. That's why I'm still involved with Lucas and Gustav. If I can stay close, I can keep a close eye on them until we can find a way to stop them. Because now they are after *all the women*."

"Bastards!" Kathleen jeered. "They were using me as part of their plan, too, right? You don't even need to tell me. I know. What a bloody fool I've been."

"And you must continue to act the fool, dear cousin. Both of you must continue to appear weak and complacent, not powerful or strong. Keep the nun's habit on to stay invisible. Because what GA7 and the Church haven't realized yet since they moved the lab into the convent is all the residual DNA from the peace-loving nuns. It's everywhere. I know because it keeps giving them false positives all the time. It's in the Holy Water in the ancient well right below the lab."

"Blimey! Mary's round about the place, she is," Kathleen cheered, as she sopped up the sauce from her butter-poached fish with a chunk of bread. "I knew there was something about the water. I saw reams of documents in the archives about it. Caught my eye about Ireland. Especially the report on a spring once held sacred to the Goddess Brigid. It said something about eighty-six percent of the Marian shrines are centered on spring wells. Real interested the Lady of Knock appeared on a rainy night, they were."

"Tell us what you need us to do, Brent. We are prepared to do whatever you need," Martha said.

"Who do you know at Vatican Radio?"

Chapter Sixty-Six

—∞—

"Hold on, sugar plum, we're almost there." Maggie coughed, her nostrils blackened by the acrid smoke billowing through the dashboard's vents. She prayed the rapidly dying car would finish the winding climb up the hill to Lilli's door.

Stella's breath was so shallow Maggie could barely hear her. She stole a glance in the rear view mirror. Stella's hair was drenched with sweat, her pallor as gray as a just-burst rain cloud.

"C'mon, you goddamned piece of shit, keep going!" she screamed as the car hopped like a drunk jackrabbit, sputtering to its death with a final burst of carbon exhaust from its tailpipe.

"Gabriel, help!" she yelled as she jumped out of the smoking heap of metal, right as he flew out the French doors.

Startled by the panic in Maggie's eyes, he reached the smoking car in three long strides. She was stunned at his strength and agility, lifting Stella up effortlessly and rushing her swiftly into the cottage and up the back stairs.

"Don't worry, mon chéri, it is not her time to go," Lilli reassured Maggie, as she rushed to her side. She took her by the arm and led her into the kitchen.

"Follow me. I must make her my special tea. It will heal her quickly. First, where is her necklace?"

"I don't know," Maggie sniveled, worried she was losing yet another loved one. "She said she took it off last night, and I told her to put it in her pocket when we were rushing from the chateau."

"It is very important you tell me exactly what happened," Lilli urged. The elderly woman reached deep into her kitchen cabinet, finally grabbing the age-darkened cobalt blue jar topped with a silver-starred lid.

At first she could not twist it open, so rarely was this herb used. She kept at it, knowing its use was critical to save Stella. Finally, she heard the pop. She sprinkled a large pinch on top of the other herbs in her white and gray marbled mortar and expertly crushed them into a viscous magic potion.

While the tea steeped, Lilli motioned for Maggie to sit at the kitchen table. "It will take a moment. Tell me what happened."

Maggie quickly told Lilli about the port-wine stained Spaniard at Lourdes and their escape back to the chateau. She skimmed over her drunken behavior and the women's plans to meet at Mary's House, still wary of Lilli. Something told her this kind wise woman had not been completely forthright–yet. She knew there were still secrets behind the veil.

"It was after we left your friend with the car that she started getting sick—or at least when I started noticing it. God, I was still so upset, and a little hung over from last night that I'm kind of hazy on all the details. I wasn't paying attention to her," Maggie said, regretfully. She knew if she hadn't been hung over all of her senses would have been clicking like clockwork. She felt shame for her weakness.

"You don't know if she had her necklace on?"

"No! Why are you so concerned about some damn jewelry?" Maggie asked, starting to get irritated, knowing now there must be more to the trinkets than even she was aware. *Time to come clean, lady.* Maggie's capacity for patience for any kind of cat-and-mouse game of intrigue was nil.

"I don't have time to tell you now, but it is very important both of you keep them on your body. There are powerful forces out there trying to harm you, to stop the women. I will tell you more later. But the necklaces will keep you safe. First, we must heal our Stella."

Having no alternative, Maggie followed the woman up the stairs, carrying the steaming cup that she hoped would save Stella's life. She was willing to table the topic—for a while.

"Good, here they are," Gabriel said as Maggie and Lilli entered the small room. Stella's color was starting to return to her cheeks. Helped along by Gabriel's continued nursing of her heated brow with the sweet-smelling cloth.

"Drink up, butter cup. You're in good hands now," Maggie said, as Gabriel helped Stella sit up to sip her tea.

"I'm so sorry. I think I may have eaten more than my share of French food. I'm sorry to put you all to so much trouble."

"You think this is *crise de foie*, an American stomach in France?" Lilli asked, aghast at such a suggestion. Realizing Stella thought she was being scolded, she softened her tone.

"Please, do not apologize. Do not be embarrassed by what happened to you. This is not another of what you call 'breaking open,'" Lilli said softly. She noticed Stella cringe.

"Stella, please do not be ashamed. You needed to be in your bed then, like being in your mother's womb. Your heart had to break open so that light could enter and the true you could emerge.

"Your biography is not your destiny. Your mother made the decision to end her life that day to stop her suffering from the cancer. It wasn't your fault. You have the ultimate power to make your own decision.

"You have gestated your grief; now is the time to forgive yourself. Be grateful for all the good in your life. If you always feel grateful, you will always be protected. You have a very important big task ahead of you.

"Every human being has pain, has suffered in this life. But it is up to you to allow your spirit to lead you back to life, to help others, to shine again. Shed your pain, don't continue to wear it like skin," Lilli said as she gently rubbed Stella's forearm with her balm.

"I really want to get better and enjoy life again. I want to wake up smiling. To be the shining star like the name my mother gave me," Stella tearfully murmured, as she collapsed back into the overstuffed narrow bed.

"No tears now. Don't worry, you will get there," Lilli said, soothingly. "Right now you must rest. I don't know what happened to your necklace, but you are now wearing another one," she said as she pulled the cherished keepsake from her apron pocket and gently placed it around Stella's neck.

"It was Dior's. It is very important that it stay on your body. I will explain later."

Maggie sat in the small chair by the window, watching the mother and son administer to Stella's needs while her brain whirled at a million miles a minute, processing the events of the last twenty-four hours. She was convinced that whoever was responsible for the murder of her husband was now after them, using the new weapons of war Jim had warned her about. He called it Spider Sweep. And she and Stella were the prey.

Maggie remembered to counteract the weapon's effects, Jim said the target should be comforted with something familiar. She knew exactly what to do. After the inaugural hair washing that frightful July evening in Vallejo when Stella had eased Maggie's terror of the Zodiac, Stella had been unable to sleep. Maggie returned the favor in a very unique way.

"Excuse me, if you don't mind, I think I know what she needs now."

"Oui, I believe you do. Come son, let them alone for the time being. Help me in the kitchen, please."

Maggie could see that Gabriel was hesitant to leave Stella, but he dutifully obeyed his mother.

She kicked off her shoes and crawled into the small twin bed with Stella, spooning as if they were one.

Barely audible, she hummed softly into Stella's ear a familiar song as they rocked gently until Maggie's final whisper: "*Together, together, that's how it must be, to live without you would only be heartbreak for me.*" Slowly, Stella's body softened and her forehead was cool to Maggie's touch.

Chapter Sixty-Seven

—∞—

Lilli's neighborhood rooster crowed good morning across his tiled red roof as she entered the guest room with her heavy sterling silver breakfast tray. Her intuition had been right about bringing up enough breakfast for two, seeing Maggie asleep in Stella's bed as she pushed through the door. The two women were still spooned together as Lilli quietly set the tray on the plain bedside table.

"Good morning," Lilli whispered, pulling back the colorful flowered curtains. "Can you sit up now, my dear?" Stella struggled to prop herself up on her elbows. "Let me help you," she said, plumping up and arranging pillows behind Stella's back.

She noticed that Stella seemed weak still, unfocused, maybe still lost in her dreams. She watched as Stella managed to get both eyes opened before grasping her throat in terror.

"Yes, it is still there. You are safe—both of you."

Maggie groaned as she tried to roll over and wipe the sleep from her eyes. "I have a feeling I'm gonna pay mightily for sleeping in this damn bed," she said as she crawled over Stella's hips trying to reach the foot of the bed. "God, I feel old." The plastic bag with Jim's T-shirt fell out of the folds of her nightgown.

"Your body hurts, no? Let me fix you," Lilli offered, studying Maggie for clues of other pain. "Here is some tea for both of you, along with our fresh honey. Sip a little of it first, then enjoy your breakfast. The bread just came out of the oven, and the eggs were laid this morning," she said, beaming with a farmer's pride.

"This tea smells heavenly, Lilli," Stella remarked as she tried to identify the bouquet: ginger, lemon and wild strawberry mixed with another essence she couldn't quite identify. She took a sip before she laid back against the pillows. Her head felt like it was stuffed with cotton.

She vaguely remembered being lowered into the small bed by Gabriel last night, his touching her brow, Maggie hugging her and singing her to sleep. Her next thought made her blush. Vividly, she remembered her erotic dream—with Gabriel. A dream experience she had never had before. Smoothing her soft cotton nightgown against her body, she hoped he would be in soon to check on her. She wiggled snugly into the mattress, pinching her arms tight to her torso in an effort to use her back fat to push her breasts upwards.

"Merci, enjoy. Stella, I know you are anxious about the events of yesterday. I will leave you two alone so Maggie can tell you what happened. I'll be back shortly. I, too, have a story to tell you," Lilli teased, leaving them with a hint of mystery soon to be revealed.

Lilli reached for her phone as she entered the kitchen, though it hadn't rang yet. "Yes, they are both here. No, she is still weak, but reviving quite quickly. You found the necklace? *Bien.* I'll report back to you this evening. I'll be introducing them to some quatrains shortly and one or two of the paintings," Lilli said before she clicked off.

Satisfied it had been a reasonable time for the tea to have an effect on the women, she walked up the stairs and gently knocked on the guest room door.

"Come in," Stella said with a smile in her voice. She quickly smoothed her hair, hoping her quick primping would suffice. Her mouth fell flat when his mother stood in the door instead.

"You were expecting my son, oui?" Lilli asked. "He had business in the village, but he will be back shortly."

Stella stammered, embarrassed by her obviousness. *Keep the shield up*, she reminded herself. "Thank you so much for the lovely meal. I'm feeling so much better now."

"*Parfait!*" Lilli studied the pair. It appeared her tea had performed as planned; they looked strong enough to continue. This next revelation would be challenging and disturbing, to say the least. Her guests had already experienced life-threatening situations; now with the enemy getting closer every day, the veil needed to be lifted a little higher. She had performed her duties as instructed, giving them little polished pearls of information to ease them into their mission. There was no going back now. The clock had begun.

"You feel better, no?" she asked Maggie, running her age-spotted hand through the American's soft curls while looking deeply into her guest's gold-flecked brown eyes, not unlike an exam in the doctor's office.

"I don't know what you put in that mortar of yours, Lilli," Maggie said, pulling back a bit, "but if I bottled it and sold it in the U.S., I'd be a millionaire. You brought Stella back from the dead! And I feel great, the best since I've arrived in your country. Look, I can touch my toes!"

Lilli smiled, satisfied with her results. The tea was enough to put them in an altered state that hopefully would make them more receptive than frightened. The time had come to enlighten them more about Nostradamus' prophecies that concerned them both—and the world.

"That is wonderful, Maggie. Now, do you both remember what I told you that first night here about my ancestor? If you're feeling up to it, I would like to tell you some more."

"So much has happened I actually forgot about that," Maggie said, sitting comfortably on the wooden bedside chair. "I think we can handle that, right, Stella?" Maggie asked.

Stella nodded her agreement.

"The floor is yours, so to speak," Maggie replied, leaning back, her knobby knees pulled tightly to her chest while she sipped her tea.

Lilli removed an abstract painting hanging on the thick plastered wall. Underneath, outlined by the picture frame's sunburned shadow, was a stainless steel door with a simple red-lighted square on its front. She pressed her thumb against the glowing light long enough for it to read her print, slowly opening the solid door of the climate-controlled reinforced steel box.

"Here, please put these on," she said, handing them white cotton gloves from her apron pocket. "I would like to show you something that not many people in the world have seen. They think they've seen it, but no," she said as she laid the ancient simple looking unbound book at the foot of Stella's bed.

"This is the real *Lost Book of Nostradamus*. Actually, only a few paintings. As reported on your *History Channel*, the paintings are by his son, César. But what they showed on television was not the whole book.

"For reasons that will become clear to you shortly, you'll understand why my family decided to release part of the book into circulation in 1994. It was, and is, necessary to use the tricks of misinformation and deception.

"Until recently these precious paintings were hidden along with other artifacts in Chartres Cathedral. However, there are those in this world who want them destroyed, no trace left behind. But these centuries-old secrets need to be told. Democracy depends on a well-informed citizenry, and these have been guarded to be released at just the right time. God time.

"Let us start with more of what I told you that first night about my great grandfather's pilgrimage on the Camino de Santiago," Lilli started, "and his journey back to Chartres."

Stella looked to see if Maggie had caught on. This was the third time in as many days someone had mentioned the Camino. The synchronicity was not lost on either of them. "Funny, did we mention two of our friends who were with us at the chateau had recently gone on the same trek?" asked Stella.

"I don't believe so. I don't know how much your friends knew of the pilgrimage. Do you know how the Camino follows the ley lines of the Milky Way? You do? Very well. That is very important.

"It was during this trip that grand-pére was introduced to the Divine Feminine. Mythology has always held the Milky Way to be the womb of the Divine Feminine, the birthplace of Isis, also known as Sophia—the Goddesses of Wisdom. During the year's long journey, he followed the ley lines of the Milky Way, studying the stars above as he talked to God—

and many prophecies came to him. He wrote of visiting many dimensions, of talking to different species, non-human.

"These beings told him of the coming of a new golden world. Told him a time would come when all three of the major religions would be united in their love for God. They said when this galaxy aligns with the earth, sun and moon there will be a rebirth, bringing a great shift in our world. This is why Nostradamus, already committed to his Hebrew training, along with Christian principles, also became a member of a Sicilian Sufi brotherhood loyal to Islam. He wanted to understand all of these religions so he could be a catalyst to serve as many as possible.

"When he returned to St. Remy he started writing his Almanac, somewhat like today's horoscopes. He wanted to let the people know the importance of our hearts and minds joining; two powerful organs that are more powerful together than anyone can imagine.

"He said we are all sparks of the divine matrix—and a time would come for the sparks to join and illuminate the world. He predicted the industrial and technological revolutions and said we would be entering a truly spectacular revolution—wisdom, a partnership culture.

"That revolution is starting now—and it will happen in the blink of an eye. Each revolution gets shorter and shorter with time acceleration. Since the 1998 Alignment, time is now twenty times faster. This is why we feel so much chaos. It ushers in change.

"Here's the first quatrain I would like to explain to you," Lilli said, lifting the fragile painting with the three women: A queen, a female pope and a sainted nun.

> *"Branch XV, 10 Quatrain 4 24*
> *On earth the sainted voice of the Holy Lady is heard,*
> *Human flame for divine will be seen to shine;*
> *It will cause Sisters' blood to be shed on the ground,*
> *Sacred temples cast into ruin by the impure of heart."*

Stella gasped. "This is about the visions, isn't it?"

"Yes, my dear, I believe so. It is the return of the goddess," Lilli added, "as illustrated by these three women; very powerful women. This quatrain represents the unleashing of the female energies of the universe.

That's the best way to describe it. We think he believed that women would rise to power in the 21st century. They will bring about the destruction of the established religious and financial institutions of their time by their beliefs. He also said that this refers to the great mother, the Earth herself, and her rebellion against being harnessed. These women represent the eternal female aspect of God.

"I'm sorry to interrupt, Lilli, but something isn't making sense to me. Stella, remember that statue at the chateau? I completely forgot about a cocktail party Jim and I once had. One of our guests, a historical architect, was telling us about the Virgin Mary and her influence on the building of Washington, D.C. She said the town was laid out like a star, with lots of references in the architecture to Mary. She's the one who told me about the statue being placed on top of the Capitol building in 1863, with a wreath of stars around her head. She mentioned all of it had something to do with the Return of the Divine Feminine.

Maggie grabbed the water book Gabriel had loaned her from her tote bag. "I thought I saw something interesting. Look at this photo, it's the tap water from Washington, D.C. See all these other pictures from other cities? Notice how tap water is a murky gray-black color? But Washington's is a beautiful crystal. In the shape of a star? Dirty stinking Washington? Can you believe it?"

"Yes. Your capitol was indeed planned using many occult symbols. It was designed by a Frenchman, you know. The city's layout is based on the star of the sea, *Stella Maris.* She is also known as the Great Mother, the First Mother and also as Mary," Lilli added, about to inform them of Washington's future, when she noticed Stella's startled look. "You are not feeling well, dear child?"

"Oh, no, that's not it. No, my Nema had told me my name meant star of the sea. But I did not know of the connection to Mary."

"I understand. You will continue to find more connections. There are no accidents. Be patient as I try to explain it all. We are all at the mercy of God time," she finished, pointing upwards.

"Maggie, you read the water books? Good. You understand about water memories and how it can be changed? My ancestor could pick out information from the cosmic grid, the Akashic records, using water. That was how he learned of the danger warned of in his prophecies. Evil forces are now using water against humankind.

"It is the beginning of the Age of the Divine, when the women must be the leaders. With Global Warming all the glaciers, with billions of years of stored memories in this water, are melting. Jesus preached by water—and his words are stored in it. But our waters are being polluted. Not by chemicals alone, but also with emotions. We cannot afford to lose the effect of those harmonic memories stored all over our planet.

"Planets are now producing a harmonic music. It sounds like Ave Maria. You noticed that they play Ave Maria twenty-four hours a day at Lourdes? This is not only as a tribute to Our Lady, but the harmonic frequency sustaining the water's magical vibrations.

"You see this picture," she said, pointing to one of the last laying in her slim stack of cryptic paintings. "Of the water, the sun, the women turning their backs to the pope, his staff in the shape of two crosses representing the tree of life, the hourglass representing time. This is the beginning of the Great Alignment.

"Here's another with ribbons, a wheel, a star inside the circle of olive leaves, the crescent moon which symbolizes the goddess, and a lamb, the symbol of Christ, with the serpent attached to all? The snake symbolizes an umbilical cord, joining all humans to Mother Earth, the Great Goddess, suggesting a coming together of all religions.

"Why did he paint the pictures if he was already writing quatrains?" Stella asked, perplexed.

"It was the time of the Great Inquisition. He was afraid for his remaining family and for himself. He had a most difficult job of warning a future generation, 500 years in the future, while at the same time keeping his messages hidden. To be successful he knew it had to be combined—the paintings and the prophecies—revealed at the dawn of a new era. Now is that time.

"He knew that images are universal to all, no matter your language or religion. Some of the first known art came from Egypt, depicting Isis by the Nile—the water. This is what my ancestor saw in his water. So many references to the Great Goddess, waiting for all the dots to be connected.

"I know you are tired, Stella, but just one more for today. It is Quatrain Century II-58. It is about our enemies, the Cabal:

> *With neither foot nor hand because of sharp and strong*
> *teeth*
> *through the crowd to the fort of the pork and the elder*
> *born:*
> *Near the portal treacherous proceeds,*
> *Moon shining little, great one led off.*

"Sometimes, to understand his quatrains, you have to start at the end and then move to the beginning. We believe the last line refers to powerful men, behind-the-scenes puppeteers, working towards their own ends. They may be in key positions of power.

"The *moon shining little* refers to those with limited psychic intuitive powers who will use great military might for the great pillage—world control, ignorant of the magnitude of damage they would be doing to us all.

"The first line refers to using all tools necessary to break through any blockage to attain their objectives."

"Are these the bad guys who chased us out of Paris?" Maggie asked, feeling dwarfed, helpless.

"We believe so."

"Who are they?"

"Most refer to them as The Elite. We will talk more about them specifically in a few hours. This is a lot of information. Rest for now."

Lilli put the paintings back in their safe harbor, as she heard her son enter downstairs. She hoped she had been successful in her attempt at distraction, covering the lower corner of the painting with her hand while she explained the quatrains. Neither women saw the image of two women painted on the last sheet—one blond, one with coppery curls.

Chapter Sixty-Eight

—∞—

"How is our patient doing today?" Gabriel asked Maggie, as he slid onto the small chair next to Stella's bed.

"Seems a lot better than the last time you saw her. Boy, she gave us a scare, huh?"

"Very much so," he said, his trauma still present from last night. He hadn't slept much since she had arrived, spending most of the night on his knees praying for her recovery. "I can stay with her for a while if you would like a recess."

"Sure. That alright with you, baby girl?" Maggie asked Stella as she grabbed her cardigan sweater and camera. Knowing she wouldn't hear any argument, she headed downstairs. "I'll be back shortly."

Now that Stella was conscious, he found himself quite anxious. He hoped he wasn't being improper checking on her while she was still in her bed—not formally dressed. The protesting creak of the chair leg was warning enough not to tempt fate as he leaned in too close and tried to smell her hair.

"I don't know if I would consider myself a patient, but I'm feeling much better. Thank you for your kindness. I think you saved my life," she said, touching his hand with a tenderness that implicated more intimacy than they had yet to share.

Gabriel jumped out of the chair, as if her touch had scorched his skin. He caught the bedside lamp right before it toppled to the floor. Immediately embarrassed by his reaction, he pushed back his hair from his forehead as he moved the chair back away from the bed. Clearing his throat, he started a different and safer conversation.

"My mother showed you the lost paintings?" he asked. "I'm sure it's a lot to take in. Do you have any questions I may answer?"

"Sure," Stella said, her ego bruised a little from his nervous reaction, but determined to find the truth. "Who are the Cabal and why would they or anyone for that matter be after me and Maggie?" Her directness shook him. He wasn't prepared to give her a quick off-the-cuff answer.

"That's a bit complicated, but also simple. It's a story about power. Perhaps I should tell you my own story. I think it will help you.

"As a young priest, I met Albino Luciani, the priest who would become Pope John Paul I. He was my mentor. Once he helped break a fever of mine, like I did for you."

Gabriel stared out the window, thinking fondly of his late friend. "He loved books. I shared many of my father's rare books with him after joining him in Rome. We would take many walks around the Vatican simply to explore. The Curia did not like this.

"His Holiness loved to play hide and seek. Kept them on their toes while we discussed sensitive matters, like the Vatican Bank. Did you know that the Vatican has 10,000 rooms and halls with almost a 1,000 stairways, 30 of which are secret?

"It was during one of our walks that His Holiness suggested I become a Bollandist. Little did I know he was arranging for my future placement and my safety. He only lived thirty-three days after becoming pope. I believe he knew his fate.

"Within hours of his papal election, the propaganda machine had started cranking against him. They even went to his university and removed all his notes and papers from his studies. Specifically, they wanted his written opinions regarding birth control."

"Why would they do that?' Stella asked, tentatively. "Aren't you all on the same side?"

"We should be, but not always. The pope believed that the Church had become a corporation. Its purpose was profits, not the Holy Spirit or salvation. As the son of a bricklayer, he was very uncomfortable with the Church's preoccupation with wealth. In his Mass of thanksgiving, he gave notice of his intentions to return the Church back to something Christ would recognize, a church for the world, free of political interests, free of big business mentality. Very radical.

"You know there is no scripture or divine revelation to justify a ban on birth control. That was man's edict, disguised as holy law. Ironically, the Vatican once owned Istituto Farmacologico Serono, the maker of the best-selling contraceptive—Luteolas.

"The hypocrisy did not escape John Paul's attention. He also didn't care if you ate before receiving communion. He said God had much bigger things to worry about," Gabriel said with a chuckle. "You know, they called him the smiling pope."

"You had great affection for him," Stella said, enjoying Gabriel's happy reminiscing.

"I did and still do. He was a brave man who knew the dangers of going against the entrenched status quo. Especially, the corruption with the Vatican bank. On his second day after being elected, he launched an investigation into the Vatican's finances. Within one week, we received a report that of the 11,000 Vatican bank accounts, only 1,650 served an ecclesiastical purpose. The rest were slush funds for the inside bankers. A judge had also started an investigation but sadly never finished. He was murdered by five gunmen at a stoplight in Rome. Soon more murders were committed, including journalists, which revealed more and more of the inner workings of Vatican, Inc.

"It was after this speech where he referred to God '*as our father; even more he is our mother,*' when the Vatican started to censor his speeches. Christo-fascism is what John Paul I called the silencing. That's when he told me he had read the Third Secret and was about to have it published." He noticed Stella sat up a little straighter.

"On the morning of September 28, the pope summoned Bishop Gustav Muench to share tea with him. He told the bishop he knew of the bank scandal and what the Third Secret was really saying. Seven hours later, the pope's housekeeper, Sister Martha, summoned me to check on him. We found the pope in bed, sitting up. His glasses were askew on his bulging eyes, and his fingers were clenched around partial fragments of a piece of paper as if something had been ripped from his hands. When the bishop arrived, he ordered the room sealed but not before I noticed that John Paul's appointment book and jewelry box were missing.

"I immediately fled to Bulgaria to be harbored by the Bollandists," Gabriel said. "I know he was murdered. He was going to reveal the Third Secret. They did not want the world to see it–ever!"

"Gabriel, that is a very dangerous thing to say, don't you think?"

"Of course. Jesus fought against the Romans' evil, and they killed him. But we can't be silent to evil. There is so much more to this story. Perhaps viewed through the prism of history would help you understand. Back in 1945, the Gnostic Gospels, about twenty of them, were found in northern Egypt in a crockery pot buried in the sand outside some caves in the Nag Hammadi desert. Some believe these precious artifacts were hidden in the jar by the monks of St. Pachomius, so they wouldn't be destroyed.

"World War II had ended and Sister Lucia had been forced to write down the Third Secret," Gabriel said as he studied Stella's face for a reaction. He could tell she was knitting all the information together, probably wondering why she was involved in all of this.

"Gnosticism was the *original* Christianity up to the 3rd century in the majority of Mediterranean countries. Gnosis is a mystical secret knowledge. The more gnosis—knowing—you had, the more you knew yourself." Gabriel noticed *that* got Stella's attention. "We believed they were hidden because, as they say, *legend is what is told when a story is too dangerous.*

"The Gnostics believed we were all part of the fabric of human nature. You didn't need a human conduit to God, such as the church. Most importantly, you could refuse to obey bishops and priests.

"Of course that all changed when Roman Emperor Constantine reinvented Christianity according to his rules. He wanted 'one god, one religion' so there would be 'one empire, one emperor.' He ordered the Gnostics be suppressed, their gospels banished, including all references to the language of emotions, imagination and prayer—and had many executed. Most importantly, all the secret texts which referred to feminine imagery for God were omitted from the New Testament.

"Jesus believed in women having an equal voice. You know, Jesus' last words were to his mother. She had been treated poorly by the Romans, too. Pontius Pilate's soldiers terrorized her for back taxes, breaking into her home and smashing her dishes, stealing her goat. He knew he was about to die and wanted his mother safe, in the land of women. That's where she lived out the rest of her life—Mary's House in Ephesus, Turkey."

Stella closed her eyes, woozy with information overload. "I thought you said Mary's House was the cathedral? I was told at the chateau about this house in Turkey. How many houses does she have?"

He smiled, understanding her confusion. "Many churches and cathedrals are called Mary's House, this is true. Yet the small humble stone house in Ephesus is where she lived after her son's death, carrying on his mission."

"So was she a virgin?" Stella asked, trying to suppress her anger at being misguided by the Church. She personally thought the whole virgin birth story was fabricated to slut shame women for actually enjoying the most natural human act.

"We all are—at one time. But no, the story has been, how do you say, taken out of context. When she was only three years old, she was selected to live with the high priest in the temple in Jerusalem, where she stayed until she was twelve. During her nine years of studying at the temple, Mary was taught to be a master weaver, a very prestigious position. They had her participate in the weaving of the veil for the temple of the Lord.

"As she grew older, the priests were worried that she would soon start menstruating, hence defiling their sanctuary of the Lord. They put a call out to widowers to come and have her as a wife. They chose Joseph when a dove flew out of his staff after a prayer service. 'You have been called to receive the virgin of the Lord. Receive her into your own keeping,' the high priest is reportedly to have said to Joseph. Hence, Mary the Virgin.

"She was just thirteen when she gave birth to Jesus—considered a child these days. Oddly, the story of the virgin birth didn't come out until one hundred years after Jesus' death.

"So most likely, she had Jesus the same way I gave birth?"

As soon as the words left her mouth, she remembered Nicki's text. It had been over twenty-four hours. Frantically, she realized Nicki had no way to reach her, as she had ditched her cell phone. She needed to find out if Nicki was safe.

"I'm sorry if I'm being impatient, but I believe my daughter is in danger, as we are. What does all of this have to do with being chased out of Paris?"

"I'm sorry I'm taking so long to explain this to you," Gabriel said, a little exasperated. "But it is a tale that started 2,000 years ago, so please have just a little more patience," he pleaded with her, with an impish smile. "I'm almost done. It is important that you know *Her* history.

"By the time of the Council of Ephesus in 431 AD, Mary had been declared Mary Theotokos, the God Bearer, elevating her to Goddess stature. Her power made the Church uneasy. By the Renaissance, she started to be depicted as weak and humble, no longer glorified. It wasn't until the 1830s that there was a grass roots renewal of Marian spirituality, especially here in France. That is when the reported apparitions started happening, starting with Catherine Labouré, a nun.

"Some say the apparitions are an alert to everyone of a rebirth. Nostradamus believed Mary was the virgin of light representing consciousness, the higher Sophia, wisdom. She appears to give us opportunities for our need to awaken, to connect with all consciousness to become One. A return to reason and rationality.

"First, she mostly appeared to children because they have yet to manifest their ego. Now she is appearing to post-menopausal women who are releasing their egos. The spiritually awake have let go of fear, ignoring religious moralists and acting more God-like.

"Defining God has always created conflict throughout history," Gabriel concluded. "There are some who do not appreciate talk of awakening and consciousness. Some refer to them as the Anti-Christ.

The Anti-Christ is not a person, *per se*, but a way of being. No compassion, just lust for power and money. It is godless to withhold care and compassion from those in need. We will all be living as anti-Christs unless we change. I believe this Cabal we talk of is the starting of the anti-Christ. For the Cabal and the Church, change is not a choice."

He stood and removed the valuable delicate fabric neatly folded in the safe. "This is Mary's scapular," he said, as he held out the ancient piece of near-transparent gossamer fabric. "She wove this tunic with her own hands to wear the night she gave birth to her son, Jesus. This is why Chartres Cathedral was built, to protect this very sacred relic. But it had to be hidden because of the politics of the Church. They want to destroy it. They understood its power.

"Remember when we were playing with the hidden dolls in the basement of that store, the City of Paris? The sparkle in the air? It was because of this doll," he said as he removed Faïence from the safe.

"She has a patch of the scapular stitched underneath her dress—this star, right here. The fabric is imbued in both Mother Mary's and Jesus' DNA; from a hidden source at the cathedral. Dior believed that Mary had obtained the highest vibration possible for a human, beyond human strife and suffering, and that her essence could somehow bring peace to the world. He said that was what he was *told* when he walked the labyrinth the first time."

"That was the true purpose why the Theater de la Mode was started," Lilli added as she entered the room. "I also have cloth from her tunic the day she watched her son take his last breath, imbued with their emotions from that day. Especially as it pertains to protecting the innocent. Part of that fabric is embedded in your stars," Lilli said. "What most people do not contemplate is that Mary was forty-six and most likely menopausal when her son was murdered. I doubt she went quietly into the night. Yet, she continued on. Her bravery and courage are embedded in that cloth.

"It is time for us to take Faïence and this holy cloth to her house, Mary's House, in Ephesus," Lilli said. "You are gathering the women there, no?" she asked, knowing full well they were. Gisele had told her so this morning.

"Son, let's arrange for the boat so you can take the women to Turkey safely. First, whenever you leave this house, you are to wear these," Lilli said, handing Stella a pair of vintage Dior gloves, lined with a tight-fitting latex insert.

"We must start being very careful with what we touch. We must guard our DNA as if our lives depended on it. Because it does."

"That might be a problem," Maggie said, as she came up the stairs, camera swinging around her neck. "Ever since I was a teen, I get incredibly sea sick. Ask Stella. Last time I sailed with her, she spent the whole time slopping up my smelly mess."

"I will take Stella then. We will leave from Marseilles in two days' time," Gabriel said, as he returned the artifacts to the safe before he took his leave from the room followed by his mother. Stella laid her head back on the pillow, exhausted.

He hoped his sermon educated Stella enough to provide her comfort. He knew the whole story but to actually participate in the precise timeliness of events as they unfolded was astounding. Like well-oiled celestial gears.

As Lilli descended, Gabriel waited and watched from the cracked door as Stella fell back to sleep. He wished he could whisper in her ear as he watched her slumber how her existence proved to him there was a God.

He wanted to tell her that every time he had blessed someone with prayer, he wanted them to feel the bliss he felt when he thought of her.

Chapter Sixty-Nine

—∞—

His just-twenty-year-old bony body ached as he entered his third hour lying stiffly on the dark side of the compost pile. The frosty nighttime temperatures caused his tired eyes to tear. Using his one clean fingertip in an effort to avoid contamination from the putrid rotting vegetables, he wiped his moist eyes as he looked through his night vision binoculars. He continued watching the graduated shadows of the Frenchman and his mother's silhouettes on the second-story bedroom wall, while his mind trailed off at the remembrances of the last time he had talked with his own mom. Too short of a visit. He knew she missed him.

Must be sharing secrets with the American women, he thought, the shadow evidencing their tight circle of heads. No doubt it was extremely important information the French were providing. Unfortunately, his listening equipment failed him, and he couldn't hear the conversation. Might have to make something up to relay back to his employer to keep him happy.

His lip reading skills weren't as perfected as he had led Lucas to believe when he signed up as a GA7 journeyman mercenary upon his return from Iraq. He had planned on taking classes on lip reading as soon as his GI benefits kicked in. Hell, who needed those skills when you had technology? He never expected technology to fail him in the south of

France. Not with a plethora of satellites in the sky and cell towers sprinkled throughout the countryside like urban billboards.

I can stop the Americans, especially women; piece of cake, he had arrogantly promised Lucas. He had heard rumors of what happened to the Spaniard and didn't want to be the next target. He wanted to get his wad of cash, attend law school or something—anything that didn't require dirty manual labor.

Time was of the essence. He didn't want to lay in the dirt all night long. His legs felt heavy like soggy rotten tree trunks, making quick strategic movements almost impossible. Time to slither over the gravel and attach the tracking equipment to the priest's car.

Luckily, because the priest lived in such a small town, his car had been easy to recognize and follow. He continued to crawl on his stomach, using his arms and elbows to drag himself across the gravel driveway. He rolled under the passenger side of the small car, reaching as far as he could up under the wheel well and installed his technology. Easy money.

Lucas had been very adamant that he not only rely on a single technology. His employer hadn't gone into detail, but instructed his operative to go "old school" and follow them physically. He did not want the targets getting away this time.

The operative, satisfied that his mission had been completed and Lucas would never be the wiser, slowly rolled out from under the car as he attempted to make his way back to his own vehicle parked in the darkness down the hill.

The pinch on his ear lobe under the knitted ski mask startled him; he batted his ear reflexively. Then it stung him. Hard. Then another. He bit his lip to squelch his cry of pain.

Soon, the bee-filled ski mask danced on his face, alive with a buzzing party of angry bees protecting their queen. He tried to run down the hill to his car, but his numb legs kept buckling, his heart tempo erratic from adrenaline and bee venom. In excruciating pain, he ripped off the ski mask to release the bees into the night while he desperately gulped for oxygen to re-fill his empty lungs.

The ex-soldier stumbled blindly into the fence of the animal pen, feeling his way along the fence line until he reached the gate and let himself in. A singular snort alerted him too late before the pigs circled and started snapping at his feet.

"Gabriel," Lilli whispered, holding up her finger to silence him. "Someone is outside. By the pig pen."

The small bedroom fell silent as Gabriel stepped lightly down the stairs to the light switch. He flipped all three switches, flooding his property with light as bright as a summer day. Walking briskly to his study, he retrieved the ancient war-time pistol from his desk drawer and headed outside.

"I'll be right back," Gabriel said, as he shut the front door. Still dressed in his normal attire of black, he walked undetected toward the muted groans.

"You—get your hands up," he instructed, as the stranger limply kicked at the pigs nipping at his ankles.

"Oh, God, please help me! Make them stop! Please," the young man pleaded, faintly.

"Who are you? Why are you here?" Silence.

Gabriel could see that the man was either playing dead or unconscious, his darkly-clothed body laying still in the muck of feces. He cautiously approached him, gun pointed, and kicked the man's foot to get him to respond.

The fattest hog was the first to swoop in—and ran gleefully into the night with the gnawed bloody foot clinched in its slobbering jowls.

Chapter Seventy

—∞—

"You must leave now!" Lilli urged her son as he rushed back into the house. "It is no longer safe here for these two."

"I agree." His stomach clenched sensing Stella's crippling fear. He found her rocking back and forth sitting in the stairwell, her blanket tightly swaddled around her body, gripped in her white-knuckled fists.

"Maggie, can you help Stella get dressed and packed? I will take her with me. Until we can arrange your travel, I want you and my mother to stay with the butcher."

"I am contacting him now," Lilli said, as she stepped quickly down the stairs with the contents of the safe. She handed the carved box to Gabriel as she put on her coat and grabbed her emergency parcel of clothes and toiletries.

"I'm taking Faïence, the tunic and scapular, the bowl and paintings with me," she said to her son, as he swiftly removed the rug over the hidden door in the floor.

"You have an escape route through the house?" Maggie asked, shocked.

"Yes," Lilli answered as she finished tossing bottles of herbs into a worn leather satchel to take with her. "Our pipeline to keep alive in the war."

"I can't leave without talking to my daughter," Stella insisted. She had no way of knowing if there were any further messages since Nicki's last text, as her cell phone was hopefully lost somewhere close to the Belgium border. It was too dangerous to call her from Lilli's land line.

It suddenly dawned on her that she didn't have the new phone number from Nicki's burner phone. The familiar shallow panting coupled with drops of perspiration on her brow began. She could feel her blood thunder against the base of her skull.

"Relax, mon chéri. Here is the salve," Lilli said, placing the container on the kitchen table as she started rubbing a dab on Stella's forearms. "You are worried, no? When you tossed in your bed with the high fever you said something about your sweet daughter. I couldn't understand everything, mostly about 'a baby.' Is she with child?

"Yes. Before we left the chateau I had told my daughter not to call my cell phone. Instead, she texted me. Said she was bleeding, but the baby was okay."

"I see. Let me ask you a few questions: What is her favorite flower? Her favorite meal?"

"What?" Stella exclaimed, her eyes wild. "Please, Lilli, we don't have time for this!"

"Please, just answer the questions," Gabriel urged.

"This will help me to help her," Lilli assured. "Your answers allow me to understand how her body processes herbs. I can make a potion to stop the bleeding."

"Lilies and lobster," Stella almost screamed, dropping the blanket as she scurried up the stairs to pack and get dressed, not caring if the Frenchman saw her jiggly-dimpled nakedness under her thin gown.

"Perfect! That is an easy one. Meet us downstairs in fifteen minutes."

* * *

"This was just returned to me by the butcher," Lilli said, as she handed a small package to Stella. "This is your necklace, oui? I think we should send this one to your daughter to keep her safe. I want you to continue wearing the maestro's. It is much more potent. The butcher will make sure to get her this package quicker than anyone else. He only needs an address."

"Tell him to use the same one as before," Stella said, surprising the elderly Frenchwoman.

"You knew he was with us in the Resistance?" Lilli asked, puzzled, looking at Stella in a different light.

"No. He approached me at the baker's after I had talked to Nicki on the phone. He knew I was your guest and could tell I was terribly upset."

"The advantages of a small community," Lilli said, proud of her village. "We have all grown up together, many through the war. After that experience, you realize the only purpose you have is to watch over each other. That simple."

"I had instructions for my daughter that I needed to get to a go-between, at the market in her town. The butcher assured me he could get the message to her without being intercepted. He put the message in a wine bottle and sent it for next-day delivery to her local grocery store."

"Bien," Lilli said as she and Maggie started handing their luggage down the steps of the underground tunnel. The butcher's sons and their hastily called friends stood shoulder-to-shoulder throughout the tunnel relaying the bags to the butcher's hiding place. "The butcher will take care of the man in the pig pen. We will be in contact before you two sail."

Stella clutched Maggie tightly, terrified she would never see her best friend again.

"Don't worry, sweetie," Maggie said. "We're tough old broads, from tough stock. They want a fight—they got one."

She whispered in Stella's ear: "He's a good and decent man, Stella. He's not disposable, and I don't want you treating him that way. Good men are not like buses, with another one coming along in ten minutes. So jump on board, darlin'—with care."

* * *

As they drove down the hill, Gabriel pulled a photo out of his inside coat pocket. "Stella, do you know who this man is?" he asked, handing her the Polaroid photo while trying to keep the car in the center of the overgrown country road. "His name is Lucas Stanchir. He wants you dead."

Chapter Seventy-One

—∞—

"This guy? You have to be joking!" Stella couldn't believe that the pasty, balding man in the photo was her nemesis. She expected some menacing thug with a crooked nose and a few zagged scars; someone more sinister-looking. Why would someone like *him* want to kill *me?* Stella blinked to camouflage the erratic twitching of her eye, the photo shaking in her white gloved hands.

Using the dawn's first rays as an excuse, she shakily put on her sunglasses while resting her head on the car seat. Staring at the car's threadbare headliner, she willed her faulty memory tape to rewind. Trying as hard as she could to flush out some memory of the unremarkable man, all that popped into her mind's eye was the image of a pig running away with a man's bloody foot, severed veins flaying in the air. An image that could never be unseen. She regretted her curiosity caused her to look out the upstairs window, now trying to disguise her gagging with a yawn.

"He is a very powerful man. And a very dangerous one."

"Oh wait! Is this about that Russian forgery Todd sold?" she blurted, sitting upright. It had to be that crime Todd had unwittingly committed after their separation. The FBI had showed up on her doorstep because she was still listed as a legal owner on the gallery. Questioned her about some Russian mob activity about money laundering by selling fake Rothkoes. She assured them that not only was she no longer involved in the business, she never would have made such an amateur mistake in the first place. The guy in the photo could have been Russian.

"No, I doubt this is about anything business-related. It's much deeper than that. It feels emotional. We don't have much time before we get to Marseilles to ready the boat, so excuse me if I bungle this question, but I must ask: Was he your lover?"

"What?" Stella recoiled and started to hyperventilate, as if she had been punched in the chest. She had been through so much with Gabriel in the last few days; trusted him to know who she was. *How could he ask such a thing?* Not only had she been celibate for years, she never once had been unfaithful. How dare him!

"Stella, I'm truly sorry if I have offended you. Please forgive me," Gabriel said, wishing he could pull over and comfort her. "However, I've met this man. He mentioned your name and his emotions were obvious, like a jilted lover." Gabriel didn't add that he understood the unrelenting pain of unrequited love all too well. "Do you know a man by the name of Brent McConnell?" he continued.

"Yes! Does he want to kill me too? Him, I can understand. He doesn't like me—I don't like him."

"Stella, you may be wrong about Brent. He is a good man. Both he and Maggie's husband were this man's employees. Stanchir is the head of GA7, a private military firm; he likes to brag that 'war is his business.' He and his family also have very strong ties with the Catholic Church, going back to WWII.

"In fact, my mother saved his father, Elliott Stanchir, towards the end of the war. She nursed him back to health at the chateau, after his plane crashed in a field nearby. Giselle and my mother ran a hospital at the chateau as part of the French Resistance. Maman said he was a difficult and bitter patient. Furious at God when he thought he would never walk again. He had begged for death, said he would not live as a cripple. She worked hard to restore his faith in God. Knowing he was Catholic, she told him the story of the three children in Fatima, Portugal and the three secrets.

"Unfortunately, instead of being comforted by the story he became hostile and demanded to know the Third Secret. He was used to getting his way, like a spoiled insolent child. Once he reached safety in Spain with my mother's help, he threatened to *out* her to the Nazis if she did not reveal Sister Lucia's Third Secret of what the Lady had said. He immediately made a visit to the convent in Portugal. Because of his threats to physically harm her fellow nuns, Sister Lucia wrote down the Third Secret and gave it to her bishop.

"Stanchir knew it wasn't supposed to be revealed until 1960 by the pope, but that didn't stop him from reading it. Powerful men get what they want—most times. Since that time, the Stanchirs and the Catholic Church have been planning on how to keep the secret from the public and how to stop the prophecy. This is why they killed my mentor.

"Brent and I both believe Maggie's husband saw too much, and Lucas had him killed. Brent's been working both sides, to keep you and Maggie safe. I have been his 'mole' at the Vatican. He's there now, with his cousin. He keeps me informed of what they are up to. I think these evil men realize now where my loyalties remain. We are both in danger.

"We believe the Third Secret is what our ancestor prophesied in his paintings—the women gathering. They want to stop the women before the secret is revealed. Unfortunately, their plan includes seeing great harm done to you and everyone you love."

"And you think this sick bastard *loves* me? This powerful man who wants me and my loved ones hurt?"

"Yes."

Stella stared silently at the passing landscape, stunned. Why would a stranger want to kill her, let alone profess some kind of twisted love for her? She wanted to ask more questions but hesitated out of fear of falling over the edge, mentally. She pulled her Birkin up to the car seat between her hip and the door and willed her leg to stop jumping up and down. She wanted a pill so bad she almost broke a tooth from clenching her jaw. Watching Gabriel out of the side of her eye, she waited until the first intersection to slyly slide the small jar into her coat pocket.

With her arms wrapped tightly around her Birkin bag as if it was a cherished stuffed toy, she wished she was back in Mill Valley. Safely nestled in her big king bed, smothered with fluffy pillows, devouring a bag of Sweet Maui Onion potato chips, zoning to Law & Order—that's where she wanted to be. Not running for her life in the south of France. About to attempt her first sail since her last with Todd.

Who decided this was my journey? I'm a middle-aged soon-to-be grandmother, flirting with a priest and headed on a get-away boat to Turkey? She touched her necklace and softly clicked her heels together—just in case. Gabriel had made her feel safe last night, but now she couldn't shake her terror. She wished she had stuffed the powerful scapular in her Birkin—for insurance!

"We should be there shortly. Are you okay?" Gabriel asked, breaking the long silence in the cramped car.

Stella nodded. She had been staring at his profile, studying his strong face, the curve of his lips. She had an impulse, maybe left over from her dream of last night, to reach over and push his hair back off his forehead. Restraining herself, she closed her eyes and reflected on her dream. It seemed so real—his hot breath warming her neck as he nibbled her ear. That's how the dream had started before Gabriel had gently lowered his naked body on top of her in a candlelit room. She unconsciously licked her lips reliving his powerful yet graceful rocking in and out of her, igniting a passion she had never known before. She remembered that she had held his head, running her fingers through his thick hair while they shivered in orgasm together as she tightened her feminine grip on his manhood. Lost in a dream world, her hips gyrated slightly in the car seat. Right before she almost let out a moan, he broke the silence.

"Are you okay, Stella?"

Startled, she dropped the Birkin, spilling the contents on to the floorboard. Horrified that her thoughts might be discovered, all she could utter was "fine, fine. Just thinking."

He grinned and winked.

Flustered, she straightened her clothes and rolled down the window. Hopefully, the cool dawn air would stave off her intense craving for a cigarette.

* * *

"You've been lucky so far that you haven't been subjected to our mistral," Gabriel said as he guided Stella into the cozy café on the pier, his hair almost dusted white from sea salt whipped into the air, his nose a rosy red.

The café looked more like a long-abandoned crab shack to Stella, snug amongst other rusted-out harbor businesses in the industrial port.

Marcel, the chef and owner of the boat, stood at window of the cook's line, gesturing with his spatula to a table in the corner, spiffy in his blue- and white-checked neckerchief. "Gabriel, please sit," he said, smiling broadly at Stella, while he flipped eggs. "Are we waiting for more?" he asked, looking about for others.

"No, Marcel, it will only be me and my friend, Stella. The others will not be sailing with us."

"Oui, understood," he replied, familiar with the brevity needed when speaking in public. "Unfortunately, my old friend, you will have to wait a few hours before you can leave. Too windy right now. Maybe later this afternoon you should be able to set sail.

"I hope you don't mind waiting, madame," the chef said as he handed them laminated menus. "It may be a little early in the day but I suggest you order our bouillabaisse while you wait. It chases the chill from your bones. Devil wind out there today. The kind that makes you lose your mind.

"You know, true bouillabaisse was invented here, right in Marseilles. Like many things in life, the secret is timing. First, you must be patient and bring it to a simmering boil. Then at the right moment, you bring down the heat. The broth and seafood mix together like the ebb and flow of the sea," he said, moving his hands together like a swimming fish. "Or, more like what happens when a woman agitates her hips to and fro when she walks, oui?" he said, eyes crinkled with flirty naughtiness. "It gives you juices and flavors rarely enjoyed, no? Then a light toss of Herbs St. Remy, delivered directly from our priest friend—*voila!*" he said, smacking his lips, obviously infatuated with the craft of cooking.

"A bowl for me, puh-please," Stella stuttered. *Had her dream caused her to emit pheromones?* The lack of practice in the art of sexual bantering left her rattled. She wished Maggie was here to at least buffer the conversation about lovers and such, steering the talk elsewhere. Terror mixed with the emotions of an awakened libido had her as confused as a barking cow. She laid her gloves next to her cutlery.

While Gabriel studied his menu, she turned to look around the restaurant.

Flash.

To the right side of her field of vision, snatches of last night's erotic dream appeared. Images flashed in front of her, on and off, like x-rated flashcards. Feelings long since forgotten started to bubble up. She squeezed her thighs together, trying to bury any urges.

Gabriel looked up at her from his menu—and again smiled. *Could he see my flashes? Does he know what I'm thinking?* She returned his smile. Emboldened, she decided that if Gabriel could ask her about lovers, it was fair play to turn the tables.

"So, do you believe that priests should be celibate?" She was surprised when she saw him continue to smile. Fearing her directness might be received as rudeness, she was quite surprised by his demeanor. As if he welcomed the opportunity.

"No. That is man's, the Church's dogma. My God never puts limits on people loving people. That's a human idea, to control. I believe I am at one with the great being that made me. The Source that formed the galaxies and the Universe. To me, God is not a separate distinct being with a rule book.

"You do not *get* love from each other. Even Jesus preached universal love with no limitations, no boundaries. Love is an energy field, like the ocean Marcel talks about. When you swim together, you love. Right, Marcel?" he asked as the chef served them their soup.

"But of course! Madame, here's love from me to you," Marcel said as he placed her soup in front of her, his flirting as second nature as breathing.

Gabriel and Stella sat silently, blowing on their hot spoonsful of the savory meal. Gabriel continued to stare at the red- and white-checkered tablecloth, until he heard the voice: *God time—now, son.*

The cue he had been waiting his whole adult life to hear, since his return from his first visit to San Francisco. He laid down his spoon, cleared his throat, ready with a speech he had practiced over and over.

"Stella, the only time I have felt truly alive is when I'm in your presence. My place in this world is to be in your world. I will keep you safe. I love you and want you to be my wife." As soon as the rushed words tumbled from his mouth, he knew he had made a mistake. At least this time he hadn't fallen into her crouch.

Stella gasped, shocked by the sudden and unexpected proposal.

"Why did you say that?" she screamed at him.

"Stop it! I can't take this," she yelled, grabbing her coat and storming out on the pier, leaving her precious Birkin sitting on the empty chair.

Chapter Seventy-Two

—∞—

"Stella, wait! I'm sorry. Please do not run away. You did that once, remember? It did not end well."

Why did I have to be so abrupt? he chastised himself. By mid-pier, he finally caught her though the force of her flight kept her in forward motion. Using all his strength, he held her arms snuggly against her frame, refusing to let her go.

She tensely waited like a snared rabbit, waiting for a window to escape. Gabriel's heartbeats slowed, signaling his relaxation; a split second in slack was enough for Stella to wriggle around and face him. She seemed a little faint with the quickness of her twirl.

"Who the hell do you think you are?" she snarled, almost spitting into his mouth. "You don't know me! You don't know what it's like to 'have me in your world!' Have you noticed how damaged I am? You know what having men in my world has done to me? They say they love me, then they fucking leave me! And now some man I don't even fucking know wants to finish me off?

"Gabriel, you don't even know women! Is it because I talked about sex and you're hard for the first time, Father Gabriel? You want to jump my bones then leave me like the others?"

"Stella, please. I *do* know you. Ever since that day in the store basement, I have felt your pain. Our connection began that day I helped you across the street after you fell. I knew that day I wanted to catch you every time you fell. But I never ever want to be the *reason* you fall. I want to hold you in my arms and keep you safe, always. Please, allow yourself to be adored, protected. Walk with me through life. I will carry your tears in my heart so you can shine as brightly as you should."

Her hair slapped her eyes, the irritation causing a rush of tears. He couldn't tell if it was her hair or perhaps her anger and pent-up hurt seeping from her bruised heart. She wanted to fight him and flee, but he wasn't willing to let her go. He had waited a lifetime for her.

She slumped against him, surrendering.

He reached for her face with both hands and pushed her hair behind her ears. He had entered a place he had never physically been in before. She softened as he hugged her, their bodies mirroring the sway of the boats in the harbor. With her so close, he couldn't talk, only hum, his hot breath warming her cheek.

She twisted in his arms to look at the sea.

Entranced by her intoxicating smell, Gabriel nuzzled the curve of her neck and began singing in French. The melody was unmistakable. The same song he had played her first night at the hilltop cottage: Sinatra's *The Very Thought of You.*

Gabriel's tight embrace apparently calmed her as she let her shoulders down cautiously with a sigh. He had no idea Todd had never held her like that. *No one* had ever held her so tight, with so much unmistakable, unconditional love.

She rolled her head back against his muscled chest, lifting her hand to stroke his face. "I don't . . ."

His quaking finger lightly pressed her lips. "Sssh, now is not the time for words. Please let me show you." He pulled her closer to his chest and cradled her in his arms as he continued with his soft song, switching between French and English. As they swayed, he lightly touched her hair, lifting a handful up to his nose.

Taking his index finger, he ever so lightly started tracing her neck to her shoulder, sliding down her silhouette to the top of her bountiful hips while the sea smashed against the dock's pillars. Like mercury, her body fluidly formed against his, the small of her back cupping his lower abdomen, her breasts rising to the heavens. Her nostrils flared as she inhaled his masculine pepperiness as it mixed well with the savory scents of the salty ocean.

As Stella looked out to the bright copper warnings of a setting sun in the vibrant blue sky, Gabriel's electric touch on her hip made her lips quiver. True molten pleasure flowed in her veins and into her loins for the first time in decades.

"Stillness is the language God speaks. Listen. You must be smiling. I can feel your vibrations," Gabriel said. "Just like God is energy, so is love. Divine energy doesn't know sin, doesn't judge, isn't jealous, doesn't avenge. With God and with love, there is never separation.

"When two want to swim together in the sea of love—they must. I have loved you since I first saw you. I have never stopped. Never. And I never will. I think you know this, no?"

Suddenly, her mouth went dry. A big angry seagull screamed at them before swooping over the water, reminding her why they were on this pier. They must cross this water, towards a treacherous destiny.

The thought of sailing made her body rigid. The memories opened her never-healed wounds—her dad leaving her for war, Todd leaving her for another man. Both of the men whom she had shared the sea with. She was frightened to sail the sea with this intoxicating man she wanted so badly. Would he leave her too? Right when she was opening to the lusciousness of joy.

Her tenseness did not go unnoticed. "Stella, please, you need to feel what it feels like to love you. I want you to love yourself as much as I do, as much as I always have. My thoughts of you when I wake, when I close my eyes at night, feel like my love for God. You fill my body with peace, my heart with joy.

"Just the thought of you changes my whole day, like my service to God. Never wavering. I want to inhale your essence, bind it with mine. Loving you is the most majestic feeling I have ever felt in my life. For this blessing, I am grateful. Thank you."

Try as hard as she could, she could no longer resist him. His words of love softened her core, her hips moving against his, her head rolling back onto his shoulder. Being with Gabriel was as easy and smooth as melted butter sliding across a hot skillet. Her body slumped against his as she turned to face him.

He lifted her chin to look into her eyes and smiled. "Close your eyes. Good. Now say my name."

"Gabriel. Gabriel," she whispered with a smile, her eyes still closed as she eagerly awaited his kiss.

The pier bounced up and down, causing Stella to take a step back to steady herself. Must be the mistral whipping up powerful waves that were pounding as fiercely as her desire for Gabriel.

No, not waves.

As quickly as she recognized the thundering sound as footsteps, she knew something had just gone horribly wrong. She popped open her eyes as two thugs, dressed in jet black, jammed a heavy dark hood over Gabriel's head, yanking him out of her embrace. The impact of the attack threw her off balance on the pier. Swiftly, his arms were handcuffed behind his back, and they threw him into their yacht like today's catch.

"Run, my love. *Go!*" she heard on the wind, as she bolted for the borrowed boat. She tumbled over the boat's lip just as a bullet whizzed past her still-warm cheek.

Chapter Seventy-Three

—∞—

The horrific crunch concussed off the fiberglass cruiser's walls. An old thick coiled rope on the boat's deck cushioned her fall, but serious damage had been done. Her front teeth punctured her bottom lip, as she tried to stifle an expletive-laden scream. Blood from her cheek and lip dribbled down her chin, staining the bold zig-zag stripes of her Missoni sweater.

Let them think I'm dead, she pleaded, as the searing pain in her right knee caused her to hang precariously to consciousness.

She watched the swiftly moving clouds high in the blue sky, their wispy softness enveloping the radiant gold Virgin Mary on top of Notre Dame de la Garde as she held her son in her loving arms, guarding the harbor.

Ringing in her ears were Gabriel's cries, telling her to run.

No! I won't leave—not now, she had wanted to scream back.

"*Flee,*" the voice said.

It was her only option if she had any hope of rescuing him. It didn't matter if she was hurt or not. No one else could save him; she had to act quickly.

Her knee ballooned, throbbing red and angry. She managed to roll on her side, crawled to the edge of the boat and listened. She had run away so fast, she had no idea how many bad guys were out there or even if they were still around.

God, please, let Gabriel be okay. I'll do anything you want, God. I'll love him like no other; I'm sorry for my sins. I know I vowed to love Todd forever, but he left me. He broke our vows. Please, God. Whatever you want, please keep him safe. As the seconds ticked away, her needy prayers of negotiation transformed into fury and revenge.

Okay, you wanna play hardball? No redemption for me, huh? Not this time, God! You're not allowed to take away another man I love. Not without a goddamned fight!

She stiffly bent forward as far as she could and somehow unzipped her high-heeled boots. Using the toes from her good leg, she pushed them off, and gripped one sharply-heeled boot in her hand like a sledgehammer. The boat was still anchored to the pier, keeping her prisoner, ripe for one shot to the head—game over.

No more being chased by the invisible, she silently pledged, wiping her bloody chin with her sleeve. I can be invisible, too.

The thud of heavy footsteps was getting closer. The thug grunted as he knelt on the pier, triggering her into action. Nicotine-stained nubs that once passed for fingers grabbed the boat's lip, banging the boat against the dock.

She held her breath, amped with rage, waiting for the one perfect moment.

Wham!

Stella speared the man's hand with her four-inch stiletto with such fierce anger, the boot stuck.

He howled, as he stumbled back onto the pier, the boot waving proudly upright, like a pinched Louboutin from a Paris sale rack before opening day.

The air burst from her lungs as her body collapsed hard on the deck. She rolled to safety of the cabin, her body in a fetal position against the inside of the door. No sound since the receding footsteps as she counted off *one thousand one, one thousand two* to the rhythm of the tide's flow. She didn't move for what felt like hours, bobbing on the harbor's now-timid afternoon waves.

Must escape, the voice urged her.

She crept back outside and pulled herself to the boat's side closest to the pier. Exhausted, she held onto the side of the boat, resting her head on her crossed arms as she tried to regain some strength and stamina.

"*Now*," the voice said.

She stood up, hopping back and forth on her good leg, while she reached for the rope. She kept pulling until the boat's bumper smacked the dock with a thump. Taking a deep breath, she grabbed the rope, and flipped it up high in the air with all her might. Finally, free to flee.

Her adrenaline pounded so hard in her temples, she momentarily lost her vision. She closed her blurred eyes, but could still see flashes in her peripheral line of sight, little glowing orbs pulsating in colors she had never seen before. She stretched her arms to the sky, waving goodbye to Mary and her golden baby. *Guide me.*

Slowly she limped barefoot inside to the steering wheel, dragging her lame leg. She looked around for the GPS and flicked it on. As its directions glowed from the small screen, she turned on the engine and gunned it out towards the open sea, the rope bouncing in her wake.

Focus! I will show you the way, the voice instructed.

As she maneuvered out of the harbor like a drunken sailor, balancing on one leg, a wicked bout of the mistral slammed into the small craft. It knocked her hands off the wheel while pitching her backwards. She was too light-headed to stand as the violent wind caught the bow and blew the boat out into the channel. Instantly, she was fast sailing at forty knots, unable to hear anything but the thunderous howling of the wind, the cries that never left the seas. Stumbling forward, Stella lunged at the wheel. Confident she had a firm handhold, she slung her body downward as a ballast against the strong gusts. She used her weight to guide the fishing cruiser, hugging the coastline until she could enter the open sea.

She wished she had the map of their charted route, but at least she had scanned it when Gabriel discussed the trip with the chef. Unfortunately, it was still on the cafe's table—along with her purse and her pills. She felt like Jell-O.

She looked up through the curved windshield and noticed the night's faint first stars twinkle, high above the shell-pink sunset. The almost-full moon was still faint in the sky.

"God is energy, it's all energy," she remembered Gabriel telling her. She knew he was right. *That's what I need—energy.* She slumped to the floor and started tapping.

"Even though I caused this," she started. "Knew he would leave me," she tapped above her bloody lip. "Caused him to go away . . ."

She couldn't finish her round, her mind fatigued by the panic brought on by her violent pursuers. Especially the one who wanted her dead. No chance to tap in the good energy. She shook.

Her hands were summer tomato red, slapped by the ferocious wind while she laid in wait on the deck; she shoved them into her coat pockets for relief. *The salve! It's in my pocket!*

She eagerly scooped out a few two-fingered chunks and started lathering it onto her forearms, then her knee and finishing on her temples. She just wanted the excruciating pain to stop. She wanted to be numb.

Lilli had warned her to use *only* a dime-sized dollop because it was such strong medicine. She didn't care; she was from the school of the "more you use, the better it works." Sitting among the stowed fishing gear, she started a new round of tapping. This time on her fear.

She had never been so frightened in her life—alone on the dark boiling sea. No rest from the onslaught of waves, one after another—each different, a warning of the power of water.

With each rise and fall of the currents of the Mediterranean Sea, she searched the coastline, afraid he was out there—Lucas Stanchir, the man who wanted her dead. She was certain he was behind the kidnapping of Gabriel. She wished she had a gun, so if he did reveal himself, she could riddle the son of a bitch's body as she emptied the weapon.

The mistral pitched the boat to and fro, splashing water into the cabin.

"Daddy, where are you? I need you—NOW! Rescue me!" she sobbed, as she tried to stay upright in her bare feet on the now-slippery cabin floor.

Her mind whirled on survival.

Must get out of these wet clothes.

Holding the wheel with one hand, she yanked her arms out of her sea-soaked coat, letting it drop to her feet, sodden with sea mist.

This was her first turn at being a single-hander. Always a co-pilot and crew when she sailed with her dad or Todd. She had watched and studied, but never had a desire to control the boat before. Another "boy job" in her mind.

They never left the comfort and shelter of the bay to venture out into the huge ocean. And never had sailed in the darkness.

She had only been on a vessel at night once—on a blind date. A yacht owned by Stanford University. Big enough to have bedrooms and a hot tub. A floating manor house that only reminded you of being at sea when you looked out the heavily brassed portholes.

"Focus."

"You can do hard things."

She wasn't going to let him go. If she was going to save Gabriel, she had to get to Turkey. With Mary's help, she would.

It wouldn't be long before she might encounter the merciless gyres; vast circular currents that could take her quickly off course, especially in the dark. With that thought, she remembered what Lilli had said about Mary's journey to Turkey. She studied the water.

She's passed this way before. The water remembers her, right?

If ever I needed you, dear Mother Mary, it's now, she spoke directly into the dark depths of the sea. Silently, she crossed herself and asked for help navigating across the choppy waters.

Please deliver me to your house.

As she stared into the black water, she wondered if this is what it felt like to go off to war. Scared, but ready for the fight. Brave and trembling. She felt like a warrior—she was ready.

She looked around the cabin for any kind of navigation tool. The previously neat stacks of paperwork were no longer, tossed about from the pummeling waves.

Friday, the laminated calendar indicated. Oh shit! Her dad would never go out sailing on a Friday; said no sailor sails on such a bad luck day.

Sunset was almost gone as she looked up into the heavens. Sailing on the San Francisco Bay at dusk, her dad had taught her some celestial navigation. She looked up again and found the Milky Way.

Staring at the center of the galaxy was mesmerizing. She would never look at it the same way after what Lilli told her about Nostradamus and the Divine Feminine being birthed from the Milky Way.

A burst of wind threatened to overturn the boat, pitching Stella to the deck. As she again stood, she saw herself in the cabin's mirror—her hair tousled and curled by the fierce moist, biting air; the slim long cut across her cheek from the bullet unable to coagulate.

Feeling a little high from the salve, she found her blood fascinating. She was riveted, thinking it so very clever for the dripping blood on her face to start sprouting rivers. Beautiful iridescent rivers, flowing with luminous life. Multi-colored rings of light burst from her forearms, her hands, her breath. Spirographed trails of electricity flowed from her fingertips.

"Stella, no one can rescue you, but you. No one has ever rescued you, but you. Open your eyes. Look at your life. Look inside. See what others see in you," her mother's voice rose from the white frothy waves as they broke against the boat's bow. She turned the nose of the boat downwind so the ghostly voice wouldn't be deafened by the ocean's roar.

"You never gave up trying to have a child, did you? And you can't give up now. Soon, you'll have a grandchild who needs you."

She could hear faint harmonic sounds surfing on the wind. Was the sea singing to her? Ecstatic, she wanted to dance, forgetting about the wheel stabilizing her. She walked outside and fell on her back, looking up into the sky. She watched as five planets—Mercury, Venus, Saturn, Mars and Jupiter, aligned.

Is this a sign, Mary? Should I follow the line in the sky?

Flash—The man in the photo, smiling at her.

Flash—Angry, rolling waves, throwing up on the yacht's deck and her new shoes.

Flash—He looks so much younger.

Flash—Sails billowing in the sky, loud guitar music ringing in her ears.

Flash—Opening their beers with his teeth. *He looks so proud of his rough skill.*

Against the darkening sky, back-lit by a dense field of emerging stars, the images whirled faster, melding together, spun together like an old time movie projection, the mighty orange bridge lost in the fog.

"*My name is Lucas,*" he said, handing her a beer. "*You go to Stanford?*"

"*No,*" the young blond girl said, taking a long swig as she tossed her flaxen hair over her shoulder.

Pop.

The young girl's shadowy face zoomed in front of Stella's face before whispering in her ear:

Can you believe this wimp? Must assume I'm a local. Typical snobby white rich nerd, living off his trust fund in beautiful Palo Alto, while the rest of us have to work to pay tuition—at state schools. Fine, I'll let him go on and on about himself while I suck down this beer and keep my eyes open for some hot fox to screw.

Stella was stunned by the phantom girl's flippant vulgarity. She wished this familiar girl would return to the ether.

"*Well, do ya?*" he sneered.

"*Do I what?*" the young girl belligerently replied, obviously irritated that he was still around.

"*I asked ya if you wanna ball me?*" he said a bit testy, narrowing his eyes while he twiddled a bottle cap between his finger and thumb.

"*Are ya kidding me?*" she scoffed, guzzling down the remaining ale with a laugh, swiveling to leave.

He yanked her arm, shoving the bottle cap into the oyster of her left thumb, her mount of Venus, between her thumb and her life line, easily piercing her young yielding flesh. Knowing it was the mound of the hand that rules love and romance, he wanted to leave his life-long mark. She screamed out in pain as she clutched her bleeding hand and fled into the safety of the party crowd. He casually leaned over, picked up the bloodied souvenir and stuck it in his pocket, vowing never to wash it.

The shadowy images dissipated into the night's atmosphere as quickly as a spring rain. Now she knew. *That wimpy guy!* Someone she'd never given a second thought to since that night.

He was the man in the photo.

Hypnotized, she watched as the Milky Way galaxy appeared to whorl and change colors, stars churning into hot liquid spirals of magnetic forces, funneling into a massive vortex. The first orb whizzed past her cut cheek, followed rapidly by ten, then a hundred, until the sky was ablaze with kaleidoscope colors of purple, yellow, red and green. Round and round went the luminescent orbs inside the vortex, faster and faster, lighting up the sky.

"Now is the time. Follow the Hol-luk'-ki."

Nema?

The blue and silver-hued beating orb morphed into her grandmother's image, gently floating before her eyes like a dandelion on a light summer breeze. *"Remember the story of the Star-People, and Hul-luk mi-yum'-ko, the powerful beautiful women-chiefs of the Star-People."*

The last time she had told Stella the legend, Nema had added a brave Indian girl, lost at sea, who had to make a decision that would forever change her life. She called her Morning Star. Said she was an Upstander, a leader, who would start a revolution. She could feel Nema next to her as the boat automatically navigated the hissing roiling water.

"Silence gives power for evil to flower. Stand Up. Sing, my Morning Star."

The orbs got denser, heating up the air. Two rushed at her, melding together and emitting a melodic chorus that spoke to her.

"Trust the Journey."

Mom . . . and Dad? Is that you? The formless substances enveloped her in a translucent membrane, causing her to reach out. "Are you there? I'm so scared. Please, I don't want to do this anymore."

Momentarily, she longed to fall into the ocean's white-tipped waves, drifting far away from her problems, her pain.

"That is not your journey!"

She could see Maggie in her mind's eye.

"Time to stop the damn pity party and fight back, girly girl!" Stella was overpowered with the urge to sleep, to close her eyes and hide.

I can't sleep . . . must tell Maggie . . . save Gabriel. Lulled into a trance, she staggered as she tapped her chest, murmuring over and over *help me, help me, they have G.* Transfixed as she watched blue electric sparks arcing between her fingers and her heart with each tap, flashing like a cosmic Morse code into the Universe, she was caught off guard when the gyres hit, turning the boat round and round. The harmony of the blue glow surrounding her was now completely eliminated by brilliant gold rays bursting from her chest and lighting up the sky. Her skin blistered as she wished she could slough off layers of her humanity. The rash violently engulfed her whole body, her skin bubbled with oozing hives.

The extreme pain caused her to scream and cry until her eyelids cramped. *Come, dive in, cool off,* the sea invited. She ripped off her remaining clothes, the wind whipping each article out of her grasp to a final resting place of flotsam on the boat's wake.

She stood at the bow, attired only in Dior's gold star necklace, now gloriously ablaze with the moon's glow, her hands outstretched to the sky as she joyfully surrendered into the bright white vortex of the Milky Way. *Trust the Journey!* the ocean sang.

* * *

The pink and gold sparkles of sunlight warmed her nude body. She opened her eyes and squinted at the chalk line horizon. It was a new day. She had survived.

The small craft was nowhere to be seen as she lay at the base of an enormous concrete hand statue on the promenade of Kusadasi, Turkey.

"You alright, lovey?" she heard her British friend ask. "Time to wakey wakey—*please!*" the lanky Black woman yelled against the sea sounds as she wrapped Stella's naked body with the silver space blanket.

"Sophia?"

"Oh! For the love of Beckham! Only knackered, not dead!" Sophia exclaimed in sheer relief. "Lovey, where's your damn clothes? Never mind. C'mon, old girl, let's get you to the ranch straight away and get you some tea—and clothes! I know there's a good story here.

"Boy, do I have a tale for you, too! And don't you bloody worry. We're all connected—and working on finding your bloke."

Chapter Seventy-Four

—∞—

Goose flesh rippled like sonic waves, shooting from her hairline down her thin arms, shaking her fingers awake as the rush of fresh air from above revived her. It was the first air movement Maggie had felt for hours, sitting on the bottom stair step in the damp stone basement.

Sharing the dank space with the butcher's hanging carcasses made her uneasy, but not as much as the lack of communication. No news from Stella since they parted. She knew Stella didn't like to text but had pinky swore her she would before setting sail. The butcher promised to let her know if her phone, left upstairs for better reception, received any notifications while she hid in the safety of the subterranean room. She had welcomed the temporary solitude. Gave her space to think and assess the situation.

The more time ticked by, the more she knew something was sliding sideways. She could feel it. Maybe she should have asked Gabriel to contact her. She trusted him to take care of Stella, knowing how much he cared for her.

The door creaked as the shaft of light pierced her eyes. "Madame, your phone pinged."

"Oh, dear God, let me have it," she said, as she darted up the creaking timbered stairs. "*They got G.*" No phone number, no identification. It had to be Stella.

Maggie almost tripped, running up the rest of the stairs as quickly as she could. Lilli was hunched over the kitchen table, madly combining various herbs.

"Something's wrong," Lilli stated matter-of-factly as she turned towards Maggie.

"It's Gabriel. Stella just texted me and said *they have G.* I have no idea who the hell 'they are.'"

"I do. First, we must get Marcel on the phone—quickly!"

Maggie tried to comprehend the rapid fire conversation in French, only capable of picking up the tense emotion in the foreign words. It was not good news.

"Oui, please put their bags in a safe place and hide the car. Someone will be there shortly to retrieve everything. Merci.

"Marcel said something happened on the pier, but can't be sure what happened. They thought it was just drunken fisherman, fighting as usual on a Friday night. But the boat is gone. He said Stella ran from the café, and Gabriel chased her. He tried to use Stella's phone that he found in her purse and texted to the only number in the address book, but kept getting an error message.

"Maggie, listen to me. Gabriel has been working with your husband's friend. The one whose cousin is a nun."

"*What?* How do you know him?" Maggie tried to calm herself. She felt stripped bare.

"I tried to warn you with the paintings. This is something that has been going on for a very long time. We think these people chasing you and Stella are the ones your husband used to work for. They had him killed—and now they want the same for you and Stella. Your husband and his—your—friend, Brent I believe is his name, found out GA7's plans on stopping you women from gathering in Turkey."

"What? What does this have to do with us?"

"Because of what the Third Secret forewarned."

"What does the Third Secret have to do with us women gathering?"

"I'm not completely sure. I can only assume from the quatrains and the painted images. I have never read it."

"Might be the time to read the damn thing, don't you think?!" Maggie blurted in shock. She would never have waited this long to remote view it.

"I've tried—many times, dear. We've tried the obvious places, like the Vatican Archives, but it still alludes us. Gabriel thinks it is still hidden somewhere in the Vatican," she said as she hurriedly loaded the herbs into her satchel. As if struck by lightning, she stopped. "I forgot. Gabriel said Sister Lucia handed him a letter when she visited Pope John Paul I years ago. Maybe there *is* a clue. I put it here in my box long ago for safe keeping.

"We must act swiftly. I need your help," Lilli said as she reached for Maggie's hand, accidentally knocking Maggie's phone off the table. They both reached down to pick it up, but Lilli reached it first. She handed it to Maggie, but not before she read the message on the screen: "xoxo—Brent."

"It's code—I'll explain later, but first let's find your son," Maggie said.

Brent's first text, not visible on the small screen, had been "enemy vibrating at hate level. Vibrate higher."

* * *

"Here is her letter," Lilli said, unfolding the fragile decades-old stationery.
"It was simply this:

> *1 John 5:6 This is he who came by water and blood—Jesus Christ; not by the water only but by the water and the blood. And the Spirit is the one who testifies, because the Spirit is the truth.*

"May I look? Lilli, does this look odd to you?" Maggie said, holding the letter up to the light of the kitchen window. "See how dark the ink is? And it's flaky. I don't think it's ink at all; I think it's blood. Let me try something." Maggie poured some water from the tap into her empty tea cup.

Taking a paring knife she dabbed a dot of water on one of the words. The two watched intently as the dried brown ink hydrated into a bright red droplet.

"I think you are right. It must be her blood. But why?" Lilli asked.

"DNA, that's why. Remember the waiter in Paris? How you instantly knew his intentions by his drop of sweat? Concentrate on her blood and see what you find."

"Of course! We must return to the basement. We can again use the tunnel, this time to the outside. We must get this to the cathedral. The butcher will get us there."

Chapter Seventy-Five

—∞—

"Much different in bright sunlight?" Lilli asked, as Maggie abruptly stopped her ascent up the Royal Portal's steps leading to the three densely-sculpted arched doors. "These images symbolize Christ's life: the door to the right is for his birth, seated on his mother's lap, the Throne of Wisdom; his resurrection on the left; and, of course, the middle one represents the End of Time from the Book of Revelation with the four beasts of the apocalypse.

Maggie stepped closer to the right door and studied the images intently. "These images don't look religious to me."

"Quite correct. Both Christian and pagan symbology are intermingled. The double rainbow of feminine sculptures arched above this doorway, or more precisely archivolts, represent the Seven Liberal Arts: music, grammar, astronomy, logic, rhetoric, geometry and arithmetic. This magical cathedral was once the highest place of learning in Europe in the 11th century. Everywhere you look there is a story being told."

Maggie gazed at the Grammar carving with the woman reading to two young boys, one playfully pulling the curls of the other. She lovingly rubbed the cheeks of the curly-head boy, her heart aching with the absence of her grandsons.

Lilli gently grabbed her hand. "Another time, we can study them. Now, we must hurry."

Maggie was awestruck when she swung open the right door, as if she was experiencing a rebirth. Ethereal rays of multi-colored sunshine beamed through the huge rose window, bathing the altar in such glorious heavenly light, she half expected to hear a chorus of angels sing. Slowly, her pupils shrank enough to fully take in the entire gleaming splendor. She stood mesmerized in the front of the altar, feeling the rapturous energy of God.

"Welcome to the Cathedral of Light, the preview to paradise," the stooped priest said, scuffling swiftly towards them. "*S'il vous plait*, this way," he said as he led them through the center of a choir of stained glass windows. "The crypt is ready for you, below. We closed two hours ago, and we have checked every inch of the church—twice. You are safe here. We have put a look-out in the north tower who will stand guard with the butcher and his sons, both here and at the entrances to the village. No one will harm you. There is everything you requested on the altar, except for the water. Let me know when you are ready, and I'll escort you to the grotto. As always, it is important that no one other than you touch this water."

"Merci, Father Pierre."

Before reaching the hidden door of the crypt, Maggie glanced again at round window above her head. It was almost identical to one of the Lost Paintings Lilli showed her.

"Quite similar, no?" Lilli said. "You must remember that this cathedral was built before common people knew how to read, so the purpose of each of these windows was to tell a story. We believe Nostradamus and César were both inspired by that window. We have reason to believe they came to this same special chamber where they were introduced to the story and then guided to paint the rest."

Lilli sat her worn satchel on the secret crypt's opulent altar. The legend was that this altar had been built on the same sacred spot once occupied by the sanctuary of Isis before the first cathedral was built. The crypt's round coved ceiling helped contain the strong magnetic forces rising from the hot spot.

With Maggie's assistance, the Frenchwoman removed the 16th century carved ivory box. "This is the box my ancestor left to me. Such beautiful craftsmanship. I believe César carved the many-breasted goddess on the top," she said as she cautiously opened the heavy double-hinged lid. Inside was a neatly folded threadbare cloth, nestled next to the nun's letter and an ancient copper bowl, trimmed with embossed sacred geometry motifs in gold.

"This is the bowl my ancestor used to travel through many dimensions. He filled it with the sacred water from below and was able to view the future so he could warn us. I am hoping to have the same luck tonight. It may be useful to add some of the letter's blood to help us view.

"This is Mary's tunic that she wore when she birthed her son. The same one Gabriel told Stella about last night—before the unfortunate incident with the young man. It is represented by the ribbons in the painting you saw.

"And," she continued as she lifted the beautiful water blue-green gowned doll from her bag, "what is attached to this doll's skirt. Dior's genius idea, of course, to bring peace to our world, before anyone even knew of the 'how and why' of DNA. I was merely following my ancestor's orders.

"Before we go to the grotto, I think you are now ready for more of the story about what these paintings mean." Lillie unfurled the canvas, not much larger than a piece of personal stationery.

"This one is the most important. It explains the Return of the Divine Feminine. You see Her in the middle of the page, heh? Mary has always been here, never left us. It's only now with the Great Alignment she can be 'observed,' to usher in the new era. You see this swirling storm here?" she points. "That is when the Milky Way aligns with the center of the Universe.

"And this ribbon at the top of the painting? I'm sure you've heard of the Apocalypse, but do you know what it means?"

"Of course. Death, destruction, the end of our world."

"Change is not always easy and peaceful. Always great chaos before change. It may be an end to the world—only as we know it now.

"Apocalypse actually means 'uncovering,' the lifting of the veil, a revelation as depicted on the center door we just saw. And that ribbon?

Is this," she said, as she lifted the fragile tunic up into the air. "The sacred veil. And it's destiny."

Maggie's jaw dropped as the energy source zapped her brain. The spray of ions from the veil felt like the ocean mist from a raging cosmic wave on her face. "Give me a minute to process this all. I actually feel a little unsteady." She was unaware her present condition was due to the strong electromagnetic vibrations emitting from the ancient cloth and in every drop of nearby water.

"I understand. I have lived with this information all my life so I forget how shocking it may be for others. Dior had the same reaction. Trust the journey."

"Let me tell you the story," Lilli said, as she laid her hand on Maggie's shoulder. "You know, we women are the storytellers. Men complain that we never forget anything. Exactly! It was designed that way. We must pass on the stories to inform humanity so history does not have to keep repeating its lessons. I say to all women—open your mouth, have courage, tell your story. But now," she said as she reached for the pull to summon the priest, "it is time we start."

* * *

"Lilli, I think we would be more powerful if we do this together. My husband once told me the reason older women are more empathic is because of our finely attuned brain waves. He said these brain waves were very powerful because they are also contagious and synchronize when two people do things together, increasing their power."

"I agree. The sister's blood has been added to the sacred water. I know my method is different than yours, but we can both start meditating on our purpose."

Due to Lilli's genetic makeup and years of experience, it didn't take long before she dropped into a trance and saw a vision. A puzzling vision. Previously, her sessions focused on the Vatican library, which contained so many secrets lost to the world. But not this time. This image was new.

It was a structure. Dark walnut stairs appeared, boxed by butter-cream yellow plaster walls. She chased the viewing up the stairs to a landing and looked around; it was the papal apartment, the ten-room suite Gabriel spent so much time in with Pope John Paul I. She had had tea in that room once.

She "opened" the wood paneled double doors into the papal sacristy. The room was lined with gold-banded glass cases, chock full of papal treasuries gifted through the centuries by all the world's leaders. Miters, papal rings, pectoral crosses, the pope's staffs and a few precious rare books.

Maggie, across from Lilli at the altar, stopped her automatic writing momentarily. On her paper were scribblings of black and white diamond tiles, similar to the same floor in the sacristy. She had run into interruptions before when she encountered geometric shapes; Jim had said it might be something to do with the powerful energy of sacred geometry.

Maggie resumed drawing larger and larger circles, as she gazed into the pinkish water in the bowl. Her head slowly rocked in a circular motion as her scribbled circles became smaller and took form. Q, then U. Maggie lifted her pen when she felt Lilli enter into her morphic field. She closed her eyes and resumed . . . R . . . A, then N. Quran?

Lilli roared with a hearty laugh, shattering the crypt's silent reverence, snapping Maggie out of her trance.

"How very clever you religious men are! Hiding the Third Secret where no one would look for it. But it is, of course, the one book that mentions Mary more than any other. In the most obvious place of all.

"It is said that the Quran must not be touched by anyone who is not pure and clean. Who else would be considered pure and clean but Il Papa? And where is the best hiding place? Right out in the open!

"Wait, something else is coming into focus. Quick, place the tunic over my head. I think I see humanely images," Lilli instructed, hoping for a glimpse of Gabriel. "I see a nun; no, wait, I see two. They are sitting in a place next to a river, bathed in moonlight, with your friend. I think they know where my Gabriel is.

"Yes, they are both at the Vatican now. Something is very wrong with my son. His hair is white. He cannot keep his eyes open or scream for help. They are torturing him," she said pulling the veil around her shoulders. "We must hurry to save him. Your friend is still in Rome? I have a plan."

"Wait, Lilli, I see something now. It may be Gabriel's location."

Seagulls danced before her eyes, diving in and out over an ocean before finally landing on the palm of a huge hand. Dusty Turkish ruins appeared in the now-murky water before it became unreadable. She scratched her left forearm, wondering where the sudden rash came from, while she pulled down the neckline of her sweater, fighting the urge to strip.

Maggie turned to Lilli to show her the sudden rash. But before she could utter one word, Lilli threw her head back and started to chant. Quickly, Maggie pulled out her cell phone and start recording, as Lilli said in Portuguese: "You must consecrate Russia to my Immaculate Heart to save the world."

Maggie could swear what came next was the Third Secret, straight from Sister Lucia's own mouth.

Chapter Seventy-Six

_∞_

A clump of stark white hair floated slowly like duck down between his feeble fingers as Gabriel cradled his head, trying to quell the searing pain. At Lucas' insistence the night before, the guards had applied electrical currents to his temples. He prayed that the passage of time would provide some relief. How long had it been since the Swiss Guards had tossed his limp body into what appeared to be a medieval dungeon? The windowless stone room had been built for a much smaller man, most likely centuries ago. He was unable to stretch his arms out or fully stand up. His only physical relief was had when he laid down, a prisoner to a hard bare cot.

He had attempted to track time by counting the number of rap songs they blasted, but quickly lost track when the denigrating phrases started regarding broken vows, disloyalty. Sleep had been impossible with the constant glare of a single flood light dangling from the ceiling. All routine GA7 torture tactics honed by their Iraqi prison staffs.

Gabriel didn't know if the psychological warfare was working, but he hated himself right now. What a foolish plan! Selfishly putting Stella in jeopardy, naively hoping his clandestine trip to the south of France had been under Lucas' radar. He thought he had an edge with God on his side. A holy advantage so he could play on the same wicked playing field and outsmart not only an immoral man but one out for revenge. He found God had no favorites.

His big mistake had been treating Lucas as a human, instead of a malignant mentally ill man whose ego blossomed by causing pain and destruction. A man in constant need of adoration, incapable of empathy. If he hadn't had such trust in their destiny, he might not be so sure that she was still alive.

What he feared most of all was her sanity. *Maybe if I hadn't been so impulsive with words of love, she wouldn't be alone in danger.* He knew her biggest fear was being abandoned by the men in her life and now he had put himself on that list. Was God punishing him? It was a hellish interior fight in his head. Was he the betrayer or was he being betrayed? Was his desire for her more important than her life?

The jangle of keys outside the cell's scarred wooden door interrupted his thoughts. Lucas entered, followed by Cardinal Gustav, who had to contort his bulky frame to fit in the room. With every inch of real estate occupied, Lucas was forced to sit next to Gabriel on his cot. Gabriel quaked like a beaten animal when Lucas' knees touched his.

"So you had her—briefly. And now she's gone!" Lucas loudly laughed, jeering inches from his prisoner's face, his thick breath stale and offensive.

"How's it feel, God man? Thought you were better than me, didn't you? Did you tell her all about our plan?" Lucas teased as he stood and backhanded Gabriel with such force, a large diagonal smear of blood traced his cracked head's path as he slid down towards the rickety cot.

Faint with pain but far from giving up, Gabriel felt a noticeable change of energy. He squinted as he tried to study Gustav. *Was he unnerved by the violence?*

Pay attention, the voice said. *They are not united.*

"I'm sure I do not know what you are speaking of, monsieur," Gabriel responded, trying to stay in neutral as long as possible.

"Like hell, you don't! Where is she? Where's Stella?" he screamed, the veins popping out on his temples from the angry rushing blood. "Tell us what the women are up to," yelled Lucas. Gabriel stared at him blankly, his pale blue eyes vacant.

"Fine! I don't have time to play games with you, Father. Baptize him!"

"What do you mean?" the cardinal gasped, horrified at what might be expected of him.

"C'mon, your kind invented the technique. You know, from the Inquisition? But you guys used vinegar. We used your techniques in Iraq, you know. Your documentation was correct; the results are more effective and speedy. But first, shove this down his throat," he said, handing the cardinal a pill.

"LSD works so well with drowning," he said, laughing like a rabid hyena. "Leaves the mind with that 'oh so fresh blankness.'"

* * *

Assured the soon-to-be retiring pope had gone to bed without his hearing aids, Gustav entered the papal sacristy. He stealthily slid the gilded green holy book from the glass case into the blouse of his priestly gown, and tip-toed down the stairs, to his waiting limo.

"What a fool Lucas Stanchir is, to think I would give up my and the Church's power to him!" he snickered as he sunk into the sumptuous leather seats of the waiting car. He now had his passport to success in the upcoming conclave.

All those years of pimping himself, it was now time to cash in on his long-ago clever ruse that would deliver him the red shoes. *Who would look for the message from the Virgin stashed in the midst of Islamic materials?*

He had been forced to find a new hiding place when that nosy Irish nun arrived. While under his tutelage, her pretended loyalty to the Church never fooled him. Did she really think her hours alone in the Archives, unsealing and reading documents would go undetected? No way would he willingly provide her any ammunition to use as a way to get back into the sisterhood.

He had the Americans to thank for his stroke of genius. After 9/11, with their increasing fear-mongering of anything to do with Islam, no one would even want to touch this dirty holy book. That was when he typed up the four-page "secret" to use as a replacement. He was surprised when the pope released the "secret" in 2000 to assuage the masses, but also felt a scrivener's pride.

Maybe they could pull this off and never ever reveal the radical real one. Changing circumstances made for new rules.

Chapter Seventy-Seven

—∞—

"God doesn't want me to eat cold pancakes!" he erupted, flipping his full plate to the floor. The two women scrambled to clean up the sticky mess off the marble floor in an effort to curtail his violent wrath.

Kathleen threw the clump of dripping paper towels into the trash as she spit out a dollop of vomit. She didn't think her contempt for "the German bulldog" could grow any stronger; apparently, she was wrong.

Martha rushed into the opulent dining room and put a steaming hot plate of pillow- soft pancakes in front of Gustav, the pat of butter in a glistening puddle on top. He didn't bother to acknowledge her existence.

"He has it—the Third Secret!" Martha said in hushed tones, as she ran the water full pressure in the kitchen sink. She prayed the rushing water combined with clinking breakfast dishes would muffle her words.

"How do you know?" the Irish nun rasped, almost dropping the bowl she was drying.

"The chauffeur told me, over his morning tea. Said Gustav had an important-looking book in his hand when he drove him back from the Vatican last night, like the kind you see in museums. Said the old beast was laughing and talking to himself as if the driver was invisible, just a part of the machinery. Said Gustav kept saying *right in here, right in here* tapping the book's cover with glee. Giggling and saying *the secret is mine.*

"So while he was taking his shower, I slipped into his office. Lo and behold, there's a new book in his book case. I know every book and its location by heart since I must weekly dust them to remove his cat's hair, with not a one out of place, mind you. The books are *always* in order. He never reads anything—it's all just to impress his visitors," she harrumphed. "But I have it! Ha! And guess what it is? The Quran! Same one Pope John Paul II kissed when the Iraqi delegation gave it to him in 1999. We must hurry to get it to Brent now!"

"Right, you are, Sister Martha! Let's go!"

* * *

"Alright, hold on I'm coming" Brent said, yanking his jeans up, his salt-and-pepper hair still tousled from sleep. "What's all the fuss?" he asked, peering through the hotel door's security lens at his flustered guests.

"We have it! The Third Secret! Here—you hold it!" Kathleen said, her hands shaking, as she shoved the heavy green embossed book into his hands, tumbling into the small room.

"The Quran? That's the secret?"

"No, it's hidden in there—I think," Martha panted, flipping the hotel door's deadlock. "Gustav brought it from the Vatican last night. I flipped through the pages and saw something. It has to be the Secret. Why would a cardinal who wants to be pope have a Quran?"

Brent opened the gilt-edged calfskin book's cover and saw the inscription to John Paul II from Patriarch Raphael I of Iraq, May 1999. He flipped through the pages until he came upon the single page, stuck into Surah 4:156-159.

Brent scanned the ayah regarding Christ's death on the cross. He was familiar enough with classic Arabic to know it said something about a false charge against Mary, mother of Jesus.

"Have you read it?"

"No, we were too afraid we would be caught by the cardinal," Kathleen said, juddering. She jumped when she heard her countryman Van Morrison's *Brown Eyed Girl* trill from Brent's phone.

"Brent, here. What? You think he's here in Rome? Yeah, we know about the 'paper.' We have it, I think, right now. I'll tell you the whole story later. Okay, I'll see if I can hook up now with the cardinal and see if he knows Gabriel's whereabouts. He may have already turned on me so you and Lilli get to the ranch in Ephesus pronto!

"Ladies, we have a situation. Martha, you said you have contacts at Vatican Radio?"

* * *

Gustav waited until the two women had left to go marketing. It was a little strange for them to go so early in the day, but a lucky break for him. He had his ticket to the throne; now he could wait and leisurely plot his takeover. He gazed around the room, sniffing in disgust at his now-shabby study. Soon, he would own a regal palace, a country even. He would be deemed infallible.

As his gaze landed on the new Persian rug, he felt a little unnerved. The Spaniard had been killed in this very room, his evil DNA still resident, his beloved Persian cat still missing; all at the hand of his mentor's own nephew. Father Marcus had saved Gustav's miserable life, and he always felt grateful for that. But torture? That was a game changer. That was a sin! He had sinned many times himself in varying degrees, but never killed anyone. He was too close to the prize to jeopardize it with blood on his hands.

After spending his life faithfully executing unsavory tasks for the Vatican, he could close that chapter and start over. Time to put distance between himself and the Stanchirs. He had done his part to stop the women, paid back his obligations. Now it was up to Lucas and his science to control destiny. Gustav was in a hurry to make right with God in an effort to save his soul.

As was his morning habit, he opened up his laptop to review his surveillance tapes. It had been a few days, what with the excitement of Gabriel's capture, and he wanted to catch up. Maybe the tediousness of the task would jump start his creative forces so he could expertly plot his future. He never paid much attention to their almost-naked bodies on the daily tapes. Didn't really do anything for him anymore after watching his housekeeper for decades.

Here, put this on, he heard his long-time housekeeper say on the tape. His coffee squirted out his nose.

He watched as the Irish one put on the nun's habit and slipped a large envelope under it, a move he had just made last night. What the hell was she trying to hide? He saw the big block red letters.

RAPE.

He could feel his blood boil, his teeth clamp. How the hell did she get that file? "Martha! Get in here. Now!" he screamed into the empty house. He twirled his chair around and looked at his bookcase. The green book was missing. Now he understood the nuns' early departure. Sneaky, disloyal hags!

He laid his massive hands on his neat desktop and stared out the window. So close to having his hand adorned by the papal ring, yet with no one in his army. He didn't even know who he could trust anymore. Definitely not his perpetua; not the Irish nun. But what about Brent? Brent was the perpetrator's cousin!

He thought hard about everything he and Brent had said to each other recently. Couldn't think of a single thing that warned him of danger, of being double crossed. He had absolutely no read on Brent.

He certainly could not tell Lucas he had found—then lost—the Secret. Lucas would kill him as quickly as he would an earthworm scurrying for safety on a stormy day. Maybe he could leverage the redhead's safety to use Brent as his pawn to carry out *his* plan—God's plan.

* * *

"I'm on my way, your Eminence," Brent said, his finger up to his lips to silence the excited sisters. "Yes, I know the location. The medieval cells under the cathedral. I'll be there in ten minutes."

"We have trouble, ladies. I can tell from his voice that he knows it's gone. And you two are obviously his prime suspects. He said he called to let me know Father Gabriel has been taken prisoner and is in the Vatican jail. I think he really wanted to see what I knew.

"I can no longer rely on him to be my ally, because of my relationships with you, Maggie and now Gabriel. Time for us to go on offense. Luckily, the jail is guarded by the Vatican police instead of the Swiss guards; not as well-trained.

"Martha, while I have Gustav away from his apartment, I'll have one of my guys meet you two there. He will help you replace all the communication ports with the jammers. I thought something like this might come up eventually, so as a precaution I pre-installed jammers in the lab. With my remote, a few flicks of the switch, and they are in total communication blackout. Lucas is supposedly on his way to the lab now. When this all goes down, he'll have no way to notify any of his GA7 henchmen. Time is ticking down.

"After you've installed the equipment at the apartment, I want you two to join the others on the March to the Vatican. I'll intercept Gustav and have him meet me at the lab. The rest is going to be up to you two and all the other nuns. Godspeed!"

Chapter Seventy-Eight

___∞___

"Nothing like good ole' Kentucky straight bourbon to help put the world right," Maggie said wearily, downing the last of her Maker's Mark before they landed. She wished she hadn't heroically thrown away her last cigarettes in Paris. A long, deep drag on some nicotine would be nirvana right now.

Lilli turned her attention away from the plane's window. If only something as simple as alcohol could ease her distress, she wished, as she wiggled the blood back into the toes of her swollen feet. It had taken them almost two days to reach Turkey, with layovers and connecting flights from Paris. It had been so long ago since she had flown, she had forgotten how brutal this type of transportation was on her body. Coupled with time acceleration and the frequency of repeated bilocations, it confused her ever-transient atoms. She looked down at her long-ago homeland. It had been a long time since she saw it from this view point. And, once again, she was worried about her son.

As soon as the pilot extinguished the plane's engine, Maggie turned on her phone. *Stella w/us. Sophia.*

"Woo hoo!" she yelped, so startling the rising passenger in front of her that he bumped his head on the opened overhead bin. His angry glare had no effect on her. She simply shrugged as she jostled down the narrow aircraft's aisle loaded like a pack mule, her quaking shoulders revealing her relief.

"Good news?" Lilli asked, certain of the answer, as she gently patted Maggie's back.

"Yes! Stella is with the rest of the women at the ranch. She made it to safety!"

Maggie elbowed her way through the articulated tunnel of debarking passengers, giddily anxious to be with all her sisters again—especially Stella. Maybe when she held Stella, she could feel normal again if there were such a thing still, amid all the chaos.

She continued marching forward while analyzing the unsolved puzzle of events. What was she missing? Something about the video perhaps? Something out of place like a popcorn hull caught on a back molar that could no longer be ignored.

As they descended from the escalator into the lobby trying to funnel out the airport's inadequate front doors, gridlock hit. Maggie stumbled into the mass of middle-aged women, a good number of them nuns. Many appeared as if they had left their homes in a hurry without time to properly dress.

"Welcome to Ground Zero, Lilli. The Great Gathering has begun."

The brown boy's hysterical crying stopped her in her tracks. She turned to her left and watched the father as he shook him and yelled *be a man*. A boy not much older than six. Like her Jason. "My teddy, daddy. Rocky!" he cried inconsolably as he tried to get free from his father's grip and run back to rescue the trampled stuffed animal. Maggie feared he would get crushed as the crowd kept moving. "Child down," she screamed. The mass of women halted.

"What's the matter, little man?"

"I want my teddy," he wailed. His mother stood back, deferring to the father. The father herded his family into a tight circle, confused and powerless. It was not good to stop inside an airport; must keep moving, keep watching.

"Let me help you," Maggie said as a nun walked up to them and handed the boy his mangled toy. He hugged it close to his narrow chest, but still he cried, unable to catch his breath. Maggie grabbed the mother's hand as she led the family in a chain out of the airport. "I'm a grandma. May I try and help him?"

Maggie sat down on the curb, holding him in her arms while he pushed against her shoulders, trying to break free. She could see the fear in his almost-black eyes as his father watched. She softened her body around his and rocked him until he calmed. Just like when she had to tell her oldest grandson that his father wasn't coming home.

"I'm Grandma Maggie. What's your name, sweetie?"

"Jonas."

"That's a noble name, Jonas. What is your teddy bear's name?"

"My father named him Alp. It means brave. But I call him Rocky because he protects me. Rocks are my friends. See? I keep them in my pocket just in case I see a terrorist. I can throw rocks at them before they blow me up" he said as he continued to shake in her arms, stuffing the reddish pebble back in his pocket.

"Baby, I'm so sorry you're afraid. I get like that too, sometimes. You know what helps me? Smiling, like this. It's my shield against the bad guys. You know how when you smile at someone, they smile back? Just keep doing that, okay. See all the grandmas here? We came here to your country to fix the bad guys, sweetie. You want to help? Next time you get mad, take a long breath or two and see if there is another way to fix things. And never ever be afraid to cry. God gave us tears to wash out all of the yucky stuff inside." Maggie looked up at Jonas' father; he was not happy with her. She stood up and leaned in close to him. "Please don't shame him for having feelings. These are our children that we waited so patiently for, had dreams for. Treat them like gold."

"Here, Grandma Maggie. Just in case your smile doesn't stop the terrorists." He handed her his favorite rock.

* * *

"You might have saved that young man's life, Maggie," Lilli said as their hired car started the long drive to the ranch where they were staying.

"I doubt that. But it felt good for me to hold a little one again."

"I think kindness to little boys goes much further than we know. If maybe Hitler had been allowed to cry, show his feelings, he might not have been so destructive. You know he wanted to be an artist, but he was rejected from art school.

"What if someone had been more kind to him? It may have saved my mother's and sister's lives. I lost them both after we were taken in 1944 to Ravensbruck, a German concentration camp." Lilli realized Maggie's surprise. "Yes, it was not only the Jews. At our concentration camp, there were 7,000 French women prisoners, and at least 1 American. We were beaten, starved, gassed. So much trauma, we all stopped menstruating.

"One day, my mother was 'selected.' They made me and my sister Rose watch while they shot her in the back of the head, in cold blood. The guards made us stand motionless for two hours in the middle of the night, watching over our mother's body. I remember that the only light on that moonless night came for the glow of the cemetery, where they were burning bodies.

"Not long after that Rose was raped by one of the young teenaged German guards. He was a mean one, that redheaded one. She became pregnant. Hopeless, she hung herself with the remnants of her tattered dress, so they say. I never saw her again.

"By the time I was rescued, I was bald, no hips, no breasts; a skeleton of seventy-three pounds. I had no family left, only Dior and my sisters from the Resistance and the other camp survivors. Dior took me to Paris; he gave me purpose. That's really how the New Look was born. My dear friend was only trying to help me look like a real woman again. He took my father's stash of blue serge we had hid in the butcher's cavern when we returned to Callian and slowly draped it on my tiny form until I had hips again! He so wanted me to smile again, like before the war. That's how he first came up with the idea for the Theatre de la Mode. It was not only to bring back beauty to France, but to help me get the taste of death out of my mouth. For a moment in time, I could pretend the war never happened, that I was still a young girl playing with dolls.

"It was while we were working at Lelong's that Dior found a gold star laying on the cobble stones on Rue Saint-Honoré, one not unlike the special one I gave him. It reminded him of our magical times at Chartres. That is how we came up with the idea of using some of Mary's veil for Faïence. A star of peace, stitched into her gown, to travel the world. Did you notice the stars in the cathedral? Stars are the oldest sacred symbol known to us. They represent the Flower of Life from the Temple of Osiris, the brother of Isis, and have a high vibrational value which is said to stimulate conscious.

"I soon expanded my sisterhood with the charming women you met at the show. We all survived because we never gave up. Never! My bond with those women will last until my last breath. We will do anything for each other. Gather the women; that is how you fight evil. Even Napoleon knew that the *sword is always beaten by the mind*. I would add the heart, too.

"Power and dominance are not values we should teach our boys. They grow up to be killers. But now I fear for my son who is such a gentle soul. I hope he has what he needs to stay strong."

Lilli shut her eyes and stilled herself so she could get a read on Maggie's vibrations. She hoped the bourbon was lubricant enough to keep Maggie calm and diffuse any disbelief, fear and anger that might arise when she finished the telling of the complete story as depicted in the painting. She had been mentally rehearsing the delivery of her preamble since they had boarded the plane. First, ease in to the telling with Maggie then hopefully the conversation with Stella might go smoother. Friends know how to handle friends. She planned to show them the whole painting after tonight's dinner.

They had yet to discuss what had happened at the cathedral. Though neither of them understood Portuguese, the message was as clear to Lilli as the painting. What wasn't clear was an image in the background, behind Lilli while she chanted. A ghostly immature, yet familiar face from another time perhaps.

"You know, chéri, how my ancestor had described the Gathering in both word and images? We have had to interpret the many symbols on our own. Back in the bedroom, there was more on that painting that you did not see. It was not the right time to tell you—but I believe that time is now. I covered the bottom right hand corner with my hand for a reason.

"The covered image is of two women. I was told they represent the Observers of the Shift. I believe they are the new leaders. One was blond, one had hair the color of yours. I think they represent you and Stella."

Maggie, who had been gazing at the Turkish landscape, went rigid. "*What the hell?* Seriously? Are you saying someone, probably goddamn Nostradamus, predicted my and Stella's destiny almost 500 years ago?"

"God has a plan for us all, don't you think? Maybe our destinies are told before we take our first breath."

"So it's was God's plan that my son died in war?"

"I apologize. I never meant to upset you. War is a hell on earth. I think that is the point Mary is trying to make. Remember we were in World War I when she told those children the three secrets. If our leaders had paid attention and took appropriate action instead of threatening the children with more violence, we may have avoided World War II. The world has paid the price for that arrogance; you have paid the ultimate price. I only survived because I had a community of sisterhood. I only *wanted* to survive because of my sisterhood. You, too, have a sisterhood waiting for you at the ranch."

Maggie figured it was not wise to speak in anger or in fear. She closed her mouth and focused on the rolling hills; they reminded her of the wild sage studded road to Dillon Beach, rustic with the promise of a peaceful sanctuary at the end. What Lilli said was true, though, about the power of sisterhood. She thought of the beach vacation she and Stella had taken when their babies were toddlers. Remembering Josh laughing, not minding being dirty with the beach sand, brought her comfort. She prayed Nicki was safe and would one day take her baby there; maybe even with her grandchildren.

That's why we are doing this, Stella. For our babies. And their babies. The time has come to stand up.

She lowered the window and whiffed the air, her nostrils wide with excitement. Horses. The familiar aroma triggered her leg muscles to tighten, her glutes to clinch. Always safer when horses were nearby.

Lilli heard the heavy sigh, felt the heartache.

"The last time I rode a horse, my Josh was still alive. My brother Bob always said that Josh was going to do amazing things. I assumed it would be with his life, not his death. I wish my son had valued his teddy bear more than the stupid guns my brothers encouraged him to play with. Maybe he would be alive today. I wish my son had been encouraged to bawl his head off when he stubbed his toe, and not man up! *Be a man* is utter bullshit. Let your boys cry. Let them release their emotions. Don't stuff it until it explodes. Teach them it's human to be scared."

Chapter Seventy-Nine

—∞—

"Sir, we have been waiting for you. You need to come see this."

The young lab tech unsteadily tottered in front of the massive electronic billboard watching the frenetic scrolling lines of blurry white 0s and 1s stream against the electric blue background. The numbers trailed across his square thick-rimmed glasses like electric train tracks.

"It's the random number generator. We started noticing the change about an hour ago. They are becoming increasingly more structured now. The 1s are rapidly reproducing. This is major."

"Have you turned on the news? Checked Twitter?" Lucas yelled, as he reached for his ringing phone.

"The President is on the phone, sir. He said it was urgent."

"This is Lucas Stanchir. It's a pleasure to hear your voice, Mr. President. *What? Oh God no! Turn on the TV now!*" he yelled at his assistant.

There in a sea of black and white, were hundreds—*no, thousands*—of nuns, filling every street in Vatican City. The TV screen scrawl read: "URGENT—Vatican Radio issues immediate call to all nuns to follow ancient Roman Water Pilgrimage to grotto at Vatican Gardens. Special announcement about the Third Secret. #GatherTheWomen."

"Yes, Mr. President, I'm watching it now. Sorry, I've been in my car and just arrived. No, I haven't talked to anyone from Liberty Group. Hello? Mr. President, are you there?"

"Someone get the president back on the phone, goddammit! NOW!"

"I'm sorry, sir, the phones aren't working."

"Then use my cell phone," he said, flinging it at her head.

"Sir, I'm very sorry. NO phones are working right now. All of our technicians are on site desperately trying to fix the problem."

Lucas' knees buckled as he sweat dripped from his brow. In the last few hours, he had started feeling nauseous, weak. He wondered if somehow he had deposited any of his DNA in the lab. He had never entered without being properly shielded.

"Where's Franco? Finally!" Lucas said as the doctor and his team scrambled into the circular tower.

"Doctor, it's time to hit the booster on Spider Sweep!" He saw the hesitation on the young Italian physicist's face.

"Now, dammit!" he roared.

"Certo," Dr. Franco responded, flustered. "Scuzi, I mean, we will do."

Franco sprinted to the control panel and typed in the special code. The blank large monitors in the round tower room started flashing non-stop horrific pictures: children screaming and crying as their skin melted from their bodies in Hiroshima, Japan; floppy-eared puppies being kicked repeatedly in the ribs until their last whimper, their once-soft eyes dangling from the sockets; crowds of pedestrians hit by speeding vehicles, laying bloodied and mangled on the roadside.

The gold-rimmed tubes, specifically reserved for the launch of the Final Phase, were unveiled. Filled with DNA taken from journalists, political leaders, celebrities, professors, ministers—anyone who could influence the masses in the shortest amount of time. Designed to infuse everyone immediately with terror.

They had planned for this implementation, but not this soon. Everyone would be paralyzed with fear—controlled by GA7. Pliable to manipulation when the grid was pierced.

"Are they normalizing yet?" Franco turned to look at Lucas; he shook his head back and forth as the 1s continued to multiply.

"Why isn't this working?" Lucas screeched, as he stumbled into a rack, his clammy hands slipping on the slick metal. "Where's the cardinal and Brent? Get them here pronto!"

* * *

Cardinal Gustav stomped into the lab as fast as his large frame would allow, huffing and puffing, releasing fumes of rotting bacteria from the bouncing fatty folds of his obese body.

He was unprepared for Lucas' appearance—sullen skin, his hair matted into thin wispy strips, plastered to his damp skull. Lucas labored for each breath as he sat limply in a chair, staring helplessly at the random number generator. Dr. Franco was kneeling next to him, trying to explain the recent test results.

"Mr. Stanchir, I'm afraid we have a problem. We thought the color of the water looked different, so we tested it. The pH of the water has changed. It appears the water is clathrating. Something is enveloping the water molecules in the test tubes and changing the electromagnetic properties. It is much more powerful than anything I've ever witnessed before. The water molecules are starting to crystallize into stars and snowflakes."

"Lucas, are you okay? You do not look well at all," the priest asked as he wiped Lucas' brow with his scarlet sash. "I was on my way to check our guest at the jail when I heard about the tweet. We must act now and decisively before they arrive in Turkey at Mary's House. Once they land in Ephesus, especially if in large numbers, it may be near impossible to turn the tide."

"I agree," Lucas panted. "Our only option is mass elimination. It worked for your people, Gustav. No reason to change tactics at this point. We have armed drones that we can launch immediately."

Gustav hid his shaking hands in the folds of his cassock. First, orders to torture and now mass extermination of the women? He swayed in place, remembering the bombs. Huddling in a barn with his terrified mother as she tried to shelter him while Allied forces dropped bombs on their roofs.

Today the pope decided to open his daily message with 1 John 4:18, preaching that the one who fears is not made perfect in love. Said fear is the mother of violence. Warned that when fear pervades a society, no boundaries exist as to the level of horrible things one human will do to another.

He knew the words to be true; he had lived it. Someone like Lucas, a white, privileged, draft-dodging American, never knew what real war was like. No boundaries as long as someone else got their hands dirty. *And you are the most imperfect human I have ever encountered, Lucas. Ready to start wars, but too cowardly to actually be in the action. Treating us like minions.*

"Having second thoughts, holy man?" Lucas asked, catching the priest off guard. "I know what you're up to. You know it's against the rules to actively campaign to be the next pope, don't you?"

Seeing the cardinal's panic, he continued. "We're not so different. We've spent our whole lives preying upon other's weaknesses and fears so we could avoid acknowledging our own. That's why we crave power. In a desperate attempt to hide from humanity our real pathetic selves.

"But you, Gustav, you are nothing like Christ. Neither is your pope. Just asexual Churchians practicing Churchianity. Rarely do you clothe and feed the masses. Everything you and I do is only to satisfy our lust for power. If the Church truly understood my science and its power, you would have been nicer. We are just a blink in the world's history. An experiment in humanity that we both failed miserably. Isn't it time to acknowledge how worthless religion is?"

"Worthless? Pope Paul VI warned the world about your kind. He told us capitalism's continual greed would call down the judgment of God and the wrath of the poor *with consequences no one can foretell.* We, in Rome, didn't start this problem. You did, Lucas! Your father and your corporations did! This whole *women problem* started when you let them think they could work outside the home and remain respectful. For God's sake! We preached to the brazen hussies not to use birth control, then you go and set us up as one of the world's biggest suppliers of birth control pills. Why would you do that? Because of *your* addiction for money!"

"Interesting opinion, Gustav. So you're prepared to make me your enemy now?" Being criticized boosted Lucas' rage for revenge. The opportunity to bully and puncture an opponent's underbelly was his chum.

"Remember, war is my business. And I'm the CEO of winning. I never, ever lose."

"Really? Lucas, you and your father's company haven't won a war in over seventy years!" Gustav yelled, instantly regretting the incendiary bomb he had just hurled.

Brent overheard the two men's loud arguing as he arrived. He stood outside the lab door, waiting for the perfect entrance. The tension from the lab room was palpable; it twitched all the connector muscles in his extremities.

He entered poker-faced, quelling his urge to charge at the seated frail man and snap his scrawny neck like a twig. As long as Lucas was alive, Brent knew his friends and loved ones were in mortal danger. But seeing Gustav is what triggered his rage. **Rapist**! Brent had to stop the cardinal before he raped Martha one more time. It was his moral duty.

"Oh, look, Lucas, your dear friend the assassin has just arrived. Let him do your dirty work!" Gustav spat as Brent swaggered into the room.

Gustav stepped back and scanned the premises, wondering if the cousin and his swine housekeeper were with Brent or with the women swarming Vatican City. Too many opponents for a rusty Hitler thug to keep track of.

"You're such a 'C-student,' Lucas," Brent said in a low angry tone as he casually surveyed the monitors. "A trust-fund bully. Your kind makes me sick." He scanned the large room, noting all personnel and the nooks and crannies where you could hide from bullets in case he needed to shelter in place. That's what made the difference between life and death in these situations.

"So you couldn't even get physics right, Lucas? You ever heard *for every action there's a reaction*?" Brent asked, sarcastically, taunting the obviously ailing man.

"You Stanchirs have been in the fear-and-hate business for so long, I think y'all got a little lazy! You forgot to pay attention to your own Achilles' heel. Love, Lucas. Accelerated! You arrogantly never factored in the power of love. It's science, pal. Higher stronger vibrations. Power versus force.

"And since you've never been grateful a day in your whole miserable, rotten life, you're ignorant of its power. Gratitude is a receiving energy; two times more powerful than love, a giving energy. It starts a chain reaction, changes up the whole structure of the energy. It's a global thing now. All that connected DNA that you thought you could use for fear doesn't have a chance against the web of love DNA. That was your fatal flaw.

"Oh, that—and not paying attention to the blueprints! The lab was built over a convent, right? You know what they do in a convent, Skippy? The nuns express their love *and* gratitude every waking moment—while putting their fingertips in the holy water. DNA deposits. Holy water that comes from their own well! Do the math!" Brent couldn't contain his joyous satisfaction when the magnitude of the situation finally dawned on the slumping Lucas. Dr. Franco tried to help Lucas back into a sitting position.

"And you!" turning to Gustav. "You offend God with every wheezy breath you suck from the atmosphere! Twisting Jesus' words and teachings to obtain power. Have you read Matthew 6:24 lately? *No one can serve two masters.* You cannot serve both God and money. How about the Apocalypse of Peter? Called you bishops 'waterless canals.' How ironic, heh?

"Don't think I'm surprised at your actions. You're not a holy man. You're a monster who advocates raping children and women as a tool of war. Yeah, I've seen the file. And I've talked to Martha! Your idea or just another G-7 project for profit?

"Ironically, it's disrespect of women that was your and the Church's downfall. You know why? Because you don't know women. Especially the older women. Their reservoirs for compassion and empathy have no limit. They sympathize with those hurt before they fear.

"So your Spider Sweep does nothing! Nada! No quivering masses like the men. Just women looking for solutions, to make everything better. If you had paid attention, you would have known this," he said, stretching the truth a bit. It delighted him to watch the two men's faces contort as they realized they were at a loss for their next action. "It has always been right in front of your arrogant noses! Why do you think the Blessed

Mother is only seen by females? Because women *see* women. They don't make them invisible.

"I know what you did to my best friend. Thought you could hide your whole damn twisted plan, didn't you, you asshole!" Brent spit on the pristine white floor, and kicked a rack, loudly jangling the fragile glass tubes, fraying more nerves.

"I'm sure I don't know what you are speaking of," Lucas said, weakly, frightened that he wasn't strong enough to protect himself or his precious glass tubes.

"Oh, now you want to play footsie, huh? Did you think I wouldn't find out GA7 was behind the murder of Jim Barnett?" he growled, his rage volcanic. "While you were rolling in all the money, you let down your guard. Bad, bad move, Scooter.

"I worked side-by-side with that man for years! You think our DNA didn't entangle years ago? I saw what Jim saw—the webs with holes. And then the planets, then the Universe. This was more than about a Gathering. You wanted to change the whole grid system, the entire global energy field.

"I've been a soldier most all of my life. And ya wanna know what a soldier's most admired quality is? It's not killing and fighting, you coward. It's loyalty, sacrificing for your fellow soldier. I get it that it's 'just business' to you. But not to us, the grunts who fight your wars. War ain't a video game. You're what we call a Blue Falcon, Lucas, a buddy butt-fucker. Blue Falcons are great soldiers as long as the commander's watching.

"Jim was something you'll never be—a patriot. And he was loyal. Out on the battlefield, there isn't a bond stronger than your troop. And you never leave a man behind!

"The truly patriotic are the brave ones who stand up and challenge those in power. Change the course, if necessary. Those women will change the course. Because they know war is a disease that happens when you degrade the life-givers—the women. It's always been the women who have saved humanity. They are nurturers, not conquerors."

"Playing your game of patriotism has a lousy rate of return" Lucas declared. "You think you have it all figured out, don't you, you inbred mongrel. Yes, you are a dog of war, trained well."

"Oh good point, Lucas! You're right about the training, dude. Watched you put all that DNA in those slim glass cylinders and then laugh as you remotely influenced Stella almost to death. So how you feeling, Lucas, buddy? Ever notice that you and Stella have the same hair color?"

Lucas' mouth went dry, sending him into a coughing fit, realizing the betrayal, the switching of his hair for hers. With the last bit of energy in his body, he pushed up out of the chair, barely making his way to the test tube centered in the rack. He pulled the bottle cap out of his pocket, still flaked by Stella's blood, as he tried to grasp the fragile glass tube. It fell to the floor and broke. As he tried to transfer flakes of dried decades-old blood into the tube containing his hair, he sliced the tip off of his index finger and mixed his own DNA with hers. Falling weakly to the floor, he reached into his sock as he rolled over and leaned on his bony elbows.

"You think people like you are valued? Your ignorance disappoints me," Stanchir said as he turned toward the two men, holding the pistol perfectly straight-armed, the red laser beam focused on the target.

"Don't!" Brent yelled, shielding his face.

The powerful gun blast blew the body against the wall as blood slowly trickled out the side of his mouth and every muscle released, sliding his big mass to the floor.

Chapter Eighty

—∞—

No one had yet been alarmed by the absence of the workaday cadence in Vatican City now replaced by the rustling of the nuns' habits. The narrow Roman streets were checkered black and white as the masses of obedient nuns acknowledged each group's presence silently. Effortlessly, like a flock of birds, they stepped into formation, shoulder to shoulder, synchronized and intent on completing the water pilgrimage to the Vatican Garden's grotto.

Martha and Kathleen joined a group, clinging closely to the right flank. They hoped their habits had allowed them the anonymity necessary to carry out their plan as they fell into footstep with the others.

As soon as they passed the last camera perched on the top of the building at the corner of Via di Porta Angelica, they slyly ducked around the corner, headed down the alleyway towards the hidden jail cell at the Vatican Gendarmerie headquarters.

"Hurry, we won't be alone for long," the French Perpetua whispered, hugging close to the wall as she quickened her step. "Follow my lead."

Martha lengthened her spine, her shoulders pinched sharply back in a "V" as she addressed the guards she assumed were retired Italian

Carabinieri. Too surly and slouchy for them to be Swiss Guard. Using the art of omission, she cleverly led the guards to believe she and the other nun were there on official Vatican business to attend to the prisoner. Something about his medication, an emergency, she had sternly offered.

She gambled right, figuring at least one guard had been subjected to the cardinal's bullying and would offer no resistance. Their pensions did not buy undying loyalty, unlike the Swiss Guards.

She prayed for mercy as she girded herself for what was on the other side of the cell door. She had heard enough stories of the atrocities which had been secretly carried out for years to be suitably frightened.

"What did that monster do to you?" she cried. The once-handsome, always-smiling French priest was huddled up against the concrete wall, a catatonic limp mass of flesh. His now-neon white hair was crowned with a bright white aura from the overhead floodlight, his mouth slackened. She softly wiped the drying froth from around his blistered mouth as she held up a water bottle to his thirsty lips. The lips shaped like hers.

Just a shell of the kind priest who had been not only her closest friend, but her ward when she served Pope John Paul I. She concentrated her thoughts as she put both hands on his bare chest, hoping the DNA of familial connection would rule out. They had to move swiftly, and she needed his trust, though she still could not reveal their true connection.

"Father Gabriel, it's Martha. Remember me?" She looked into his sapphire blue eyes now cloudy and pale, searching for a spark of his soul. She thought she saw a flicker, some kind of activity around his left iris. Convinced it was enough for her to work with, she continued. "I'm here with Brent's cousin, Sister Kathleen. We are going to get you out of here."

"Father Gabriel, I'm Kathleen, Brent's cousin. We haven't much time. I apologize for what I have to do now and pray to God for guidance. I have to inject you, Father, with medication. I don't know if you understand what I'm saying. And I pray to God we don't damage you further," Kathleen said, as she inserted the thin needle into his chest wall, expertly between his ribs.

Within seconds, his breath stopped. They heard the squeak of an opening car door. Within minutes, they loaded Gabriel into the waiting hearse.

Chapter Eighty-One

—∞—

"Bloody hell, you're finally here!" Sophia exclaimed, yanking Maggie into the crowded motel suite.

Maggie swung her head around so furiously looking for Stella, the hitchhiking spider web from the motel room's rustic screen door whipped-sawed into a tight furry ball on the back of her curls. Her own worry knot.

"I thought I'd never hold you again," Maggie cried when she spotted Stella. She squeezed her tightly as she burrowed her wet face into Stella's toga. "I'm so sorry I wasn't there to protect you."

"Things happen for a reason. Right, Lilli—no accidents? Maggie, I'm here. I'll always be here," Stella calmly said, as she sprinkled light kisses on the top of her friend's head. "Everything will be fine soon." She lifted Maggie's head by the chin as she looked deeply into her best friend's eyes.

Maggie returned the look, confused; something had changed. It wasn't the fact Stella was cleaned-faced, her wavy hair obviously air-dried. This wasn't the Stella she expected, this radiant goddess holding court in an airy, white caftan surrounded by an aura of confidence. She had prepared herself for a frantic, twitchy Stella; perhaps a catatonic, broken

Stella, disappointed and terminally damaged. Certainly a Stella in need of rescuing. That Stella appeared not to exist anymore. This Stella was calm, steady, reverent.

"Honey, we don't know yet about Gabriel or Nicki. But Lilli and I feel we will hear soon." She winced, hoping new Stella wouldn't crumble.

"Then we will wait, as we have for the Third Secret," Stella said calmly, her hand caressing her star necklace coupled with another: an eye-shaped glass amulet, cobalt blue with a white center dangling from a gold cord.

"Isn't it beautiful? It's called the Nazar. It wards off evil. Sophia bought them by the dozens at the market."

"These Turks love to haggle, so I got a great deal, Maggie! Here's one for you, deary," Sophie said. "I'm sorry, would you like one too?" she asked, addressing the graceful stranger standing by the door.

"I would be honored," Lilli said, bending her head to accept the gift.

"You must be Lilli. My name is Sarah, wife to that plucky live wire handing out necklaces. Stella told us about you at the chateau. Here, please sit," she said, pulling out the dinette chair. "Let me get you a cup of tea. We have some proper pastries left over. Get comfortable. Or do you prefer to freshen up? No? Okay. But warning, you might want to sit down as we catch up with each other. Got a doozy of a story! So does Stella."

"Okay, I'll start, if you don't mind, lovey," Sophia said as they wedged themselves around the faded yellow Formica table, while Sarah busied herself with refreshments for all. Stella graciously nodded her agreement and sat.

"Remember at the chateau I told you ladies I would be going to Catalhöyük, Turkey, after we left Lourdes? Let me tell you, it was mind blowing! It's believed to be the first dedicated city, begun 9,000 years ago, in 7,500 BC. The women of this community were glorified as givers of life and worked hand in hand with the men for the common good, an equalitarian civilization.

"We think they were the first agricultural civilization. However, first and foremost, they were a community of artists. They chose the site of their city based on the artistic materials available in the surrounding earth. The soil was really bad for growing food so they had to walk miles to plant. Some believe Catalhöyük is the site of Eden. But get this: they lived there for at least two thousand years, women and men, with no bloody war!"

"Really?" Maggie exclaimed as Stella nodded her head yes, obviously a rehearing of the story.

"Amazing, huh? So one day there I was, end of the day, tired, grimy, my dry tongue encrusted in sand and craving a cold frosty pint! The sun was setting, and I was sitting on one of the cubicles over a burial pit. You see, they built their city in layers, one for each generation. And below each layer, they buried their dead in small holes. I know, kind of creepy, but you get used to it in my business.

"Anyway, I was sitting there, blurry-eyed, trying to get my focus back to present day. My eye lands on this oblong hole in a wall, rimmed in red. In those times red symbolized blood and was thought to be magical. As long as a woman bled, she could still give life. I just stared at it until I was compelled to stick my hand in. And I pulled this out." Sophia showed Maggie the obsidian icon.

"It's called the Mother Goddess, the Lady of Heaven. She dates back 20,000 years, we think. Someone at our site has held one that dates back maybe 800,000 years. And you'll love this. These Mother Goddesses icons all have huge hanging breasts, bulging bellies, wide hips. They glorified our curves! Actually, the multi-breasted ones like this represent the nourishing of life. Some of the goddess icons have extremely oversized breasts since woman was able to breast feed to keep humans alive. The religion of the Life Givers.

"As I examined the icon, I swear I started feeling weird shit! I thought my exhaustion was making me bonkers. My hands started tingling, and when I looked down at them—no bloody edges! Frigging scary as hell, I tell ya.

"But wait, it gets better. I felt a light pressure on my thigh and when I looked down, I saw finger outlines on my pants, but no fingers. I was stunned, couldn't move, couldn't talk. Wisps of plasma or something started swirling around me, kind of like those whirling dervishes you see here, yah? They gained substance like a hologram and started to multiply. Blurring together, different women from different times, morphing through dimensions, dressed in gowns of bright white, saffron, copper rose, blood red. And then—this will blow your mind—the smell of roses. What's that all about?"

"You mean like when you saw Mary—or thought you saw her?" Maggie asked.

"Exactly the same!"

"It's the Shift, Maggie. And this magical place," Stella added. "Wait until I tell you what happened to me.

"I went to another world. That's the best way to describe it. Like the Wizard of Oz—on acid. I escaped on our boat when they captured Gabriel and soon was lost on the nighttime sea. I got caught up in this swirling vortex, made of colors I've never seen before or *heard* before. Yes, the ocean sang to me. Remember in the Wizard of Oz how all of Dorothy's farmhands were the characters she met in Oz? It was kind of like that! Except it was all of you—my family. Everyone started as floating orbs." Stella noticed Maggie twirl her watch nervously.

"And I saw the man who is after us, Maggie—Jim's employer, Lucas Stanchir. I apparently rejected him once. I doubt his motive for all this evil is only because of that, but it gives me insight into the type of man he is. The next thing I remember was opening my eyes and seeing Sophia and Sarah. Naked except for my star necklace, wrapped around the base of giant hand sprouting doves on the Esplanade!"

"And this is where it gets spooky," Sophia said.

"You mean *spookier*, don't you?" Maggie asked, unsure if she wanted to hear more.

"I knew exactly where to find her because *this* 'woman' told me." Sophia held up her recovered icon over her head, like a trophy.

"Without moving her lips, I heard *seek the hand that holds peace.* Crickey, what the 'eff does that mean, ya know? My ever-so logical spouse said 'let's noodle this,' and we figured it out. We remembered seeing the hand statue on YouTube when we were planning our trip here. It held doves, birds of peace. So we hurried to Kusadasi, and there she was— naked as the day she popped out!"

"Sophia, tell her what else you heard that day," urged Sarah.

"Oh, yeah, sure. She gave me a message for you, Lilli. She said *Trust the Journey.*"

Lilli smiled. "Would this, per chance, have happened yesterday in the afternoon?"

Sophia nodded her head quickly, yes.

"Ah, but of course. Maggie, I think we now know what *confiar a viagem* means, don't we? Anyone speak Portuguese?"

Chapter Eighty-Two

—∞—

The wizened Turkish woman ambled to the middle of the compound's courtyard, waving her raggedy dish towel at the dusty slow-moving donkeys loitering around the dinner bell, impeding her nightly ritual. She wiped her greasy hands on her apron, latched onto the frayed rope and tugged it hard. By the last brassy peel, her sister had joined her in the courtyard. A cook, like her sister, she had just arrived that morning from California where she ran the Click Café. "It's been a long time since we hosted so many, but I'm happy to say we are now ready for service," the sister said, wiping her brow.

Throngs of ravenous women, led by Lilli, Maggie and Stella, began to flow out of the low-slung ranch motel. Enticed by wisps of succulent aromas perfuming the sunset-lit air, they treaded the wide, sloping path towards the hidden meadow. Once a huge horse barn, the enormous round dining hall now resembled a massive wooden beehive now abuzz with queens from every nation.

They were met by a group of Indian and Asian women as they entered the capacity-filled hall with walls draped in a billowing sea of luxurious turquoise silk. Quickly and deftly, they painted a God seed on each woman's forehead. Similar to the Fibonacci spiral, they started with a dot on the third eye that ended in a circular flourish in glow-in-the-dark white paint.

"The color of alpha waves," Stella said, fingering the fluttering silk, "like when you meditate. It's an excellent conductor for connection." She glided into the crowd and waved her hand for her friends to follow. Strings of brilliant kaleidoscopic light fanned out over her head from each fingertip similar to flowing streamers from a child's bicycle handles, in the wind. Throughout the dining hall, the vaporous energy resembled the early morning smoke from a wakened river, bending and curling in harmonic curly-cues around the room. But no light was as brilliant as the moonbeam shining down through the round skylight with celestial pride on the icons on the altar.

"Stella, would you join me at the altar? It is time for Faïence to join her sisters. Sophia, please bring the Mother Goddess too."

Lilli led the sacred procession of three towards the dining room's center and the circular multi-tiered dais. Each of the seven tiers held feminine icons from throughout history, including the original *Notre Dame Sous Terre*, The Lady of the Underground from Chartres Cathedral. Following Lilli's silent instructions, Sophia stepped forward to place the black obsidian goddess, mother to them all, at the tall apex of the altar, centered above Isis and the Virgin Mary.

"Welcome, my fellow apostles. My name is Lilli St. Remy Aubert. By now you know we have all been called to this ancient land of women to gather for a historical event, centuries in the making. Though our ultimate purpose may not yet be clear, it will be revealed shortly. In God time.

"Tonight, I would like to start our ceremony with a poem from the altar of the Temple of Sais, which is dedicated to Isis, Goddess of the Moon, Goddess of Resurrection:

> *I am she who separated the heaven from the Earth. I have instructed mankind in the mysteries. I have pointed out their paths to the stars. I have ordered the course of the Sun and the Moon. I am queen of the rivers and winds and sea. I have brought together men and women. I gave mankind their laws, and ordained what no one can alter.*

> *I have made justice more powerful than silver and gold. I have caused truth to be considered beautiful. I am she who is called the goddess of women.*

Before Lilli finished the first line, she was joined by a chorus of the women present who stood and recited the poem along with her.

> *I, Isis, am all that has been, that is, or shall be; no mortal man hath ever me unveiled. The fruit which I have brought forth is the Sun.*

"As we know, art is the sacred tool for preserving our human stories. Tonight, we add two more storytellers to our collective gallery of remembrances. Just like the women depicted in the beautiful statues on the altar—Artemis, Isis, Cybele, Diana, Athena, Sophia and, of course, Mary—we women have been chosen for this historic ushering in of the Shift, what some call the 'end times' or the 'lifting of the veil.'

"For those of you who have not yet met her, this is Faïence. Though she is quite young compared to the others, she is the reason we are here. Since the end of the last world war, she has patiently been spreading Mary's DNA around the world like drops of water in the pond that ripple out into an ocean of compassion to all humankind. In honor of the Mother of the Heavens, she wears this star," Lilli said, lifting Faïence's full skirt. "It is made from the tunic Mary wove and wore when she gave birth to her son. The love she felt that day delivering her special baby is imbued in this fabric, as is His DNA.

"And yesterday, we were introduced to what may be the Mother Goddess, the Lady of Heaven, dating back at least 20,000 years, found not far from where we dine tonight. She is the oldest art we have found yet, informing us the story of the Goddesses is still unfolding. They both are home now with their sisters."

Lilli placed Faïence in the middle of the second tier, hesitant to part with her for the final time. Small sparks of light bounced among the other goddess icons as they appeared to communicate in a secret silent code.

"We are gathered here in the land of the Mother Goddess to usher in the next era of evolved humanity. We are at the end of the Mayan

Long Count. The Amargi, a return to the mother, what some call the Return of the Divine Feminine, has begun.

"Our art tells us that for thousands of years all ancient tribes on our earth were headed by women. These mothers were our first religious leaders, our healers. Tomorrow evening we will gather at the Great Theater of Ephesus. The same theater where the Apostle Paul caused a riot when he tried to vanish the goddess Artemis from the land of the Ephesians.

"As Matthew said *we have come to the place where we've been directed.* In this land there was once harmony, man and woman working together. As a community they labored and provided needed shelter, food, comfort and joy. But most of all they revered women because they had the ability to keep the species alive, not only with their bodies but also with their hearts.

"As one of our holy sisters preaches on a bus in America: *We let our hearts be broken, to touch the pain of the world, so we can release hope into the darkness. We see those who hunger to be seen, who hunger to be understood.* That is our purpose—to take care of each other.

"We start tomorrow with a visit to the home of Mary where she fled after suffering the unimaginable pain of witnessing her son being tortured and nailed to a cross. She was comforted here in a gnostic sisterhood and allowed to heal before starting her next mission of continuing her son's ministry. Some say she was buried in the surrounding hills.

"So now, please enjoy this wonderful meal, and get to know each other. Share your stories. Tomorrow morning, we will all meet in the courtyard at 9 a.m. sharp."

As Stella walked to their table, she thought she could detect protests from the heavily laden wooden tables; their creaking begging her to help lighten the loads they bore. Barely any bare wood could be seen on the round table tops between all the shimmering, luscious dishes.

"Intoxicating, isn't it?" Lilli said, walking behind Stella. "It's called mesa. Everything you could desire, from hummus to shrimp and courgette fritters which are eaten with an ice cold blend of Raki and water. When we are all seated, those huge platters of salt-baked sea bass will be cracked open and filleted by the waiters."

Stella noticed ceramic jugs of red wine placed every few inches down the center of the long main table. What caught her eye was not only the more-than-generous offering, but the actual vessels. They had the same star and wave motif as her bread bowl back home, given to her by Nema. The jugs also had the addition of an embossed snake encircling the jugs' rims.

It wasn't until they almost reached their group when Stella spotted her. Seated among the familiar Lourdes crowd was the addition of Mary Rose of Rwanda. Mary Rose rushed to hug Stella, trying to stem her flowing tears as she helped her patron into a chair across from her. "They all came, Stella," Mary Rose said gesturing to the crowd, while deftly pouring Stella some wine with her lone remaining hand.

"What an amazing night," Maggie said, as she filled her plate. "With all this chaos, I haven't had the time to delve deeply into research of Ephesus yet. I'm curious as to the connection of Christianity and the Goddesses," Maggie said as she dug in and peeled some grilled shrimp, the buttery lemon sauce dripping in rivulets down her forearms.

"Christianity was launched here by the Apostles," Bernadette offered. "At that time, it was the richest city outside Rome and home of the first bank. But more importantly, it was known as a great center of learning. Much writing took place here, documenting Jesus' teachings. Many early church leaders lived and worked in Turkey."

"But for Mary, it was a city that was dedicated to the worship of the Mother Goddess. The temple of Isis is not far from the Temple of Artemis here, one of the Seven Wonders of the World," Sophia exclaimed.

Bernadette continued, "We now think most of the Gnostic Gospels were written here, as was Revelation—right out in the bay on the island of Patmos. Its author, the Jewish prophet John of Patmos, some believe to be the descendent of the apostle John who brought Mary here.

"One Sunday he said he was 'in spirit' and heard a loud voice. A divine being appeared who announced *what is going to happen soon* to bring the *end of time.* John thought it was Jesus. Maybe it was, though what's interesting is his vision most likely occurred after Mary died. And now she's here again, talking about end times? The Book of Revelation is about our worst fears, and if you survive all of that, you have the gift of new life, hope and joy—resurrection. Sounds like maybe the first apparition to me." Bernadette impishly winked at everyone as she took a sip of wine, hoping to engage some lively discussion.

"Maybe she came here for another reason—like protection," Sophia said. "This *is* the land where woman warriors began, too. Amazons. Probably out of necessity due to the violent third wave of the Kurgan Invasion back in 3000-2800 BC. The Kurgans were a nasty lot of bullies. Aryans or Indo-Europeans, the same race Nazis were based on, who came from Northeast Europe—or today's Russia. Their leaders were powerful priests and warriors who worshiped male Gods of War.

"The Kurgans changed everything in this peaceful land. Based their prosperity on violence and organized warfare, but more specifically the demonization of women. They feared our kind. They roamed the lands stealing cattle and women which led them on a journey here, the wealthy southern Sumerian cities. That's what started the domination culture and ended the Goddess culture of partnership. The male-war God v. the life-giving Goddess.

"This land is rich with stories starting with the myth of Isis and Horus as the great mother giving birth to the child of light only to be reborn 3,000 years later into our modern age as the Virgin Mary and her son, Jesus. Same stories for Attis, Krishna, Dionysus, Mithra—all virgin births on December 25th, resurrection after three days, star in the East alerting births, twelve disciples, performing miracles.

"My apologies, Sister, I hope I'm not offending you. Not my intention. I know this makes Christians uncomfortable and maybe even angry. But it is something we should consider, don't you think? As an anthropologist, I can't ignore history and its stories. My colleagues are starting to conclude that this is the birthplace of the Goddess Master Mind. An embedded energy that remained united until disharmony arrived with the Kurgans. Maybe that's why *we* were gathered *here* to usher in the new era."

"This changed everything," Lilli interrupted, holding her beef kabob up to the table's diners. "For thousands of years the old Natural Religion worshiped the power of Mother Earth, a water-from-the-earth religion where the community fed everyone. Their partnership culture is reflected in the art you are now finding. In fact, the bowls you are eating out of represent some of the first art in existence, glorifying water and connection. Then profit was introduced by the domestication of animals."

"Some of my female evolutionary scientist friends think we became erect so we could gather food in containers," Sophia stated. "Pottery was invented by these pre-historic women to give to others, according to them. Before they changed the myth of the serpent as something sinful—ya know the whole Eve-eating-the-apple tosh—the snake was seen as the cycle of life. The sensual snake shedding its skin represents death and rebirth. Some say biting its tail is the assimilation of male/female energies, a partnership.

"But real change occurred in 1961, when Catalhöyük was found. A partnership community that existed long before the Mayan Long Count of 3115 BC. Paintings were found of what were first assumed to be bulls. Now we believe they were depictions of the womb and Fallopian tubes, heavy with seed."

"Millions of women have been tortured and killed over the centuries since the twisting of Jesus' words. The Christian church feared women's powers. Especially the occult tradition of healing by older women. It was the healers they called witches and so, started burning them," Bernadette replied.

"We healers know that menopause is a natural progression that doesn't need interference by chemicals. Menopause is our time to regather and reevaluate—focus," Lilli added. "It is our gateway to a deeper gnosis of compassion. Mother earth gave us plants for a reason along with the language of the rain and the stars. We knew that being in balance with all was the key to happiness and health. We all were created with powerful bodies that can heal themselves once you go within."

Maggie's cell phone vibrated on the wooden table, clanging into her cutlery with an incoming text. "*We have G & paper. On our way. Srs. K & M,*" the white-on-blue text glared from her phone. She quickly wiped her mouth and threw her napkin onto her plate.

"Stella, follow me!" She grabbed Stella's hand and rushed for the front door.

Sophia swiftly caught them before they could exit, her lanky shoulders cupped inward like a protective shield: "Psst, ladies—gotta be super careful out there; getting dodgy. That's why I bought the evil eye amulets.

Since we arrived, I've seen some shape shifters around. Like the images I saw at the dig, but cold and dark. Be careful what you share. Look for the purple auras; they're the safest."

* * *

"He's okay, Stella. I just received news that Gabriel has been rescued. Stop! I know you have a ton of questions, but that is all I got for you right now. Just a short text, from Brent's cousin, I believe. Appears the cranky old nun was on our side, after all. Anyway, she's on her way here with another nun—and a document. That's all she said. I hope it's the Third Secret. All we got is the video in Portuguese and no translators.

"I'm sure they are being monitored very closely. Apparently, the other nun is well connected with Vatican Radio—and with Gabriel according to Brent. All those nuns are the ones who jumped on social media and the airwaves to get all these women here now. You should had seen the airport! But no information about Nicki. I'm sorry."

Stella stood still and gathered her thoughts. "It's almost breakfast time in California. I'm going back to my room to try calling."

Stella fumbled with her key in the darkened doorway, the yellow bulb long ago burnt out. She almost missed the message taped to her dusty screen door.

> *I see you. Retrieve your note marked with a red dot stuffed into the message fence at Mary's House. Explicitly follow the directions. Do not disappoint me again. Best, Lucas.*

Chapter Eighty-Three

—∞—

They had barely gotten Bernadette's wheelchair loaded into the hired turquoise dolmus when the driver quickly handed everyone headphones. "Welcome, welcome, ladies! We are about to embark on a sacred trip to our Mother's house. Do you know how they found her house? Listen, listen," he urged, as he tapped his ears and hurriedly got back behind the wheel.

Stella put on her provided headset, but turned off the sound having heard the story before in Lourdes. She closed her eyes and breathed slowly, without thought. Silence is what she needed to center herself for the courage to face her enemy.

Soon, the circus train fleet of vans and tourist busses jugged into the mountain-top parking lot as women from all over the world disembarked, ready to pay homage.

"Ouch!" Sarah shook her hands. "I just got shocked on the door handle, big time. My whole body is vibrating, as if I plugged into some energy source."

"You have, my dear," Lilli said as she grasped Sarah's offered hand and lowered herself onto the cracked asphalt. The sun glinted off the frozen sprouts of sea grass everywhere, making them slippery. Lilli welcomed Sarah's kindness as she carefully navigated around the greenery. Suddenly, her spine stiffened as she scanned the parking lot, sensing a presence long ago remembered.

"The Ninth energy wave, correct, Sophia?"

"That's the expert consensus. We're in the Ninth Wave of the Mayan Calendar known also as the Universal Wave or Underworld. It's the highest level of consciousness humans have ever achieved. Lore has it that universal consciousness would feel like pulses. Maybe that's what you're feeling, my love? A shock of consciousness. My heart is beating as frantically as a Keith Moon drum solo."

"We have to be prepared," Lilli warned, as she looked around the crowd. "Something like this has not happened for many centuries. The power of our increasing numbers, baby boomers I believe some call you, is what humanity has been waiting for. The power of numbers. They say there was a beautiful ringing in the air when Mary passed over. Maybe it's her love energy."

Maggie was the first in line of their group, guiding them past the tacky souvenir booths on the trek up to the small hill to Bulbul "Nightingale" Mountain. They walked on the stone path up to the solitary house. Maggie slowed her pace so she could glance at the postcards, looking for orbs. She still hadn't shown her photos to anyone. Her orbs were getting so numerous that they blocked the photographed image. They stopped and bought small plastic bottles for the holy water.

As they came around the corner towards the stone house, Maggie was struck by the sight of the lone tree by the front door. She could feel a sadness. She wondered if Mary planted it when she arrived. *A singular gnarled tree as a memoriam for a lost son?* She decided she would plant Italian Cyprus around the ranch when she got back—tall, strong, evergreen—a suitable memorial to her men.

"See this Y-shaped cross in the oratory?" Lilli asked Stella, as their group was allowed to enter. "It's a mixture of woods: the pale stem is cypress, the brown arm is cedar, and the other arm, a yellow palm-wood. The piece on top a smooth yellow olive-wood. Some think it represents the cross Jesus died on. I have always thought it represented the Great

Gathering, the Y in mixed woods for women's wombs from around the world. A mixture of woods to symbolize our uniqueness, our oneness."

Stella was trying to pay attention. She had yet to share Lucas' threating note with Maggie. Or information about her new visions. Since using Lilli's salve, she could see different moments in time—all at the same time. Sporadic and vague happenings, she hadn't mentioned yet to anyone. But now she might have to talk. Since entering Mary's House, she had been entranced by a ghostly image that seemed interested in communicating. The woman was in a sleeping alcove hidden behind a billowing white cloth, lying on a low-laying lounge. Weak and pale, encased in a purple aura, and wrapped in a cloth from her head to her toes, she was surrounded by women grievers.

Stella heard her whisper. She leaned in.

"She was my sister."

Stella looked around to see if anyone else had heard or seen what she had. Nothing.

The too-short tour was over. As Lilli started to emerge from the stone house she stumbled, falling into Maggie's arms. She pointed her trembling finger towards the picnic area. "I know that essence. I smell her. She's here!" Lilli said. "Rose? Are you Rose?" Lilli called, walking towards two nuns seated at a far picnic table.

Martha stood and tried to answer but her voice could not be heard.

Lilli climbed the concrete steps and hugged her long-lost sister.

"Yes, Lilli. It's me," she sobbed as she handed the green book to her older sister. "I believe this contains your message for the world."

* * *

Having slipped out of Mary's House before the rest of her group, Stella was glad for once for a crowd, giving her coverage to swiftly worm her way back to the Wall of Ribbons. The red dot on the white paper looked like a bull's eye. She made a bee line to retrieve it.

Go to the Seven Sleepers alone, or terror will reign.

She put her hand over the old scar from the bottle cap and closed her eyes. After a few moments, she smiled, nodded her head and headed for the bus instead, to wait for the others.

"Stella, are you awake?" Lillie whispered as she lowered herself into the seat next to Stella. "My prayers have been answered. I have been reunited with my sister, Rose. She brought me the Third Secret."

Stella rubbed her fists into her eyes, trying to fully wake. Standing in the busses' aisle was Lilli's sister. Stella jumped out of her seat and yelped. "*I know you.* I saw you in the park!"

Chapter Eighty-Four

—∞—

It was a solemn stroll among the ancient town's now crumbling marble statues lining the Marble Way, once walked on by Cleopatra and the Virgin Mary as they each made their own pilgrimage to the Grand Theater. Bases of what once were columns of grand burial tombs guided their path, the only signs attesting to the grandeur of what once was there. Embedded in the pavement was a square of marble with graffiti of a crown, a woman's left footprint and a heart. Another story.

This is how it should feel, Stella thought, walking amongst all the women dressed in white. *This is church. Harmony. Peace. Oneness.*

"Says Cleopatra's sister was buried in Ephesus," Stella said, slowing to read the posted historical marker.

"So was Luke, according to legend."

"Lucas?" Stella hissed, mishearing what Maggie said. Even she was shocked by her outburst after such a long peaceful existence since the vortex. She felt a sudden warmness on the back of her neck; similar to the sensation on her blind date when Gabriel stared at her.

"What's going on, Stella?" Maggie asked, jerking her to the side. "What was your message on the wall?"

"How in the hell *do you* do that?" Stella had flushed the red-doted message at Mary's House in case it had any tracking devices on it.

"Good old holy water from the spring under Mary's House. I was washing my hands in it while you were flushing. Pretty easy, actually—especially with that red dot."

"Lucas left me a message last night on my door to retrieve that message. It warned that if I didn't meet him at the cave of the Seven Sleepers that terror would reign. I didn't go, Maggie," Stella said, bravely. "I'm hoping with our connective power we'll all be safe. If I die, I die. But what about the others? Do we need to alert everyone?"

"Not anymore, sweetie. We two together are a fierce force of sisterhood to be reckoned with. Besides, no men here today." Maggie tightly grasped her best friend's hand. She couldn't remember a time when she felt stronger. Which helped her right now to have the conversation.

"Speaking of sisters, Lilli sure is happy. What a shock to find your sister alive after so long."

"Indeed," Stella replied, craning her head to read more historic signs, trying to avoid further engagement on the topic.

"Stella, hon, spit it out! I see a little of old Stella still lurks behind those baby blues of yours. I'm thinking the same thing. I never saw your Highway 101 woman, but I remember the lady in Golden Gate Park."

"Sophia warned us about shape shifters. But there's more."

"More?!"

"Since the whole lost-at-sea incident, I sometimes can see between dimensions—at the same time. I have no control of it. It just happens, somewhat like Sophia said she saw at her archeological site. Not only have I seen Lilli's sister, Rose, as the woman in Golden Gate Park and at the highway exit, but I see faint images of others. I recognize souls I have known before. I have abilities I never had before, experiences of other worlds."

They slowed as they reached the entrance of the massive stone Great Theater. The majestic amphitheater was situated between two rolling hills in a valley that slopped towards the once-bustling Ephesus port on the Mediterranean Sea. One hundred rows high, enough to hold over twenty-five thousand people as they faced and honored the water.

They watched as women, distanced by decades of the business of living life, ran into each other's arms—hugging, smiling, and weeping with joy. As the crowd grew thick, the women glowed with the familiar colors of last night's gathering, illuminating both the theater and the surrounding hills.

"Stella, look at all these women! They all have vials of water. See the flag decals? Must be from their homelands. I have never seen so many flags, not even at the Olympics."

Stella stared at the crowd and watched as translucent columns of watery images formed, weaving in and out of the crowd:

> Harriet Tubman, Maya Angelou, Jeanette Rankin, Petra Herrera, Molly Ivins, Esther, Celia Sanchez, Mother Theresa, Helen Keller and Corazon Aquino. Shirley Chisholm, Nora Ephron, Elizabeth Glaser, and Coretta Scott King.

A voice buzzed in her head: "Great is Artemis of the Ephesians."

* * *

"It is time. The world is ripe for peace," Lilli started. "God time." The crowd of 25,000 females hushed. Stella and Maggie hurried to stand as witnesses next to Lilli on the ground-level stage, their backs to the sea.

"We have been gathered here in the home of the goddesses to observe the Shift. The veil has been symbolic throughout history from Greece and Rome, from the nun's habit through to the wimple of Medieval Europe to the hijab. Meant as protection, it has also been used to limit women, hide them. No more. We start the new era by lifting the veil."

Lilli pushed her opaque hood back off her head. She was dressed in Jewish ceremonial garb, exactly as instructed by her ancestor. A red and yellow striped over-garment was draped on her back, held at the shoulder by a single cloth-knotted button. The stripes helped to keep the energy flowing up and down. Underneath, she wore a brown undergarment, a good absorption color, girdled at her waist, full sleeves to her elbows. Her hood was her only head wear, which she removed to allow energy an escape route to the heavens above. Mary's scapular was loosely wrapped around her neck.

"At the beginning of the Mayan Long Count in 3115 BC, men of war invaded this sacred land. Always a land of peace, the goddesses knew nothing of their world. The goddesses lived in a giving world; these invaders were takers. A peaceful community working in partnership became a community dominated by brawn and aggression. They called the goddesses a cult; that is how the demotion of women began.

"Since that time, governments have been at war. Religions have been at war. But not their countries. Look around—women from all over the world are here. We are not here for war.

"We all love a god or a creator in our own way, whether as a Christian, a Jew, a Hindu, Muslim, or Buddhist. The universal force of everyone's god is love. An energy not bound by time and space. But our world has forgotten that force.

"As I said last night, we are the Shift's apostles. Many of you have lost a child, many in war. Women pay the price of war with their grief and pain. It takes courage to stand for peace. Women have this bravery. We must realize the power of our energy and learn how to use it. We always had the power. We are the doors to peace. Women are tired of cleaning up after war, picking up the broken pieces of our communities and loved ones. We will not clean up after another one. Where there is injustice, the whole earth suffers. We are all connected.

"We are now in a time where we have to choose: *live in chaos or in connection.* Choose what makes you feel better. You can no longer sit out and observe. Now, we must feed the field. Be open and kind to everyone you meet. Smile with your heart. Feed the field so we can all connect in peace. It is time for us to weave a web: a web of love. Every time you feel fear—stop, breathe, focus on your heart, and send out a beam of love full blast. Two becomes four, four becomes eight.

"I am the descendant of the famous seer, Nostradamus. He left my family paintings that told us of this Shift, a planetary alignment that would bring earth changes. In his quatrains, he predicted there would be a new awareness in western civilization. He said there would be an accelerated rate in the conjunction of the planets, a shift when war *might* be avoided. This natural occurrence when the Shift would happen and the degree to which it happens would depend on the awareness people have mentally and spiritually.

"He referred to women as 'sisters who see,' who have a clear perception of multidimensional mental messages and who can most easily receive revelation, if only they unite and refuse to be divided by the dictates of lower interests. Many of us here have been visited by a womanly vision. We think she is Mary, the never-ending light.

"Your soul, your flame, is eternal. You physical body was born on a certain date, and it will die on a certain date, but your flame never is extinguished. But it's your choice of what your flame shines its light on when you are here on this earth.

"To feed the field, we must still our minds so we can talk with God. To sing together in silence is how we will settle our disputes in the future. The more time spent in the splendor of silence, the easier it is to know God, know yourself.

"I think it is no accident that Mary's sister, Elizabeth, mother of John the Baptist, taught him the power of prayer mixed with water; what we now call baptism. Water absorbs and memorizes that love energy, then moves it along in the stream.

"From this day forward, men must ask our permission before they can put our children in harm's way, killing other women's children. As our Liberian sisters said: **we no longer ask, we tell. We no longer abide and obey, we lead.**

"We must be more wall than window. Time we stand as One and we say NO!

"We lift the veil, and we say NO!

"Ignorance, not sin, causes suffering. LIFT THE VEIL.

"Teach. Speak up. LIFT THE VEIL."

"Sing it, sistah!" Sophia yelled from the side of the stage, her sinewy arms raised to the heavens as she shook her jazz hands.

The women started chanting "lift the veil," flooding the theater's magnetic field with the high frequency of their vibrations. Spontaneously, the women started praying, humming, whistling—all in tune with the harmonic hum coming from the long-dead port to the west. An other-worldly light emanated from the women's hearts before interlacing into an all-encompassing, pulsing, sparkling web as far as the eye could see. Stars crystalized in their vials of water as they felt the low rumbling under their feet. Slowly off in the distance, the resurrected aqua harbor gently started to roll in, making its way peacefully into the valley between the hills.

Unbeknownst to the raptured participants, their collective field had melded with the revived water and created magnetized wormholes; global nooks and crannies of quantum foam began transmitting the whole experience across the planet.

"Singing is spirit. Silence is prayer. Singing is to be one with the Divine, the Mother of All. Have faith, not fear. Keep singing in silence. We will now all be connected.

"The time has come to lift the veil. Time to read what Mary wanted us to know so many decades ago. The Third Secret. It is God Time.

"It is time to share your gnosis, your wisdom," Lilli advised as she held up the quickly typed page from the translator. "Rejoice!"

"*The shoes*!" Stella spat, as her attention was grabbed by the unusual-looking nun swiftly moving towards them from the crowd.

"What the hell?!" Maggie whispered angrily.

"Those are *not* women's shoes!" Stella screamed as she lunged at Lilli to shield her.

His frail arm moved through the night air, white knuckles clinched on the gleaming hilt, the index finger heavily bandaged. He couldn't be stopped, as he flipped his nun's costume to the stage.

The tip of the blade easily glided through her soft chest wall, plunging into her heart. She stood for a few seconds, before she fell to the ground, bleeding. The crowd hushed.

"Remember the paintings, mon chéri," Lilli whispered as Stella cradled the dying woman in her arms. "This is now your responsibility," she said, trying to hand Stella the twinkling scarf.

"Remember, I am only a thought away. Look between the drops."

An emerald green whirling column of light streamed upwards from the crown of Lilli's head, round and round in an eddy of death as her earthly form morphed first into the Virgin Mary and then Isis before majestically ascending to the heavens as a glorious luminescent orb.

"I've waited my whole life to see this. It does not disappoint," she said on the wind.

Lucas crumbled into a fetal ball on the marble stage, as seven women circled him. Always an emotional cripple, he was now stunned speechless by his emotions. Not quite sure what the feeling was as he had never known love before. He was rendered immobile by their force field that locked him to the cold cracked marble.

Stella knelt down and dabbed her left index finger in the remaining pool of Lilli's blood and turned to the whimpering shell that was Lucas. "I'm sorry you are in so much pain. You needed someone to love you," she said as she marked his forehead with a stripe of blood before marking her own. "I give you life. Amargi, return to the Mother," she chanted as she placed her hand on his heart. The remaining circle mimicked her actions.

Stella reached over and picked up Lilli's scarf and the bloodied paper. They were right; it was just twenty-four sentences, one page.

"This is what Sister Lucia wrote. The Third Secret. It is dated January 9, 1944:

> *The Lady revealed a vision of thousands of women in white robes, a Great Gathering, facing the Source water in the west that once flowed in between two hills.*
>
> *In her hand contained seven stars which she said would once again shine when the women joined the singing of the nightingale to lift the veil.*
>
> *She said the Divine Mother, clothed with the sun, the moon under her feet, and on her head a garland of twelve stars, will return when these stars shine brightly in the womb of the sky.*
>
> *She will heal the earth after the planets align and usher in a return to peace after the Seven Squares are completed, ending the great disharmony and chaos throughout the world.*
>
> *"Gather at my house, those without seed, to join with the daughters of Abraham, Jesus, and Muhammed, Artemis and Isis.*

The Time of the Water Bearer has come.

Time to 'look at the pond, not just the fish,' and welcome the Sophia of Christ.

No tree has branches so foolish as to fight among themselves."

Our Lady then opened her hands and rays of bright light appeared as she said, "I am the Thought that dwells in the Light.

She who exists before the All.

I am the Invisible One within the All that moves in every creature.

I am the perception and knowledge who poured forth the water.

It is I who am hidden within radiant waters.

Live simply and listen to God in your heart.

Be in nature, do not be attached to things, a slave to silver.

Live for the power of love, not the love of power.

Those who have denied your Knowing yet profess that they cannot see you will try to stop you.

Sing in silence for strength.

Sing in silence and know heaven within.

Sing in silence as you become One.

Blood will be shed by me, but know that I am still here.

Look between the drops.

You will find me there.

Your only purpose is to serve each other."

EPILOGUE

"Just as the horizon is not the edge of the ocean, death is not the end of your eternal life," Gabriel preached, as they all watched the floating white lilies form a circle. "Water is life. We return you so that you will come forth again." He motioned gently for them to come to the bow.

"In his remembrance, Doug suggested that you make one wish for someone else as you return his earthly ashes to the sea."

Stella and Nicki held Todd up in between them and guided him to the boat's edge, tearfully feeling his heart break as he made his formal goodbye to his husband. Lilly wiggled in between the women so she could hold her Grandpa Todd's hand.

Though Doug had been dead for some time, Todd had wanted to wait until the fifth month of Nicki's pregnancy with the twins so the whole now-healed family could gather to say their goodbyes. He said he didn't want to take any chances. It wasn't until after Stella and Todd had assisted with the water birth of their Virgo granddaughter Lilly, that he told Stella how much her—their—miscarriages had wounded him. They had respectively left the bungalow so Nicki and Carlos could start bonding with their new child, snatching a bottle of the Sanchezes' special tequila as they snuck out into the Harvest Moon-lit vineyards to celebrate. That's when his whole story drunkenly poured out.

He told his ex-wife that he had loved Doug since high school; his one true love that society forced him to shun, hide as a dirty secret. That is, until Doug had received his fatal diagnosis: multiple sclerosis. Todd could no longer live an inauthentic life now that Doug needed him. That was why he had left Stella.

He had apologized in a drunk crying jag for being so mean to her, not being honest. Stella now understood his pained face when he held sweet Lilly for the first time. He was welcoming a new life while knowing someday soon he would be saying goodbye to another. The circle of life. They had pledged that night to honor each other as they once did as a united family.

As she stood in orange glow of the Golden Gate Bridge with her daughter and granddaughter, Lilly broke their solemn silence. "Mommy, I'm hungry. May I have a sandwich with Nema Stella's special bread?"

"Go," Stella laughed, as her phone rang. Lilly scampered down into the cabin, with her swollen mother waddling behind.

"Good news, Dib?" she asked, wiping her nose on her thick 49er sweatshirt sleeve before mentally switching gears. "Do we have a tentative grandmother committee in each war zone on every continent?" Stella asked, as she took her first sip of her ice-cold dirty martini, her smiling husband had handed to her with a kiss. Now settled in her favorite seat— co-pilot—she ran her hands through his thick white hair, his thick black eyebrows glistening in the salty spray, while he handily took the wheel.

"Sounds like you have it taken care of, as usual. Thank you. We are sailing under the Golden Gate Bridge right now, so soon I'll be out of range. Get some rest, my sister friend."

Stella, like millions of women across the globe, was exhausted after the exhilaration of the Women's March the day before. There was a collective months' long exhaustion across America from the unfolding fast-paced nightmare that was happening in Washington. From her meditated communications with her mother-in-law, she knew it would get worse before it got better. Their battle against the Elite was not yet over.

"Great chaos before change," Lilli had once warned. "They will try to exhaust you into apathy with constant crises. Pay attention. Feel better. Gather the women."

As she disconnected from the phone call, she took a deep breath of the zesty sea air and reflected on everything that had happened since that long ago November evening.

Now, she was the founder of the *Lilli Council*, a newly formed international peace-keeping organization. Ironically, the idea grew from a conversation with Brent at her chateau wedding to Gabriel. Brent warned that even though Lucas had dissolved his GA7 Empire as a plea bargain for a life-time prison sentence for the three murders—the Spaniard, Cardinal Gustav and Lilli—there were still others right behind him ready to step up and take GA7's mantle. The last gasp of patriarchy with their never-ending war business model would be brutal. Then the election happened.

Stella flew to Maggie's horse ranch where, with her friend Brent's help, she had opened up a horse riding program for Wounded Warriors to help them cope with post-traumatic stress disorder (PTSD), depression and anxiety. Brent also needed a place to stay on the East Coast as he testified before numerous Congressional hearings about the Liberty Group's and the Elites' crimes. Lucas had also agreed to give evidence in exchange for avoiding a death sentence. Soon, all the for-profit prisons would be brimming with wealthy men whose money could not save them.

The two friends had arranged for their cherished new friends, the Liberian women, to join them in an emergency "noodle session." After much discussion, it was decided it was time for binding international dispute resolution committees, run independently by the grandmothers. Using the 1915 Women's International League for Peace and Freedom guiding principles of working together, utilizing non-violent means, the women vowed to promote political, economic and social justice for all. Like ancient indigenous tribes, these committees would address issues of gender, militarism, peace and security.

They proposed that all disputes with other countries had to be presented to the Lilli Council first, outlining all efforts at resolution before being authorized for armed combat as a last resort. Each resolution council was headed by grandmothers that would review and resolve disputes in 260 days, a nod to the time from conception to birth in human timing.

At first, some rogue countries, including the United States, gave the women no attention. While old white men arrogantly ignored their request, they were mobilizing to institute global changes quickly.

Sophia and Sarah had suggested the "One Thought" campaign, inspired by the success of Maharishi tactics used for the Great Gathering. It was created and promoted by Dibrovna's daughter, Sylvania, now a successful innovator of social media messaging. They based it on the Lourdes conversation that with collective thought, no man could have erections while war raged. Within one week of no sex, leaders of all waring countries came to the bargaining table. The rapid numbers generators almost fried at Princeton right before the historic agreement had been signed. It may have been the one time everyone in the world was getting lucky.

Her life had changed radically since that fateful night in the Turkish theater. Though she thought of death in a different way, she still grieved. So did her husband, Gabriel. Now they had each other to help through the dark times of the process.

He had stayed at the Chateau for almost a month, going to the waters at Lourdes every day. He still stuttered when he was tired, and at times it was easier to get around in his wheelchair. Some of the bones in his crushed ankles hadn't healed correctly, but he wasn't willing to have the bones broken and reset. He was determined to spend every moment he could with his lovely wife, Stella. They were married at the chateau, standing in the fountain.

They decided after Lilly's birth to split their time between Northern California and Callian. They sold the Mill Valley house, at an incredible profit, and bought a working organic farm in Petaluma. Stella had been surprised at Gabriel's growing skills. But he reminded her he had had the best teacher in the world and traditions had to be continued.

Though Stella still owned the Third Act, she changed the way she did business. Profit wasn't so much a motive as was selling story-telling art and financially supporting artists. Dibrovna was now the chief executive officer of all of the businesses which now included a co-housing project at the winery and its self-sustaining arts/business incubator. For all intents and purposes, the store belonged to Dibrovna. All Stella requested was her help to set up her organic garden and show her how to raise chickens.

At Lupe's insistence, the Sanchez family had gifted five acres of prime grape growing acres to the newly-married couple so they could build a co-housing project where Nema could live. Not long after returning to the States after the Gathering, Stella and the very pregnant Nicki pulled the comatose Nema out of her nursing home to live at the winery under Rose's care. Within a month of Nema's stay, with the help of Rosa's and Lupe's cooking and Lilli's salve, she was acting as the self-appointed general contractor.

The self-sustaining community made special imbued silver-star jewelry, one-off embellished clothing, while they farmed. They worked furiously making their organic chutneys which sold out faster than the wine in the gift shop. Their project was based on the Sumerian tablets of the Goddess Nanshe of Lagash who was worshiped as "She who knows the orphan, knows the widow, seeks justice for the poor and shelter for the weak."

Martha/Rose had comforted Stella after Lilli's memorial. Rose explained that indeed she was a shape shifter whose purpose was that of a guardian angel, sent by Nema to watch over her just as she had watched over Gabriel. She and Kathleen now headed up the gentle new pope's committee on sexual abuse and human trafficking. They also obtained priestess hood with their clever leveraging of all their stashed documents. The Church had no choice.

"Mom, you might want to come down here and look at this," Nicki yelled. She had set up Lilly to watch videos while she ate her snack.

"Lilly, come over to grandma—slowly. Remember, no running on the boat."

"Look, Nema Stella!" Lilly said excitedly, pulling Stella over to the monitor. "It's the Lady who talks to me at night. Why is my head floating above hers?"

Stella, knowingly, looked lovingly at her granddaughter and replied, "Must be something in the water. It's always the water."

Excerpt from the Gnostic gospel, *Thunder, Perfect Mind.*

For I am the first and the last.

I am the honored one and the scorned one.

I am the whore and the holy one.

I am the wife and the virgin.

I am the barren one,

And many are her children.

I am the silence that is incomprehensible.

I am the utterance of my name.

ACKNOWLEDGEMENTS

Much of this story is fact-based. If you are interested in finding out more, I suggest the following books:

The Mayan Code, Time Acceleration and Awakening the World Mind, Barbara Hand Clow, 2007, Bear & Company

The Divine Matrix, Bridging Time, Space, Miracles, and Belief, Gregg Braden, 2007, Hay House

The Intention Experiment, Using Your Thoughts to Change Your Life and the World, Lynne McTaggart, 2007, Free Press, a Division of Simon & Schuster

The Hidden Messages in Water, Masaru Emoto, 2004, Atria Books

Théâtre de la Mode, Fashion Dolls: The Survival of Haute Couture, Essays by Edmonde Charles-Roux, Herbert R. Lottman, Stanley Garfinkel, Nadine Gase, Colleen Schafroth and Betty Long-Schleif, Second Revised Edition 2002, Palmer/Pletsch

Christian Dior, The Man Who Made the World Look New, Marie-France Pochna, 1996, Arcade Publishing

Revelations, Visions, Prophecy, & Politics in the Book of Revelation, Elaine Pagels, 2012, Viking

The Gnostic Gospels, Elaine Pagels, 1979, Random House

The Chalice & The Blade, Our History, Our Future, Riane Eisler, 1987, Harper & Row

The Miracles of Mary, Bridget Curran, 2008, Inspired Living, an imprint of Allen & Unwin

Mary's House, The Extraordinary Story Behind the Discovery of the House Where the Virgin Mary Lived and Died, Donald Carroll, 2000, Veritas Books

Reading the Enemy's Mind, Inside Star Gate – America's Psychic Espionage Program, Paul H. Smith, 2005, A Forge Book

A Store to Remember (I. Magnin), James Thomas Mullane, 2007, Falcon Books

About the Author

Karen Clark is a true Renaissance woman whose vast lifetime career ranges from an Italian-trained fashion designer, litigation paralegal, carpenter and wood floor mechanic to concert promoter, personal historian, pet and house sitter, landscape designer and IT/word processor at the ad agency that brought you the *Pet Rock*. Like most midlife women who have gone through the "Change," she now spends her time on artistic activities such as writing and spending time with her grandchildren—and yelling at politicians on television.

Singing in Silence is her debut novel. Her next book is *NestQuest*, her memoir of the twelve years it took to write this historical novel while suffering a brain injury from workplace bullying which led to homelessness at age sixty. Her journey to find her own home led to wanting to know more about the history of her brave ancestor's quest for a home in America, culminating in driving herself through England, Ireland and Scotland in 2015. That journey revealed Mayflower ancestors, including the pilot of that famous voyage and her ten-times great grandmother who was one of the original Separatists. She has learned to Trust the Journey.

Visit Singinginsilence.com

Contact: info@singinginsilence.com